LOVE'S PROMISE

"Beth, we belong together. I'm not going to let you go."

Beth felt scorched by the blaze in his eyes. His lips came down on hers firmly, possessively.

Deep inside, a traitorous part of her was responding to Cy's passionate entreaty. She willed herself to give nothing back. When he released her, she stepped away.

"What I understand, Cy, is that you were dishonest."

"Beth, I should have told you. There are no words for how sorry I am for doing it all wrong and causing you to hurt."

His eyes caressed her lovingly. "I'm not going to let this be the end for us, sweetheart. . . ."

LOVE'S PROMISE

Adrienne Ellis Reeves

Pinnacle Books
Kensington Publishing Corp.
http://www.arabesquebooks.com

ACKNOWLEDGMENT

To my husband, William, who continually gives love and support and sacrifice of time; to the Summerville Writers Guild for their encouragement and professional understanding; to Helen Somers for her generous and expert assistance; and to Lisa Black who helped solve a worrisome problem.

PINNACLE BOOKS are published by

Kensington Publishing Corp.
850 Third Avenue
New York, NY 10022

First Printing: November, 1998
10 9 8 7 6 5 4 3 2 1

Printed in the United States of America

Chapter 1

''This is the day!'' Beth Jordan declared, shutting off her computer and standing up. ''I'm out of here.''

Aretha Symonds turned from the filing cabinet. Her thin lips turned down disapprovingly and her penciled eyebrows rose. ''Don't tell me you're going to go through with this. The last time we talked about it, you said you'd decided not to.''

Beth ran a comb through her short reddish curls and put on fresh lipstick. ''Don't care what I said,'' she countered in a light voice. ''I'm going to do it. Have a good weekend, girl.''

''You, too,'' Aretha said, wondering how in the six months since she'd come to Jamison Realty, Beth Jordan could still surprise her by doing the unexpected. She watched Beth get into her dark green Honda and roar out of the parking lot. Aretha's plans for her weekend suddenly seemed dull, and she closed the filing drawer with a slam.

Beth darted in and out of the Friday traffic impatient to cover the distance from Jamison to the other side of Charleston. She was half listening to the rapid beat of the music on the radio when an exasperated driver blew his horn at her too sudden lane change. She searched the rearview mirror for a traffic cop and slowed down a tad.

Spanish moss hanging from the trees looked spectral in the late January afternoon. Beth, a lifelong resident of the South Carolina Lowcountry, hardly noticed it, her thoughts focused on her weekend possibilities. There's a new club opening downtown, she thought, maybe Art will call and we can check it out or a bunch of us could go. That'd be fun.

A red light caught her at an intersection where an impressive brick church stood. It made her remember how she'd missed church the last two Sundays. The light changed, and she drove on thinking she definitely had to get to church this Sunday no matter how late she got to bed tomorrow night, and after church she'd have dinner at Aunt Elly's.

Beth always packed her weekends with activity in the hopes that along the way she'd experience something stimulating and exciting. She was on her way now to do something she hoped would lift her out of the doldrums she was in and add verve to her life.

She put her right turn signal on and swung into the huge lot of Charleston Motors, one of the premier establishments on the famed Auto Mile. Ignoring the clutch of waiting salesmen on the porch, she walked quickly down one of the aisles of new cars to the one car she'd been considering for several months. As she stopped in front of a blazing red Saturn, a balding man with a gray mustache came from the next aisle.

"May I help you?" he asked in a pleasant voice. He was sure he'd seen this slender young woman with smooth brown skin, firmly set lips, and luminous brown eyes on the lot before. His selling instinct developed over twenty years in the business warned him to be very careful with this customer. "I'm Max Gregory," he said, extending his hand.

"I'm Beth Jordan," Beth said and shook hands briefly. "What can you tell me about this car?" She'd read that Saturn people were trained not to resort to pressure tactics to sell a car, but she had yet to meet a salesman who didn't in one way or another.

"This is our top-of-the-line sports coupe, Miss Jordan," Mr. Gregory said. "Let me mention a few things about how the car is built first. These panels are made of a dent and corrosion resistant polymer.'' He pointed to the car's side panels. ''The halogen headlights are standard equipment. It has a four-cylinder engine and power rack-and-pinion steering, which means it responds to the slightest touch.'' He moved to the back of the car. ''This model comes with a rear spoiler.'' He pointed to the raised bar across the back, which was one of the features Beth particularly wanted. In her view it made the car look even sportier and more distinctive.

Mr. Gregory opened the driver's door and with a gesture invited Beth to sit in the car. To her surprise the interior of the car was black. ''Is this the only interior you have?'' She had expected a complementary shade of the red exterior.

''This model also comes in a rich gray,'' Mr. Gregory said. ''As you can see, it has bucket seats in the front and the driver's seat has an adjustable lumbar support and cushion height.'' He showed her where the lever was that made the changes. ''The steering column is also adjustable and is leather wrapped.'' He explained that the AM/FM stereo had four six-inch speakers and that the digital clock was reliable. ''Cruise control is available in this model also,'' he said as he described the rest of the instrument panel and the five-speed manual transmission controls.

''Does this model come with a sunroof?'' Beth asked.

''Yes, that's an option, a power sunroof that can tilt. You can also have an inner sliding shade and dual map lights. An option I strongly advise any driver to get is our security system.''

''What does that include?'' Beth was particularly interested in this. Last week she'd had a scare when she was approaching her car after shopping until nine, and a man had suddenly appeared on the opposite side of her car. As it happened, he went on by and got into a car two down from hers, but it made her think seriously about the system several of her friends had described and how it made them feel less helpless.

''Our system,'' Mr. Gregory said, ''includes power door locks, a door alarm, an engine immobilizer, a power trunk-lid release, and it lets you open your door by pressing on a button while you're walking to your car.''

''How do you like the inside, and is your seat comfortable?''

Mr. Gregory asked as Beth fiddled with the steering wheel adjustment.

"It's fine," Beth said. She'd already noted cupholders in the back as well as in the front, the two coat hooks, and a vanity mirror on the passenger side.

"I'll get the key, Miss Jordan, and you can drive it around the lot to get the feel of it. Back in just a minute."

Beth touched all of the instruments, stroked the leather seats, adjusted her cushion up and down, and inhaled the new car fragrance. The car had everything she wanted and more. It was sporty and fine looking, and it gave her a sense of luxury. Now if I can find a way to pay for it, she thought, as Mr. Gregory returned and handed her the keys.

Beth drove around the lot several times and was all the more impressed. The car's motor was quiet, but you could feel its power. It had responded superbly to her touch, and she could see herself skimming down the highway to Atlanta, to Savannah, even to Washington, D.C., in this sleek, smart, scarlet beauty. What an adventure that would be! The act of driving was a joy, it made Beth feel free and untrammelled.

Mr. Gregory was waiting for her when she pulled up. He opened the door for her. "Did you like the way it handled, Miss Jordan?" He was confident that the car had pleased this young lady.

"Yes, very much."

"What car are you driving now?"

"That's my '93 Honda Civic there," Beth said, indicating where her car was parked.

That had been the beginning of talking about the purchase of the Saturn. Beth had thought that when they went into the office the subtle pressure might begin, because so far her conversation with Mr. Gregory had been pressure-free. But she was surprised. The Saturn was priced at $22,500 plus tax, and they would allow a trade-in price of $5,200. There was no haggling and no disappearance of Mr. Gregory to talk with his manager and return with a better offer. Instead Mr. Gregory spoke of the Saturn service, which included policies Beth hadn't experienced elsewhere and then left it for her to decide.

Beth took Mr. Gregory's card and thanked him for his time, and he said he hoped she'd return.

Devastated, Beth drove slowly out of the lot. The Saturn had everything she'd ever desired in an automobile but she hadn't counted on it at over sixteen thousand as the absolute maximum, even with the Honda as a trade-in, and she wanted the car with all of the options. A stripped-down version might be all right for some people, but not for her. The tilting sunroof, the cruise control, the security system, and the other options—she wanted it all.

The problem was that fifteen thousand was the maximum she could put into a car, and even that would leave her finances dangerously low for any emergencies that might occur. She was willing to take that risk, but more than that she couldn't pay, and she definitely was not going to borrow from her parents nor take out a loan to make up the twenty-three hundred dollar difference.

In her depression Beth drove unthinkingly and found she'd missed the turn to put her on the interstate to Jamison, so she made her way to a street that roughly paralleled the Ashley River and linked Charleston with Jamison. The divided lanes, two aside, carried a moderate amount of traffic, and Beth returned to the problems of buying the Saturn. She'd kept her '93 Honda in excellent condition. Surely it was worth more than the fifty-two hundred Mr. Gregory had offered. In the ads she'd read that a '91 Honda had a value of five thousand, so her '93 should have at least seven thousand dollars in value, considering it had all of the options including a tape player which worked.

The cars ahead of Beth began to slow, and their brake lights came on. She knew there was no traffic signal for the next few blocks, so why were they stopping? Then in the distance a siren screamed. All of the cars stopped momentarily as two ambulances, lights flashing, raced by. Must be a very bad accident up ahead, Beth thought. She automatically noted the time as five minutes after six, and resigning herself to a long wait, searched the radio dial until she found the station that played jazz and easy swing. Marilyn McCoo and the Fifth Dimension were singing gaily about going up, up, and away.

I haven't heard that in years, Beth mused, but it sure fits me right now. That's what I wish I could be doing. She looked longingly at the sky. The air up there might be able to sweep away the discontent and restlessness that had plagued her the past few months. Now it looked like she wouldn't even be able to buy the new Saturn, which was to be an antidote, something to lift her spirits and give zest to her life.

Beth had been inching along in the traffic but now came to a full stop. Out of the corner of her eye, she saw something familiar and turned her head to see what it was. Directly beside her in the right lane was a scarlet Saturn exactly like the one she'd looked at and driven.

She looked to see who was driving her car. The dark-skinned man at the wheel was looking straight ahead, stretching his neck to see beyond the next car, so Beth felt safe looking at him. His head was shaved and he was wearing a diamond stud in his left ear. He had a trim mustache and small goatee. He wore a white shirt with a tie and jacket. Must be coming home from work, Beth thought, and wondered why she didn't recognize him if he was on his way home to Jamison. Suddenly the man turned his head as if Beth had called to him, and they looked at each other for a long moment.

The line of cars began to move again, and Beth turned away to attend to her driving. Two cars in front of her eased into the right lane, and when next she looked in the rearview mirror, the scarlet Saturn was several cars back. Traffic was moving more steadily now, and Beth kept driving until she reached an intersection. The light turned red as she approached it. Cars in the right lane turned right, and suddenly the Saturn was beside her again.

She turned her head cautiously to find that the man had lowered his window and was waiting for her to notice him.

He glanced at the red light above. "Excuse me, but do you live in Jamison?" he said rapidly.

"Yes," Beth said unhesitatingly.

"So do I," the man said. "My name is—" But the rest of

it was drowned as people then began to blow their horns, Beth was embarrassed to see the light was now green.

Beth drove on with the Saturn staying right beside her. Twice the man looked at her with a friendly smile. At the next intersection the man slowly turned right with a light tap of the horn and a wave of the hand. Impulsively Beth raised her hand in a wave and tapped her horn good-bye.

Beth smiled at herself. This certainly wasn't the first time a stranger in a car had sought her attention, but she'd never been compelled to an immediate and continued response. But this man looks like he'd be interesting to know, she mused, and after all he is driving my car. That bit of fallacious reasoning made her smile again, and she felt a breath of lightness in her spirit as she turned at her intersection and drove to a section of Jamison called Willow Wood.

When she was ready to leave her parents' house, her dear aunt Elly had spoken of a vacant apartment near her own large house. Beth had been glad to be near Uncle Sim, the five children, and her favorite aunt Elly, her mother's older sister. She saw her uncle's Ford in their driveway and the cars her cousins, Jannie and Lucious, had proudly acquired in the past year. Often one of her five cousins would drop by as soon as they saw her car, but Beth hoped no one would come this evening. At least not yet. She wanted to be alone for a while and relax. Later she'd be ready to go out when Art called or do something else, as she rarely spent a Friday night without social activity.

In the kitchen Beth opened the refrigerator but saw only a head of lettuce, a piece of steak, and the remains of a macaroni and cheese casserole. Nothing looked appetizing. She'd order something in or eat out, and meanwhile she'd drink a Pepsi and see if her Belk bill was in the handful of mail that had been in the box. Shoes off and the Pepsi beside her, Beth stretched out on the worn chaise longue she'd brought from home and placed in the corner opposite her bed. She switched on the lamp beside it and began to go through the mail. She discarded three advertisements, looked at her phone bill and reminded herself to talk less frequently to her friend, Clio, in

Atlanta. Then she found the Belk bill and opened it with some apprehension. Forty-five dollars; that wasn't too bad, even though last month she'd vowed not to put anything new on it after her Christmas shopping. Here were her *Essence* magazine and under it several flyers from local markets. As she picked one up, a small envelope fell out onto the floor. Beth shook the flyers to see if anything else was stuck in them then looked at the letter. The return addressee was Arthur Woods, the man she'd been dating for several years.

What in the world is Art writing to me about? Beth thought idly. I was expecting him to call any minute. She opened the flap and extracted a folded page covered in Art's precise script. Dated two days earlier, it said:

Dear Beth,

Last night I got engaged to Evelyn Hardy, and I want to tell you myself right away. I, at least, owe you that. Beth, you and I have been seeing each other for nearly three years on a pretty regular basis, but it seemed there was nothing permanent in the future for us. Evelyn and I are both interested in the business, and we both want to start a family soon. I don't know what else to say, Beth, so I'll just wish you happiness and thanks for all our good times together.

Art

Beth's eyes opened wide in sheer astonishment. Surely she had misread the note. She read it again slowly. Art engaged? Who was Evelyn Hardy? Her mind demanded an answer to that before she could feel anything else. She knew no one in Jamison by that name. She ran through all of the people she and Art knew and had associated with in the time they'd been together. She vaguely knew an Evelyn Gilmore, but that Evelyn had a husband and several children.

It must be someone out of town. Then she remembered that once when they were visiting Art's family in Winnsboro, his hometown, they were looking through some family albums. One of the pictures was of Art, looking young and very handsome, dressed for his senior prom. When asked, he had identified the pretty girl beside him as Evelyn Hardy. "What's she doing now?" Beth had asked. "Teaching school in Columbia last I heard," Art had answered and turned the page.

No wonder I haven't seen much of him these past two months, was Beth's next thought. They usually saw each other nearly every week and more often if something was happening. He'd gone home for both Thanksgiving and Christmas this year, and that's probably why. He'd been courting Evelyn.

Beth began to feel angry and hurt. She vividly remembered Art bringing her home from the Labor Day party and, taking her in his arms, he kissed her over and over with unusual fervor. "Why won't you marry me, Beth?" This was the third time he'd asked, and Beth gave the same answer she'd given the other times. "I'm not ready, Art."

She liked Art a lot—enough to date him more than anyone else, and Art had from the beginning said he loved her. He wasn't exciting, but he was a source of comfort and stability in her life. Then James Ellington had returned to Jamison, and the crush she'd had on him in high school had almost instantly flamed into something more on her part—but James had discovered his love for Glennette Percy, and they had soon married. Beth had gone out of town so she wouldn't have to attend their wedding. Then she resumed going out with Art.

People thought of them as a couple and took for granted that their wedding announcement would occur in due time. They'd get a wedding announcement, but it would be for Art and Evelyn. People will look at me in pity and wonder what it is that keeps me from securing a husband, Beth thought. James had chosen Glennette—and now Art, her old dependable, had chosen Evelyn. How could he do such a thing without a word of warning? He could at least have told her he was seeing Evelyn. Beth had never accepted an engagement ring, and it was an unspoken agreement between them that they were free to see other people.

Art owned his own garage and was establishing a limousine service. His social time was limited, and Beth hadn't known him to take anyone out but herself. How many people had known he was wooing Evelyn Hardy? They say the other woman is always the last to know.

Beth couldn't sit still any longer. She felt hurt and angry, humiliated and rejected, but most of all just plain wretched and unhappy. The feelings of dissatisfaction and restlessness she'd had must have been her intuition telling her this was going to happen. She looked for an outlet for her feelings and ended up taking down the venetian blinds and cleaning them—a job she usually avoided—but now she attacked the dirty blinds with energy. Then she mopped and waxed the kitchen floor. She felt empty but couldn't force herself to eat. The telephone rang several times, but she didn't answer it. She was in no mood to talk with anyone.

Her thoughts went round and round, darting from one aspect to another of her relationship with Art and then with the other men she'd dated until now. Most women at her age of twenty-nine were married or engaged, but she was neither. No one wants me, was her dismal conclusion. She looked around for something more to do. Taking out the vacuum cleaner, she used it with all of the attachments to clean the apartment more thoroughly than it had been cleaned in many months. Finally, she was tired enough to go to bed.

In the shower she thought of Rhonda Hayes, her longtime friend. Rhonda was a good listener, she was discreet and she was wise. Maybe she could talk with Rhonda about this debacle. But even Rhonda couldn't change the facts that stared Beth in the face as she waited for sleep to come.

There's something wrong with me. I'm stuck in the same old job, I can't get the car I like, and worst of all, no one wants me.

Chapter 2

Beth had been on Rhonda's mind, and she made a mental note to call Beth after the committee meeting. Rhonda pulled her car into the parking lot of the Martin Luther King, Jr., Community Center in Jamison. She'd left her husband, Henry, still eating his dinner so she could be here on time and she hoped the other members of the Helping Ourselves Project committee wouldn't make her hurrying meaningless.

She noticed that several of the steps were rickety as she mounted them and crossed the porch to the door. Thank goodness they were all here, she thought, as she greeted the other members and slipped into the vacant chair beside James Ellington.

Reverend Elijah Garner opened the proceedings with a few words of supplication that the Almighty would bless their efforts today. Bill Barnes, chairman of the North Jamison Community Council, which managed the center, stated the agenda for the evening. "As you know, in a few months it will be time to present the Helping Ourselves Project award to a person, persons, or organization that has given the most service to the black community. Tonight we have to begin deciding who will receive that award. You people have been asked to serve on this committee because you represent a good cross section of the community. Any general questions before we begin the discussion?" One hand was raised. "Yes, Attorney Ellington?"

James Ellington, a tall man with a long face and laugh lines around his eyes, said he'd been away from Jamison when the award was established, and he'd appreciate knowing exactly how it and HOP began.

Reverend Garner folded his hands comfortably across his stomach, and his keen eyes fixed themselves on James. "It began because of a wonderful woman named Maude Cokley. She made it her personal business to get in her car and make the rounds, visiting folks in need, especially those who lived in isolated places. She'd do a little first-aid or plain nursing if that was called for; nursing had been her career. She bought people food, did their mail for them if needed, or helped them with a bank or government matter. She did it all out of a need to serve and help people—and as a result, a lot of the people were then better able to help themselves and others. A few people who knew what she was doing decided such service should be noticed and appreciated by the community. So Miss Maude was given an award, and the Helping Ourselves Project was established to encourage that same spirit in others."

Zenobia Masters, a smartly dressed woman from the Black Professional Women's Club added, "It was fine the first few years, and the community took it seriously."

"One year the churches got together and established the playground with all of the play equipment for kids under eight," Bill Barnes recalled.

Dr. Earl Felder, a dentist, said, "My youngest son still goes there."

Ammie Clay, the black female Community Relations police officer in Jamison said, "But ever since then the project has gone downhill."

"How do you mean?" James asked.

"People don't seem to care anymore," Ammie replied.

"That's right," Rhonda agreed. "The last few years interest has dropped so much that it's been hard to find outstanding service that deserves recognition."

"Who was it given to last year?" James asked.

"Two women who were tutoring children after school," Dr. Felder said.

James was puzzled. "Wasn't that a real community service?"

"Indeed it was," Reverend Garner pronounced. "The disappointing thing was that it had no competition. The whole idea of setting up the project was to encourage many such services by the people of the community for the people of the community."

For a moment there was silence. Then Bill Barnes, noted for cutting to the heart of the matter, made a suggestion. "Let's not give the award this year. Why should we if no one is deserving of it?" He looked around the table challengingly.

"What about Hettie Williams, who took in the Marshes when their house burned down?" Rhonda asked.

"That was a good thing to do, but that sort of helping out in time of need happens all of the time," Reverend Garner said. "I can think of three or four other examples."

"I don't like to see us not give it," Zenobia protested. "That is a shaming thing and makes it even less important in people's eyes."

"I'm the new one on this committee," James said, "but I'd like to suggest that we try something different. We still have six months before the award is to be given, right?"

"That's correct," Bill Barnes said. "What did you have in mind?"

"I hadn't worked out the details," James admitted, "but I am wondering if there's a way to get community organizations and businesses directly involved."

"You mean by having them compete in service projects? I don't see how that would work," Dr. Felder said.

Zenobia said, "They couldn't do that, but they could involve their employees who live in Jamison."

"What would they do?" Ammie wanted to know.

"Maybe the employees themselves could come up with some kind of project that would help the community." Rhonda became visibly enthusiastic as she talked. "You couldn't have all of the employees who live in Jamison because that could get unmanageable, but we could ask these organizations and businesses to nominate one or two people."

"Then to increase their interest in doing something outstanding, we could put people together in teams," James said, "but the people would be from different organizations."

"Before we go any further with this idea, let me have a show of hands to see if there's agreement to give the award this year, and that we devise a method to involve the business and community organizations." All hands were raised. "Good. Now let's proceed with definite ways to do this," Bill Barnes said briskly, looking at his watch.

At the end of the hour, it had been voted to ask ten organizations and businesses to nominate two Jamison employees, and these twenty people would be put into ten teams. Each team would be briefed and watched over by a committee member. The teams would be encouraged to use grass-roots support services as much as possible but could also ask their sponsors if necessary. The award recipients would be selected by the committee for the June ceremony. The value of the service to the entire community would be the main qualification.

The committee had immediately obtained names from as many of the sponsors as possible. They made up the teams by drawing names until they got two people from different organizations.

Rhonda volunteered to be responsible for two of the ten teams. Her first call was to Beth, but there was no answer. She called again the next morning. "It's me, Rhonda," she said when Beth finally picked up the phone. "Were you busy? I can call back."

"I was just deep in sleep," Beth said drowsily.

Rhonda's astonishment sounded in her voice. "But it's nearly eleven on a beautiful Saturday morning, girl." She knew that Beth never slept late. Too many things to do to be wasting time in bed was what Beth always said. "Are you sick?"

"No, but I didn't get to bed until about four."

"Oh, you and Art must have been to that new club we were talking about. I called you, but there was no answer."

''No, I didn't see Art. I stayed here in the apartment. I was in the mood to do some cleaning.''

Rhonda reacted to the somberness in her friend's voice. ''Well, I haven't eaten yet so I'm bringing us some breakfast, See you in a while.'' Rhonda hung up quickly before Beth could tell her no.

Beth had barely put her clothes on when Rhonda rang the bell and hurried in with a basket into which she'd put sausage, eggs, grits, biscuits, and strawberry preserves. ''I gave Henry the last piece of fresh fruit I had,'' she said, making herself at home in Beth's kitchen after giving one searching look at Beth's drawn face and weary eyes. ''You make the coffee, and I'll do the rest. Henry went into the post office early, but I didn't get out of the bed until nearly nine, and I went out into the yard instead of eating right away.'' She talked on about inconsequential things while putting the meal together.

Rhonda had brown eyes and heavy long hair brushed back from her square face this morning and tied with a cord. She wore jeans and a long-sleeved green shirt. Her socks were green worn with scuffed brown leather slip-ons. She was a little self-conscious about her nose, broken as a child, and now just slightly askew to her pleasant face, but Beth, watching her, felt it added character to her face. Content to watch Rhonda work, she was still feeling numb from the night before and physically tired from working so hard in the apartment.

''Your cleaning work shows,'' Rhonda said, turning over the sausage and stirring the grits. ''You could dance on this floor it looks so clean and waxed.'' She served the food at the small table under the window. What Rhonda had to say to Beth could wait until her friend regained some color in her face and she felt able to tell her what it was that had changed the lively upbeat Beth she'd always known into this sad quiet person, who was pushing her food around on the plate.

''I'm not very hungry this morning,'' Beth said apologetically. ''I guess I haven't been up long enough.'' Ever since Rhonda's call, Beth had been considering telling Rhonda about Art's letter. Rhonda was happily married to Henry Hayes, who had provided for her in every way, so that instead of continuing her teaching career she'd been able to stay home and do community work, which was her main goal. Rhonda had been especially interested in her two best friends, Beth and Glennette, finding the same happiness she had in marriage. Glennette was on her way since marrying James Ellington after he returned from Alaska three years ago. Rhonda's been keeping up with Art and me so I ought to tell her, Beth thought. I wouldn't want her to learn about it from anyone else.

As if reading Beth's mind, Rhonda pushed her plate away and said, "What's happened, Beth? Don't try to tell me it's nothing because I know better." Her voice was sympathetic but firm.

Beth took Art's letter from her pocket and handed it across the table. "This was in my mail last night," she said.

Beth watched as Rhonda read the letter, surprise and dismay showing in her face. "I can't believe this!" Rhonda looked at the letter again. "Evelyn. Who in the world is Evelyn?"

"A hometown girl from Winnsboro who teaches in Columbia."

Rhonda shook her head in slow disbelief. "Art has always been crazy about you. Anyone could see that. Did you two have a fight or something?"

"No," Beth said. "In fact, he hasn't been around so much lately, but I just put it down to his working hard in the business."

"Do you know Evelyn? Have you seen them together?"

Beth explained about seeing her picture in the album, but that was all she knew.

Rhonda read the letter once more then returned it to Beth. It was obvious that the news had a major impact on her dear friend, but she wasn't sure about the nature of that impact. The intensity of this affair had always been on Art's side as far as one could see, but perhaps Beth had felt more deeply than it appeared.

"How are you feeling about this, honey? You want me to have Henry beat him up for you?" She hoped this might lighten Beth's mood.

That unlikely scenario of mild-mannered Henry going up against a well-muscled younger Art brought a reluctant smile to Beth's eyes. "Thanks, but that won't be necessary," she said dryly. "When I first read the letter, I was astonished then angry then hurt then sad and a whole lot of other things," she said slowly. "That's why I couldn't go to bed, and I had to keep myself moving and busy doing something. This morning I just feel numb."

"Everyone's going to know pretty soon," Rhonda mused aloud. "If the girl's from Winnsboro, they'll probably get married there, but Art will have to bring her here to Jamison because of his business."

"I know. I can just see people looking at me and feeling sorry for me, but I don't want anyone's pity." Beth's voice was stronger, and she sounded more like the person Rhonda knew.

"You can't control what people think," Rhonda said, "but you can show that this isn't going to make you hide."

"You know me well enough to know I don't believe in hiding," Beth said defiantly.

"I know you don't, and that reminds me of what I was calling you about last night," Rhonda exclaimed. "Your news made me forget it. You've been loaned by Jamison Realty to be on one of the ten teams for the Helping Ourselves Project this year."

"I've never heard of teams in connection with HOP," Beth said. "Anyway I'm not interested in that right now, and my boss can't lend me without my consent."

Rhonda knew that when Beth Jordan got that stubborn look it was hard to move her. She used all of her persuasive techniques to capture Beth's attention for the project and her consent to at least give it a try. "I'm inviting the two teams I'm responsible for to dinner this coming Friday so they can meet each other and learn what they have to do. Come out and help us, Beth. This is one way you can show you're not going into hiding, and it'll give you something different to think about." Rhonda waited to see how Beth would respond to this.

Beth turned her coffee cup around on the saucer, thinking of Rhonda's last point. "Who's the other person I'll be working with?"

"I don't know him myself, but he's someone from Alumax."

Rhonda waited another moment. "You'll come, won't you, Beth?"

"How can I say no?" Beth's wry smile did not reach her eyes. "After all, you gave me breakfast."

When Rhonda left a little later, she said. "I'll see you Friday at seven, but I'll talk with you before then, girlfriend."

"Okay, Rhonda. At least you and HOP need me."

Chapter 3

Rhonda Hayes looked critically at her table set for four guests plus Henry and herself. The low centerpiece of fresh flowers looked very decorative, she decided, but it might interfere with conversation, so she put it on the sideboard and in its place set a small crystal bowl filled with colored glass balls. That's better, she thought, as she saw how they caught the light and sparkled. She smoothed the rose tablecloth, pleased with how it complemented the china with its edging of tiny roses and delicate green vines. She hoped her guests would be pleased also and would feel comfortable and relaxed.

Beth had thought the week would never end. Aretha had pounced on her Monday as soon as she got to work "I waited because I wanted to see the new Saturn," she said with a curious look.

"It's still on the lot," Beth said.

"You decided against it after all," Aretha said approvingly.

"I looked at it and drove it. I'm still considering it." Beth's tone of voice put a period to the subject as she sat down at her computer and began work.

It had been a busy week for the real estate agents who provided Beth extra work as she prepared their computer listings of properties. She stayed late several nights, working to assist agents coming in from successful showings thankful to have something to do other than go home.

Beth was in a peculiar state of mind. She had lost her equilibrium as a result of Art's letter. She felt abandoned and desolate. Yet she knew that if she were completely honest it wasn't because she'd been deeply in love with Art. She liked him well enough, maybe even loved him a little but had never been able to accept an engagement ring from him. So why did she feel unstable and confused? Was she so shallow that pride was her main concern—and what folks would think since Art had left her rather than the other way around? She hated to think only her pride had been hurt, but if it wasn't that, what was it? Beth knew herself to be somewhat frivolous as far as going around with people and finding ways to be entertained. It was a lifestyle developed from an inner rebellion against the way her mother had raised her to be prim and docile. The late-born child of Minnie and Merdis Jordan, Beth had been strictly raised with vanity of any sort discouraged by a loving but protective mother. Beth had tried to conform, but the outward-looking, gregarious, and fun-loving ways of her father's people were more attractive to her nature. Once old enough to be out from under her mother's control, Beth put enjoyment and gaiety as necessary components to whatever she was doing. The fact that this gave rise to some gossip that was untrue, she ignored. She knew that she tended to be unconventional, but that was all. She wondered if that was part of the reason Art had rejected her. By the time Rhonda's dinner meeting arrived, she was still out of sorts.

Friday morning she decided not to go—she was in no mood to meet people and pretend an interest in HOP. Rhonda wouldn't be too surprised, Beth reasoned, because I said I wasn't sure. That's a shabby and selfish way to treat your friend, her conscience said—she needs you there, and you're thinking only of yourself. By the end of the workday, Beth resigned herself to doing what she should do instead of what she wanted to do.

She dressed in a pleated skirt in blue and black tones with

gold medallions around the bottom. The matching vest worn over a long-sleeved white blouse had gold medallions on it. Black T-strap shoes went on over sheer pantyhose that showed off her long legs. The image in the mirror didn't suit her when she looked. Beth's face was square with high cheekbones and a jawline that could be too firm when she set it. Her lips were full and well shaped, her eyes dark and wide. She had taught herself to use a minimum of makeup effectively, so she took a blusher now to highlight her cheekbones and applied a dramatic red lipstick. Her thick auburn curls were framing her face, but she still needed something to set off the outfit. She tried on a pair of elongated gold swirl earrings. They caught the light and complemented her honey-colored skin. Satisfied, she put on her coat, picked up her bag, and left the house.

"Come in, Beth," Henry said, his thin face with its scraggly eyebrows and kind eyes lighting up with a smile.

Rhonda was immediately behind him. She pulled Beth into her arms for a brief hug. "Thanks for coming, Beth."

The bell rang again, and she opened the door. "Loretta. Come in." Loretta Daniels, administrative assistant to one of the directors at the Jamison Medical Center with only ten years to go before retirement, greeted Rhonda and Henry warmly. Then she turned to Beth. "I haven't seen you for a while, Beth. How are your mom and dad?" Beth had known Mrs. Daniels all of her life, and she attended the same AME Zion church as the Jordans.

"Mama's trying to get over a heavy cold that's kept her up and down since the holidays. Seems like she can't shake it. Daddy's trying hard not to catch it."

"I knew I hadn't seen her at church lately. Please tell her I asked about her, and I'll try to get by to see her."

Another ring of the bell brought in Windell Myers, loan officer at the bank in the Plaza. A stocky man with a smooth face and mixed gray hair grown fashionably long in the back, Windell was well known to the black community in Jamison as a facilitator of many small business and personal loans.

As the small group moved from the doorway into the living room, Beth excused herself. In the bathroom mirror she looked to see if the nervousness she felt was apparent. At some point this evening, Loretta was sure to ask her about Art, who lived two doors from the Daniels family, and Loretta had a proprietary interest in him and his welfare. She'd always hoped Art and Beth would marry, so Beth knew she'd have to tell Loretta that Art was marrying Evelyn. She hoped that when the moment came her dignity and intelligence would help her. That decided, Beth cooled herself with cold water on her face then redid her makeup and combed her hair. I guess I'm ready for the evening, she thought, as she left the safety of the bathroom.

She went directly into the kitchen to where Rhonda was putting last-minute touches on the plates of salad. Beth picked up three. "I'll put these on," she said and took them into the dining room. Rhonda brought the other three.

"What else needs to be done?" Beth asked.

"You should be in the living room with the other guests," Rhonda said, returning to the kitchen with Beth behind her, "but it would be helpful if you could fix the glasses. They're cooling in the fridge, and there's water and iced tea to be put in pitchers."

"I know where everything is, so you attend to the stove and leave this to me," Beth said, opening the refrigerator.

"The other team member came while you were in the bathroom," Rhonda said as she carefully slid the roast onto a silver platter.

"Who is it?" Beth asked politely.

"A guy who works at Alumax but lives here in Jamison. I hadn't met him before, but Henry seems to have either met him or heard about him."

"What's his name?" Beth finished filling the glasses with ice then put them on a tray.

"Cy," Rhonda answered as she placed the last of the browned potatoes around the glistening roast. She stepped back to see the platter. "Does that look all right?"

"A sprig or two of parsley would add something if you have it. It sure smells good." Beth watched as Rhonda tucked small curls of the bright green herb among the golden brown potatoes.

"Do you know him?" Rhonda asked.

"Who? Oh, you mean Cy. What's his last name?"

"Brewster. There, how does that look?"

"Looks great, and ready to be eaten. No, I don't know that name at all. You take the meat, and I'll bring the vegetables."

When all of the food was on the table, Rhonda stepped into the living room and invited Henry and the guests to come to dinner while Beth went back to the kitchen to get the beverage pitchers.

"Henry, here at the head, Loretta here," Rhonda said, indicating the seat to Henry's right, "and Windell, here," indicating the seat opposite Loretta. Rhonda turned her attention to Beth, who brought in two full pitchers, watching them carefully until she deposited them on the table.

"Beth, I'd like you to meet Cy Brewster, our fourth team member," Rhonda said, "and Cy, this is Beth Jordan."

Beth looked across the table at the man standing beside Rhonda. There was a jolt of recognition between them as they gazed at each other and then said hello.

"Beth, here, please," Rhonda said, indicating the chair beside Windell. Cy Brewster instantly moved around to pull out the chair for Beth. "Thank you," she murmured and felt a current of awareness as his arm lightly brushed hers.

"Cy, you're here, opposite Beth," Rhonda directed as she sat down at the end of the table between them. "Henry, will you bless the table, please?"

Beth bowed her head in wonderment that sitting across from her so close that they could touch each other was the man with the scarlet Saturn.

Chapter 4

Cy Brewster couldn't believe his good fortune. So close that he could look into her eyes and see that they were as velvety dark as he thought they were sat the girl he'd been trying to find. He'd already made a few discreet inquiries of a friend or two about a Jamison girl who drove a dark green Honda but without success. Now here she was, and she'd remembered him just as he had remembered her. Maybe his luck was changing, he thought, as the blessing ended and he raised his head to look at her again.

Beth Jordan. He said the name to himself. He liked it. It fit her, he thought, as he made conversation with Mrs. Daniels on his left and accepted food from Mrs. Hayes on his right. Without being obvious he looked at Beth's hands. The only ring she wore was what appeared to be a birthstone ring.

''Iced tea, Mr. Brewster, or water?'' Beth asked.

''Water, please,'' Cy said and handed her his glass. ''Please call me Cy. Mr. Brewster sounds much too formal.''

Beth smiled, and when she handed him the filled glass and he said, ''Thanks,'' she replied, ''You're welcome, Cy.''

Cy was thinking how easy it was to listen to Beth's low-pitched voice when Mrs. Hayes asked, "Have you been in Jamison long, Cy?"

"Only a few months," Cy said. He had answered this same question in the living room while Rhonda and Beth were in the kitchen, so he addressed himself to them. "We're from Charleston, but my folks have wanted to live in Jamison, so now that Dad's retired they bought a place on Zinnia Lane. My older brothers and my sister live in New York and Atlanta, so I came to live here also, a block or so away from them in the Waterford apartments."

"I've been here only fifteen years," Rhonda said. "I'm from Spartanburg, but Beth is a native." Rhonda deliberately drew Beth into the conversation not only as a good hostess but with the thought that if Beth found Cy interesting, she might decide to participate in HOP with him as a teammate.

Beth had been listening but did not raise her eyes from her plate until Rhonda spoke her name. She couldn't ignore such an obvious cue. "My parents and I have never lived anywhere but here," she said, looking across at Cy. "Mama was a Bowman, and they've been here forever, it seems. My daddy's from upstate."

"So you're an only child?" Cy wanted as much information as he could politely get.

"Yes, but I was practically raised with a bunch of first cousins."

Beth saw a glint of mischief in his eye as Cy asked her innocently, "Did they keep you from being lonely, or spoiled?"

"It certainly helped the loneliness. As to being spoiled, that's not for me to say." Her voice held a hint of challenge.

Rhonda had excused herself and gone to the kitchen to replenish the food. The others at the table had been discussing the latest political scandal. Cy picked up the nearest dish and, using it as an excuse, leaned across the table and offered it to Beth. "Perhaps I'll be able to say after I know you better," he said softly.

Beth felt a tingle as Cy's probing gaze held her own. She took the dish and offered it to Windell, who passed it across the table to Loretta Daniels. As Loretta took it, she looked across the table at Beth and caught her eye. ''How's Art?'' she asked casually. ''I haven't seen much of him lately.''

Beth said just as casually, ''Oh, you hadn't heard the news? He's getting married to a girl from home named Evelyn Hardy.''

There was an instant of silence at the table. Both Loretta and Windell tried to hide their shock. Beth picked up her glass, willing her hand not to tremble as she held it. Cy's social antenna told him immediately that this announcement from Beth carried much more than what was apparent on the surface.

Rhonda, now back at the table, picked up the ball. ''Yes. I heard that, too. I understand Evelyn's been teaching in Columbia, but I guess she'll get a job here as soon as she can.'' She turned to Cy. ''I don't know if you've met Art Woods. He has the local limousine service and also a body shop on Green Street.''

Henry now did his part. He'd been slicing more of the roast beef and, picking up the platter, urged Loretta to have some.

That wasn't so hard, Beth thought. If I can do it once, I can do it anytime I need to. She glanced around the table, assessing reactions. Poor Loretta. The shock still showed, although she was putting on a brave face as she spoke with Henry. Windell had Cy engaged, but Cy looked at her speculatively from time to time.

Dessert was served and over coffee in the living room Rhonda reviewed the Helping Ourselves Project and how the ten teams had been selected. Loretta and Windell would be Team Three, Beth and Cy Team Four.

''What kinds of things are the teams expected to do?'' Windell asked.

''Anything that improves the general welfare of the community. I don't want to give you specific ideas. The committee's looking for vision and creativity—that's why this year we thought of teams. It's our hope that from your different backgrounds you'll come up with an expanded variety of ideas that will truly enhance our community life.''

Loretta was looking at the notes she'd taken. Windell and Beth looked thoughtfully into space. Cy's face was bright and lively. ''What're you thinking, Cy?'' Rhonda asked.

"I was just going over some broad areas of possibilities like recreation, education, healthcare, the arts, and housing," he said.

"The economy and finances, too," Windell added. Loretta nodded her agreement.

"What about transportation, civic and religious affairs," Beth said. "Would they be outside what the committee's looking for?"

"It all depends," Rhonda said. "I'll be your liasion with the committee, and I'll be in touch with you on a regular basis. As soon as you've decided what your team wants to do, let me know."

"The deadline is when?" Cy asked.

"Last week in May. The award ceremony is in June."

Rhonda's initial mention of the HOP teams had made little impression on Beth. Her thoughts and emotions had been focused on Art and the news in his letter. She'd come tonight more out of a sense of debt to Rhonda than an interest in HOP. At dinner when Loretta asked about Art, Beth had surprised herself with the simple announcement of his engagement to Evelyn Hardy. A sense of release had followed and later, when Rhonda explained again about HOP, Beth found herself listening carefully. Working with the project would give her something to think about and an outlet for energy. Having Cy Brewster as a teammate wasn't a bad thing either. He was a stranger, an unknown entity, and that should add some zest to the next few months. As she came to this conclusion, Rhonda was saying, "If there are no more questions or comments, I take it that your two teams are prepared to begin."

Loretta looked at Windell. "When I get back to the office Monday and look at my schedule, I'll give you a call to arrange a meeting."

Windell nodded. "I think we'll be able to come up with something helpful to the community," he told Rhonda.

"That sounds encouraging. Beth and Cy, what about you?" Rhonda was hopeful that Beth had been won over and would make a commitment.

"I'm ready anytime," Cy said, looking at Beth.

Beth looked at Rhonda. "We'll get together and think of something," she promised.

Rhonda didn't try to hide her enthusiasm. "I can't thank you four enough." Her wide smile covered them all. "The committee will be as happy as I am to know you've agreed to participate and we'll look for great things from Team Three and Team Four."

Cy was feeling cautiously optimistic. Like Rhonda he hadn't been sure that Beth would be working with him. He didn't know why she was holding back, but he'd hoped everyone else's interest would carry her along.

Sometimes good things happen when you do what you're supposed to do. When Gary Raeford, his supervisor at Alumax, had told him he'd been selected to represent them, he'd agreed at once to do so. It had been explained that he'd have a partner from another organization, but how could he ever have expected it to be the girl he'd been looking for since seeing her from his car? Why he felt attracted to Beth the first time their eyes had met he didn't know. Finding out would be part of the fascination in working with her these next few months. Cy made himself a promise to do all he could to keep their work together not only interesting but challenging because he had a feeling Beth Jordan was the kind of person who would respond to challenge.

Henry brought in the coats from the bedroom. Beth moved to get hers, but Cy took it and held it for her. "Where do you live, Beth?" Her coat and her skin carried a faint fragrance which Cy couldn't identify but found pleasing.

"At 440 Willow Creek Road in Willow Wood subdivision. Do you know it?"

"Yes, I do. My number at the Waterford apartments is 62A." Cy watched the graceful way Beth's hands moved as she adjusted her long silk scarf. "I'll call you tomorrow or Monday if I may to see when we can get together." Beth looked at him thoughtfully, and Cy smiled reassuringly. "We need to get Team Four on the road and not let the other nine get ahead of us."

Beth's answering smile did not reach her eyes as she gave Cy her telephone number.

"Cy, I wanted to ask you about a guy I used to know at Alumax," Windell said coming up and, as Cy turned to him politely, Beth told Rhonda and Henry good night and left.

On his way home fifteen minutes later, Cy took a detour past 440 Willow Creek Road. One light burned in the apartment, where the green Honda was parked.

Good night, Beth, Cy thought. He wondered if the sadness in her eyes had something to do with the man named Woods. He wanted very much to know about that.

Maybe the next time he saw her, he could do something about bringing her smile back.

Chapter 5

''Beth Ann?''

''Morning, Mama. How're you feeling today?'' Beth had dashed to get the telephone as she came in from picking up the Sunday paper.

''A little better, got a little more strength in my legs.'' Minnie Jordan's strong voice still had a raspy edge to it.

''I'm glad to hear that, Mama. How's your appetite?''

''It's better, too, though I don't feel much like cooking.''

''Good, because I'm bringing a pot over for you and Daddy. Okay?''

''We're right here. I'll wait till I see you then because there's something I want to talk to you about, Beth Ann.''

Her mother's voice sounded heavy with meaning, and Beth felt an involuntary contraction of her stomach muscles. She had been putting off telling her parents about Art's engagement to Evelyn Hardy while still intending to do so before mentioning it to anyone else. She had not foreseen being at Rhonda's dinner—and Loretta Daniel's direct question. Now as she carefully placed her pot in a box in the trunk of the Honda, she thought it was surely Loretta who'd informed her mother so they could talk about what had happened. The two friends had always wanted to see Beth married to Art.

Merdis and Minnie Jordan lived twenty minutes from Beth in a modest two-bedroom house. Merdis, lately retired from long employment with the state's largest lumber company, had embarked upon a list of house repairs and small furnishings. It seemed to Beth that each time she came home, her father had something new to show her. He opened the door, a tall, thin man with a long smooth face showing scant signs of his sixty-eight years except for wrinkles around his brown eyes.

"Smells like something good's in the pot," he said as he reached to take it from her.

"Be careful, it's still hot," Beth warned.

"Your mother's in the kitchen, and when she's through I want to show you what I just built," Merdis said, leading the way through the living room and into the kitchen.

Beth hung her jacket over a kitchen chair. "You're looking better, Mama," she said. Last week her mother had looked gray and dull-eyed. Even though the grayness was gone, and the brown eyes in her full face looked clearer, Beth could see sadness and disappointment in them.

"Sit down, Beth Ann." Minnie indicated the chair across from her and got right to the point. "What's this Loretta told us about Art?" she asked sternly.

Merdis pulled out a chair next to Beth. "First, let's tell Beth exactly what it was that Loretta said, Minnie. She said that you said Art's engaged to another girl." His voice made a question of the statement, and it was to this that Beth responded.

"That's what I said because that's what Art told me in his letter." Beth's voice was calm, but under the table her hands were clenched tight.

"In a letter? He didn't tell you in person?" her mother said in disbelief.

"We haven't seen much of each other lately, and he went home to Winnsboro for Christmas. I thought he was just busy with his businesses," Beth explained.

"No big quarrel, no falling out?" Merdis asked.

"No, Daddy. Nothing like that."

"Who is the girl?" her mother demanded. Beth related what she knew about Evelyn Hardy.

"But didn't he ask you to marry him, Beth Ann?" Minnie's voice was sharp with anger and disappointment.

Beth nodded her head affirmatively, not trusting herself to speak.

"The problem was you liked him, but didn't love him?" Merdis asked slowly.

Beth turned to her father gratefully. "I guess that's what it was, Daddy. That's why I could never wear his ring," she managed to say.

"Then why did you keep him hangin' around all this time? No wonder he got tired of it and found someone who'd appreciate him." Her mother's eyes pierced Beth with disapproval. "You've got to change your flighty and frivolous ways, miss, or you'll never get married. No real man's going to put up with that kind of carrying on!"

"That's enough, Minnie," Merdis said sharply.

With tears rolling down her face, Beth picked up her bag and rushed from the house. It wasn't until she was several streets away that she began shivering and realized her jacket was still hanging over the kitchen chair, but she didn't turn back. She barely got the Honda into the driveway and herself into the apartment before the hurt and misery from her mother's words overwhelmed her. Beth slid down against the door. She put her arms around her knees and laid her head on them as deep sobs poured from her.

Beth knew that her mother's way of looking at life was very different from her own, but nothing her mother had said since Beth was an adult had been so filled with disapproval, so biting it had an edge almost of scorn and contempt.

The kernel of truth in that indictment tore at Beth. What did she do in her life other than try to enjoy herself and hold down a job? She wasn't involved in anything serious or worthwhile. The last challenging task she'd done had been to learn a new software program, and that hadn't taken too much effort.

Her mother had called her flighty and frivolous and in his letter Art had said there didn't seem to be anything permanent for them. Did that mean she was so light-minded that she was incapable of a serious, responsible commitment? Maybe she needed to face the fact that she had this flaw in her character. As this thought occurred to her, Beth's tears dried up. She sat looking into space, feeling empty and despondent. At last, she got to her feet and in the bathroom washed her face over and over with cold water. The mirror showed her eyes were still red and puffy. As she dabbed at them with a soft towel, her stomach growled, making her aware she'd had only a cup of coffee when she first got up, and now it was afternoon.

In the kitchen Beth began to warm up her part of the food she'd made to take to her parents. Its fragrance suddenly made her ravenous. She quickly mixed corn meal batter and, too hungry to wait for it to bake, began making it into corn cakes on the griddle. The doorbell rang, and she hurried to answer it before the cakes needed turning.

"I took a chance that you might be home, Beth," Cy Brewster said with a friendly smile. " I also took a chance that you might let me in, even though I didn't call first, if I brought you some extra special Ben and Jerry's ice cream." He held out the sack, and Beth automatically reached out to take it while her mind was still taking in the fact of Cy's presence at her door.

A look of alarm crossed Cy's face as he sniffed the air. "Something's burning, Beth."

"My corn cakes!" Beth ran to the kitchen followed by Cy. The overheated griddle had blackened the cakes, and smoke had begun to fill the air. The burner was red-hot, and the heat from the griddle's handle almost made Beth drop it as she moved it to an unheated burner. Cy turned from opening the windows above the sink.

"If you'll open your back door, I'll set this outside to cool off," he said, wrapping the handle with a towel then picking it up with a pot holder. As they carried out the maneuver and returned to the kitchen, Beth said, "If you hadn't—" at the same instant that Cy said "If I hadn't—" Beth's legs suddenly felt a little wobbly and, not wanting Cy to notice, she sat down on one side of the kitchen table and gestured for him to sit.

''If I hadn't rung the bell when I did, you wouldn't have burned your corn cakes.'' Cy finished his sentence. ''Is that what you were going to say, too, Beth?'' Cy said with a little smile.

Since his first look at Beth when she opened the door, Cy had been troubled by the sadness in her face and the evidence of a long crying spell. His first inclination had been that he should turn around and go home. Then he smelled the smoke, and his only thought was Beth's safety. Now that the danger was past, and he was sitting across from her, he wondered what could have happened since the dinner Friday night at Rhonda's to cause Beth so much sorrow.

Beth was trying to get her bearings. First, her mother had slapped her down verbally, and she'd come home to try to deal with that wound. Then out of nowhere comes Cy Brewster, the man in the red Saturn, whom she had just met formally Friday night. A few seconds later the kitchen is nearly afire, and Cy jumps right in. Too much is happening too fast, she thought, as she gently rubbed her smoke-irritated eyes. She knew they must still be red and swollen because they felt sore. At this point she didn't care how she looked to Cy as he asked was that what she'd been about to say.

''Yes, it was,'' Beth said candidly, ''but it isn't true. I could have turned off the burner before going to the door.''

''Or moved the griddle off the burner,'' Cy offered with a smile hovering around his mouth.

''Or waited until I'd turned the cakes,'' Beth responded with a lighter tone.

''Or not answered the door at all,'' Cy said, hoping to erase some of the sadness from her face. Beth wore faded jeans and a pullover that had once been a vibrant rose. Now its softened tone blended well with the unadorned brownness of her skin. Cy thought how you could see more of what a woman is like when her face is bare.

''Now that's a thought,'' Beth said, pushing back her hair. She had meant to do something with it today, but that would have to wait. She focused on Cy for the first time. In his black jeans and black turtleneck with his diamond-studded earlobe, his mustache, goatee, and shaved head he looked . . . what was the right word? Rakish, maybe? Interesting, certainly. Something a little enigmatic about him despite his outward easy friendliness. "What would you have done had I not answered the door?" Beth was curious to see how his mind worked.

I finally have her attention, Cy thought. Now if I can just get her to laugh. "What would I have done?" he repeated. He raised a finger. "One, I could have gone home, but I don't accept defeat easily." He raised a second finger and smiled as he leaned a little across the table. "Two, I like a little better. I might have sat in my car and waited for you to look out to see who'd been ringing your bell so persistently." There was the beginning of a smile on Beth's face as he raised a third finger. "Three, and this is the one I like best," he said confidingly. "I would have beat a tattoo on your door and windows while yelling, 'Yo, Beth, let me in!' " He threw back his head in a mock yell.

Beth's smile widened and became a laugh at this outrageous picture. The more she thought of it and the likely reactions of her neighbors, the more she laughed. "You are crazy," she told Cy appreciatively.

"You're absolutely right," he said delighted to see her laugh. He reached across the table and touched her hand. "A little craziness helps us to get by." Her fingers were long, slim, and warm to his touch. Before he could stop himself, an irresistible impulse made him lift her hand and hold it against his cheek. He closed his eyes, marveling at the softness of her skin. He heard Beth's sudden indrawn breath and released her hand, chiding himself for all he had meant to do was make Beth laugh, not come on to her in any way.

Cy leaned as far back in his chair as he could. "Now about those corn cakes," he said. "You must have been getting ready to eat and the least I can do is to make you some more if you don't mind showing me where things are."

Beth, anxious to act as if nothing had happened, and that

her hand wasn't still tingling from the way Cy had held it to his cheek, said, ''Don't tell me you can cook as well as beat a tattoo on a door.''

''Sure can, girl. I'm thirty-three, so I've been a bachelor a long time, and I finally decided I'd better learn to cook if I wanted to eat good.'' He sent an easy smile across the table.

''I really did want the cakes to go with a new soup I made, but I used up the rest of the mix,'' Beth said. ''I've got cornmeal if you know how to make them from scratch.''

''That's mostly how I cook.''

''Then you make them, and I'll find something for a salad and dessert. Oh, the ice cream! What did I do with it?'' Beth jumped up and looked around.

''I think I saw the bag in the sink,'' Cy said, his eyes following her every movement, his senses still stirred by her hand on his cheek.

''I like your kitchen,'' Cy said as he watched Beth put the ice cream in the freezer and set out the ingredients he needed. The cream-colored walls had a coral border. The sink with its counters and cupboards on each side, and the refrigerator to its right, was opposite the stove, which had cupboards above it and a large workspace on its right side. The oblong table and four chairs were at the far end of the rectangular space. Sunlight poured into the room from the two large windows, which were above the sink and decorated only with a coral valance over cream miniblinds.

''So do I,'' Beth said, taking out a mixing bowl. ''It's one of the main reasons I chose this apartment. I think this is everything you need,'' she said as Cy came over to the counter. He quickly mixed his batter and heated the heavy skillet she gave him. Beth turned on the burner to heat the soup while she mixed a green salad and set the table. Each was engrossed in thought, and there was no real conversation as they prepared the meal.

Beth was trying to think of anything but Cy because so much about him was very different from what she'd found in Art. Her mouth curved in a smile, recalling the door tattoo idea—and Cy, glancing at her when he thought she wasn't noticing, wondered what she was smiling about. Art had no interest in the cooking she enjoyed, and here was Cy . . . totally at home in her kitchen.

"Coffee or something cold?" she murmured, knowing he'd prefer coffee.

"Coffee, please." Every time she was near, Cy felt his senses respond to her and to the faint fragrance that seemed to emanate from her. There was danger here and, as he poured the last of the batter, he resolved to shut off his emotions and stay strictly to the business at hand, the Helping Ourselves Project.

Beth filled the coffeemaker and plugged it in at the table. She brought two dark blue mugs, some sugar and cream, and surveyed the table. Cy turned from the stove. "Ready?"

"Mmmm," she said affirmatively.

Standing beside Cy at the stove, Beth held the deep bowls for him to fill with the steaming soup. She carried them carefully to the table, and Cy followed with his plate of delicately browned corn cakes. They bowed their heads, and Beth said grace.

"Tell me about this soup," Cy said after tasting it. "I don't think I've ever had it before."

"It's a new one for me," Beth said. "I love dried beans, and I wanted something other than chili with my red beans after I'd soaked them. I put in chunks of beef, pork, and chicken cooked in garlic, onions, and oil, added potatoes, bay leaf, and tomato paste to taste. Do you like it?" Beth hoped he did—somehow his opinion was important to her.

"You can see I do." Cy's bowl was nearly empty. "There's a spice I can't name that gives it a distinctive flavor."

"I tried some allspice, is there too much?"

"Not for me."

"Your corn cakes are just right," Beth said and made a small childlike smacking sound as she ate a piece to show her appreciation. The comfort she felt sitting and eating the meal they'd put together was reflected in her eyes, and Cy responded with a warm smile. Get on with the project, he reminded himself, before you lose yourself in this quiet intimacy and touch her again.

"Have you thought of any way our team can approach this project?" he asked.

Beth was glad for the questions, so she could drown out her mother's "flighty and frivolous" still in the back of her mind. Wasn't she being exactly that in feeling this attraction to Cy, whom she had met only two nights ago and knew nothing about? Cut him off and stick to business, she admonished herself as she answered, "No, I haven't. Have you any ideas?"

By the time they had finished their meal and were drinking coffee, they'd tossed around some of the things they felt would benefit the community. Both liked the idea of helping set up small businesses, perhaps a children's day care, a fix-it shop, a bakery, an outlet for crafts, even a day care for senior citizens or a center for young people.

"You and I have made a lot of contacts with people through where we work," Cy said, "and you know practically everyone in town, having lived here all of your life. That's in our favor. What about your work time?"

"Marty Armstrong owns Jamison Realty, where I work," Beth said. "He told me I could use my computer setup there anytime. I already have a key for the nights I work late with some of the agents. How much free time do you have away from your work and your social life?" Beth bit her tongue. She hadn't meant to put in those last four words. Cy's social life, which she was certain must be quite full, was not her business. She busied herself pouring more coffee to avoid looking at him.

"I have very few calls upon my time away from work, since I long ago decided to do only what I choose to do," Cy said, "as against what others may want me to do."

Sounds egotistical to me, Beth thought as she stirred her coffee. But then she wondered if Cy had simply expressed in words the concept she herself had been following. Look at where that concept had brought her.

Cy saw Beth's face settle into soberness and pondered what it could be that kept making her sad. "Where do you want to go from here, Beth?" he asked gently. He felt safe in leaving the next step to her. He did not think she would pull away from the project now no matter what her personal problems might be. If she did, he promised himself he would use every type of persuasion at his disposal to pull her back in. He had no intention of losing track of her again.

"Let's each of us do some more thinking on the types of micro-business operations we've talked about, and next time we meet we can decide on one. All right?"

"Fine with me." Beth looked tired and Cy got up. "Thanks for the good food, Beth. Next time I'll call first so you won't have to worry about burnt food nor me beating a tattoo on your door." He was trying to leave her with at least a little smile.

Beth led the way from the kitchen through the living room. Cy's attention was caught by a large framed picture of a younger Beth surrounded by a group of other children.

"Are these the first cousins you told me about last night who kept you from being lonely?" he asked.

"They're the ones," Beth said, "my aunt Elly's and uncle Sim's kids." She pointed to each one as she named them. "This is Lucious, he's the oldest and Jannie is just a year younger. Then Nelson, Annette and Toria. This one next to me was Bobby. He and I were the same age." She pointed to a bright-faced boy with lots of hair. "He was killed in an accident. I often wonder what he'd be like all grown up. We were best buddies, and I still miss him. We could always talk about anything." Beth put down the picture and turned to Cy.

Cy's face was grave, his eyes remote. He seemed to wrench himself back to the present. "Yes," he said, "we do wonder that. Where do your cousins live?"

"Three houses down the street."

As she opened the door Beth said, "Thanks for coming, Cy, and for the ice cream and the corn cakes."

"It was all my pleasure," he answered formally. He did not try to lighten the serious look on his face, and Beth wondered what had put it there as he said, "I'll call you soon, Beth," and turning, went away.

Chapter 6

Beth wondered if the sun would ever shine again. It had been gray, rainy, and cold for two days. As she splashed across the lot to her car, she decided the last thing she wanted to do was go home to a dreary and lonely apartment. She passed her driveway a little while later and stopped down the street at her aunt Elly's house.

''Where've you been, girl?'' Jannie said, opening the door. At twenty-three Jannie looked a possible eighteen to her dismay. Her petite size and innocent-looking face made it necessary for her to continually prove her age with her ID. ''Daddy was just saying you haven't been over for days.'' She closed the door and raised her voice. ''Hey, everybody, look who's here!''

''It hasn't been that long,'' Beth protested as she followed Jannie into the kitchen and greeted her aunt and uncle.

The large kitchen with its round table where most of the meals were eaten was like most of the house: clean, cheerful, bright, and more comfortable than smart with all the signs of a big family whose income went more toward education than decoration.

Uncle Sim, his heavy body seated in a chair at the table, looked up from his paper and put out one arm to pull Beth into a brief hug. "How you doing, Beth?" His dark eyes looked knowing and kind.

"I'm okay, Uncle," Beth said and moved on to Aunt Elly, who was busy at the stove.

Aunt Elly looked a lot like Beth's mother, but Elly's gentler nature made her brown eyes soft, the lines in her face pleasant and open and her generous mouth ready to smile. Beth often pondered how the two sisters were so different, yet their upbringing had been the same, and both had found good husbands. Maybe her mother would have been happier with a whole brood of children like Elly, who'd had six over a span of fourteen years. Lucious was out of the house now, but Jannie, Nelson, Annette and Toria kept the place full of noise and activity that could get on Beth's nerves occasionally but was mostly welcome and enjoyable.

Aunt Elly turned from the stove where she was stirring gravy. "You can put that kiss right here." She turned her right cheek. Elly and Beth were the same height, and there was enough family resemblance for Beth to have been Elly's daughter. She'd been anxious to see her niece ever since Minnie had called about Art's letter. Twice she'd sent the kids to see Beth, but they hadn't caught her home. "We'll just have to wait until she's ready to see us," she'd told her husband.

"Go put your plate on the table," she said after Beth kissed her. "Yes, ma'am," Beth said fervently, looking at a platter heaped with chicken.

Jannie went to the foot of the stairs. "Dinner's ready." Doors opened and music went off as Annette, seventeen, and Toria, a year younger, came downstairs. "Nelson!" Jannie called again, then went back to the kitchen. After a few minutes Nelson, eighteen and tallest person in the family, appeared just as everyone was quiet for the blessing. Nelson stood motionless until his father raised his head. "Hey, Cuz," he said, sitting down next to Beth.

Conversation at the table, while the chicken, rice, gravy, and succotash got passed around, was a jumble of school gossip from the three still in high school. Beth basked in the warmth of the family atmosphere, watching her young cousins—fondly known as Nel, Net, and Tory—tell anecdotes one after the other. They tolerated school but were anxious to get out of it and be able to decide what they thought they wanted to do next. Beth remembered her feelings at their ages and how exciting that future had seemed then. In the next pause in the conversation, Beth said, "I guess you've all heard about Art Woods."

"Minnie called," Aunt Elly said, "but if you don't mind, could you tell us yourself?"

Everyone looked at her as Beth related the basic facts of Art's engagement. The younger girls sat enthralled at this true-life shattered romance—it was better than the soap operas they saw. Jannie was horrified, thinking how she would feel if her sweetheart, Timmy Sexton, would send her such a letter.

"That's awful!" Her voice was full of outrage. "Why didn't he at least come and tell you in person?"

'He's chicken, that's why," pronounced Nelson scornfully. Net and Tory added their two cents' worth to the effect that Art must be crazy because Evelyn couldn't possibly be in the same class as Beth.

"Now let's not go wild here," Uncle Sim said. "Art Woods is a good man. Beth wouldn't have spent time with him otherwise, and he's been in this house at this table more than once." He looked at his youngest son, Nelson. "But you have a point, Nel. He should have been man enough to tell Beth in person. You remember that if you're ever in that situation." He looked at his son until Nel said, "Yessir."

Aunt Elly asked, "Would that have made you feel better, Beth, honey?"

That question hadn't been raised with Beth before as the only people she'd discussed it with had been Rhonda and her parents. She didn't mind it being raised now, because in all of her growing-up days she had been accepted as part of this family—where one's ups and downs were freely shared in an atmosphere of goodwill and trust, even though opinions and comments might be totally opposite.

Beth nodded her head affirmatively. "It would have been hard. I'd no idea what was happening. But if Art had come and talked with me about seeing Evelyn, and told me how he felt, I could have a better understanding . . . and I think it wouldn't have hurt so much."

Jannie burst out, "But wouldn't you have been angry? I know I would have been!"

"I probably would have been at first," Beth admitted, "but being able to talk it all through with Art would have helped a lot."

"I don't see how he could do that, being engaged to you," Tory said, a puzzled look on her face.

"They weren't engaged, silly," Net said. "You never saw Beth wearing an engagement ring." Her sixteen-month superiority over Tory was plain in her voice. She turned to Beth. "One thing about it, there's plenty other fine men out there, Beth."

"That's enough, Net," her mother said.

"Which reminds me," Nel said, "whose red Saturn was that I saw Sunday? Didn't I see a dude with a shaved head get out of it?"

Again all eyes were on Beth. "That's just a team member for this HOP thing Rhonda Hayes got me into."

"What's HOP?" Net asked. Beth explained the project and this year's implementation of it and how her team was thinking about small-business ideas like a day care or a fix-it shop.

"I was talking to a girl I went to school with about that," Jannie said. "She's home, taking care of three children while her husband works, but they're barely making it. She said two friends want her to get a license and keep their kids, but she doesn't know if she would qualify for a license."

"That sounds like the kind of thing we might be able to help with. What's her name?"

"Loraine Dillard."

"I wonder if that's the same girl Rhonda's mentioned to me. Where does she live?"

"Probably is because she lives the next block down from Miss Rhonda," Jannie said. "You'll see if you can help her?"

"You can count on it," Beth promised.

As Aunt Elly served banana pudding for dessert and conversation became general again, Beth felt cheerful for the first time since getting Art's letter. The open discussion about it and the invittation to express her feelings in the supportive affection of the family was healing. Even the pain of her mother's words was blunted now, and she could think of them without flinching.

Later, when Beth was thanking Aunt Elly for dinner, her aunt said, "I know my sister's tongue can have a sharp edge to it. She knows it, and she told me she's sorry for what she said. Try not to let it upset you, Beth, you know what I mean, hon?" Her eyes met Beth's in a plea for understanding.

"I hear you, Aunt Elly," Beth said, "and I'll try."

A few moments later Beth parked her car in her driveway. The security light, which came on automatically in the evenings, made the apartment look welcoming to her for the first time in many days. Once inside she felt energetic enough to do something about her hair, but first she turned the stereo to her favorite jazz station. As she passed the telephone, a flashing light on the answering machine signaled a message. She pressed the button and heard Cy Brewster.

"Beth, this is Cy. Hope you're feeling well. Could we meet after work Friday? How about dinner at the Palmetto Tree? I can pick you up at seven. Think about it, and I'll call you later."

Beth reversed the tape and played the message again. Cy's voice sounded deeper than in person. It was pleasant to her ear and, as she listened, she closed her eyes and again saw Cy taking her hand and holding it against his cheek. When the message ended, she went to the kitchen and on the calendar above the counter penciled in *dinner/Cy* on Friday's date.

In the bathroom Beth set out what she needed to transform her hair from auburn red to dark brown. Changing its color and style had been her habit since she'd discovered at sixteen that her hair had the body and texture to lend itself to experimentation. She'd taught herself to develop the necessary skill with scissors, styling combs, and dyes. People who knew her accepted her frequent change of appearance as part of who Beth Jordan was.

At the end of two hours, the auburn curls were gone. Beth's hair, now a deep lustrous brown, lay like a shining cap, trimmed short with straight bangs across her forehead. Small flat half-curls outlined her face. She deftly applied eye makeup that went with the new hairstyle and decided she liked the total effect.

It was nearly ten when the telephone rang as she was cleaning up the bathroom.

"Beth, this is Cy. I hope this isn't too late to call, but I just got in." Cy's voice was a little anxious.

Beth smiled as if Cy could see her. "It's all right, you said you'd call back later." Should I tell Cy now about Loraine or do some work on the day care myself first? she wondered.

"Can Team Four get together Friday evening at seven?"

"Yes, but we don't have to go out to dinner to discuss the project," Beth said.

"You can think of it as a working dinner if you want to," Cy said. "I'll pick you up at seven."

At his end, Cy hung up the telephone quickly. He'd been afraid Beth might not go out with him, and he thought the longer they talked the more reasons she might find not to go. He wanted to sit across the table from her again. This time he would study Beth Jordan.

Studying and analyzing people was a mental activity he'd pursued since high school days. This was the interest that had led him to human resources work and community service. With Beth Jordan he had a personal interest. Why did he see an underlying sadness in her? What kind of person was she? How far could he allow himself to respond safely to the attraction he felt without overstepping his self-imposed limits and endangering his secret?

Maybe he'd find out the answers to these questions on Friday.

Chapter 7

"Call for you, Beth. Can you take it?" Aretha Symonds said.

"Yes, thanks." Beth looked up from her computer, pushed the button on her telephone and positioned the receiver between her ear and shoulder without taking her eyes from her screen. "This is Beth," she said.

"This is Taresa, Beth. Cathy and I are going to see that new movie that opened Friday at the Oakwood. How about meeting us there at seven?"

When Beth didn't answer immediately, Taresa said, "Come on, girl, you've got to get out sometime. We'll even treat you, and you know that's something because our Cathy isn't much for getting up off her money!"

This got the laugh Taresa wanted as Cathy's ability to pinch a dime was well known, but the teasing about it didn't bother Cathy at all. "Hard as I work I mean to keep this money," she always said referring to her job as a fifth-grade teacher.

"Okay, Taresa. See you at seven," Beth said.

Here was the day she'd been dreading, but as she returned the telephone to its cradle Beth found she was relieved. Eventually she had to rebuild contact with the people with whom she and Art had been a couple for more than two years. In the core group of Taresa and Romy, Cathy and Bay, Betty and Vernon, Merlie and Howard, Beth with faithful Art at her side had been looked at as the person ready to do or dare for enjoyment—as long as it wasn't too outrageous, dangerous, immoral, or illegal. Now all of that was changed.

Since Art's letter Beth had spent her free time alone, coming to terms not only with Art's abrupt departure from her life but also with her mother's unflattering analysis. Minnie had told her sister, Elly, that she was sorry to have said that to Beth, but she hadn't told Beth. They hadn't spoken since that Sunday. Despite this Beth believed that parents who love their children know what they are like. Therefore even though she often saw matters differently from her mother, deep inside she could not dismiss Minnie's judgment as insignificant.

Instead of going straight home from work, Beth took long drives and ate in unfamiliar restaurants. She walked around in malls and stores. She even spent time in the area libraries. During this irregular activity pattern, she had discovered an unsuspected pleasure in her own company.

"Beth, could you please pull up the Green River Development file for me," Lana James said as she ended a client interview.

"Coming up," Beth said. Occasionally during the rest of her busy day, Beth, anticipating seeing Taresa and Cathy, came to the decision that she was going to hold on to her less social lifestyle. She needed more time to discover if this direction would become her true north or turn out to be a temporarily distracting detour.

Taresa, square face, square body, and long legs, and Cathy, trim and tailored, were waiting in the theater lobby as Beth entered. As they went to meet her, Taresa said softly, "She's changed her hair." "Which means she's going to be okay," Cathy said.

"Sure good to see you, girlfriend," Cathy said.

Taresa looked at Beth closely and hugged her. "You doing all right, hon?"

"I'm fine, and I'm glad to see you two, " Beth answered.

It was good to see these longtime friends. As they laughed together at the romantic comedy and later had some food at a nearby restaurant, Beth thought maybe she'd been wrong to cut them off, especially when Cathy began complaining.

"I've got to tell you, I was a little pushed out of shape when you didn't return my calls," Cathy said, neatly cutting her sandwich in half, then taking a bite of the kosher dill. "I was worried about you."

Before Beth could answer, Taresa said, "I told Cathy you probably didn't feel like talking to anyone yet. Not even to us."

Beth was glad Taresa understood. "I didn't mean to hurt anyone's feelings. It wasn't personal. It took me a while to get over the shock. I'm used to the idea now."

Cathy began saying something about what was going on, including a dance that was coming up. Beth ate her chili—it was the way she liked it, spicy and piping hot. She was reminded of the bean soup Cy had eaten at her table the previous Sunday. She could feel the way he had gently held her hand to his cheek and closed his eyes.

Cathy's sharp voice impinged on the sweet memory. "Did you hear what I said, Beth?"

"You were telling me that the Over-Thirty Club is giving a dance at the hotel center. When is it?"

"Valentine's Day," Taresa said. "Romy took his car to Art's shop the other day," she went on. "Art said he was bringing Evelyn to the dance so she could begin to meet people." Her glance at Beth was anxious.

Taresa was considerate about people's feelings, and Beth thought how sensible Romy was to have pursued Taresa until she promised to marry him. At their October engagement party, people had teased Beth and Art about being next. It suddenly occurred to Beth that this might have been the event that made Art decide to cut his losses. Like Romy he, too, had been in long pursuit of his love but without success and rather than continue, he began to look elsewhere and rediscovered Evelyn.

These thoughts flashed through Beth's mind and, with this

new insight, she said, "Sooner or later I'll have to see Art and meet Evelyn, so it's all right."

"You want to come along with the rest of us?" Cathy asked. "Bay and I can pick you up."

"Thanks, Cathy, but I'll manage." Beth wasn't going to hide in a crowd. Going where she wanted to go was what she'd always done whether in a group or by herself, and she wasn't going to stop now.

Beth's next two days at work were very busy as activity picked up after the holidays. She lacked the time and energy to do anything about Loraine Dillard's child-care problem and decided that could be a safe topic for discussion with Cy Brewster at dinner on Friday.

A steady rain was falling when Beth awakened Friday. Splashing in rain puddles and feeling the rain on her face were childish pleasures Beth had never outgrown. Water was a friendly element to her and being in it a refreshing experience. She put on a yellow rain slicker, matching hat, and short black boots over woolen pants and sweater. The moisture-laden air was welcome to her as she got into her car, and she looked forward to her day.

When Marty Armstrong called her into his office at ten o'clock, she wondered if her optimism had been wrong. The owner of the realty agency could be unexpected in his actions and sometimes unfair in his assessments and expectations. His saving grace was that he would listen to what a person had to say. Beth had left other jobs because of her outspokenness if she thought an action or policy was unfair, but with Marty she was going into her sixth year because they had respect for each other.

An avuncular man with mixed gray hair, he was dressed in his usual blue slacks/white shirt/navy jacket/red tie outfit that deepened the blue of his eyes. With an expansive gesture, he invited Beth to sit in one of the two upholstered chairs opposite him.

"Wet morning," he said genially as he closed a folder and drew his weekly calendar sheet toward him.

"Sure is but I like it," Beth said.

"Can't say I do, but the rain's needed. It's been drier than a hound dog in August." Marty looked absently at the falling rain then he flipped the calendar sheet back. "I see it's been a week since you and Mr. Brewster met with Mrs. Hayes and she told you about HOP. You come up with a plan yet?"

Beth knew that Marty's plan for anything was to start immediately then work hard and fast until it was completed. That's how Jamison Realty had grown from two people in a cubbyhole twelve years ago to fifteen agents plus support staff in their own building today. She hurriedly pulled her thoughts together on the ideas she and Cy had talked about.

"We've considered small-business ventures run by community people for the benefit of the community, such as a children's day care, a fix-it shop, a center for teens, a day care for seniors, a bakery, and an outlet store for local crafts." Marty wrote the items down as Beth named them.

"Which one did you choose to work on?" Marty looked at the list consideringly. "Some will be easier to do than others in the limited time you have."

"We know a person who wants to operate a day care and who already has potential clients," Beth answered smoothly. "We're meeting tonight to discuss it."

"Don't discuss it too much. Get to work on it. Anything I can do to help?" His pen was poised over the paper ready to record Beth's needs.

Let me get out of here before he pushes me farther into this corner, Beth thought and stood up. "Not at the moment, Marty. I'll keep you informed."

"All right then," Marty said. "I'm looking for Team Four to win!"

I guess I'm not going to be able to take my own sweet time on this, Beth grumbled to herself. Between Marty on one end and Cy on the other, I won't have any peace, so I might as well go to work on it. At her computer she pulled up the zoning restrictions for the area where Loraine Dillard lived. Yes, a house on her street could be licensed for day care as long as the space and safety requirements of the Department of Social Services were met. Next she called Rhonda Hayes.

"Rhonda, this is Beth. My cousin Jannie told me your friend, Loraine Dillard, wants to get licensed for child care, and I need to know about her house."

"Is this a Team Four project?"

"I hope it will be."

"Good! Loraine has three bedrooms, one and one-half baths, living room, kitchen with dining area, and a fenced-in backyard."

"No porch?"

"Yes, in the back. Have you and Cy gotten together yet?"

"Once and we're meeting again tonight. That's why I need the information."

"Let me know if I can help." Rhonda replaced the telephone thoughtfully. She hoped that this accidental pairing of Beth with Cy Brewster would prove to be fortuitous in several ways. For one thing their combination of skills and resources should produce good community projects. Rhonda's other concern was more personal.

She had watched Beth's and Art's association from the beginning and had never been convinced of a depth of feeling on Beth's part, or that they were truly matched. When James Ellington had returned to Jamison, Beth's reawakened interest in him had surfaced strongly. Rhonda, friend to both Beth and Glennette Percy, who soon turned out to be James's true love, had been sorry for Beth and admired the way she hid her hurt and disappointment.

Rhonda thought it was more habit than commitment that kept Beth seeing Art. She'd discussed with her husband, Henry, how long Art would hang on. She'd sensed at her dinner that Cy Brewster was interested in Beth. He had the kind of presence and personality that she thought Beth would find intriguing. Cy was still an unknown entity, Rhonda thought as she made a notation on her Team Four page. I have a good feeling about this. It's been only a week since my dinner, and they've already met once. They're meeting tonight, so at least Beth isn't backing away.

Cy, leaving his office promptly at five, was thinking the same thing. He couldn't keep from being keyed-up at seeing Beth again. She had been in his thoughts many times during the week. Every time he went home, he was afraid to play his messages in case there was one from her with some kind of excuse for not going to dinner.

The rain was tapering off, and an occasional star was visible in the night sky as he pulled up at Beth's apartment. He took his oversized black umbrella with him and rang the bell.

The porch light went on and the door opened.

"What? No tattoo on my door?" The lady at the door smiled as she opened the screen. "Come on in, Cy."

Cy stepped in. He was speechless. The auburn curls he remembered were gone. The whole aspect of this person facing him with amusement in her eyes had changed.

Lest Beth think he was too overwhelmed, Cy put on a stern face and asked, "Do you do this often?"

"Do what?"

"Change into another person. Because if you do, I'm going to have to get out my psychology book and begin keeping notes."

Beth executed a graceful pirouette. "Do you like the change?" Beth's shining brown hair hugged her head, and a few small flat curls added to the framing of her face. Sleek, stylish bangs along with the shape of her eyebrows and eye makeup gave her a new exotic look. She was wearing a long burnt orange knit skirt that swirled around her hips and topped her brown boots. Her close-fitting orange top had a scoop neck, and from her ears hung long amber earrings.

Cy studied her, and a slow smile lit his face. Not only had Beth's physical appearance change, but in the six days since he'd seen her, he felt in her a lightening of her spirit.

Beth raised an inquiring eyebrow, eliciting an answer to her question.

"I like the change very much," he said, and she dropped her eyes demurely. "However," he said, and she looked up at him again, "I found the original model quite fascinating also. This just makes everything twice as intriguing."

Beth started to ask what he meant but knew Cy wasn't referring to the business they were supposed to be involved in as Team Four. "Is it still raining?" she asked as she moved toward her all-weather coat lying on a chair.

"Yes, a little," Cy said as he moved quickly to hold the coat for her. Again he inhaled the faint fragrance of her skin, and as she nestled into the coat, he had to resist the impulse to press a kiss on the spot behind her ear that was tempting him. The strength of the temptation surprised him, and he stepped back sharply.

Outside Cy settled Beth in the passenger seat. As he started the car, Beth—who had been noticing all of the Saturn's features, including the rich gray color of its interior—observed, "You're driving my car, you know."

"What do you mean?" Cy turned the corner smoothly.

"Do you remember the first time we saw each other at that stoplight?"

"I'll never forget it."

"The reason I was looking was because I'd just come back from the Saturn dealership where I'd been talking to a salesman about this same model."

"All this time I've been thinking it was myself who was the attraction," Cy said. He looked at Beth mournfully. "You really know how to bring a man down."

"You can take a tiny bit of credit for yourself," Beth said, smiling. "I did tell you I lived in Jamison, which is more than I've ever done before with a highway Romeo."

Cy looked amused. "Is that the name women give to guys who try to get their attention in cars?"

"You didn't know that?"

"No, I didn't. For your information, Miss Jordan, like any other guy I've noticed ladies in cars, but you're the first one I've actually talked to." Cy hoped Beth believed him because it was true. Something had compelled him to make some verbal contact so he would not lose her.

Is this a line or the truth? Beth wondered as she glanced at Cy. Cy put his hand on hers. "Believe me, Beth."

Beth instinctively turned her hand into Cy's. His hand tightened on hers. Both looked straight ahead as the emotional energy inside the car rose. Say something, Beth told herself, as the warmth from Cy's hand began to communicate itself.

"I'd been wanting a Saturn for some months. Although I had no business doing it financially, I decided to go shopping for one that day after work. This model is the one I looked at and drove. I loved everything about it."

Beth's hand felt smooth and vital and confiding to Cy. He hadn't expected the way her fingers had curled about his. He could taste the sweetness of it in his throat. He slid the car into the slow lane so he could hold her hand as long as possible.

"Were you having trouble with your Honda?"

"None at all. I wanted something sporty, and I thought this car looked sleek and smart. I liked the way it handled."

"That's what appealed to me too." Cy looked at Beth with a smile. "Since we both like it, we'll have to see how many places we can find to go in it," he suggested.

This topic wasn't turning out to be as impersonal as Beth had thought, so she tried another.

"I remember that you said your family came from Charleston. Were you born and reared there?"

"Thirty-three years ago on April twenty-third," he said. "Both my parents' families have always lived in Charleston. Dad drove a city bus, and Mom worked off and on in the schools. My oldest brother, George, lives in New York City, not married yet. The next brother, Winston, lives in Atlanta and has two kids. My sister, Alicia, lives in Atlanta also and has three children. I'm youngest and like George, still single."

"You and George don't believe in marriage?" Beth had pictured Cy's family as he described them. If Cy was thirty-three then George must be nearly forty. In a city like New York, he certainly met many eligible women, yet wasn't married. Cy had good looks, a good job, an attractive personality and also was still single. Perhaps the two brothers had had bad experiences in their relationships but not wanting to ask that question outright, Beth asked another.

"Just the opposite," Cy said. "I believe in it so strongly

that I decided long ago to take my time in finding the right person. The first choice has to be the only choice for me.''

Twice before Cy had felt the need to state his concept of marriage to a young lady he was seeing with whom he felt he might become seriously involved. Each time the person had been turned away by his need for serious commitment. This was only the third time he'd been in Beth's company. He was surprised that he'd confided in her his deeply held principle of marriage instead of giving her some meaningless statement. He wondered what Beth's response would be.

Cy's answer was a surprise to Beth. There was no doubt of his seriousness and Beth, glancing at him, saw a different Cy than the one who would beat a tattoo on her door. Was that how she felt about marriage, that the first choice had to be right because it would be forever, even though the ease of walking away from one's vows seemed so prevalent? You stuck it out and made it work like her parents had done and like Aunt Elly and Uncle Sim were doing despite tragedy and hardship.

''There would have to be a feeling of absolutely belonging to each other to make that possible,'' she murmured.

''Yes. Absolutely belonging to each other.'' Beth's choice of words indicated to Cy that she understood the implications of his statement.

Ahead was a busy intersection where Cy would have to turn left then pull into the parking lot of the restaurant. The light turned red as they came to the intersection. Cy raised Beth's hand and turned the palm to rest against his cheek. For a long moment he held it there then released it as the light turned green. Beth let her breath go and hoped Cy couldn't hear how fast her heart was beating.

The Palmetto Tree was filled at this Friday dinner hour. As Cy and Beth waited to be seated, each tried to overcome their intense awareness of the other. They talked about the newly decorated restaurant, the weather, and issues involving two local school elections that were making daily headlines. Finally, a waiter led them to a comfortable table for two, served them beverages and rolls, and brought their orders for prime rib and steak Diane.

"I have a lead on a day-care situation that might be just the thing for a project," Beth said, determined to make this the working dinner Cy had mentioned and thus keep away from personal matters.

"Tell me about it," Cy said.

"A young married woman named Loraine Dillard, who lives on the same street as Rhonda Hayes, has been asked by several friends to keep their children. Her husband works. She stays home to take care of their three kids, two girls and a boy, four, three, and eighteen months. Loraine told my cousin Jannie that she'd like to get licensed for day care but doesn't know what the requirements are and if their house is suitable."

"Why doesn't she go on and do it on an informal basis like so many people do?"

"Her friends told her they would bring their kids only if she got a license. She can charge more if she gets a license, also."

"I wonder about the zoning in that neighborhood," Cy said, remembering that Rhonda Hayes's house, roomy and smart on the inside, was modest but well kept on the outside.

Beth explained in some detail the zoning codes in Jamison and how Loraine was lucky that her small area did permit private day care because it was an older neighborhood rather than one of the new developments. Cy admired Beth's grasp of the information and the competent way she explained it. His professional background in human resource management told him she was undoubtedly a valuable employee in the real estate agency, but what else might she be able to do? What were her career interests?

Cy's close attention and obvious interest drew more information and ideas from Beth. Over the remainder of the meal, they discussed what they would need to find out and what the possibilities were for Loraine's day care to become a reality. Cy spoke of two women at Alumax who lived in Jamison and were unhappy with their present child-care situation; its uncertainties caused them to be late for work. They could be referred to Loraine. They decided that the next step would be for Beth to talk with Loraine and get back to Cy.

As they went out to the car, Cy thought of how Beth had

managed to keep the conversation on business during dinner, and that was fine, but he had other plans for the drive home. There were still many questions about Beth to which he wanted answers, and one was pressing.

Beth congratulated herself on how well the dinner had gone. Sitting across from Cy in the restaurant had been a totally different experience from sitting across from Art. She had to admit in fairness to Art that what made the greatest difference was her own reaction. If she were going to be completely honest with herself, she would even have to say that the strong pull she felt toward Cy was not like anything she'd felt for Art. But who was being honest? There was no way she was going from Art Woods into a relationship with Cy Brewster and thus confirm that she was flighty, like her mother had said. As she settled herself in the car, she decided there would be no hand holding on the way home. She casually crossed her arms and leaned back in the farthest corner of the car seat.

Cy, searching the dial for music he thought Beth would like, started to tell her, "Message received," but smiled to himself and was silent. He wasn't yet sure how she would take that kind of teasing. But he was determined to get one bit of information from her.

Two blocks had gone by while they listened to soft jazz. Then Cy glanced at Beth, sitting back with her eyes closed and said, "Did you have a busy week?"

"Yes." Beth opened her eyes. "Business is picking up after the holiday drop, and I've stayed late a couple of nights, so I'm glad the weekend's here. How about you?" She turned her head toward him.

"The same. We've been hiring as well as beginning some fairly major departmental changes, which means a lot of work for us. Then I try to look in on Mom and Dad two or three times a week. This week Dad's had a bad cold and wanted me to do some things for him."

Beth involuntarily leaned a little toward Cy and abandoned her protective stance. "I'm sorry to hear that. Has he gotten any better?"

"Not yet, so he's staying out of the rain. How's your mother?

I remember you were telling Mrs. Daniels that she hadn't been well."

"She's better now," Beth said.

"One of the things Dad wanted me to do for him," Cy said after a moment, "was to take his car in for some work. We don't know anyone here yet, but I remembered Mrs. Hayes saying that the Woods you all were talking about had a shop. So I took it there." He gave a quick glance at Beth. She was again leaning back in her corner with her arms crossed. "Woods and I had some conversation, then I picked the car up the next day and he'd done a good job. I was impressed by his work and his shop." Cy stopped. He'd spun out the story as long as he could to give Beth time to decide her response. There had to have been a connection between Woods and Beth. He wanted to know what it was from her, not from someone else.

"He is a first-class mechanic," Beth said. "Been in business a long time."

"Beth," Cy said gently, "when Mrs. Daniels asked you about Woods at the dinner, I got the strong impression that there was something between the two of you, and therefore your answer was a total shock to her." He took his eyes off the road to look at her. She was looking at him, her face set in sober lines, her eyes giving nothing away.

"I'm not asking to be nosy," Cy went on, "but I do want very much to know. I don't want to ask anyone else or listen to gossip."

Answer the question and get it over with, Beth told herself after thinking about it. She looked straight ahead as she gave Cy the facts.

"Art and I had been seeing each other regularly for quite a while. We were never engaged, although he wanted to give me a ring. Two weeks ago with no warning I received a note from him saying he'd become engaged to a girl named Evelyn Hardy. They grew up together in Winnsboro. She's a schoolteacher in Columbia."

A muted sax and a tasteful bass filled the silence with a sweetly mournful sound. To Beth's horror she began to feel sobs rising in her throat. She hurriedly opened her bag to find the lozenges she carried and popped one in her mouth. Instead of having a soothing effect, the lozenges set off a spasm of coughing.

Cy looked at her with concern. He patted her between the shoulders. The coughing subsided, and Beth dabbed at her eyes.

"All right?" Cy said.

"I'm fine. I think I swallowed the wrong way." Beth felt slightly embarrassed but thankful that at least she hadn't burst into tears after telling Cy about Art. He would certainly have made the wrong conclusion about her feelings.

Cy was digesting what Beth had told him. Had there been an earlier quarrel? Or had Woods grown tired of waiting for Beth to make up her mind? But what he wanted to know most of all was how Beth felt about it. Undoubtedly her pride was hurt, that was understandable. But had she found that she did care for Woods after all, and was that why Cy kept feeling in her a sense of sadness?

He read Beth's little flurry a few moments ago as a diversionary tactic, conscious or subconscious on her part.

"Thanks for telling me, Beth," he said softly and left it at that. The rest he would discover later. He hoped that in time Beth would develop trust in him and then she would tell him how she felt.

Cy had no idea that Beth was now fighting the urge to tell him the whole story. Instinctively she knew Cy would understand. He would probably even help to put it into perspective for her from the male point of view.

But that would have to wait. Still she felt more relaxed and she gave herself up to listening to the sound of the music and the swish of the tires on the street and the comforting nearness of Cy Brewster.

Chapter 8

''Rhonda, could you give me Loraine's telephone number, please?''

''Sure, Beth,'' Rhonda said and read out the number over the telephone to Beth. ''So Team Four got its plan going when you met last night?''

''We talked it through. The first thing is for me to see Loraine, and I'm going to try to do that this afternoon,'' Beth said.

To Rhonda's ear Beth's voice had more energy, and she sounded more like the vibrant person Rhonda had known before. ''You sound good, honey,'' she said. ''You feeling better?''

''You know the old saying. You can't keep a good woman down,'' Beth said with a laugh.

''And we both know you're a good woman,'' Rhonda responded, joining Beth in laughter as they ended their conversation.

Beth hung up and realized that she did feel better than she had in a long time. Better might not be the right word. What she felt was purposeful. She had something to think about and to do outside of herself, and that was a good feeling. She dialed Loraine's number, hoping the young lady would be home on this Saturday morning.

Loraine answered the telephone, and Beth identified herself as Jannie's cousin. "Jannie said you'd mentioned that you wanted to get licensed for day care, Loraine. I belong to a community group whose purpose is to help people get started in small-business projects. I wondered if I could drop by today and talk with you about this?"

Loraine didn't answer right away. Beth hastened to add, "I know you don't know me, but Mrs. Rhonda Hayes knows me very well. Maybe you'd like to call her first and call me back. She gave me your number just a few minutes ago."

"If Miss Rhonda gave you my number then it's all right." There was relief in Loraine's voice. "I'll be home all day. You want to come about two?"

"That'll be fine, Loraine, and thanks. I'll see you then."

When Beth pulled up in front of the Dillard home, she tried to assess the outside appearance as she thought the licensing agency might. The front yard was neat, and what she could see of the back had a chain-link fence. The house was made of brick, and the painted trim looked fresh and unbroken. The surfaces of the walk, steps, and porch were secure and smooth.

The door opened before she could ring the bell.

"Hi. I'm Beth," she said to the young woman with a square face and deep-set brown eyes. Two small girls stood next to her, looking solemnly at Beth.

"Come in. I'm Loraine, and this is Tisha and Terry." Tisha, three, and Terry, eighteen months, sat quietly as Loraine told Beth how they couldn't afford the child-care costs to enable her to get a job. Since they had to have more income, the idea of keeping other children seemed a good way to make money. As Loraine showed Beth through the house, Beth could see it was clean and orderly. She also saw that the Dillards had only essential furniture with a few odds and ends to make the place comfortable. Beth thought this would leave lots of space for the other children.

"How many children do you think I could keep?" Loraine asked anxiously.

''That's something we'll have to find out. I know there's a certain number you can have, and that includes your own.''

''My oldest, Tony, is out with his dad. Tony's four going on five.''

''He's home all day with you and the girls?''

''He will be until the fall.''

''Have you put in a written application yet, Loraine?''

''I'm not sure where to send it or what to say.''

''Why don't you call the Department of Social Services on Monday and tell them you want to keep some children in your home. They'll send you the application, and we can take it from there.''

One of the essentials for a family day-care home Beth knew about was that the applicant had to submit some letters of reference. As she left Loraine, Beth was confident that she could write Loraine a positive recommendation. That went very well, she thought, and was anxious to hear from Cy so she could tell him all about it.

Cy Brewster's Saturday had begun with a call from an organization to whom he gave his services as often as possible.

''Cy, we got a guy here needs to talk to you. Can you come?''

''Be there in an hour,'' Cy promised. On his way he thought how the time he gave to the organization was important to him. What would Beth think about it? She was still an unknown quantity that drew him despite himself.

He pulled into the parking lot of an ordinary-looking two-story house.

Cy was ushered into a familiar room furnished with a couch, two chairs, bookshelves, and tables. The walls were painted a muted green with a border at the top of a floral pattern, which was repeated in the drapes and cushions. This was the library of Vesey House, established by a consortium of churches and community groups as an intervention program for young people when they reached a danger point in their lives. Marcus Jay, who ran the house, thought that Kwesi Michaels was at such a flashpoint, and that Cy Brewster was the best person he knew to help Kwesi see where he was going.

Marcus, a heavy man with steady eyes, large features, and a voice that he never raised, came into the room followed by a fourteen-year-old boy neatly dressed in jeans and a T-shirt. His hair was closely cut, his skin clear, and his features unexceptional. But as he politely acknowledged the introduction Marcus made before leaving the room, Cy could see that the boy's eyes told another story. They were angry and scornful and a little afraid.

There was no foolproof way to do these sessions, Cy knew. If you began with ordinary conversation so each of you could get a feel of what the other was like before attempting the hard part, the other person was liable to think that he was being softened up or that you were pretending an interest you didn't have. Nevertheless Cy could do it no other way. His interest was sincere regardless of what the other thought, and the tension level usually went down before the crux of the matter had to be addressed. This happened now, as in a relaxed position in a cushioned chair with Kwesi opposite in a similar chair, Cy led the conversation into sports, television, movies, and music. Kwesi answered easily.

"Is Jamison your home, Kwesi?" Cy asked.

"Charleston's my home," Kwesi said.

"Mine, too. Where'd you live?"

"Over by Hampton Park."

"My folks are from the same area," Cy said. As they began comparing notes, they found their houses were three blocks apart and that they knew some of the same people. Cy could tell Kwesi some things about Hampton Park when he was Kwesi's age that Kwesi didn't know.

Then Cy said, "The reason I'm here is because when my folks retired, they moved here. I came to be close in case they needed me since my other brothers and sister don't live here. How come your folks moved?"

"They diidn't," Kwesi said. "They sent me to live with my uncle. It's not right, it just ain't right at all!" Anger was strong in his voice now.

"Tell me what's not right, Kwesi," Cy said.

When Kwesi was twelve, he'd started hanging around with a group of boys on his street, some older, some younger. For a long time they were just boys playing, running, scuffling, shooting baskets in the park on weekends—and no trouble at all. By the time he was thirteen, one or two of the boys had tried shoplifting and gotten away with it. They shared candy and gum with everyone. It was so easy that soon most of the boys had joined in, including Kwesi. Kwesi got caught with five candy bars one day. Because he had just turned thirteen, he was released to his parents, who confined him to the house for two months except for school. The word got around in school, and some kids thought he was dumb for getting caught. A few weeks later Kwesi's teacher's wallet was stolen with one hundred dollars in it. A note appeared on her desk printed in block letters: K. M. TOOK IT.

Unshed tears shone in Kwesi's eyes when he came to this part of the story. "I told my parents and everyone else, I didn't know nothing about Miss Fort's wallet. Nothing! But they didn't believe me because I'd been caught stealing the candy. The police were going to take me to Juvie, but my dad got a lawyer right away. They couldn't find any time when I had the chance to get the wallet. It turned out to be a girl who did it. Miss Fort gave her two F's, and they were always arguing. She sneaked into the teacher's restroom when Miss Fort was alone in there and snatched the wallet real fast. Then she left the note about me. My parents said I had to get away from that environment and sent me out here."

"I can see you had a bad time over the wallet, Kwesi," Cy said. "But what brings you to Vesey House?"

"I don't want to be here, I want to be home. Uncle Matt won't let me go anywhere except to school and church."

"Where does your uncle live?"

"Way out on the north side of town. I don't know what he's scared of. There's only three other families that live near him, and the don't have any kids my age."

Cy asked the same question again in the same even tone. "What brings you to Vesey House?"

Kwesi shrugged. "I've had a couple of fights at school when kids tried to push me around."

"How're your grades. Kwesi?"

Again the shrug. "I don't want to be at this school. They don't like me, and I don't like them."

"Where do you want to be?"

"Home."

"Do you think you'll get to go back home any sooner if you get into trouble here?"

Kwesi looked both defiant and sad at the same time as again he shrugged. Cy could barely hear his mumbled "No."

This was the start Cy was looking for. In the next hour Cy and Kwesi discussed in detail all of Kwesi's grievances. Then they talked about what Kwesi could do at home and at school to make things easier for himself.

Cy's reading of Kwesi was that he was a good kid who'd gotten off the track and was on his way to building up a king-sized grudge against everyone because of the unfair accusation that he'd stolen the wallet. He'd let that incident outweigh the initial crime of shoplifting.

Once that was in perspective, Cy could work on helping Kwesi adjust his attitude so that anger would no longer be his motivating factor. This would take time, but Cy was confident it could be done and told Marcus so after Kwesi had gone.

"I agree," Marcus said. "That's why I wanted to get you two together before Kwesi did something that would put him in trouble again. Thanks a lot, Cy. Wish we had more men like you."

There probably would be if they'd gone through what I did at Kwesi's age, Cy thought as he drove away. I wonder if Beth likes working with kids? She hasn't mentioned it, but there's still so much I don't know about her. Wonder if she'd go for a ride tomorrow?

The thought of having Beth beside him as they rode along country roads, a favorite pasttime for Cy because of the tranquility it brought him, was so attractive that he knew he shouldn't do it. He pulled into his driveway, went in the house, and called her.

"Beth, this is Cy. Am I interrupting anything?"

"Hi. No, I just got in a few minutes ago from seeing Loraine Dillard."

"Good. The Saturn is at your service tomorrow afternoon. Perhaps you'd like to go for a ride, and you can tell me about it."

"Thanks, Cy, but I can't. I'm going to see my mom and dad after church."

Cy did not give up easily. "Will you be long, do you think?"

"Depends. I really can't say, but thanks for the invitation."

Cy saw he wasn't going to persuade her, so he said, "I'll call you tomorrow night, then." He rang off quickly so Beth wouldn't tell him about Loraine. He needed that excuse to call her the next night.

As Beth did her laundry she mused on how the mind works. She'd been reluctant to visit her mother but knew she should. When Cy invited her to the Sunday ride, she immediately envisaged herself in that lovely car beside Cy, the two of them shut off from the world for a space, each comfortable with the other. Her desire to say yes was so strong that she instinctively did the opposite and decided to visit her mother, although she knew she would have to confront the pain of their last encounter. But the longer she put it off the more difficult it would be.

Minnie Jordan was peeling potatoes at the sink when she saw Beth's Honda turn into the driveway. It was not in her nature to be demonstrative, but she loved her daughter with a depth equaled by nothing else in her experience. Minnie passionately wanted Beth secure in a good marriage and had pinned her hopes on Art Woods, who had held Beth's attention longer than anyone else. That was why she had said words to Beth she had regretted ever since. Maybe she could put it right now that Beth was here.

"Where's Dad?" Beth asked after she'd greeted her mother.

"Went to the store for me, but he'll be right back. Can you stay and eat? It'll be ready soon."

Her voice held more than an invitation as she looked at Beth, and it was to this that Beth responded. "I'll be glad to. What can I do?"

"In a minute you can set the table, but now just sit here and tell me what you've been doing."

Beth began with the story of Rhonda's dinner. Her dad came in, and they all talked about HOP and what it had done in earlier years. Minnie and Merdis were interested to hear what Beth's team was doing. By the time dinner was over, the constraint Beth had felt at first had dissipated.

The closest Minnie Jordan could come to a spoken apology happened when her daughter was ready to go. Minnie brought the jacket Beth had left when she hurried from the house. Minnie laid it over Beth's arm and patted her arm affectionately.

"You feeling better about things, Beth?" Her eyes and her voice held the apology.

"Yes, Mama," Beth said and laid her cheek against her mother's.

"I'm glad," Minnie said. "I need some new shoes. Maybe you can go with me to find some one evening?"

Beth's eyes widened. "Of course, Mama. Call me when you're ready."

Beth loved shopping and often tried to persuade her mother to go, especially when the older woman said she needed a certain item. Minnie rarely went. Beth saw this concession from her mother as a major move to patch things up, and as she drove home, she knew she'd done the right thing in visiting her parents today. She looked at her watch. It was only three-thirty, and she wondered if Cy was out riding around.

She turned the corner into her street, which was only two blocks long, and the first thing she saw was a red car. Her heart skipped a beat. As she pulled into the driveway, Cy came to open her door.

"Hello," Beth said. "I thought you were out riding."

"I never got started. I messed around at home, and then I

had this impulse to drop by to see if maybe you were back yet."

"I'm back."

"Can we go for a ride?"

"Sure."

Five minutes later they were on the road that led into the countryside. Neither one had said a word. Beth nestled into her corner and looked at the winterscape of pine trees, some bare branches of other trees, matted leaves, and an occasional stream. Soft music from a tape flowed around them.

They crossed a bridge over a sizable stream. "This is one of Daddy's favorite fishing places. He used to bring me here when I was a little girl."

Cy smiled. He could imagine how Beth had looked as a little girl with long skinny legs and big eyes. "What was your hair like then?" he teased.

"Thick. Mama had a time with me when it needed to be washed. It hurt like everything, and that's one of the reasons I decided early on to take care of my hair myself."

Cy touched one of the artfully arranged curls framing her face. "I like what you do with it." His voice was affectionate.

Beth smiled at him and found herself wishing she could put her hand on his face. His skin looked so smooth, and she very much wanted to see how it would feel against her hand. She deliberately turned away and looked out of the window to resist the temptation.

Another mile passed. They saw a group of three or four small houses back from the road in a clump of trees. "We used to know the people who lived there," Beth said.

"What happened to them?"

"The old people in the family died within a few years of each other, and the children moved away."

Cy told Beth about his grandfather, Seth, who was born in Beaufort County, South Carolina, in 1868, shortly after his parents had been freed from slavery. When Seth was fourteen, he ran away and months later ended up in New York. His life had been full of adventure, and he didn't settle down to raise a family until he was fifty.

''Fifty?'' Beth questioned with disbelief.

''Fifty,'' Cy said smugly. ''He's a legend in the family. Seth and his young wife had three boys in quick succession. My dad was the last one. Seth died in 1969. Lived to be 101. Always said it was because of the hard living he did.''

''Did he come back here?''

''Only for visits. Said New York was too much in his blood, and it was too slow for him down here.''

Beth shook her head at Cy. ''You're making this up, Cy Brewster,'' she declared.

Cy held up his hand. ''Scout's honor. I'll show you pictures of Grandfather and his whole family when you come to my apartment. He liked having his picture taken, and we have a lot of them.''

Beth laughed. Cy was the most entertaining man she'd ever met. She also liked the way he did things on impulse. She, too, was impulsive. Sometimes it didn't turn out right, but that was the chance you took. Better than everything cut and dried.

''That reminds me, when are you coming to my place?'' Cy asked.

Beth was taken off guard. ''I haven't been invited to your apartment,'' she said.

''Miss Jordan, would you please come to my place for dinner one night this week?'' Cy said in a formal tone.

Was this another of his impulses? She'd better put him on hold for a while. ''I can't say so far ahead. Depends on what's happening at work.'' She rushed on before Cy could say anything more. ''Speaking of work, let me tell you about Loraine Dillard.''

Cy listened attentively to all that Beth told him. He said his understanding was that since Loraine already had three children of her own, she probably would be permitted to take in only three more. ''Six is the limit. Does she know that?''

''No, that was one of her questions. I wonder if only three children would bring in enough money to make it worthwhile?''

Cy had made a wide semicircle, and they were now on the way back to Jamison. Here and there people were beginning to turn on house lights.

"I'll get that information tomorrow," Cy said. "I'll ask a couple of women at Alumax from Jamison what the going rate is."

Their route into Jamison took them past the high school. "Did you go to high school here?" Cy asked.

"All four years," Beth said. "I had a lot of fun, but I couldn't wait to grow up and be on my own. I thought the world would change so much." Her voice was wistful.

"You haven't found that to be so?" The tinge of sadness was present again in Beth. Cy asked the question, hoping her answer would reveal its source.

"It's seldom what you expect it to be, is it? What about you? Did you go to high school in Charleston?" Beth asked, thinking he had probably been a smart student in class and out and likely got into a little trouble now and then. She looked at him speculatively.

"Yes, I did, and I guess there's a teacher or two who wishes I hadn't been there. But I made some good friends and some of them I still see."

He left the street with the high school and turned into Main Street. Most of the stores were closed because it was Sunday. Parking lots at restaurants were beginning to fill up for early dinner.

"Wish I'd met you in high school, Beth," Cy said.

"You do? Why?" Beth wasn't sure what to expect.

"Because then I'd already know a whole lot about you. I'd know what kinds of things you like or hate, what you're interested in, what bores you, what makes you happy, what makes you sad, what kind of flowers you like, what kinds of places you like to see, what your taste is in movies and books." Cy's voice had grown quiet and reflective. He was looking straight ahead, but Beth felt the impact of his words.

If Cy knew all of that about her, he would know more than anyone else knew—maybe even more than she knew about herself. There was danger in letting someone know you that well unless there was a strong foundation of trust.

"You'd probably learn a lot about me that you wouldn't

like,'' she said lightly. '' 'Where ignorance is bliss, 'Tis folly to be wise.' ''

Cy realized he had let his private thoughts about Beth come out, and they had scared her. Still it wasn't a bad move entirely to let her know his deep interest. He matched the lightness of her tone and, as he pulled up at her apartment, said, ''I prefer the other saying.''

''What other saying?'' Beth asked as she got out her key.

'' 'Wisdom is the principal thing; therefore get wisdom.' '' He opened her door. ''You must have learned that Bible verse too when you went to Sunday school.''

''I did, and I've got to hand it to you, Cy. You're one up on me there. I can see I'll have to brush up on any quotations I use with you.''

Chapter 9

The first part of the week passed quickly for Beth. Work kept her busy at the agency. Monday night she went to a church meeting, and Tuesday night she took her mother shopping for shoes. The rapprochement with her mother lifted a weight from Beth, but it did not erase the meaning of the adjectives Minnie had used. Frivolous and flighty lingered in Beth's subconscious.

When Cy called to tell her the ladies he spoke to said they paid forty-five and fifty dollars a week for child care, she kept the conversation to a discussion of Loraine. When Cy was ready to branch out from the business at hand, Beth found a reason to get off the telephone.

Clio Stewart called Beth from Atlanta Wednesday night, complaining that she hadn't heard from her. Something must have happened, and she wanted to know what it was. Beth told her about Art.

''I don't believe this!'' Clio and Beth had the kind of friendship which permitted total openness. Neither told other people what they told each other. Their confidence in each other's support and discretion had never been compromised. So when Clio said, ''How come you didn't tell me right away?'' Beth responded with the truth.

"So much has been happening so fast that I didn't know myself what I was feeling."

"Do you know now?"

"I got the letter one week—and the very next week I met this new man because Rhonda got me involved with HOP. You remember that?"

"Sure. Just before I moved here, I was on a subcommittee for it one year. Tell me about the new man."

Beth had been at the table doing her nails. She moved to the couch, made herself comfortable, and began describing Cy Brewster to Clio.

"His name is Cy Brewster. He's a little bit taller than me, has a shaved head, moustache and goatee, smooth like dark chocolate. Has a diamond stud in his left ear and dresses in a casually smart style. He's thirty-three and apparently has never been married from what he says." She told Clio how they'd seen each other from their cars then met at Rhonda's dinner.

"Romantic, girl. Tell me more."

"The day after we met at Rhonda's, he showed up at my door with some kind of reason and we had a small meal together."

Clio waited a moment. When Beth didn't resume the story, Clio knew something disturbing must have occurred. Surely this man hadn't made some terribly wrong move with her friend. "Go on, honey," she said. "What happened?"

"I'd been to see Mom and Dad just before he got there. Mama was really upset about Art breaking up with me." The repressed memory of all that her mother had said surged up, not just the two adjectives. "Mama asked me why did I keep Art hanging around all this time, that it was no wonder he got tired of it and found someone who'd appreciate him. She said I'd have to change my flighty and frivolous ways or I'd never get married, that no real man's going to put up with that kind of carrying on."

Beth's voice broke on the last few words as all of the original pain reasserted itself. She swallowed hard. She would not cry again about those cruel words. Gradually she regained her composure as she listened to Clio's agitated voice.

"Girl, I don't want to say anything against Miss Minnie, but that was a hard thing to say. You didn't keep Art hanging around. He could have said good-bye anytime he wanted to. He's a real man in charge of himself and what he wants to do, so I don't know where she's coming from. I hope to goodness you didn't take it too much to heart, honey. Did you?''

''I guess I did, Clio. After all, when your own mother tells you something about yourself, you generally listen to it. To tell you the truth, I think maybe I have been a little frivolous because I'm not into anything except the job and shopping and then doing whatever I feel like doing. You've been working with the homeless since you went to Atlanta. I've never done anything like that.''

''If you feel like that then it's a good thing you're involved in HOP.''

''That's what I thought. When Rhonda first asked me I said no, but now I'm glad the agency put me in it. The only problem is that my teammate is Cy.''

''Let me guess. The problem is that you like him. Right?'' Clio was a large-framed woman with an oval face, dark eyes and hair, and an easy smile which broadened now as she thought of her dear Beth attracted to this new man who sounded most interesting. Clio liked the way he'd shown up at Beth's the next day after he met her. Didn't let any grass grow under his feet. She doubted he'd turn out to be another Art Woods.

Beth echoed this thought. ''Cy's not like Art at all. We like so many of the same things. He cooks, likes to go for rides in the country, and you don't have to talk to him to keep him entertained. He's funny and quick thinking. Makes me laugh in spite of myself. I get the feeling that he knows something is bothering me, and he tries to lighten things up when we're together.''

''What's your take on how he feels about you?''

''Clio, I honestly don't know. I can tell you what he's done—like the day after I met him and he came over, we were sitting at the table. He took my hand and put it against his cheek. He held it there with his eyes closed for what seemed like a long minute.''

''What a sweet thing to do, girl. Did he say anything?''

"No. We both went on as if it hadn't happened. He's been persistent about seeing me. Last week he took me to the Palmetto Tree for dinner, and on the way home he asked me about Art. Said he truly wanted to know and didn't want to listen to gossip from anyone So I told him the facts."

"What was his reaction?"

"He didn't ask for any more details, just thanked me for telling him about the letter."

"Sounds like he's an up-front guy, honey."

"On our way to dinner, he said he'd never spoken to a woman from his car before. I thought maybe that was a line. He said, 'Believe me,' and put out his hand. We held hands all the time he was telling me about his family and what he thinks about marriage."

"This gets better and better," Clio said. "What does he think about marriage?"

"That he believes in it so strongly that the first choice has to be the only choice for him, so he's taking his time finding the right person."

"What did you say?"

"That the two people would have to be sure they belonged together. Then he put my hand to his cheek again."

"Have you seen him since then?"

"I told him I'd be busy Sunday, but he came by anyway on the chance I'd be free. He was waiting for me when I got home and we went for a ride. It was so nice, Clio. He's a smooth driver, and of course I love the car. We talked a little. We're very comfortable with each other. He said he wished he'd met me when I was in high school because then he'd know a lot of things about me that apparently he wants to know."

"What kinds of things are we talking about?"

"What I like, what interests me, what makes me happy or sad, what I like in flowers, books, movies, places I'd like to see."

There was silence as Clio digested what Beth had said, and Beth thought about Cy telling her in effect that he wanted to know her inside and out.

"What do you think about this, Clio?" she asked.

"How long has it been since Rhonda's dinner, Beth?"

"Twelve days."

"Counting the dinner you've seen each other four times and talked on the phone. He hasn't tried anything other than to hold your hand. He's already told you how he feels about marriage. Seems to me that he sees you as more than a casual date, that he's willing to take the time to get to know you better, much better. There's no doubt in my mind that he feels a strong attraction from what you've reported." Clio's voice was serious as she gave her analysis. "But the big question is how do you feel, Beth?"

"I admit to a certain attraction," Beth said cautiously.

"Is it a rebound from Art?" Clio asked bluntly.

Beth forgot her caution. "No, Clio, this is nothing like I ever felt about Art. That's why . . ." she started to say then stopped.

"Why what?"

"Why I can't give in to it. I'd be just like Mama said, so flighty that a week after Art breaks up with me I take up with a perfect stranger!"

The strength of feeling in Beth's voice made Clio realize the impact Miss Minnie's words had made on Beth. Time was going to be needed for Beth to recover and regain her self-confidence. If anything was to come of this, Cy Brewster would certainly need a lot patience. Meanwhile Clio comforted her friend as best she could.

"I have never thought you were flighty or frivolous, honey. You and Cy Brewster are adults capable of making your own decisions about your feelings. I'll be looking forward to meeting him eventually. Any chance that you two might come to Atlanta?"

"I always like to go to Atlanta," Beth said, "but you know I don't do weekends with men."

"You know I didn't mean that, girl. You stay with me, and he stays wherever—but you could drive up together and go to a show and visit me."

"Actually Cy has a brother and a sister who live in Atlanta," Beth recalled.

"There! You both have a perfect reason to come, and on the way you can get to know more about each other," she said laughingly. "There's nothing like traveling together to bring out the worst in people."

Talking with Clio was always fun, Beth thought with a smile. She replaced the telephone and returned to the manicure. Their conversations helped her to get issues clearer in her own mind as well, which was one of the reasons Beth valued the friendship.

In having to relate to Clio the events of the past three weeks, Beth had to acknowledge that something was going on between her and Cy. It hadn't been stated by either one, but the undercurrent was there whenever they were together. That was why their hands touched, why he came by when he wasn't supposed to, why she went out with him unhesitatingly Sunday afternoon, why he wanted to know everything about her, and why when she saw him or thought of him or heard his voice she was filled with warmth.

The telephone rang again. This time it was Loraine, who said she received a large packet of information from DSS in the mail, and would it be possible for Beth to go over it with her? Beth said she'd be by after work tomorrow, and Loraine thanked her.

That's what I'm going to do, Beth told herself firmly. I'm going to concentrate on working with Loraine and any other idea that comes up for HOP and put Cy Brewster in place as my teammate and that's all. Deciding that whatever was going on with Cy and herself could be thus contained, Beth took her shower and went to bed.

When Beth arrived at Loraine's the next evening, she could see why Loraine wanted assistance. The application itself was long and involved. To be a registered family day-care home required letters of reference, statements from parents, zoning approval, and a criminal background check, which cost nearly fifty dollars. The registration was valid for one year. To be a licensed family day-care home was more involved and costly, but the license was valid for two years. In both cases the number of children was limited to six at any given time.

As they waded through the material, Loraine decided that

the best option was to get a license rather than being registered. A list of regulations and suggested standards was included. It was evident that a certain amount of money was going to be required in order to meet the standards and become licensed.

''We don't have this money, Beth.'' Loraine had a frown on her as she looked at the figures. ''We're struggling to meet the bills every month—there's no extra.''

''That's the kind of thing our team might be able to help with. We'll look around for some grants or loans that are set up to help people get started in a small business.''

The next day Beth called Cy at his office.

''This is Mr. Brewster's secretary,'' an efficient voice said.

''I'd like to speak to Mr. Brewster, please.''

''He's in a meeting. Is there anything I can help you with?''

No, there isn't, thought Beth then smiled at herself for feeling affronted. Cy Brewster had always been so accessible to her that this being put off seemed odd. She left her name. Cy called her back ten minutes later.

''Beth? Sorry I wasn't available when you called. How are you? It's been much too long since I've seen you or talked to you.''

His intonation evinced such interest that Beth found herself reassuring him that she was all right. ''Loraine's going to need some immediate money that she doesn't have, Cy. We went through all the application requirements from DSS when I was over there last night.''

''I wondered if that's where you were, I called twice last night,'' Cy said.

''There was no message on the machine.'' Beth was surprised.

''Lady,'' Cy said with a little chuckle, ''if I left a message every time I called you just to hear your voice or pass the time of day, you'd need a new tape on the machine every week.''

''I didn't know.'' Beth's response was involuntary.

Cy's voice became intimate and quiet. ''Honey, there's a lot you don't know yet.''

The silence between them was palpable, and Beth felt a shiver run through her body.

"Beth?" Cy's voice caressed her name.

Beth cleared her throat. "What I called you about, Cy, is that Loraine is going to need some money." Beth heard herself repeating what she'd already told Cy. "What I mean is do you know any way we can get her the money? It would have to be a grant, not a loan, because she wouldn't be able to pay back a loan anytime soon."

"How much does she need?"

"If we could get two hundred, that should make it possible for her to pay the fees and get a few items for the kids that she'll need. Two fifty or three hundred would be better because then she could stock up on some supplies to get her through the initial months and pay for the unexpected."

"You're satisfied that she will be responsible in her use of the money?"

"I believe so, and Rhonda Hayes vouches for her, but you need to meet her for yourself, Cy, since this is a team project."

Cy jumped at the opportunity. "That's a good idea. How about this evening? Could we run over there? Whatever time suits you, I'm available."

He doesn't let any grass grow under his feet, Clio had said. "I'll see if she's going to be home and let you know," Beth agreed and later called back to say Loraine and her husband would be home.

Josh Dillard opened the door and invited Cy and Beth in. A tall well-built man with a ponytail and heavy eyebrows in his square face, he shook hands with Cy and spoke formally to Beth as Loraine introduced him.

"I knew some Dillards in Charleston," Cy said. "Henry Dillard and his family. Related to you?"

"Distant cousins," Josh said. "You from Charleston?"

"For several generations. My folks and I moved here recently. They're retired, and my dad always wanted to live here."

"You'll find lots of Dillards around this area," Josh said. "Most of us are related. I got a cousin over in the next block, and if Loraine can get her day care going, she's thinking that after a while she may be able to have the cousin help her.''

Beth was interested to see the proud way he spoke about his wife. The difficulty Rhonda had mentioned between the Dillards had apparently been resolved.

A tour of the house and yard followed, with Loraine pointing out the kinds of small repairs and painting that needed to be done.

''No problem doing the work if I can get the supplies,'' Josh said. Beth showed Cy the papers from DSS and, after assuring Loraine that a grant would be possible, Cy and Beth took their leave.

''Before I left the office, I arranged for a sum of two hundred dollars for the Dillards from one of our community funds. I think they'll handle it well,'' Cy said as he ushered Beth into the car.

''But you hadn't even met them yet.'' Beth was surprised.

''You had, and Mrs. Hayes knew them well. I figured I could trust your judgment.'' Cy was matter of fact. ''Do you think your company could provide another hundred?''

''I'm sure it can and will. Marty wanted to know how he could help, so I'll let him know that one hundred dollars is needed to make the team's first project a success.''

The February night was clear and the air was brisk. ''I love this kind of weather,'' Cy said, driving the car slowly up the street.

''So do I.''

''Look, there's a park with swings,'' Cy said. ''Let's go swing.'' He turned the Saturn into the park before Beth could say no. ''I love to swing, and I haven't been in one for a long time.''

Cy jumped out of the car and opened Beth's door. ''Come on. I'll race you to the swings.'' His eyes were sparkling and his face mischievous as he waited for Beth to start even with him.

What he didn't know was that in high school Beth had been a good sprinter and, despite the fact that Cy had longer legs, he beat her by only a step or two.

They were both laughing as they fell into the swings. "You nearly beat me," Cy said protestingly as they began swinging.

"I was a pretty good sprinter in high school," Beth confessed.

"Do you run or jog or work out now?"

"Only when the spirit moves me. Do you?"

"Not as much as I should, but I try to keep in shape."

Gradually they increased their speed. They went higher still side by side, not talking now but looking at each other. Beth was euphoric. The air was like wine, the stars high and bright. The rhythm of the smooth ascent and descent was intoxicating. If she weren't careful, she would fly off into the air with this wonderful man.

Cy knew he could touch one of the diamonds shining above if he tried. He was filled with excitement at being with this marvelous woman. Beth met him on so many levels. She understood and responded to the childlike sense of play that was a part of his nature. Cy felt his heart swell as Beth looked at him with a brilliant smile.

With unspoken accord, they slowed their swings until they stopped. Beth held out her hand. "You can't go on the playground unless you spend some time on the merry-go-round."

Cy took her hand and they ran across the grass to the merry-go-round. Cy started it with a hard spin and they jumped on.

"How did you get into personnel work, Cy?" Beth wanted to know more about this man, who was growing into her consciousness.

"It began with an interest in people. In high school and in college, I was always trying to get people into clubs and organizations where I thought they would fit. Most of the time the fit turned out right. A friend told me I should do that for a living. I was a business major anyway, so it wasn't hard to specialize in management of human resources."

"I've been meaning to ask you what college did you go to?"

"University of South Carolina. How about you?"

"I went to State in Orangeburg."

"Was it a party school when you were there?"

"A party school?" Beth was indignant. "Yours was the party school from what we heard at State!" Her tone of mock outrage was belied by the mischief in her eyes.

"It might have been for some people but I, of course, was a hardworking, totally virtuous student."

"I can just imagine. You were probably the guy who showed up on Tuesday all primed for a Monday exam. He'd partied so hard on the weekend that he slept all day Monday."

"We heard that same story, but it happened on your campus," Cy said.

Beth shook her head in disbelief. Cy told a story about a scrape his roommate got into. Beth countered with one of her own and threw back her head in laughter.

This is the first time I've seen Beth happy, Cy thought. The sadness that's always been in her eyes is gone. "I'm so glad I've met you, Beth!" Cy's words burst out spontaneously.

"Why are you glad?" Beth wanted to know. The echo of laughter was still in her face, but a wariness had come into her eyes that made Cy careful.

"It's so hard to find a grown-up playmate who'll swing in the park and enjoy it. Do you play ball? Swim? Go on picnics?"

"I like whatever appeals to me at the moment, which includes some of the above—or might be throwing Frisbees or running a race. And winning." Her voice held a clear challenge.

Cy took it up. "You want to race again?"

"I'll beat you this time," Beth declared, jumping off the merry-go-round and running swiftly to the car.

Cy, taken by surprise, reached the car several seconds later. "That wasn't fair," he protested.

"Who said anything about fair? All I said was that I could beat you, and I did." Beth was still smiling at Cy's chagrin.

Cy looked at her speculatively. "I'll give you this one but . . ."

"But what?"

"You just watch out for the next time." He opened the car door.

"I can see I'm going to have to start practicing again to really get in shape," Beth said, settling into the car.

Later as Cy walked her to her door, Beth said, ''I don't know when I've had so much fun.''

''Same here. How about dinner tomorrow or Sunday?'' Cy said.

Beth started to say she was free on Sunday then remembered her vow to stick to business with Cy and restrict the emotion between them. Cy saw the hesitation in her face. Perhaps it would be just as well if she said no, because he was getting in over his head.

''Thanks, but this weekend is full,'' Beth said. ''Let me know when the money is available for Loraine.''

As Cy drove home, he wondered if he should begin seeing someone else. Last year he'd dated Liz Evans. Maybe it'd be a good idea to see her again and put the brakes on the way Beth was taking over his thoughts. If he continued with her, his secret would be in danger. That he needed to avoid if at all possible.

Chapter 10

The noise in Kimberly Raeford's house, where she and Rhonda Hayes were giving a baby shower for Glennette Ellington, engulfed Beth as she was drawn into it Saturday afternoon. She was later than she'd meant to be, and the large room seemed crowded with women. Rhonda found a seat for her near Glennette.

''You're looking wonderful,'' Beth told Glennette. ''No problems with the baby?''

''None at all,'' Glennette said. ''I don't see you much, Beth, not like when you and Rhonda and I used to hang out. What're you doing these days?'' Glennette's brilliant dark brown eyes looked at Beth affectionately. Glennette had always been a beautiful woman, but now in her approaching motherhood there was an added quality of serenity that made her breathtaking.

No wonder James could see only Glennette when he came back, Beth thought. I never had a chance. Beth had liked James when they were all in high school. When he returned to Jamison, Beth felt a resurgence of interest in the grown-up James, which he seemed to return briefly. Then he and Glennette found their love for each other and married.

"I'm still at the realty agency, but Rhonda also got me involved in this year's HOP work."

"James told me about it. He's on the committee this year. What do you think about it?" Glennette asked curiously.

"At first, I wasn't interested," Beth said truthfully. "But the more I get into it, the more I like it. Our team is helping Loraine Dillard get set for a day care in her home."

"That's what Rhonda said. I hope it works out because the Dillards are trying hard to make it and hold their family together. While I have you, Beth, will you come talk to my Girls Club about learning the computer?"

"Be glad to. These kids need to be computer literate. Call me when you need me."

Someone else came to talk with Glennette, and Beth moved about talking to other people including Emily Brooks Walker, who was nursing her new baby.

"What does Peter think of his brother and sister?" Beth asked after admiring baby Caroline. Peter was Emily's son by her first husband, Peter Brooks, who had left her a widow when Peter Junior was a baby. Peter, now a young man in his twenties, wasn't in Jamison often. "I haven't seen him for several years," Beth said.

"David and I don't see him as often as we'd like," Emily said, "but he's happy about the children. When he's home, David Junior follows him around like his shadow," she said proudly.

Rhonda beckoned Beth over to talk with a slim young woman with hazel eyes and dark hair worn in a stylish twist and tied with kente cloth.

"Kimberly, I don't think you've met Beth Jordan. Beth, this is Kimberly Raeford." Rhonda left the two to get acquainted and began to prepare the table for the food.

"You have a lovely home," Beth said. "It feels so warm and and welcoming." The room they were in, and the others Beth had seen, were furnished with a combination of bright and subtle colors that was echoed in an assortment of sitting places in which comfort was the primary consideration.

"I'm glad you like it, Beth. You said just what I said the first time I came into this house after I met Gary, my husband."

Kimberly had been anxious to meet Beth. Cy Brewster, her husband's assistant in Human Resources at Alumax, was a frequent visitor in their home. Lately in his conversation, Beth's name had been mentioned as he spoke of the HOP work to which Gary had appointed him. His admiring comments about his HOP teammate had made Kimberly curious to meet Beth because of her own affection and respect for Cy.

"I think we have a mutual acquaintance—Cy Brewster." She watched a little color creep into Beth's face. "Cy works with Gary at Alumax, you know."

"Then you probably know that Cy and I are Team Four for HOP," Beth said. Here was someone who knew Cy and could tell her about him. "I don't know him well yet, but he seems to be very efficient."

"Gary says he's the best," Kimberly said simply. If Beth wanted assurance about Cy, Kimberly was willing to give it. "Cy is knowledgeable, resourceful, and hardworking. Gary says he can rely on him absolutely." Beth was drinking in Kimberly's description of Cy. "If you want my opinion, Beth, I think you're lucky to have Cy as your HOP partner because he loves working with people."

Kimberly had heard the story about Art Woods and Beth but hadn't met the participants. She thought Beth looked stylish in her well-cut olive green knit dress topped with a silky scarf of emerald green and royal blue. Kimberly sensed that even though Beth showed interest in the comments about Cy, there was an uncertainty and reserve below the surface. In an effort to put Beth at ease, Kimberly said, "You know, Beth, Cy drops by often. Why don't the two of you come over sometime? Gary and I would love to see you."

She smiled at Beth. "As an extra added attraction, you'll meet my son, Adam. He's eight his next birthday and thinks he's at least twelve."

"I know how that is from being around my aunt Elly's five kids," Beth said.

"You will come see us, won't you, Beth?" It was important to Kimberly that Beth understand how welcome she was.

"You can count on it." Beth thanked her and moved away for another guest who was waiting to speak to Kimberly.

"What's for breakfast, Mom?" Cy was on the phone after coming in from his early Sunday run.

"How about pecan waffles?" Iva Brewster knew all of Cy's favorite foods and tempted him into coming to Sunday breakfast as often as possible.

"I'll be over in twenty minutes," Cy said and went in to shower.

"No matter what I do, I can't make my waffles taste like yours," Cy said appreciatively later as he buttered his second one. "What do I do wrong?"

"Maybe you over beat your egg whites or stir them into the batter instead of folding them in gently," Iva said. "Here, have some more ham and how about some applesauce?"

"Your mother worries that you're too thin," George Brewster Senior said. George and Iva were both comfortably fleshed with round faces, brown eyes, and graying hair. They had that similarity of countenance that sometimes happens in couples who have been married a long time.

Cy accepted what his mother served him. "You'll make me put on the ounces I just ran off," he teased.

"Seriously, son, are you trying to lose weight?"

"Not really, Mom. I'm trying to get back in shape and be able to win a race."

"You racing one of the kids you counsel?" George asked.

"Haven't done that lately, but a young woman beat me in a race the other day."

Over long years of experience, both parents knew that the way to encourage their children to talk about their friends of the opposite sex was to show only a casual interest.

George shook his head. "That's hard to believe Cy, unless she's tall with longer legs than yours."

''Beth isn't taller than I am, she was just faster off the mark. Then I discovered she'd been a good sprinter in high school.''

''So when's the next race?'' George said as he filled his coffee cup from the pot on the table and offered some to Cy. ''Which you of course will win.''

Cy found that he wanted to talk to his parents about Beth, although he hadn't known it until he said her name. ''Of course I will.'' Cy echoed his father's certainty.

Iva looked at the two of them fondly. ''Men!'' she said in mock disgust. ''Personally I'm pulling for Beth—what's her last name, Cy?''

''Beth Jordan. She's my teammate on HOP. I told you about it. We're trying to come up with workable ideas to benefit the community, so we meet now and then. The other night we went to the home of a young woman who's trying to begin a licensed day care in her house. On the way back we stopped in the park to swing, and Beth beat me running back to the car.'' George and Iva exchanged the briefest of glances.

They had a special interest in the well-being of their youngest child. Cy had gone through rough times in his early years. As an adult he'd developed into a responsible person who spent much of his free time working with young people. They knew he also went out, and occasionally he'd mentioned a girl he was seeing. He had yet to find the young woman who would be his partner in life and give him the devotion they felt he desired and to which he could respond.

George leaned toward Cy. ''Next time,'' he said conspiratorially, ''you set the race for a longer distance.''

''I bet Beth'll still win,'' Iva said, looking at her husband combatively.

''All right, you two.'' Cy laughed. ''Don't fight. I'll let you know who wins.''

That was what George and Iva had been angling for in egging each other on, because there was something in the way Cy talked about this young lady that told them he was more than casually interested. The race was nothing except as an indication that, in addition to Beth being someone Cy could work with, she was also a person who could share in the play activities that were important to him.

In the afternoon Cy stopped to see Gary and Kimberly Raeford. "I met your friend Beth Jordan yesterday," Kimberly said.

"You met Beth? Where?"

Gary glanced up from the Sunday paper, alerted by the tone of Cy's voice.

"She was here at a shower for Glennette Ellington." She didn't add anything more, waiting to see what Cy would say.

"Nice person, isn't she," Cy remarked offhandedly.

"I thought so and very attractive. We had a little conversation about your project."

Cy made no reply but watched Kimberly so intently that Gary took pity on him. "Put the man out of his misery, honey," he told his wife. "Don't tease him anymore."

Kimberly looked at Cy affectionately. "I mentioned that you worked with Gary. She said she didn't know you very well yet. It was clear to me that she was hoping I would talk about you. So I did. I told her that Gary says he can rely on you, that you're resourceful and hardworking."

"Did she say anything?" Cy asked.

"I could see that she still wanted more," Kimberly said thoughtfully. "So I gave her my personal opinion that she was lucky to have you as a partner because you like working with and for people."

"For that you get a chaste kiss on the forehead," Cy said, suiting the action to the word. Gary looked on tolerantly.

"Before she left, I told Beth that you drop by often and invited the two of you to come over sometime. She promised she would."

"You two are real friends," Cy said seriously.

Gary said, "That reminds me, someone sold me a table at the annual Valentine Dance next Saturday. Why don't you and Beth share it with us, Cy?"

"She may already have a date, but I'll ask her," Cy said.

Beth had been to church on Sunday then spent a relaxed

dinner hour and afternoon with Aunt Elly and Uncle Sim. The girls had rented a movie about growing up in Harlem.

"I can't wait to grow up and go to New York and see for myself what it's like," Toria said.

"After you get there, you might wish you hadn't gone," Net said.

"What do you know?" Toria flashed. "You haven't been anywhere."

"No, but I know what I read and see," Net said from her one-year superiority.

"But I want to know for myself," Toria insisted. "Beth liked New York, didn't you?" She turned to Beth for confirmation.

"I sure did. I thought it was very exciting." Beth had spent a two-week vacation in the city when she was twenty-two and had always promised herself to go back. But every vacation period after that presented a reason to postpone the trip, usually financial.

The city had been a revelation to her, so filled with an infinite variety of people, activities, sights, experiences. Remembering it now as Net and Toria talked of what they wanted to see, Beth wondered how she had stayed away so long.

I'm positively going again before this year is out, she promised herself. This time I'll go to the Apollo Theater first and check it out. Her cousin Bobby had always declared that one day he'd be a performer at the Apollo and was getting ready for it by constantly putting on shows for Beth to watch. Twenty years had passed since he'd been killed accidentally, but he'd been closer to Beth than anyone, and she still missed him.

"Let me fix you a plate to take home, hon," Aunt Elly said when Beth got ready to leave. "You'll be hungry later on."

Beth accepted the food gratefully. She had just finished eating it about eight o'clock and was watching a news show when Cy called.

"Am I speaking with the up-and-coming Jackie Joyner-Kersee of Jamison, South Carolina?" Cy spoke in the clipped phrasing of an interviewer.

"You are indeed," Beth said as she made herself comfortable

on the couch and prepared to enjoy this conversation. "I hope you're prepared to get beaten again at the next race?"

"Not a chance, girl. No way will that will happen twice."

"We shall see what we shall see," Beth pronounced, reminding herself that she'd better do some serious practicing because she'd never be able to catch Cy off guard again.

"How's your day been?" Cy wished he could see Beth. Sitting next to her and having this conversation was what he wanted to do. But the telephone was better than nothing.

"Not too bad. Went to church then spent the afternoon at my aunt Elly's. After dinner we all looked at a movie Net and Toria had about growing up in Harlem, and that led us to talking about New York. I'm sure you've been there." Beth was confident that a man as sophisticated as Cy Brewster had been to New York. Then she remembered that his older brother lived there, the one who was still single like Cy.

"It's my favorite city, and George being there gives me an excuse to go fairly frequently. Do you like it?"

"I spent two weeks there about six years ago and I loved it."

"You mean you haven't been back since?" Already Cy was seeing himself taking Beth to his favorite restaurants and theaters, to the museums and the neighborhoods.

"No, but just talking about it this afternoon made me promise myself that I am going before this year is over."

Stay cool. Don't push, Cy told himself. "Maybe we can coordinate our schedules," he said lightly. "George and I would love to show you some of our favorite places."

Beth smiled to herself. "That might work, we'll have to see. What did you do today?"

"Went for a run, had pecan waffles with my folks, and had a visit with the Raefords. Your name came up."

"I guess Kimberly told you I was there yesterday. She was very friendly and invited me to come over."

"I have an invitation from them for both of us to share their table at the Valentine Dance next Saturday. May I have the pleasure of taking you, Beth?" Since Gary had mentioned the affair, Cy'd been thinking that maybe Beth had decided not to go since that was surely an event she and Woods had always attended.

The dance had receded in Beth's mind. Her attention had been on HOP and Cy and her own feelings. Yesterday at the shower it had been mentioned, and it occurred to her that if she wanted to go with someone she could probably ask Cy—but she didn't want to do that. Now he was asking her, but it wouldn't be the two of them alone. This made it possible for her to say yes.

"Thank you, Cy, I'll be glad to go."

As Cy replaced the telephone, all he could think of was that he would finally hold Beth in his arms. On the dance floor, of course, but she would be in his arms!

I have all week to get myself together to see Art and Evelyn and decide how to handle it, was Beth's thought as she ended the conversation. Tomorrow I'll start shopping for a knockout dress!

Chapter 11

One Monday Beth told Marty Armstrong that one hundred dollars was needed to complete the grant that would enable Loraine Dillard to begin her day care. He gave her the check with the proviso that when that was done she would let him know the next idea Team Four would be working on. Beth told Loraine that as soon as she received the rest of the grant, she'd bring it over so the application could be mailed.

After work she looked for a dress for the dance but found nothing that suited. It wasn't until Wednesday, on her lunch hour, that she happened upon a dress in a small shop on a side street. The lined silk dress, the color a subtle tangerine, fitted as if it had been molded to her body. "It was made for you," the clerk said. Beth agreed and paid the one hundred twenty-five dollars gladly.

Thursday she received the grant from Alumax and took the entire amount to Loraine. They looked at the finished application to be sure it was complete. Beth explained about the grant and what it was to be used for and that she'd appreciate receipts for the purchases or at least a list of them.

Cy called Beth to find out if she'd received the grant, which went out later than he'd anticipated. She told him she'd taken it to Loraine.

"I meant to call you sooner, but it's been a rough week and I've been getting home late, so I was afraid to call. How are you?" Cy's voice was solicitous.

I wonder what keeps him out late, Beth thought as she said, "I'm fine, Cy."

"Beth, may I ask you something?" Cy was hesitant, making Beth almost afraid to say yes. He hurried to add, "You don't have to answer if you don't want to."

"In that case, ask away."

"I've been wondering if you're nervous about meeting Woods and his fiancée at the dance."

His voice, friendly and concerned, touched Beth. She answered him as honestly as she could. "Yes, I am. But I know it has to be done sooner or later. I guess a social occasion like the dance is a better place than by ourselves. I think that would be more awkward."

"He'll probably be just as nervous as you are, Beth."

"You think so?"

"I'd sure be nervous in his shoes, because I wouldn't know if you were going to make a scene or what after what I'd done."

Beth had only been thinking of how she was feeling. Cy's comment made her see that Art might be uncertain about her public reaction, and that gave her a sense of power. She decided to be so gracious, so poised, that everyone would marvel at her. Not by a glance would she let her composure slip. After all she was going to be dressed to kill, and she would have as her escort Cy Brewster, who had more presence than Art Woods any day.

Beth thought of this conversation as she was dressing for the dance on Saturday. She'd spent a leisurely time picking up the heels that had been dyed to match the dress, giving herself a pedicure and manicure, taking a scented bath, and doing her hair and makeup.

With the dress she wore a necklace of triple strands of gold chains set with glossy onyx ovals. The same gold-set onyx ovals hung delicately from her ears. Beth looked at herself critically and knew she had never looked quite so stunning. A satisfied smile touched her lips as she carefully dabbed her favorite perfume at her wrists and ears.

There was a single chime at her door then a gentle tattoo. She opened the door quickly. "I heard your tattoo, Cy, come in."

Cy's first reaction as he stepped inside was to the gaiety in Beth's voice and the smile in her eyes. Then he looked at her as she stood before him.

"You are ravishing," he said slowly, his eyes taking in the full effect of her toilette. "Ravishing!" he repeated softly.

Beth felt enveloped in a warm glow. His eyes held hers as he came close and put in her hand a boxed corsage.

"This is for you, sweet Beth," he said softly. "And this is for me." He raised her face to his and kissed her.

Beth, taken by surprise, was motionless. Cy's lips felt warm and firm. There was neither passion nor demand in his kiss, but she knew the line beyond friendship had just been crossed.

She drew back and looking at the box said, "Thanks, Cy."

Cy was shaken by the kiss. He hadn't planned it. It just happened when he saw her. She looked so lovely, and she seemed happy, and before he knew it he'd kissed her. She hadn't kissed him back, but he had the feeling that the impulse to do so was nearer than either of them thought. If he'd embraced her as he wanted to do and kissed her a little longer, perhaps she would have put her arms around his neck and kissed him back. The thought made him shiver inside.

Get yourself together, he ordered and turned his attention to the corsage Beth was lifting from the box. "I didn't know what you'd be wearing," he said as they looked at the tiny red and white rosebuds. "I can see they won't go with your gown."

"I know what," Beth said, glad to have something to do to get past the awkward moment. From the dish cupboard she took a shallow crystal bowl. "This is to float blossoms in, and we'll put it on our table at the dance."

Conversation in the car for the twenty minutes it took them to reach the hotel where the dance was being held was jumpy and inconsequential. Cy's brief kiss had somehow become a part of the warm glow Beth had felt when he looked at her. It was with her inside the car and made her want to keep looking at Cy. It was hard to pay attention to the conversation.

Cy was worrying about getting through the evening of dancing. What had happened to the self-control that life's hard lessons had taught him? He was acting as young as Kwesi, dealing only with his wants and ignoring self-discipline.

The parking lot was already nearly filled with cars. They hurried from the car into the building. ''I didn't realize it was so windy,'' Beth said. ''Excuse me while I fix my hair.'' Cy got in line with their coats at the check stand.

A couple of women came in and out while Beth was making repairs to her makeup and hair. A young woman hurried in with her curly hair obviously in need of combing. She looked at it in the mirror.

''I spent so much time at home getting every curl to lie just right,'' she said sadly.

''I know what you mean, it's happened to me too,'' Beth said sympathetically.

''Yours looks great,'' the girl said, glancing at Beth while working on the curls she could see in the front.

''Would you like me to see what I can do in the back?'' Beth suggested tentatively.

''I'd sure appreciate it.''For a few moments there was silence as they brought order out of disorder.

''There,'' Beth said, looking at the young woman whose black scoop-necked dress set off by a gold choker and earrings now was enhanced by the soft curls on her head.

''Thanks so much. I was already nervous enough because I'm new here and I just couldn't go out there with my hair in a mess,'' she confided as she renewed her lipstick. ''My name's Evelyn Hardy,'' she said, turning to Beth with a friendly smile.

''I'm Beth Jordan.'' Beth returned the smile instinctively while another part of her mind was assessing the woman who was going to marry Art Woods. Evelyn's round face was pleasant, and when she smiled two dimples appeared. Her eyes were brown, and she carried herself well. She hadn't reacted to Beth's name, so Beth assumed Art had not told Evelyn about her.

They left the ladies' room together. Beth, knowing Art would be waiting for Evelyn, was prepared to see him. Art's smooth brown face registered shock, quickly covered up with an uncertain smile as Evelyn hurried to him and laid her hand on his arm.

"I'm sorry I took so long, but I had to do my hair over." She included Beth as she said, "Beth helped me."

Before Evelyn could go on, Beth said easily, "I know Art." "How are you," she asked. "I haven't seen you for some time," she said pleasantly.

Beth could see his jaw muscles tighten, a sure sign of discomfort with him. "Nice to see you, Beth," he said. With Evelyn standing close and looking at him proudly, he said, "This is Evelyn Hardy, my fiancée."

At that moment Cy appeared beside Beth. "Congratulations to you both," Beth said graciously. She turned to Cy. "This is Art Woods and his fiancée, Evelyn Hardy, Cy Brewster," she said and watched while the three of them greeted each other.

"We'll probably see you later," Cy said and with an arm around Beth's waist, ushered her into the ballroom.

As they made their way through the crowd, looking for their table, Cy said quietly, "That sure happened fast. How do you feel?"

"Relieved," Beth said and told him how she and Evelyn had met. As she finished her story, they came to the table where Gary and Kimberly welcomed them and admired the rosebud centerpiece Beth put on the table.

The Over-Thirty Club gave two big dances a year, one for Valentine's Day and a Christmas Holiday Dance. They were the highlights of the social scene because attention was paid to every detail. The tables that rimmed the large ballroom were laid with white tablecloths. A tall red taper sat on a lacy red heart in the center of the table. The buffet tables against the wall on each side were filled with salads, meats, breads, and desserts. Beverages were brought to the tables by waiters. Decorations of lacy hearts and flowers appeared tastefully around the room. The club always hired a band, and this evening they interspersed lively numbers with mellower favorites and a few waltzes to match the romantic theme of Valentine's Day.

Between dances with Cy, Beth took him around to meet people she knew. Her old group—Taresa and Romy, Cathy and Bay, Betty and Vernon, Merlie and Howard—greeted them enthusiastically, exclaimed over Beth's appearance, and insisted they join them for a while. Two extra chairs were produced and as they talked, Cy was interested to see another aspect of Beth. It was easy to see that in this group Beth was a highly valued member, and they missed her.

"Some of us went to the skating rink last week," Taresa said. "Remember the time we went and you led a conga line, Beth?"

"That was some fun," Romy said. "Do you skate, Brewster?"

"Love it and most other sports," Cy said.

"You two need to come with us next time, for sure," Cathy said.

"Art brought Evelyn over to meet us a little while ago," Betty said casually.

Beth knew everyone was watching for her reaction. "Cy and I saw them out in the hall," she said.

Cy wanted Beth's friends to know that he was aware of the history, so he touched her hand lightly and said, "Tell them how you and Evelyn met."

Beth told of seeing Evelyn in the ladies' room but not knowing who she was until they were ready to walk out.

"What'd you think of her?" Merlie asked.

"I thought she was friendly," Beth said. "I liked her."

After Beth and Cy left, there was silence for a moment. Then Howard, the most observant of the group said thoughtfully, "If Brewster stays in the picture, Art will soon be just a memory."

"Poor Art," Betty said.

"I don't see anything poor about him," Vernon said. "Dropped one nice-looking girl and picked up another who's going to marry him and help him in his business."

''Seems to me he's doing all right,'' Romy agreed.

The other men pitched in while the women said the men had it all wrong, that Art had been so depressed and discouraged at not getting a commitment from Beth that he'd decided to be content with second best and had wooed his old high school girlfriend. The friendly argument was enjoyed by all until they gradually returned to the dance floor.

Beth was having a good time. It was great to be out again among people she hadn't seen in months, to feel more like the Beth who used to go out at least once a week. Still she knew she wasn't quite that same person.

It was almost as if she'd begun to grow again, she thought dreamily as she and Cy danced to ''Let Me Call You Sweetheart.'' Everything about Cy's dancing pleased her. They seemed to move as one person and he held her just right. She and Art had danced a lot over the years, but their styles had never fit as far as Beth was concerned. Art liked to talk while dancing. Beth loved dancing for its own sake and loved to be caught up in its rhythmic pleasure.

Cy seemed to feel the same, speaking only now and then. As the muted brasses played, he murmured, ''Enjoying yourself?''

''Oh, yes,'' Beth said forcefully and shivered inside when Cy held her closer and whispered, ''So am I.''

While the band took a break, Cy and Beth joined Kimberly and Gary at the buffet table and with plates piled high went back to eat.

''This is the first time I've been to one of these affairs,'' Gary said. ''They do it well, don't they?''

''They pride themselves on taking care of business down to the smallest detail,'' Beth said. ''You don't become a member of that club unless you're prepared to work hard. They raise a lot of money with these dances and use it for several charities.''

''This food is better than the usual hotel fare,'' Cy said.

''That's because this is Leah Givens's cooking,'' Kimberly said decisively. In answer to the inquiring looks from Cy and Beth, she said, ''She's a wonderful cook and caterer. I used to work for her.''

Gary looked at her lovingly. ''We were courting, or at least

I was during that time, and I didn't think too kindly of Leah then.'' Kimberly blushed.

Beth was curious to hear the story. Gary, tall and dark with prominent cheekbones, was obviously older than his wife, and Beth had been wondering about them.

''We met in front of the library,'' Gary began. ''My daughter, Amanda, knew Kimberly from some modeling she'd helped the girls with.''

''That was the show Glennette put on,'' Beth said, remembering how she'd left town that weekend so she wouldn't have to attend and see Glennette with James Ellington. Without thinking, she put her hand on Cy's in thankfulness to have James and Art in the past.

Cy had spent the evening attuned to every cue he could pick up to help him know more about Beth, as this was the first time they'd been in the company of people she'd known and with whom she'd shared experiences. He was hungry for all he could discover about this woman who was filling him with intense emotions and sensations.

What a joy she was on the dance floor, pliant and responsive in his arms. Through his reverie, he felt Beth touch his hand, something she'd never done before. He instantly took her hand in his while his mind played back what she'd said about Glennette's show. What in that remark had triggered her gesture?

Gary was going on with his story. ''I was trying to see Kimberly, but she was always so busy with her son, Adam, or her job in the bookstore or something. Then the Christmas season came, and she began working with Leah in the evenings and on weekends.'' He gave a huge sigh.

''But obviously you didn't give up,'' Cy said.

''Not me. I knew what I wanted.'' Gary's simple statement held such feeling that Kimberly blushed again. Cy instinctively looked at Beth and held her hand more closely. He saw a faint color rise in her face as she returned his glance.

''Shortly before Christmas we had a tree-trimming party at my house,'' Gary said.

''I remember that well,'' Cy said. He looked at Beth. ''It was a great party. Good food, dancing, all of us trimming the tree and then singing carols. That was the first time I met you, Kimberly."

Kimberly nodded then looked at Cy teasingly as she told Beth, "Watch him carefully, Beth. Cy was the life of the party with all of the single girls."

"That's not fair," Cy protested amid the laughter of the other three.

"Tell us the rest of the story," Beth said to Gary.

"On Christmas Eve she accepted my ring." Gary raised his wife's hand to his lips. They looked at each other as Kimberly said softly, "We were married a few weeks later."

Gary, a reserved man, was slightly embarrassed at the depth of feeling he'd displayed. He broke the enchantment that had held them all by relinquishing his wife's hand and taking a sip of coffee. He touched his napkin to his mouth and looked around the room. "I see the band is coming back."

Beth blinked her eyes and looked around. She felt as if she'd been in a fairy tale or a lovely dream. Now she was back in reality. But why shouldn't the promise of love become as real for her as it had for Kimberly and Gary? She knew this was the second marriage for both of them. Had love seemed as real their first time around and then faded away, she mused as she danced with Cy. Maybe Cy could tell her what happened. But not now. Now was for dancing, but the image of Kimberly and Gary looking at each other with unguarded love wouldn't go away. She sighed.

"What is it?" Cy asked.

"Just thinking of Kimberly and Gary," she said.

"Me too." Cy held her closer.

Beth wanted to look at him to see what his eyes might reveal but was afraid to do so. There was already a strong unspoken intimacy between them, and the Raefords' love story had added another element. Beth wasn't sure where all of this was leading and was relieved to have the current broken when one after another of her old friends asked her to dance. Howard had just returned her to her table when Art appeared.

"Dance, Beth?"

How familiar this felt and yet so different at the same time.

Beth followed Art's lead without even thinking and waited to hear what he had to say.

"Beth, I know I should have talked to you instead of writing the letter," he began.

"Yes. You could have at least called if you didn't want to talk face to face. Why didn't you?" Beth looked at Art.

"I was embarrassed. But that wasn't all. It took a lot for me to face up to the fact that no matter how long I stayed around you weren't going to marry me." He looked at her intensely. "Tell me the truth, Beth. Were you?"

Confronted with the question she'd never had to answer, Beth found she knew what to say. "No, Art, I'm sorry."

They danced in silence for a few moments. "I needed to hear you tell me that so I won't have to wonder about it," Art said.

Beth had thought about telling Art when she saw him how hurt and angry his letter had made her, but now that didn't seem to matter. If anything, she wished she could think of how to comfort him. She was not going to use the corny line about how they'd always be friends. She said the only honest thing she could think of.

"Evelyn seems to be a very nice person, Art. Have you decided on a date yet?"

"She has to finish out the school year in Columbia, so we're thinking of late May."

On the way back to the table, Art said, "Thanks for all the good times, Beth."

"I'll always remember them, Art."

Cy was returning to the table as Art was leaving. Beth was talking to Kimberly as he sat down. When Gary and Kimberly got up to dance, Beth and Cy turned to each other.

"How did it go with Art?" Cy asked.

"All right," Beth said. Her eyes were so luminous and soft that Cy was impelled to ask the next question, even though he knew he had no right to.

"Is it over, Beth?"

"It's over," she said with certainty.

Cy felt a surge of joy and triumph. His shadow opponent

was gone! But in this setting he could do nothing except take Beth's hand and pull her gently into his arms to dance.

Beth felt like she had come home, and when Cy whispered, "I'm so glad," she answered, "So am I."

The band leader announced that the final dance would be "My Funny Valentine," and the lights would be dimmed for the most romantic effect on this most romantic of days.

The red candles on the tables were lit, casting a soft glow on the dancers swaying gently to the music. There was scarcely any sound of conversation, just the swish of skirts and the brush of soft leather on the polished floor as the dancers moved rhythmically.

Cy put both arms around Beth's slim waist. He'd been wanting to hold her thus all evening. She laid her cheek against him and linked her arms lightly around his neck.

"You're my valentine," he whispered and feathered a kiss across her cheek.

Beth heard the words and felt the kiss. From her dreamlike state, she stroked the back of his neck once, lingeringly.

When the dance ended, Beth and Cy blinked in the sudden bright lights. They didn't look at each other, but their hands were clasped tightly as they returned to the table to say good night.

Fifteen minutes later they were finally in the Saturn. Cy drove past the street that led to Beth's apartment.

"Where're you going, Cy?" Beth asked.

"For a little ride. I can't take you home yet, Beth. The evening doesn't feel like its over." He turned to look at her. "Come sit close to me."

Beth had not put herself in the far corner of the seat, but she wasn't close enough for him to put his arm around her. She hesitated, uncertain if that would be wise given the emotional climate.

"Please, Beth."

Beth moved as close to Cy as she could without impeding his driving. Cy put his arm around her. She leaned against him and closed her eyes for a moment. There was a faint fragrance of a man's cologne that she had once thought of giving Art but had decided it didn't suit him. It suited Cy, she thought as she nestled against him.

Her movement made Cy catch his breath. If he wasn't careful, he'd have them in the trees that lined the road. Better try some conversation. "How'd you enjoy the evening?" he asked.

"Much more than I expected to," Beth said. As the miles unrolled before them, they discussed all aspects of the evening, laughing and talking together quietly and confidingly like old friends. As they returned to Jamison, Cy said, "Were you satisfied with your conversation with Woods?"

"Yes, but I was more surprised than anything else."

"How do you mean?"

Beth told Cy what Art had said. "I thought when I saw him I would want to put on him the hurt and anger I felt when I first got his letter. But tonight I didn't want to do that. What I felt most of all was relief, like a weight off of me."

The Saturn came to a noiseless stop under the shade of a huge oak tree on a quiet street. At two o'clock in the morning, no lights were on in the houses, and they had the space to themselves. Cy gave Beth his complete attention.

"I liked Art a lot because he's a nice guy and then because he was so opposite to me," Beth went on. "He was steady, responsible, generous, and kind. When I'd be acting flighty and thinking only of myself or what I wanted to do, he could pull me back just by being himself. In many ways we didn't match at all. We were never particularly interested in the same things, but he'd go along with me, and I tried to be interested in his business for his sake."

Beth suddenly heard herself telling Cy all of these things. She hadn't meant to. What in the world would he think of her now?

"Go on, honey, I'm listening," Cy said mildly. "Let me hear it all."

"He asked me to marry him several times, and I always felt a little guilty when I said no. I kept thinking maybe next time I'll say yes. But I couldn't." Beth paused and Cy was quiet. There was still a resolution to come, and he wanted to hear it from her.

"Tonight he asked would I ever have said yes. When he asked point blank like that, I knew that I wouldn't. I couldn't because I didn't love him. What I felt was a deep affection, not love. But I didn't see that until tonight."

Cy still waited, giving Beth all the time she needed to work through her feelings. The fact that she was sharing those feelings with him said that she had developed trust in him. He had to be careful not to do or say anything that would harm that trust.

"Now I can see that Art did the wise thing. He said in his letter to me that there was nothing permanent in the future for us, and he was right. He saw it and I didn't."

All of this time Beth had still leaned against Cy, his arm holding her close. She was looking straight ahead at the branches dark against the sky as she tried to sort things out. Now she sat up and turned to look at her companion. "What do you think, Cy? Does all that make sense to you?"

"What makes sense to me, Beth, is that apparently from the beginning Woods was like Gary Raeford, he knew what he wanted. You didn't, so you just went along with the program. It also makes sense that eventually he would have to make a decision about what to do since he was not going to get what he wanted."

"Would you have written a letter?"

"I like to talk to people face to face," Cy said, "but I'm not going to fault Woods for his approach. It was a hard thing to have to do."

What Cy wanted to add was that if he'd had any chance at all with Beth, he couldn't see himself letting her go. Never. But he sensed a need to be cautious. Beth was still thinking about what she saw as a relationship in which she might have been at fault. Her analysis of it had dissipated much of the emotion he'd felt from her on the dance floor. Better to wait for a cue than to barge in prematurely.

Beth leaned against him again with a feeling of contentment. "Thanks for listening, Cy."

"Anytime."

"It's getting late," Beth said. "I'm ready to go home."

Cy started the car. The late show was playing music for

Valentine's Day. As the car moved soundlessly through the empty streets, Beth began to feel again the sweet closeness with Cy that the dancing had evoked. Cy was remembering how responsive she'd been in his arms. No words were spoken, but communication was taking place.

The Saturn turned smoothly into Beth's driveway. In one quiet movement Cy put on the brake and, with the music still on, took Beth in his arms. He was sure he'd read her mood correctly.

Beth, moved by the emotions of the evening and elated to be free of the Art affair lifted her face to his. The first kiss was tentative and brief. The second one was a little more assured. Then Cy gathered Beth as close as he could in his awkward position behind the wheel.

''My sweet valentine,'' he whispered tenderly.

Beth put her hand on the back of his head and stroked it. Cy was thrilled. She brought his mouth down to hers and this time the kiss was more exploratory and extended. Beth pulled back when she felt she might explode. Her heart was beating furiously, and deep in her stomach there was an unfamiliar sensation.

''I really must go in now, Cy,'' she said.

Chapter 12

Beth's fingers flew over the keyboard. Work had become a positive pleasure. In fact everything in life had taken on a brighter aspect. It was as if the resolution of the Art affair had torn away a veil, a veil she hadn't realized was there. The fact that Cy Brewster called every day added a certain zest as well.

Cy, elated at achieving the breakthrough he sought from purely business to personal with Beth, now felt it circumspect to return to business as a guise for calling. He was sure that if he pressed the personal issue too fast, Beth would retreat.

''This is Team Four checking in,'' he would begin. ''Any news today?''

Beth was happy to play the game. It kept matters on the even keel with which she felt comfortable. She and Cy would discuss how Loraine was doing and throw around other possible projects they had heard or read about. Then the conversation would become more personal about people they knew, what was happening at work, their likes and dislikes, reactions to what was going on in national and local politics.

Their conversations were so wide ranging and intriguing that Beth looked forward to them each evening. ''Have you ever been to a station of the Underground Railroad, Beth?'' he asked one evening.

When she said no, he promised to take her to one he knew of in Charleston. He mentioned an exhibition of Egyptian sculpture he'd once seen at the Metropolitan Museum of Art. ''It made me long to go to Egypt, and I will one day. Have you ever wanted to go there?''

Another time when they were commenting on the death of a local prominent person, Cy said thoughtfully, ''I was reading the other day about reincarnation. What do you think of the concept?''

No other man Beth had ever dated could hold a candle to Cy for stimulating, intelligent, and entertaining conversation. Perhaps James Ellington, but she hadn't had the opportunity to talk with him like she was talking with Cy. Cy fascinated her.

Glennette Ellington called Beth to remind her that it was the coming Saturday at one o'clock that the Girls Club would be meeting at the community center for Beth to speak to them about the benefit of knowing computers. When Beth arrived, she found a group of ten high school girls talking and laughing as they were sweeping the floor and arranging the chairs in one of the smaller rooms.

Glennette was cleaning off the chalkboard. ''Thanks for coming, Beth. Sorry we have to meet in here. This room is so dingy, but all the others are taken.''

Glennette had organized the Girls Club some years earlier. The initial activity had been learning to make their own clothes. Now the young girls learned about manners, modeling, etiquette, personal health, cooking, career options, and anything else that might benefit them. Membership fluctuated as the girls grew older and their places were taken by younger ones.

After Beth made her presentation about computer literacy and its importance both in the present and the future, the girls asked questions about how much it paid, how did she get her job, and did she like it.

''You going to stay right there?'' one girl asked.

''Until something much better comes up,'' Beth answered.

"Once you get a good position, you don't leave it unless you're very sure that what you're leaving it for is going to be better for you in every way."

Glennette thanked Beth for coming. As they lingered talking, Glennette said. "If I could find someplace else to hold these meetings, I would. The center is getting so rundown it's depressing. But we've always met here, and sometimes we have a better-looking room than this."

"I noticed on the way in that it's looking shabby. Why doesn't the council do something about it?"

"Not enough money. It takes all they can get to pay taxes and utilities and keep the activities going. Not to change the subject, but how did you enjoy the Valentine Dance? You looked marvelous."

Coming from Glennette, who was acknowledged to be the most beautiful woman in the Jamison community, Beth felt that was high praise indeed. "Thanks for the compliment," she said. "I was lucky to find that dress. As for the dance, I had a good time. Cy Brewster and I sat with Gary and Kimberly Raeford."

"I know you and Cy are Team Four," Glennette said. "How is that going? Is he easy to work with?" Rhonda Hayes, an old friend of both Glennette and Beth, had confided to Glennette her hope that Beth and Cy might find more in common than HOP.

"He's easy to work with, has good ideas, and follows through. We've both been to see the Dillards, and it looks like that day-care idea is going to come about."

Beth told Glennette good bye and left before the conversation turned personal. She wasn't ready to discuss Cy with anyone except Clio. As she crossed the floor of the central large room which was being prepared by a group of young people for a Sunday activity, some high school boys erupted into the room from the hall.

Beth was surprised to see Cy in their midst, talking with one of the boys. As he saw her, he detoured from the group, bringing the boy with him. They greeted each other, and Cy said, "Miss Jordan, this is my friend Kwesi Michaels."

''How are you, Kwesi?'' She thought the boy must be fourteen or fifteen. He was neatly dressed and said hello in a civil manner, but there was a wariness in his eyes. As he joined the other young people, Beth wondered what Cy was doing with the boys—perhaps the same thing she'd been doing with the Girls Club.

''You come here every Saturday?'' Cy asked.

''No, I came today because Glennette asked me to talk with her Girls Club about computers. How about you?''

''I meet with some boys here quite often. I called you before I left home, but I guess you were on your way here. I wanted to ask you to come to dinner tonight.'' Cy had awakened that morning with the thought of Beth coming to dinner. Maybe she wouldn't, but he had to ask. Sooner or later she would consent if he kept asking. In her eyes now he saw hesitation.

''I want to show you I can make something other than corn cakes,'' he said with a smile and saw an answering smile in her eyes. ''I also have an idea for our next project that I'd like us to talk about.'' He hoped that would be the persuading touch.

''That does sound inviting, Cy, but tonight I'm busy.''

''Tomorrow?''

''What time?''

''Five suit you?''

''I'll see you then,'' Beth agreed.

Beth had been curious about Cy's apartment. How would it reflect his taste and personality? She was intrigued when, as he opened the door and welcomed her in, the first thing she saw was a sculpture. It stood on a marble-topped table against the wall in the living room. It was no more than twelve inches tall, but it dominated the room and drew her to it.

Carved from wood and finished in various shades of brown and black, it represented a group of people and children who seemed to spring from the ground. It had a vibrant power that made Beth want to touch it.

''May I?'' she asked, her hand hovering over it.

''Of course.'' Cy watched her face, delighted at her response.

He'd felt the same way the minute he'd seen it in a small gallery in Charleston.

Beth's fingers traced some of the faces and marveled at how the artist had brought such feeling to them. You could even feel the differences in the textures of the skin. But there was more to it than that.

"There seems to be a sense of purpose in the group that's holding them together, but I don't know how the artist achieved it." She looked away from it for the first time, turning to Cy inquiringly. "Does it have a name, a title?"

"It's called 'Community,' " Cy said.

"I see the aptness of the name," Beth said.

"I'm so glad you like it," Cy said.

The room with its dining alcove was not as large as it had seemed at first, and Beth now observed how Cy's placing of two comfortable chairs and a couch with small tables and tall lamps were strategically done. On each side of the door were tall live plants. Cy had made room for his books in the dining alcove, where two walls opposite the table were lined with bookshelves. The only other item in the living room was a compact oak entertainment center, housing a television and stereo equipment.

Two windows opposite the couch were draped in the same striped fabric that covered the couch. Beth thought that the plum and emerald colors set off by a rich gold gave a lushness to the room. Another aspect of Cy Brewster was tucked away in her consciousness.

Beth opened her bag and took from it a small parcel wrapped in green and gold foil. "A host gift for you." She extended it to Cy.

"You are the only gift I need," he said, his eyes warm and smiling. Beth felt the heat rising in her face. She watched his hands as they opened the package. Inside the box was a jar of blackberry preserves.

"My mother made these, and they're so good I thought you might like some to go with your toast or biscuits. Or even your corn cakes. Speaking of that, you're not letting anything burn in your kitchen, are you?"

Beth sniffed the air anxiously. She intended to divert Cy's attention. If she didn't move, she was sure Cy would take her in his arms so strong was the feeling coming from him.

"I don't think so," Cy said, "but let's go see." Cy's kitchen was decorated in white and dark blue. It had a window over the sink and a counter for eating and serving. Beth sat at the counter on a high stool and put her feet on the rung.

"Anything I can do?" she asked as Cy put rolls in to warm.

"Not a thing, thanks. I was just waiting to finish the potatoes. They're best if eaten right away."

He was gently stirring minced garlic in a little olive oil over a low flame. When the garlic was a pale golden color, he added it to the boiled and drained quarters of unpeeled red potatoes.

Beth watched with interest, and Cy showed off a little as he mashed the hot potatoes with the garlic, warm milk, and sour cream. He flicked a glance at Beth to see her surprise when he added a little cider vinegar along with the salt and pepper.

"I can't wait to taste it," Beth said.

"You'll love it," Cy said smugly.

Cy had covered his glass-topped table with brown linen, which set off the white plates trimmed in gold. They brought in the food then Cy seated Beth. He couldn't resist the need to touch her, so he laid his cheek against hers. "I'm so glad you're here," he said softly.

"So am I," Beth said. How was she going to eat when the pit of her stomach was quivering, and she was going to have to look across the table at Cy. . . . Already she was afraid that her hands might tremble, so she held them together tightly in her lap as Cy blessed the table, then cut slices from the bottom round of roast beef. Broccoli flowerets and carmelized carrots joined the roast beef and mashed potatoes to make a colorful plate.

"It all looks so good," Beth said as she accepted a roll.

"But how does it taste?" Cy watched while Beth took her first forkful of the potatoes.

"They're wonderful," she said, and Cy smiled with relief. "How did you get the idea to fix them this way?"

"I read recipes sometimes, especially of foods I like. I came across this one last year and tried it. I wanted to see what you thought of it.''

By this time Beth had tasted all of the food. ''Ever thought of opening a restaurant?'' she said appreciatively.

''Never. But speaking of businesses, I've an idea for the next project for Team Four.''

Beth felt intuitively what Cy was about to say.

''I've been looking at the community center, and I think we can do something to spruce it up and make it more attractive. What do you think?'' The look on Beth's face made him add, ''What's the matter? Did I say something wrong?''

''I knew you were going to say that,'' Beth said with certainty.

''We're on the same wavelength,'' Cy said, relieved.

''Glennette told me yesterday that it's getting so rundown, it's depressing to hold her club meetings there. This morning when I woke up, the first thing on my mind was the same idea you had.''

''It's a big undertaking,'' Cy said.

''There's the large room, the kitchen, the office, two bathrooms, and four other rooms plus the halls, the porch, the closets and other storage space—so you're right. A huge job. Glennette said the council in charge hadn't done it because their money pays the taxes and utilities and keeps the activities going. There isn't any left over.''

The center conversation kept them going through the rest of dinner. After Cy cleared the table, he brought in a lemon meringue pie and coffee.

''Don't tell me you made this pie yourself!'' Beth exclaimed. The swirled peaks of meringue were golden brown, and the pastry looked flaky and tender.

''That's a sexist remark,'' Cy protested.

''It is and I apologize,'' Beth said. ''Did I hurt your feelings?''

Cy laughed. ''Honey, you didn't hurt my feelings. I was only teasing you. This is my favorite dessert, and I save it for very special occasions.''

Cy had been cutting the pie, but he put down the knife and

held out his hand to Beth. His dark eyes held hers intently. She put her hand in his. He pressed it to his cheek then put a kiss in the palm. Beth understood the message but did not take the kiss from her hand. Matters between them were moving too fast already, and she wanted them to slow down, even though her emotions were in turmoil.

Cy scolded himself silently while he explained to Beth that sometimes his pastry was good, but other times he had to use a good commercial kind. He always made the filling and the meringue himself. ''I learned how through trial and error, and it took many months, but it turns out pretty good now.'' *Take it easy, or she'll eat her dessert and walk right out.* ''I use real lemon. Is it too tart?''

''No, that's one of the things that makes it good. This kind of pie is often bland. The lemon is covered up by the sugar and cornstarch.''

''I'll help clean up,'' Beth said after dessert was finished.

''You don't have to do that,'' Cy said. ''I'll do them later.''

''No fair,'' Beth said, picking up her plate to take into the kitchen. ''I let you help in my kitchen,'' she reminded him.

Cy had shown off his cooking skills to one or two other young ladies, but no one had felt as right in his kitchen and at his table as Beth. He felt in harmony with her for reasons he couldn't list as one, two, three. He just knew that the more he was around her, the stronger the tie grew—and yet his objective mind told him that Beth Jordan of all people was not the person with whom he should fall in love.

Beth, making casual conversation as she worked, was afraid that she was in serious danger of going overboard where Cy was concerned. Why couldn't she have met him before she ever started going around with Art and wasting all that time with him? Here was the man—who from the first meeting of their eyes—had drawn her to him. Could there be any truth in the concept of soul mates? I'm not at all sure that I can keep on resisting, even if it does prove I'm flighty and frivolous, she thought as she put the glasses in the cupboard Cy indicated.

The conversation they were both trying to maintain died a

natural death as they completed their chore. Beth started to say something, and found she had to swallow first.

"Where does this towel go?" She looked around for the rack.

"Right here." Cy's voice was husky as he reached for the towel and drew Beth into his arms. For a second Beth stood rigid then with a sigh relaxed against Cy and laid her head against his neck.

Cy breathed in the fragrance he had come to associate with Beth as he laid his face against her soft hair. He closed his eyes and stood holding his precious Beth in his embrace, her slim body warm and soft in his arms.

Beth was sure she could feel her heart and Cy's heart beating in tandem. As she stood in his embrace, she found a longing to copy Cy's gesture. She raised her head and laid her hand on his cheek. In her eyes and in the gesture, there was a tenderness that made Cy feel weak. He started to speak, but Beth laid her finger against his lips.

"No words," she whispered.

His rational mind heard her command and applauded its wisdom, while his heart was yearning to express itself. Bending his head, he touched her lips with the same tenderness she had given him. When he opened his eyes and looked at Beth, she had such a look of warmth and expectation that he gathered her close and kissed her repeatedly until she drew away.

Beth had to wait to catch her breath, but her eyes, wide and bright, never left Cy's. "I'm not playing with you, Cy," she said softly, "but I don't want us to get beyond ourselves. Okay?"

Cy could not trust himself to speak. He nodded his head in acquiescence and reluctantly let Beth go.

Still they stood looking at each other. "I said I'd show you pictures of Grandfather Seth," Cy said.

"Another time. I know I need to go," she said quietly.

"Another time then," he said as lightly as possible. "That will give me something to look forward to. Let me get your coat," he said as he ushered her from the kitchen.

"It was a delicious meal, Cy," she said.

Cy held her coat and, as she put it on, he turned her around and began to fasten the three front buttons.

Beth felt as if she were mesmerized. She could not stop looking at Cy. He finished the last button and looked at her. Wordlessly they leaned toward each other for a last lingering kiss.

Cy walked around the apartment after Beth had gone, touching this and that, not even seeing what he was doing. This was his way of thinking through problems. What was he to do about Beth? She had said she was not playing with him, and in his heart of hearts he knew beyond a doubt they were falling in love with each other.

He'd been around too long to mistake the signs. He was sure that some residue from her relationship with Woods was holding her back, but that would pass with time if he could stay in the picture and develop the foundation for love which they had begun.

But should he stay in the picture without telling her everything? Yet if he did, what were the chances that he could stay? He had to stay. The prospect of no Beth in his future was too bleak, too lonely, too cold.

Beth relived the events of the evening all the way home and as she puttered around the bedroom deciding what to wear to work the next day, she went through each sweet segment, savoring it all again and found herself standing in front of the closet with two different outfits she didn't recall picking out.

She sank down into an easy chair after putting the clothes back. She needed to seriously examine her position.

In high school Beth had experienced the usual short-lived infatuations. Only the memory of James Ellington had survived that era. Later she had gone out with a number of people to movies, parties, and dances, her vivacity and readiness for enjoyment making her a popular date.

Then she'd begun going out with Art Woods, whose steadiness she found restful, and she spent her social time with him until James returned to town. That mutual interest flared only briefly. Then Beth and Art went on as before—but considering her past, Beth acknowledged that no one had elicited the feelings she had for Cy.

All the months she'd gone out with Art—all the kisses they'd shared, the conversations they'd had, pleasant though they'd been—faded into dullness compared to these past weeks with Cy.

Everything about him was interesting to her. She'd loved being in his apartment and seeing what he saw every day. Now she could imagine him there. She wanted to meet his parents, and that would fill in another part of his picture.

Suddenly Beth laughed. She was thinking about Cy just as he thought of her when he said he wanted to know everything about her. Now she understood. I would love to have a picture of him. His dear face with its expressive dark eyes, the broad forehead, the well-shaped mouth, the way his mouth felt on hers, the way he held her in his arms, the way they fit together so wonderfully well when they were dancing.

Beth closed her eyes. She could feel herself again in his arms, held so close and tenderly. The memory suffused her with its warmth and sweetness.

Beth reminded herself that she was supposed to be examining her feelings in order to come to some conclusion. But as she prepared for bed, all she could conclude was that Cy Brewster was taking up more and more of her thoughts, that she loved being with him and all that she knew of him, and that she didn't know what this said about her flighty and frivolous character.

Chapter 13

Loraine Dillard's day-care license arrived the following Thursday.

''I'm so glad,'' Beth said when Loraine called to tell her the good news. ''Is there any help our team can give you now that you know you're in business?''

''Can you go with me to get supplies? We could go Friday evening after Josh comes home, so he can keep the kids, if that's all right with you.''

''I'll let you know,'' Beth promised.

Cy was free, so after work he picked up Beth then Loraine. For the next three hours, they looked for the best bargains in suitable toys and play furniture for small children. By the time they unloaded tiny tables, chairs, a playpen, and other items at Loraine's, they were all tired.

''That was fun,'' Beth said later as she and Cy sat at her table having sweet potato pie and coffee.

''I'd no idea there was such a variety of toys and prices,'' Cy said. ''I usually send my brother and sister money for them to buy whatever the birthday child wants, so my experience is very limited.''

''I've been buying for my cousins for years and for friends

who have small children. I like looking at the new toys as well as the old ones. I guess it's the kid in me still.'' She smiled drowsily across the table at Cy.

She looked adorable to Cy, and he felt his heart contract as he watched her. ''Would you like to have children?'' he asked softly.

''I've always wanted a lot of children,'' she said dreamily.

''Me, too.'' Cy said the words so softly that at first they did not penetrate Beth's thoughts. When she heard them, she looked at Cy. The message of love and desire he sent in the silence was so unmistakable that Beth felt herself blush all over. She instinctively put her hands on her burning face. She snatched at the first thing she could think of to change the subject.

''Speaking of kids, Cy, tell me about the one you introduced to me at the center. Kwesi, was that his name?''

''Yes, Kwesi Michaels.'' His racing heart gradually slowed as he related Kwesi's story. His seriousness told Beth this was an important matter to Cy.

''Is he doing any better since you've been working with him?''

''He doesn't seem so frustrated because he's met a friend or two in that group you saw at the center. His uncle still keeps him on a tight leash.''

''Do you think he should have more freedom?''

''Yes, but not until he's shown his uncle he can deal with it.'' Cy was pleased at Beth's interest. He'd started to tell her about Kwesi before, but having her ask was so much better.

''You're a good man, Cy, taking your time to work with Kwesi and the group,'' Beth said approvingly.

''Not really,'' Cy answered. ''It's a tough life out there for so many kids. If they don't get a little help now and then, too many get lost.''

Beth thought she saw a shadow in his eyes, and there were lines of concern on his forehead.

''You sound like you know from experience,'' she said sympathetically. Probably something happened to one of his brothers or a close friend when they were all young.

''We've all had experiences growing up and I—'' The ringing of the wall phone interrupted Cy.

''Excuse me,'' Beth said.

''Hello.'' Cy saw her face light up. ''Hey, yourself, girl!'' She covered the mouthpiece and told Cy, ''This is my best friend from Atlanta.'' Cy started to leave the room, but Beth stayed him with her hand.

''Yes, I am busy and I want you to meet someone, Clio. Clio Stewart, say hello to Cy Brewster.'' Beth handed the instrument to Cy.

She watched his face as he greeted Clio. She hoped they would like each other but hadn't planned on this kind of introduction. However, when she heard Clio she couldn't resist. Now Clio would have some idea of Cy when they discussed him in their heart-to-heart talks.

Cy had been looking down at the table as he and Clio exchanged insignificant chitchat, but now he looked up as he told Clio, ''It's been nice talking to you, too, Clio, and I look forward to seeing you in person.''

Beth thought that was the end of their conversation. Then Cy said, ''Yes?'' and after listening for a moment, his face grew serious. His voice was quietly emphatic as he said, ''You don't have to worry about that, Clio.''

He handed the phone to Beth, who said, ''I'll call you later.''

''What is it that Clio doesn't have to worry about?'' Beth asked. It must have been important by the way Cy's face and voice had changed.

''I'm sure Cliio will tell you her side of the conversation when you talk with her,'' Cy said lightly. ''It's getting late, and I'm going. Thanks for the pie and coffee.''

Leaning across the table, he cupped Beth's face in his hands. He looked at her intently. Beth was sure he was about to tell her something, but he closed his eyes and kissed her instead. ''The pie was good, but this is sweeter,'' he murmured.

Beth was wondering at Cy's somewhat abrupt departure as she straightened up the kitchen then called Clio.

''What did you think of Cy?'' she said immediately.

"I liked his voice, and I thought he sounded confident and warm. I liked what I heard."

"He said you'd tell me your side of the conversation when I asked him what it was you didn't have to worry about. I wondered about it because he got so serious."

"At first we talked about the weather and about Atlanta, nothing much. I was just trying to get a feel for him. Then I said, 'It's been nice talking to you,' and I hoped we'd meet in person. Just before he handed the phone back to you, I told him there's one thing more I wanted to say. He said, 'Yes?' I said, 'You be careful, Cy Brewster, and don't be messin' with my friend, Beth.' I didn't say it mean but in a friendly way. When he said, 'You don't have to worry about that,' I got the feeling he was totally serious."

"Don't you think you came on a little strong, Clio?"

Beth could almost see the shrug Clio gave. "Maybe I did, and if you think so I'll be glad to apologize, honey. But I don't want you to get hurt all over again, so I was giving friend Cy a fair warning. That's all. So what else has been happening with you two? Any dates, et cetera?"

Beth laughed. "I'm not sure what you mean by et cetera, but he did take me to the Valentine Dance, and I talked to Art and met his fiancée." She told Clio about the evening and what a relief it was to be through with Art.

"Have you decided what you feel about Cy now that Art is out?"

"I asked myself that same question. All I could decide is that I love being with him, and he's different than anyone else I've met."

"Sounds good to me. Wish I could meet someone who makes me feel like that," Clio said wistfully.

The conversation turned to Clio's social life, and when it was over Beth still wondered a little about Cy. She had the feeling that something had happened that changed the atmosphere, and that's why Cy had left—but she couldn't put her finger on what it could be. My imagination is being overactive, she decided and went to bed.

In the next few days, Cy and Beth discussed more details

of what they would like to accomplish at the center. Beth made an appointment for them to meet with the council on Wednesday of the following week.

Beth thought the center looked less dingy in the evening under electric light than in the glare of the sun. Even so, places where paint had begun to peel were evident, and the floor of the room where the council sat had most of the finish gone.

Bill Barnes, chairman, called the meeting to order promptly. Noted for his efficient organizational skills, Bill had held the post of chair for the past decade. A short, well-dressed man who was sometimes pompous, he was also evenhanded in meetings. Matters moved along and things got done while a reasonable harmony was kept. He now called for Marge Sinclair to read the minutes after Reverend Garner had offered an opening prayer.

The minutes read and approved, Bill Barnes introduced Beth and Cy. ''We all know about the HOP work going on. The two members of Team Four want to lay a proposal before the council. You have the floor.''

Beth began. ''Cy Brewster and I have completed our initial project, assisting Loraine Dillard to open a licensed day care in her home. We are now ready to start on one that we hope will have the support and approval of the council. In fact, we can't proceed without you.'' She drew a deep breath. She didn't know how this idea would sit with the council, so she watched their faces as she said, ''We'd like to work on this building and do whatever it takes to get it in better condition.''

Cy came in easily, sitting beside Beth and looking around the table at each person as he enlarged upon the theme. ''We know this is a big task and undoubtedly one you've been thinking of yourselves. Beth and I couldn't think of any way to better serve the community in general than to do whatever can be done for the building most people in the community use.''

They certainly had the full attention of the council. Willamae Hines and Jimmy Groves were both ready to say something, but Jimmy Groves was first.

''What do you propose to use for money?'' As treasurer, he

knew to a penny the income and outgo of funds and knew also that much as the center needed painting and repairs, the money simply was not available. Had it been, the work would have been done.

Cy addressed Mr. Groves. "We'll want to discuss this with you, of course, but we want to involve all of the community in it. Our idea is to have organizations of every kind as well as families, individuals, and businesses all adopt a certain part of the task. For instance, someone would be responsible for the painting of this room, someone else for redoing the floor. If plumbing or electrical work needs to be done, we'll see if we can get a plumber or electrician to donate the work." Cy and Beth went on with more details, stating their case with enthusiasm and persuasiveness.

Willamae Hines wanted to know if they'd made a list of what they wanted to do. Beth said they had and passed around copies for the seven members. Marcus Jay, Vesey House director, who knew Cy as a counselor for his agency said, "I'm impressed. Your list is very thorough."

"We also have a list and yours looks almost like ours," Rhonda Hayes said.

"This represents a tremendous amount of work. Do you really think you can get enough people to volunteer not only their time but to buy the supplies they'll need like paint?" Reverend Garner asked looking up from the list. "We're talking about hundreds of hours of work you want volunteers to do."

Beth said, "We asked ourselves that question, Reverend Garner, and we frankly don't know. But we're willing to give it a try. We thought we'd have a series of meetings to tell people about the idea and get people to sign up. We want to make a beginning as soon as possible because if folks see something being done, it might inspire them to pitch in."

Cy added, "We're also planning to apply for some grants to help pay for supplies."

Bill Barnes looked at his watch. "The council will have to discuss this and get back to you. Are there any more questions from anyone?"

Marge Sinclair said, ''I just want to thank these young people for having this idea and offering to carry it out.''

Beth and Cy left with the promise from Bill Barnes that the decision of the council would be given to them within the next few days.

''Do you think we convinced them?'' Beth asked as they stood talking at her car.

''I'm not sure,'' Cy said. ''I think Mr. Groves and Reverend Garner weren't entirely persuaded. I couldn't tell what Mr. Barnes was thinking.''

''I know Rhonda and Marge Sinclair will support us. What about your friend, Marcus?''

''I'm pretty sure he will. You know, Beth, as we were talking to the council, I began to see it from their eyes, and I could see this is a huge proposition. Putting this building in order will take a lot of sustained work. You've lived here all of your life. From what you know of the people, do you think we can find enough folks to do all of this work?'' He looked at her searchingly.

Beth hadn't thought of the undertaking in those terms. Now she did.

''This is my first time to be involved in a project like this,'' she began as she looked at Cy. ''But Rhonda and my aunt Elly have been doing community work for years, so we can get some ideas from them. I think we also have to know from the beginning that some people who sign up won't show up, and that there'll be a small group of committed, hardworking people who'll do most of the work. It's always like that, no matter what you set out to do. But I think we can get it done.''

''It will mean a lot of work for you and for me. We'll have to stay on top of it from the word go,'' Cy warned.

''I intend to do just that,'' Beth declared. ''I'm determined to make it work for Team Four,'' she added. ''Are you up to it, partner?'' She challenged him with a smile.

''I'm up to it,'' Cy said. ''I'm especially up to anything that involves you and me together,'' he said softly. ''Are you up to that, partner?'' He kissed her tenderly.''Are you, Beth?'' he whispered as he kissed her good night.

''Yes,'' she said as she returned his kiss.

Chapter 14

Rhonda Hayes met with Beth and Cy on the weekend.

"The council approved your proposals," she said. Beth and Cy smiled broadly and gave each other a high-five.

"There are conditions, however," Rhonda went on, "and after you hear them, you might want to reconsider." She hoped they would decide to go ahead, not only because the center needed the work but also because Beth and Cy were becoming more than a team. It was what she'd hoped would happen.

"Tell us the conditions," Cy said.

"First, every task like painting a room must have a specific person supervising the work. The council doesn't want a group of teenagers, for instance, trying to take on a job that they are eager to do but don't know how to do. It's too easy for something to go wrong."

"That makes sense," Beth said. "Actually Cy and I plan to be on hand for each task that is done.'

"That will please the council," Rhonda said. "Next, every person involved in a task must sign a simple form releasing the council and the center from responsibility for injury." She looked to see if Beth and Cy understood. "We carry the usual insurance, but it would not cover the kind of activity you're proposing. People must understand that. That's another reason each task must have a responsible adult supervising it.''

''Understood. You'll give us the form?'' Cy said.

''I have it here, and you can make copies as you need them and return the signed ones to me. The final condition is the easiest. The council would like to have regular progress reports, and I'm to be your liaison person.'' Rhonda handed Beth and Cy each a copy of the conditions for them to initial.

''Do we contact you when we need to work in a certain room to be sure it's free at that time?'' Beth asked.

''Yes, that's the kind of thing I'll do. Do you know yet where and when you'll begin?''

Cy and Beth looked at each other. ''We thought,'' Cy said, ''to begin with the large central room because when people see it looking good, it should encourage them to help with the rest.''

Beth went on. ''It's always best to do the largest and hardest job first, and that's what the central room is. What do you think?''

''I think you're right,'' Rhonda said. ''When will you begin?''

''Hopefully ten days from now,'' Cy said.

''That won't give you time to hold all the meetings you spoke of, will it?''

''Not all of them, no, but we want to make a beginning. Then as we talk to folks, we can invite them to come see what's happening and to become a part of it.'' Beth was very positive, and Rhonda thought to herself how Beth had changed from the person who wanted nothing to do with HOP when first approached.

''Let me know anything at all that I can do to help. I'm behind you on this one hundred percent,'' she said in leaving.

For all of the following week, Beth and Cy worked separately and together to put the pieces in place to make what they referred to as ''center rehab'' a success.

Each space in the center was assigned a number. Each number had a list of the specific tasks to be done to rehabilitate that space. To each task was attached the needed supplies. Essential skills for the tasks were listed, and persons known to have those were noted and contacted. Key persons were contacted and asked to give their services. Beth and Cy met with two core groups one night and with Reverend Garner's church another night. Rhonda cleared the calendar for work to begin in the central room. Both Beth and Cy researched funding sources, and Beth stayed late at the job doing the paperwork.

They were working in Beth's apartment Saturday night late, going over the lists and seeing where they stood.

"David Walker will supervise the work, but you and I will be there also," Cy said. "Emily Walker's business will supply the painting materials, and they'll also bring a crew of workers." He looked at Beth with admiration. "That was a great idea of yours to ask the two of them."

"I remembered that Emily was on the council for a few years and that the council helped David when he first came here to get material for his book. They're both solid people. If they say they'll do something, you can count on it. Did I tell you Emily is also going to provide food for the workers?"

"That's great. I've eaten at her Letters and Lunch, and the food is first class." Cy looked again at his list. "Len Nesbit, who owns the big hardware store, will supervise the floorwork. Did you say he'd related to Mrs. Walker?"

"He's her brother-in-law," Beth said. "Emily's younger sister, Sue Marsh, and her husband, Chuck, who both are at the high school, are going to bring some kids to work on the floor under Len and Chuck."

"Pardon me if I stretch," Beth said, suiting the action to the words. She gave a big yawn. "I feel like I could sleep a week. But when I get in bed, my mind stays busy going over our lists and thinking of what I have to do the next day. I'm definitely not getting my usual sleep." She stretched again.

Cy, watching her, felt the usual stirring within himself. All these days of being with Beth after work, sitting across the table from her as they ate and then worked or went to meet with someone, had confirmed his feelings for her. He was certain that Beth was the woman for him, the one he'd been searching for—but how could he tell her? What would her response be? Each time he asked that question of himself, he shied away from the answer.

''You know what we need to do?'' Cy put a gentle hand on Beth's neck and began to massage the tight muscles there.

''Ummmmm. That feels so good,'' Beth said, eyes closed. ''What do we need to do?''

''Take tomorrow off. No work, no lists, no planning. Monday is set and if anything comes up, we'll deal with it on Monday. What do you say?''

''I say it sounds great,'' Beth murmured. ''You'd better stop because you're putting me to sleep.'' She opened her eyes and straightened her back.

''I'll pick you up, and we'll go someplace and relax. Not a single word about center rehab. All right?''

''Very much all right, you're a genius. Ten o'clock?''

''Don't eat, sleep in, and we'll have breakfast out.'' Cy cradled Beth, now so relaxed and drowsy she could scarcely keep her eyes open.

''Good night, my little sleepyhead,'' he whispered.

Sunlight came through the miniblinds in Beth's bedroom, its rays warming her and waking her from a deep sleep. Through the open blinds she could see blue sky and the branches of a tall tree. Recent rains then days of warm sun had made tiny green buds appear. Spring is right on time this year, she thought.

Beth had a sense of extreme well-being. All aspects of her life were going well. She'd received a raise on her job and a commendation from Marty Armstrong. But that wasn't the main thing. The big reason was finding out that she, Beth Jordan, could do something worthwhile and like doing it. She was developing skills in working with people and finding ways to get things done. She felt more vibrantly alive than she'd ever been.

Then there was Cy. Beth smiled to herself at the thought of him. Over the weeks of work with him, they'd become so close. We're a great team, she thought, because we each want the same thing: to make the project successful. We're willing to work hard and support each other to reach the goal. Now we almost know what the other is thinking.

I feel sometimes that we're part of each other. When he kisses me we melt into each other. The memory of those kisses and embraces flooded Beth with intense sensation.

Suddenly the alarm went off. Beth jumped out of bed. After her shower she dressed in a multicolored pair of silk pants with her favorite colors of yellow, black, orange, and white. With them she wore a bright yellow cropped jacket with long sleeves and zippered front. In each ear she wore three tiny linked circles of yellow, orange, and black. Soft black slip-ons completed the ensemble. She looked at her image in the mirror and was pleased with what she saw.

A few moments later she opened the door to Cy. His eyes devoured her. "You look wonderful," he said and took her in his arms. "I could eat you with a spoon," he said, punctuating each word with a kiss.

Beth, flushed and excited, said, "I'm afraid you'd get a bad case of indigestion. Let's go get some breakfast. Maybe that'll satisfy you."

"I know what will satisfy me," Cy said as he started the car, "and it isn't breakfast."

Beth blushed and started a conversation about the strange sound she heard in her car the previous day. Already she was quivering inside and blushing every other minute, even though the day with Cy had just begun.

Cy had awakened at six with a deep longing for Beth. He couldn't put it off any longer. Today he had to tell her how he felt. Just seeing her at the door, so striking in yellow, orange, and black, with her eyes luminous and face glowing had made him nearly lose his control. He wanted to blurt out all of his feelings then and there. But he knew this was neither the time nor place.

They went to a small restaurant for breakfast. There were a number of other people enjoying the waffles, ham, eggs, and grits. Beth could only pick at her food. She seemed to already be filled with anticipation and tension, leaving no room for mere food.

''I heard from Clio yesterday,'' she said.

''How is she?'' His eyes lingered on Beth's face. He found he was having trouble eating because all he wanted to do was look at Beth.

''Fine. She said she's coming here for the award banquet and that she's looking forward to meeting you.''

''How long has it been since she was here?''

''She was home for Christmas.'' Beth took another sip of hot coffee. The muscles of her throat felt taut, and every word she spoke felt weighty.

She could not keep herself from observing every motion and gesture Cy made. She watched him now as he buttered his last piece of toast. His knife strokes deft and clean, he broke a piece, took the knife again and spread a small amount of orange marmalade on the square of toast. He lifted the square to his mouth. His even white teeth bit down on it, and his firm lips moved as he chewed the toast.

She unconsciously licked her lips, leaving them moist, and her eyes glistened.

He stopped chewing and she raised her glance from his mouth to his eyes. Cy had been watching Beth watching him. Now with his eyes holding hers, he took her hand, opened the palm, and pressed on it a fervent kiss. He closed her hand and gave it back to her.

Beth opened her hand and slowly kissed the place where his lips had been. Still looking at each other, Cy, his voice barely audible, said, ''Ready?'' Beth could only nod.

They stood. Cy put money on the table and with his hand loosely riding the small of her back, they walked to the car and got in.

Still without words they turned to each other. Cy held her as close as he could. Beth put her arms around him as tightly as she could. For an endless time they stayed embraced, then at the same moment they moved to look at each other.

''Oh, Beth,'' Cy whispered, too filled with emotion to say anything more.

Beth closed her eyes and kissed Cy as if she were drowning. The slam of a car door and the voices of children startled Beth, reminding her that they were parked in a car lot in broad daylight. Embarrassed she pulled away from Cy and tried to regain her composure.

"Where . . ." she started to say but had to clear her throat and try again. "Where are we going?"

"I thought we'd take a drive down to Saint Helena and look at Penn Center. I've been there only once, and I'd like to go with you."

"I haven't been in years, not since they got the funds to take care of it."

Cy was still looking at Beth. "Why don't you drive for a change?" he asked. Cy wanted to fill his eyes with Beth, not look at the road. He thought also she might enjoy driving the Saturn.

"May I?" Beth smiled. "I'd love to drive."

It took Beth a few miles to recall how the car had handled when she drove it on the lot, but soon she became accustomed to it.

"What a marvelous car!' Can we have the sunroof open?"

Cy showed her where the controls were, and then the warm breeze was blowing in upon them.

They spoke little on the ninety-minute trip down. Once in a while one or the other would remark on the hamlets they passed on the rural roads. The land they passed through had remained relatively untouched, and the quiet peace of the surroundings soothed them. They would look at each other and smile or touch each other gently, briefly.

Beth, who had always liked the act of driving, felt released. The blue skies, the balmy breezes, the fragrance of the grass, the nearness of Cy, and the smooth power of the car made her giddy with delight.

How well she drove, Cy thought. Like she did everything else she put her mind to as far as he could see. He hadn't known her for years, but what he'd learned of her filled him with admiration. Yet for all her competency, she had a vulnerability that made him want to cherish and protect her from whatever it was that shadowed her. He didn't see it in her now as frequently as when they first met, but it was still there.

Beth slowed the car as she drove through the coastal town of Beaufort. The many boats anchored at the marina were swaying, and the breeze made small ripples in the water. Cy, watching Beth's reaction to the scene, said, "Shall we stop here on the way back?"

"I was thinking the same thing," Beth said.

"I know," Cy said, his smile tender and knowing.

They crossed the bridge to Lady's Island and soon came to Frogmore on Saint Helena Island, seven miles east of Beaufort. Beth turned off the main road and found her way down a dirt road to the complex of buildings known as Penn Center.

Before them stood a number of white buildings, large and small, dotting the acre of land planted with the immense live oak trees indigenous to the Low Country. There was no one about, only the trees, the buildings, the soft southern breeze, and Cy and Beth.

"It's so tranquil," Beth said.

A plaque on the large structure on their right stated that the Penn Center was started in 1862 by Pennsylvania missionaries as a school for freed slaves. The school closed in 1951, and the center's focus shifted toward community organizing and support activities as a nonprofit organization funded mainly by private grants. The first building with its formal style and long windows looked to Beth like the main auditorium.

"I can see the students sitting at attention on their wooden benches, listening to the principal or minister," she told Cy as they looked through the windows.

"The opportunity to get any education at all must have been a wonderful thing to them," Cy said.

Hand in hand they strolled from building to building, looking in all the windows. Dormitory-style buildings were on the other side of the main avenue along with a residence.

"When I come here," Beth said, "I feel that if I sat still long enough and put myself in the right frame of mind, I would see people from those times moving back and forth. Some of them are my ancestors." This was a feeling Beth had never put into words before, but talking with Cy was like talking to herself.

"I know what you mean, honey," he said softly. "You can almost feel them around you."

"Do you have any relatives down this way, Cy?"

"Not that I know of, but my dad has a couple of friends here he used to visit. One was named Hayward, and he talked to Dad about how worried he was that the life of these South Carolina sea islands was going to disappear entirely unless the land developers could be stopped."

"You mean they'll become like Hilton Head?"

"That's right. Hilton Head used to be a black farming community when Hayward was growing up, just like the other sea islands. Now that beautiful land has been taken over, the blacks pushed out or used only as low-paid workers for the luxury resorts and retirement homes."

"Can't anything be done to prevent it happening here?" Beth looked around at the unspoiled landscape.

"One of the main programs here at Penn Center now is land retention. The people are being educated about the need to file their deeds, clear up heirship land titles, and pay their taxes on time. They even give loans from the private grants to the most desperate cases."

Beth shook her head. "Such a shame," she said sadly.

Cy saw her becoming despondent. "Don't be sad, honey."

Beth turned to him. "We have to do something to help. Maybe we can give money to the grant fund."

Her look of entreaty and the fact that she said 'we' broke Cy's last defense.

"We will, I promise," he said huskily then took her in his arms. "I love you so much, Beth. I can't hold it in a minute longer."

Cy hardly knew what he was doing as he rained kisses on her face, her hair, her neck, her mouth. The words were out at last, and he felt a vast release. He held her closer and whispered her name.

Beth was overwhelmed. A feeling she had never known existed filled her entire being. Every cell of her body seemed to vibrate with happiness. This is what love is, she thought, dazzled with its light and joy.

Beth caressed the back of Cy's neck. As he held her she said so softly he thought he might be imagining it, "I have something to tell you."

"You may tell me anything in the world, sweetheart," Cy said tenderly as he pulled back to look at her.

There was a light in her face, but her expression was very serious. "What is it you want to tell me, dear?" Cy asked, and he braced himself for whatever might come.

Her brilliant eyes looked deeply into his, and his heart began to thump in his chest for what he saw there.

"I'm so glad you love me, Cy," she began bravely. Then her voice filled with emotion broke, and all she could do was whisper, "Because I love you with all of my heart."

Chapter 15

Lumbering into the parking lot beside the Saturn, a big blue and white bus with Paradise Tours on it pulled to a stop with a blowing of exhaust.

The enchanted moment that had lifted Beth and Cy outside of time and space came to an abrupt end. A large group of people began to emerge from the bus and stood looking around curiously as they waited for the tour guide to collect the crowd.

"Let's go," Beth and Cy said simultaneously.

Cy opened the door on the driver's side for Beth, but she seated herself on the passenger's side. After he had carefully guided the car out past the bus and onto the road, he smiled at Beth in invitation. She immediately nestled against him, and he put his arm around her.

Beth was light-headed with happiness. She gave a little gurgle of laughter as she held Cy's hand.

"What is it, sweetheart?" Cy asked, smiling in response.

"This morning I couldn't eat breakfast, and now I understand why."

"Why?"

"I was so full of love, there was no room for food."

"I was almost as bad," Cy said. "This morning I woke up

early with such longing for you, I knew I couldn't go another day without telling you how I felt.''

The look between them grew in intensity and time. Cy's awareness of Beth shut out even the highway until an angry motorist blew his horn and startled them both. Cy had begun to veer into another lane of traffic. Sweat popped out on his forehead when he saw how dangerous his driving had been through inattention.

Beth moved away and sat in her corner. ''I won't say another word until we get to Beaufort,'' she offered.

''That wasn't your fault, honey. It was mine, but I agree. I didn't realize traffic had become so heavy.''

Twenty-five minutes later the car was safely parked, and Beth was walking on the beach hand in hand with Cy.

The other walkers, recognizing lovers, smiled at them in passing. When they found a deserted spot, they sat down against some rocks. Pleasure craft and fishing boats plied the blue waters. Occasionally a scarlet or bright blue water scooter sped by, the rider trying to control it as it trampled the waves like a bucking horse. White birds sailed down from the sky to land on the water, skimming it until they found food then flew away with it in their beaks. Over all was the seductive tropical breeze and sunlight.

The movement of the water, the boats, the scooters, the birds and the colors imprinted themselves on Beth's mind so vividly that she knew they would be with her forever. They were all a backdrop for the flooding sensations she still felt from the moment Cy had said he loved her.

''I can't believe that you love me,'' Cy said. ''It seems too good to be true.'' He stroked her hair lovingly, then he turned her face to his and looked at her anxiously. ''Are you sure, Beth?''

''I'm certain,'' she said. ''Why do you find it hard to believe?'' Her look, direct and filled with love, went straight to his heart.

''Because I know I don't deserve it,'' he said, his eyes shadowed.

"You're being modest," Beth said and leaned back against him in utter contentment. "I know you deserve it."

After some time on the beach, they explored the waterfront shops and strolled along the main street. The drive back to Jamison was as quiet as on the way down, but there was a difference in the atmosphere. Emotional tension, anxiety, and anticipation were released by the satisfying assurance each felt in loving and being loved. Their glancing and touching were openly tender now without the need of being veiled.

"Where would you like to eat?" Cy asked as they entered Jamison.

"Why don't we go where we had breakfast? This time I think I can do better."

"You hungry, baby?"

"Famished!"

"That makes two of us," Cy said, and they laughed together.

They ate their way steadily through baked chicken with rice and gravy, succotash, hot rolls, and peach cobbler.

They entertained each other by making up stories about the other diners, which then reminded them of other stories of people and places. The enchantment of being with each other heightened their delight in all they said and did.

Beth leaned across the table, her eyes bright with unshed tears. "Oh, Cy," she whispered, "I'm so happy."

Cy was too moved to answer in words. He swallowed hard. All he could do in this public place was squeeze her hand and hope she could read his love in his eyes.

Ten minutes later as they stood at Beth's door, Cy said, "I won't even ask to come in, sweetheart. It's been a long and wonderful day, and tomorrow we'll both put in twelve hours of work. So get your beauty sleep and dream of me." He took her in his arms.

"Kiss me, Beth, and tell me again," he whispered.

Beth, secure in his arms, tilted back her head. "Tell you what?" she teased gently.

A look of uncertainty came over Cy's face. "Can't you say it, Beth?"

Beth had meant only to tease, not cause him pain. "Of course

I can because I do,'' she said. ''I love you, Cy,'' she said almost fiercely and, pulling his face down to her, kissed him with all of her heart.

Cy responded to her kiss, pulling her tightly into his arms and kissing her over and over. ''You mean more to me than I can ever tell you, Beth,'' he said. Then in a quieter tone, ''Let me just hold you before I have to leave you.''

They stood embraced, resting against each other as their heartbeats returned to normal. Finally, Cy reluctantly took his arms from around her. ''See you tomorrow, sweetheart,'' he said and left without looking back.

Beth stood, bemused, until the Saturn pulled into the street and with a small salute on the horn, moved away, and turned out of sight.

Beth could not believe what had happened. She had finally found love. Love had found her after all of these years. The feelings she'd experienced for James Ellington and Art Woods were nothing compared to what she felt for Cy. She'd had no idea about this kind of emotion that came from depths within her of which she'd been totally unaware. She moved through preparations for bed dreamily. Later as she lay in bed thinking of all that had transpired, she understood with a new insight that this love, although wonderful now, would grow and deepen as she and Cy grew to know each other more fully.

Every day is going to be an adventure now, she thought as she snuggled into the covers. I can't wait to see him tomorrow.

Cy was filled with alternate joy and despair. Beth loves me. She told me so three times, and while she's saying it I can believe it. But how can I accept it and hold on to her? She still doesn't know all about me. How can I tell her? I know I have to tell her. I should have told her a long time ago before we fell in love. Now what am I going to do? If I tell her, how can she still love me? I want her to love me as much as I love her. But if I don't tell her, she'll despise me when she finally knows.

Over and over his thoughts swirled in his mind. When he fell asleep at last in the early morning hours, it was from the exhaustion of his inner battle. He awakened on Monday morning unrested and looking forward to seeing Beth at the center with both joy and guilt.

Marty Armstrong stopped at Beth's desk to pick up some data sheets Monday morning. "What's the latest news on Team Four?" His blue eyes sharpened as he looked at her. "You're looking like things are going well."

Beth hoped she wasn't blushing as she spoke quickly to keep Marty from further inquiry. "Things are going fine, Marty, and tonight we're actually beginning work on the center."

"That's the best project you could have chosen. You know, over the years we've sold a number of houses all around the center, and it's a shame to see how it had begun to go down. Keep me updated, and let me know if you get in a bind." With a decisive nod, he picked up the sheets and went back to his office.

Beth filed away in the back of her mind Marty's offer of help. She didn't want to ask him for money again until she had used up all of her other sources, but it was comforting to know the offer had been made.

Beth arrived at the center that evening after a hurried sandwich and change into work clothes. David and Emily Walker were already there along with Rhonda Hayes.

David, a tall man with a pleasant but firm voice, had just begun to instruct the group of six people who had volunteered to help him with the painting of the large central room. It had been emptied of all furniture except for three large tables end to end in the center of the room.

"We've all done enough painting to know that a paint job is only as good as the preparation that goes before it," David said. "We want to make this a good job that will last for many years. So first we'll clean up the walls and ceilings and fill all the nail holes. Then we'll paint the ceiling on half of the room first then start painting the walls on that same side. Do the same with the other half of the room. Put a second coat on the walls. Doors and windows last."

Beth felt Cy's presence. "Beth," he said softly and touched her hand.

"I looked for you when I came in," she whispered.

"I was in the back, stacking the chairs we moved out of here." They stood together, glad to be close again, as David began assigning people to working groups.

Beth and Rhonda worked together cleaning a wall, while Cy helped two other men to go over the ceiling. At the end of an hour and a half, David called for a break.

"I'm using muscles I didn't know I had, and they're groaning," Rhonda complained as she and Beth stopped work.

"You're not alone." Beth turned her neck this way and that to relieve it and at the same time try to see where Cy was.

Emily Walker had sandwiches, snacks, and coffee set out on one of the tables. Rhonda and Beth took their food and sat on the floor against a wall. Beth saw Cy go to the table and select some food, exchange some words with one of the men, then look around the room. He's looking for me, she thought, and felt like she used to feel in high school when she wanted the attention of a certain boy. Come sit by me. Don't go sit with that man.

Cy finished talking to the man, and they laughed together. Then he walked directly over to Beth.

"How's it going?" he asked as he slid down to sit on the floor beside her.

"Slowly," she said.

"Achingly," Rhonda added.

"I think I'll have a permanent crick in my neck from looking at the ceiling," Cy said. "I must say, this food and coffee helps."

"I'm going to get another cup of coffee," Rhonda said and excused herself.

Cy immediately turned to Beth. "How are you, sweetheart?" he asked softly.

Beth looked at him from under her lashes, "Wonderful," she answered just as softly, "now that you're here close to me."

"I wish I could tell you how much I want to hold you in

my arms this instant and kiss your sweet mouth.'' The longing in Cy's voice made Beth wish the same thing. She felt herself grow warm.

''You make me blush all over. Maybe we need to talk about something else.''

''Why, certainly, Miss Jordan.'' Cy was very formal. ''I hope you had a good day at work.''

''Thank you, Mr. Brewster, I did. How about you?''

''I had a terrible day, thank you.'' He was rewarded by a startled look from Beth, who wasn't sure if he was being serious. ''My problem was that I hardly slept last night because I was thinking of you, Miss Jordan. So today I was tired and also anxious because the day didn't go fast enough so I could come here tonight and see you.''

Beth looked at him again from under her lashes. ''Oh, Cy,'' she murmured. ''What am I going to do with you?''

''Love me, Beth. Please love me.'' Cy's voice, for her ears alone but filled with urgency, made Beth tremble.

''Break is over,'' David Walker announced. ''I hope everyone is ready to put in another hour and a half.''

Cy grasped Beth's hand and pulled her up from the floor. ''I enjoyed eating with you, Miss Jordan,'' he said as they started back to their respective workstations.

''The pleasure was mine,'' Beth said.

Emily Walker was clearing up the food with Rhonda's help. ''Surely something is going on with Beth and Cy.''

''I sincerely hope so,'' Rhonda said. ''I think they fit together well, and it's past time for Beth to find a man she can truly love.''

''You didn't think Art was right for her?''

''He's a nice person, but the feeling was always on his side, not hers.''

When work was finished for the night, Rhonda, Cy, and Beth were the last to leave. They made the rounds of all the rooms to see that all was safe and secure, then Rhonda locked the door after Cy put out the lights.

''A good beginning,'' Rhonda said. ''But am I tired! It's nearly eleven.''

"It feels so good to see that we're on the way," Beth said.

"Thanks to Team Four. See you two tomorrow," Rhonda said.

"May I see you home?" Cy asked Beth.

"Of course." They had come in their own cars, so Cy followed Beth. At her door Beth said, "Come inside for a minute." She was sure the lady across the way had seen them on the porch Sunday night. From now on their good nights would be safe from prying eyes.

Cy closed the door behind him with one hand and with the other stayed Beth as she started forward to turn on a light, although illumination from the soft lamp in the front room kept the foyer from being dark.

"Baby," Cy whispered.

The tenderness in his voice took the strength from Beth's limbs. His hands slipped inside her coat, and she melted against him.

In the glow from the lamp, she could see his eyes glitter, and she watched in fascination as his mouth slowly descended upon hers. With a sigh she surrendered herself as Cy drank again and again all she had to offer from her lips.

The world began to turn for Beth as the embrace grew in its intensity. Unsure of what was happening to her, Beth put her hands against Cy's chest.

"What is it, sweetheart?" Cy's voice was husky.

"I need to say good night," Beth whispered.

"I should have said it sometime ago, but I was so hungry for you." He smiled at her and caressed her face. "Shall I pick you up tomorrow? There's no need for us both to drive over."

Beth agreed, then she reached up and kissed Cy quickly and said, "Good night, Cy."

"I'm taking the hint," Cy said ruefully and with another kiss was gone.

Chapter 16

Beth began to see ceilings and walls in her dreams. The work on the center was laborious and tiring. Each night she fell into her bed wearier than she'd ever been. She was also more exhilarated than she'd ever been. As the work progressed, a sense of achievement came to her. The work crews showed up night after night, and a camaraderie developed which made the evening's work pleasant.

One night she couldn't go to the center. She went instead to speak to two groups about helping in the coming weeks. They signed up to assist with two of the smaller rooms. When she returned the next night, the original pale green, which had begun to look dingy and gloomy, was gone. The first coat of a glowing cream-colored paint transformed the hall, making it light and inviting. It looked much larger.

"Doesn't it look wonderful," she exclaimed to Cy, her face beaming.

"It's beginning to," Cy agreed. "We've still a long way to go, and we need more workers."

"The sorority said they'd do one of the smaller rooms, and so did the businesswomen."

"I'm meeting with a fraternity next week and a churchmen's

group who might be interested in helping. They may give a small donation, too,'' Cy said.

''I know we've just begun,'' Beth said as they walked over to the central tables to get their work equipment. ''When I was a child and had something hard to do, Mama used to tell me to keep working on it. 'Little by little adds up' was one of her favorite sayings, and I hated to hear it. But it certainly applies to this.''

By the end of the first week, the ceiling was painted and the walls had their two coats of paint. A little work had been done on the windows and doors, and one-half of the floor had been scraped by the crew working under Len Nesbit.

Saturday afternoon as Beth and Cy were working on the windows, Cy said, ''I think we should stop in another hour and let people go home. We've all been working so hard this week. What do you think?''

''I agree. A few people mentioned working tomorrow, but I don't think anyone should.''

Cy's announcement was greeted with enthusiasm, and by three o'clock the workers were gone.

''I've some errands to run for Mom and Dad,'' Cy said. ''What are you going to do?'' he asked as they stood beside Beth's car.

He was concerned about Beth, who despite her energetic work showed signs of tiredness in her face. He knew she got home late at night and was up the next morning with at least twelve hours of work ahead. If only he had the right to take care of her! He would take her home and put her to bed and let her sleep as long as she could. He knew she wasn't taking the time to eat properly, so he'd cook a tasty nutritious meal and sit across the table from her as they ate it. Then they would go in and lounge on the couch and listen to music or some entertaining television show until it was time to go to bed. Cy was so far away in this lovely fantasy that he didn't hear Beth's reply to his question until she called his name.

''Cy?''

''Yes?''

''You asked me what I was going to do. I answered, and

you were looking right at me but you didn't hear me. Where were you?'' She gazed at him curiously.

''I was in a lovely place with you.''

Beth waited to hear more. When Cy didn't continue, she said, ''Aren't you going to tell me about this lovely place?''

''Not now,'' Cy said, holding her hand to his lips. ''Later. What did you say you're going to do?''

''Go to the cleaners, do some shopping, and try to do some house cleaning before I fall into bed.''

''Don't forget to eat. Want me to bring you some dinner?''

''I'll pick up something while I'm out.''

''Can we spend some time together tomorrow after you've rested? We've had only these snatches together all week.''

''I'd like that very much. Why don't you come over for dinner?''

''I don't want you to do all the work. I'll come over, and we'll cook together. I'll bring a steak and dessert, and you can fix the rest.''

Thoughts of Cy were with Beth off and on through the rest of Saturday and while she was preparing for his visit on Sunday. She tried to analyze why he affected her so differently from anyone else she'd known. Why did I fall in love with him and not with Art? When I first looked at him in his car, I felt something. He's not as conventionally good looking as Art or as James, but to me he's more attractive than they are. I love the strength I feel in him. He's all male. I know I could lean on him if I needed to. He's kind, and with me he can be so gentle but he's not soft. He's so good with people, and I admire that in him. I've been watching him all week at the center, and he's the one who keeps his eye on everyone. I hadn't expected that of him, but he seems to do it naturally. He steps in when the least little problem comes up, and it's resolved before it gets bigger. How did he learn to be so good with people?

Beth cleaned the salad makings and put them in the crisper. She prepared potatoes au gratin and fresh green beans with pearl onions. She set the table with a lavender linen set, crystal, and candles.

As she showered and dressed in a slinky peach pants set, she began to tingle in anticipation of seeing Cy for an uninterrupted evening. They hadn't been alone for more than a few moments since last Sunday. Was it only a week ago that he'd told her he loved her? It seemed a much longer time had gone by than seven days.

Beth was at the window when the Saturn turned into the driveway and Cy got out. She stepped back so he couldn't see her. In his smart brown wool check slacks and cream shirt with a dark chocolate crewneck sweater, he looked sumptuous. She licked her lips unconsciously and flew to open the door before he could ring the bell.

Cy stepped in swiftly, pushed the door closed, and in the blink of an eye they were in each other's arms. Beth was lost in a vortex of emotion as Cy kissed her gently at first on her lips then again but not as gently on her face, her hair, and her neck. The faint spicy scent of his cologne and the taste of his mouth inflamed her. She pressed closer to kiss him again. He returned the kiss fervently then kissed her on a spot below her ear. The sensation was electric!

"Cy," she murmured. "Cy." She spoke a little louder and took his face in her hands.

Cy stood still. "I'm sorry, baby, did I upset you?" His eyes were dark and stormy, but his voice was full of concern.

"No," she said. "I was just, I mean I . . ." She stopped in confusion, not knowing what it was she wanted to say. She looked at him helplessly.

Cy searched her face then understanding illumined his countenance. "It's all right, baby," he whispered. He loosened his embrace then kissed her cheek.

"I'm going to get the food," he said and went out. Beth looked at the door still a little dazed. What food was Cy talking about? Then she remembered the steak and dessert.

Cy walked slowly to his car, glad of the air in his face. He needed it to blow into his head, which was so filled with longing for Beth that he was having trouble keeping himself in control.

I have to do better than this. The evening's just begun, and I'm acting like a kid that doesn't know any better. He opened the trunk and took out the basket of food. Just being near her makes me feel like a kid again, he thought, but I'm not. I'm supposed to be a grown man. So act like it, Brewster!

In the kitchen they turned on the broiler for the steak and put the raspberry-chocolate mousse in the refrigerator after Beth had admired it. She began putting the salad together and mixing a dressing while Cy attended to the steak. The potatoes and beans were warming. They talked as they worked but about nothing in particular: the weather, their jobs, what they'd been doing since they left each other yesterday afternoon.

It seemed to Beth they shared the space smoothly and unselfconsciously. You'd think we'd been working together in this kitchen for years, we never get in each other's way. She handed him the oven gloves just as he needed them. He opened the refrigerator when her hands were full before she could ask. We're so easy together, she thought contentedly.

When it was all ready, they put the food on the table. Cy pulled out Beth's chair. When she was seated, he tipped her face back. "Thank you for this, honey," he said and brushed her lips with his.

He took his seat opposite her, and Beth said grace. The steak was tender and juicy, the potatoes creamy underneath their cheesy top. The green beans and pearl onions were a hit.

"I like green beans this way, but most people don't know how to do them right," Cy said appreciatively. "Have you always liked to cook, Beth?"

"I learned the basics of cooking from my mother when I was growing up, but I didn't start liking it and experimenting with it until I got out on my own."

"When was that?"

"When I finished college, I was twenty-one. I lived home more than a year after that, working here and there until I got the job at the realty agency and saved enough paychecks to move out. That was six years ago."

"Have you always lived in this apartment?"

"Yes. I was lucky to get it, as it had just been renovated. I liked it because it was near Aunt Elly and Uncle Sim. How about you, Cy? Did you move out on your own right after college?''

''I moved out when I was twenty-three. My first apartment was only two rooms because that was what I could afford then. I was working two jobs, and neither one paid much, but I liked the work.''

''What were you doing?''

''I was assistant manager for a youth shelter, and at night I did some counseling for another program.''

Beth recalled other references Cy had made to such involvement with people. ''Was there ever a time when you weren't interested in helping people one way or another, Cy?''

Cy skirted the direct question. ''I think everyone is to some degree, don't you?''

''Not like you do,'' Beth said.

''Look at all the people who are volunteering in this job at the center. Look at yourself,'' Cy said.

Beth cleared the table, and Cy got the dessert. While they were eating it, Beth picked up the topic again. ''That's what I mean. These people have been good enough to volunteer when we ask them. But very few people work continually helping others as you do, Cy. I think it's admirable.''

Cy smiled at her. ''What's admirable is the way you work so hard on this. Look at the way you did the whole day-care project with Loraine. I did practically nothing, but you put in lots of hours. You're the one I admire.''

''I wish you wouldn't.''

Cy had been finishing up the meltingly rich mousse. He looked across the table to see if Beth was serious or being appropriately modest. She was looking down into her coffee cup, and her face was set. When she raised her eyes, Cy saw again the sadness that he had first associated with her. Maybe now he could find its source. But not here. He stood up.

''Why don't we take our coffee into the other room,'' he suggested.

''Good idea,'' Beth said. ''I'll bring the pot.''

Beth's living room was bright with color. A deep coral couch stood opposite a picture window flowing with drapes that matched the couch. To the space on the left were two chairs, one cranberry red and the other in a stubby oatmeal fabric. Between them was a piecrust lamp table. On the other side of the room, a heavy square table filled with books and magazines stood beside a navy blue chair and hassock. An entertainment center stood on the wall beside the picture window. Beth had reserved one wall as a gallery of personal pictures.

Cy paused to look at the display, and Beth paused also. He pointed to a photograph of Beth glowing in her cap and gown at her college graduation with a man and woman standing on each side of her.

"Your mom and dad?"

"Yes."

"They look like nice people. I know they were proud of you."

Beth nodded. "I think even Mama was proud of me that day."

As Beth pointed out the people in other pictures from her childhood and college days, Cy's gaze returned again to the picture of her parents. Her remark about her mother had many implications, and he wanted to see what Mrs. Jordan's face revealed. She was not a bad-looking woman, and Beth had her eyes but generally looked more like her father. Mrs. Jordan's mouth had a severe line, and her eyes were watchful. In the photograph Beth and her father had wide smiles that lit up their faces. Mrs. Jordan looked as if she wanted to join them but couldn't.

"Where's Clio?" Cy asked.

"The last time she was here, Clio took down the picture I had of her and promised to send me one she liked better. I liked the one I had, but she didn't."

"What didn't she like about it?" Cy asked as they sat on the couch, and Beth filled their cups.

"Clio and I are the same height, five seven in our stocking feet, but she has always carried some weight. Runs in her family. So although she exercises to keep fit, she's still a big girl. Someone took our picture when we were out jogging, and

I loved it. I'm not sure why she didn't like it. We were laughing, and the sun was shining. We looked so carefree and happy.''

There it was again: her wistful reference to happiness. Cy had to try to find out why she felt this way. Her vulnerability touched his heart and made him want to wrap her in his arms against anything hurtful.

''Beth,'' he began, ''would you tell me something if I asked you?''

She looked at him in surprise. ''Of course I will if I can.''

''At the table you said you wished I wouldn't admire you, and you were very serious about it. Why do you feel that way?''

''I've done so little,'' Beth said, ''and I didn't even want to do that at first. When Rhonda first asked me to be a team member, I said no several times.'' She looked at Cy to see what his reaction was. Would he be disgusted or embarrassed for her? All she saw was interest and the desire to understand.

''But you did come to Rhonda's dinner.''

''I decided to at the last minute only because she'd been so kind to me. I thought I could at least go to the dinner.''

''Why did you decide to be on the team?''

''You three team members seemed so interested and took for granted that I was also. I didn't want to let Rhonda down.''

Cy knew there was more to it than team membership. ''Nothing in the concept itself appealed to you? The idea of doing something not only to help the community but to inspire other people to go beyond their own interests?''

Beth looked down. If I answer that honestly, Cy will see the kind of person I am. It's like I told him, there's nothing to admire.

Cy, watching her face intently, saw her uneasiness. He took her hand in his. ''Sweetheart, there's nothing you can tell me that will change how I feel about you.'' He tipped her face up so he could see her eyes. ''Don't you know that?''

His voice was gentle, his eyes held only tenderness. Beth felt reassured that she could be open and honest with him.

''I've been one of those people you described, Cy. I've been concerned with my own interests—and those were going to work and doing whatever else I wished to do as far as enjoying myself was concerned. I supported various community affairs when asked. But generally speaking, the kind of attitude you described, I'm sorry, Cy—it just wasn't a part of me.'' There. It was out as baldly as she could state it. Now he knew that deep down, she was a self-absorbed person.

That attitude wasn't a part of me, either, thought Cy. Not until it was made to be a part of me.

''You know what I think,'' Cy said thoughtfully. ''I think the capacity was always there, but nothing had happened to awaken that interest in you. I've always thought of you as a warm and caring person. It's obvious that people like you. They respond to you, and you respond to them.'' Again his eyes searched hers. ''What or who made you think otherwise?''

Cy felt Beth's hands grow still in his, and a veil came over her eyes. I've touched it—whatever it is that makes her sad. This was the moment he always looked for in counseling when he knew that a critical issue had been reached. Sometimes he pressed hard and persistently to bring forth the issue. But this was Beth, his dear love. What he wanted here was not for himself but for her to discover the root of her sadness so she could work through it. Let it go. Be healed. Be the whole healthy person she could be.

Beth listened to Cy in wonder. How could he see her as a warm and caring person? She believed he was in love with her, but love happens when and where it will. It doesn't necessarily endow people with admirable qualities. She could only think that Cy kept talking about a different kind of Beth than the Beth her mother had summed up and described with precision and emphasis. Cy seemed to be mind reading when he asked who made her think otherwise, and she couldn't but react.

Cy put both arms around her and nestled Beth against his chest with her face turned away from him. Perhaps it would be easier for her to tell him what he wanted to know if she didn't have to look at him. Cy was fairly certain now that the comment Beth had made that even her mother had been proud of her on graduation day reflected the central issue.

''Are you comfortable, honey?'' he said softly.

''Yes,'' Beth said as she felt herself begin to relax.

''Now can you answer my question?''

Beth took a deep breath then began slowly to tell him what he wanted to know. She described unsparingly the scene with her mother when her mother found out about Art's leaving. She told how she'd run from that scene to her own apartment when Cy knocked on her door with the ice cream.

Cy—remembering how anguished her eyes had looked that Sunday afternoon and the brave front she'd put on, even allowing him to stay and have the soup and corn cakes with her when all the time she was in pain—felt a lump in his throat. He hugged her tighter and laid his cheek on her hair.

Beth went on to describe the days she'd spent alone after Art's letter. How she'd reviewed her life in light of Art's rejection and her mother's indictment. Then her voice trailed off.

''What conclusion did you come to, baby?''

''That there was more truth than not in what Mama said. That I was a flighty, frivolous person and shallow, not doing anything worthwhile and not able to keep a man.''

Again Beth stopped. Cy knew there was more. Perhaps the hardest thing she yet had to say. He would help her if necessary, but he'd wait and see if she could say it herself.

They sat quietly. With his arms around her, she felt secure and safe. She'd come this far, surely she could say the rest. His support was such that now she almost felt as if she were talking aloud to herself. Unconsciously she moved against him for the sheer pleasure of feeling his protectiveness.

''Then I met you,'' Beth said. Cy hadn't realized he was holding his breath until he let it go. How he admired her courage and honesty!

''I saw you in your car,'' she went on, ''when I was on the way home. I got home and in my mail was Art's letter. Exactly seven days later I saw you at Rhonda's, and I felt something between us. Each time I saw you the feeling grew. I kept telling myself that I can't let this happen. I tried to resist it. But it happened anyway in spite of myself . . . so here I am going from one man to another in a week's time and being flighty and shallow just like Mama said I was.''

Cy's first reaction was anger at Beth's mother. How dare she belittle Beth because Beth didn't love Woods! It wasn't her business in the first place and then to say such hard cold words to her daughter was indefensible. He couldn't imagine his mother or father taking such an attitude to any of their children. What kind of woman was this who could so scar her grown daughter with that accusation? The fury in him made him put Beth gently aside. He got up and walked over to the window, his back to Beth and his hands clenched in his pockets.

Beth was devastated. Out of the shelter of Cy's arms, she felt cold and alone. It had been a mistake after all to open herself to him. He'd given her the impression that she could tell him anything. She'd acted on that belief and as a result had driven him away. She blinked her eyes quickly to hold back the betraying tears and tried to erase the misery she felt from her face. With a tremendous effort she made herself ready for whatever he had to say.

Cy turned and came to stand directly in front of Beth. His face was stern, his eyes cold.

''Beth, I mean no disrespect to your mother,'' he said, ''but that was a terrible and unforgivable thing she said to you. She wasn't the one who had to decide about Woods. That was only between you and him. It might not have turned out the way she wanted it to, but it wasn't her business. You're a grown woman, not a fifteen-year-old kid. She should never have said what she did and given you all of that pain you've been carrying.'' His eyes softened. ''Come here, baby.'' He pulled her up and into his arms. ''I'm so sorry you've been hurting all of this time over that,'' he said, stroking her back.

Beth could not hold back the tears now. She'd thought she'd pushed Cy away, but instead he'd been upset on her account. Beth had always fought her own battles. Only with her mother had she been vulnerable beyond her own strength. To find that strength in Cy unhesitatingly and freely given was an unexpected gift. She leaned against him now and let her heartache ease itself until the sobs stopped. He pulled out a large clean handkerchief and tenderly dried her eyes, crooning to her all the while.

When Beth was quiet, Cy sat again on the couch and cradled her in his lap. Could he match her courage and honesty? She couldn't see what there was in her to be admired, but he knew what it had taken for her to tell him her inmost pain. He knew because he hadn't been able to bring himself to the same account. The risk of losing her if he did was a consequence he could not contemplate.

Beth's eyes were closed. She looked drained, but her face was composed. Cy felt his heart swell within him. This was the woman he'd been looking for all of his life. Tenderly he caressed her face. Beth opened her eyes and smiled. Cy knew it would take more than anything he could say to permanently erase from Beth's consciousness the pain of her mother's harsh words. But he had to try.

"Sweetheart, how did you and Woods meet?"

"He'd moved here from Columbia by the time I got home from college and was part of the crowd I went around with."

"Did you like him right away?"

"No. We sort of drifted together and began going around about three years ago."

"When we were on the way home after the Valentine Dance, you said you realized you had a deep affection for him, but not love."

"That's right."

Cy paused. He had to ask the next question so she could see she wasn't to blame for how she felt.

"Had you ever been in love, Beth?"

"Not until now."

Cy felt the fire blaze up in him. It was all he could do not to crush her in his arms and love her with all of the pent-up emotion in him. He gritted his teeth and swallowed hard.

"When you and I met," Beth went on, "it was totally different. Even before we met formally, when I saw you in your car and we looked at each other, something happened for me."

"For me, too, sweetheart," Cy said.

Cy thought of how he should put the next point. "Suppose you and I had met on some occasion when you were out with

Woods, like at the Valentine Dance or some party. Would you still have been attracted to me?''

Beth thought of the other men she had seen and talked with during the time she was going out with Art and before. None had secured her attention, although some had tried. The chemistry between Cy and her had been instantaneous and unmistakable. She couldn't resist it, no matter how hard she tried.

She had been resting quiescently against Cy as she answered his questions, but now a wave of longing enveloped her without warning.

''You were irresistible to me,'' she whispered, her eyes soft and yearning. ''Kiss me, Cy.''

The control Cy had been holding on to vanished. With one strong hand he held Beth to him. With his other hand he supported her head and searched her eyes. ''What do you want, baby?'' He'd heard Beth clearly the first time, but he wanted to hear her say it again. Prolonging the anticipation made the event itself all the more exquisite in its pleasure.

Beth's mouth went dry. She moistened it with the tip of her tongue. A fiery gleam lit his eyes. ''I want you to kiss me,'' she said and watched, mesmerized, as his lips came down to claim hers.

The universe turned again and again as they kissed each other, drank all they could and gave all they could. Beth couldn't get close enough. She had the peculiar feeling that she was surrounded with fire. She'd never experienced anything like it and wasn't sure what to make of it. All she knew was that she couldn't get enough of Cy.

We're rapidly reaching the boiling point, Cy thought. I didn't mean this to happen. Reluctantly he lifted his head and held Beth to him, gently stroking her back and trying to still his own raspy breathing and runaway pulse.

''See what I mean?'' Beth murmured when she was calm.

''I understand perfectly because you're irresistible to me,'' Cy answered. After another moment Cy returned to his theme. ''Do you see the point I'm getting at, honey?''

Beth reviewed his questions. ''You're saying that I fell in

love and that it had nothing to do with time or anything else. When it happened, it happened."

"That's what I'm saying. It's the way love is, and we don't have much control over it. We can accept it or reject it, but that doesn't change the fact that it happens. Don't carry any guilt in your mind about when it happened to you, sweetheart. Let's just both be thankful it happened for us."

Cy watched her expressive face as Beth considered his analysis. He knew the instant she weighed it against her mother's words and found it adequate. It might take some time for it to permanently replace those words, but the healing had begun. In her eyes he saw a newfound trust. She gave him a smile of great sweetness.

"Thank you, Cy."

Cy hid her face on his chest and rocked her in his arms. Fear and anxiety gathered within him. He knew he did not deserve her trust. But how could he go on without her? Every day she became more precious to him, more necessary.

Beth felt the tension in Cy. "What is it, Cy? What's the matter?" she asked anxiously.

She tried to read his eyes, but he had shuttered them. Beth felt a coldness in the pit of her stomach. She had opened herself fully to Cy, telling him all that he had asked. Why couldn't he do the same?

Cy was aghast. He had not realized that she could read him so well. Yet why shouldn't she be as aware of him as he was of her? He would have to be more careful.

Beth drew herself away from Cy. "Can't you tell me what's wrong?"

Cy made himself smile. "Nothing's wrong that we can't make right, honey." He put her on her feet and stood beside her. "It's getting late, and we still have the kitchen to clean up."

He isn't going to say any more, she thought. His lack of trust and openness chilled her, but she would not let him see her hurt. The work in the kitchen went swiftly with surface conversation but none of their earlier easy laughter and friendliness.

At her door Cy said, "Shall I pick you up tomorrow for the center at the usual time?"

"No, thank you, Cy. I won't be coming from home."

"Thank you for dinner," he said.

"My pleasure." If he doesn't open the door, I'll open it for him and usher him out. I'm not the one who withdrew, he did.

"Sweetheart, let's not part like this," Cy said with a big sigh. He took her gently in his arms and held her. She could still feel the tension in him, but she had done all she could do to help him with whatever it was. Beth felt sad and troubled.

She kissed him on the cheek and opened the door. "Good night, Cy."

Chapter 17

The first day of April awakened Beth with balmy breezes drifting through her bedroom windows. She'd been dreaming and, as she opened her eyes, she tried to snatch at the remnants of the delightful feelings the dream had brought. Maybe she should spend more time in bed asleep, she reflected as she went about her preparations to go to work. Dreaming was better than waking these days.

Her awareness of a barrier set up by Cy was a reality she hadn't been able to destroy. They traveled to the center separately each evening. Her heart still turned over each time she saw him, but the oneness she'd had with him was gone. Their friendly conversation at the center was superficial. Several times she'd felt his intent look, but when she looked up he'd turned away.

The beauty of the day lifted Beth's spirits as she drove to work. The morning sky was already a flawless blue, and the sun promised an eighty-degree temperature later. The air had a soft and soothing quality. For the first time since Sunday, Beth began to hope that Cy would be able to trust her and say what was on his heart. Until he did, they could not regain what they'd had or move forward.

Marty Armstrong asked her to come into his office after the end of his midweek session with the agents.

"Where are we on the center, Beth?" he asked.

It amused Beth that Marty now took a position of partnership in the rehabilitation that Team Four was effecting at the community center. She did nothing to discourage him, because she knew the time would come when his financial help might be crucial.

"We're putting the finishing touches on the main room, the hall," she said.

"You're that far along ?" Marty was pleasantly surprised.

"We've had a great group of workers who've been faithful in showing up, and they work hard. The ceilings and walls have been done. The floor has just been finished, and we're completing the windows and doors tonight." Beth couldn't help but be a little proud as she listed the completed tasks.

"I'm impressed! What's next?"

"The second largest room gets done next, and a new group will be coming in to get started on it."

"When will it be done?"

"Depends on how faithful the workers are."

Beth had been working with Marty long enough to know that when he was looking pleased and a little smug, something was going to happen that he'd arranged. He had that look now, and she prepared herself for the announcement. She hoped it would please her as much as it was pleasing him.

"The people working on this next room are a good mixture of adults and young people from Mount Calvary Church," she went on. "One of the deacons is an experienced carpenter, and he'll be in charge, so it should go well."

"I've been able to arrange a little event that should help the project along," Marty said. "Channel Fifteen is quite interested in the story I told them. They're going to come to the center next Wednesday night, a week from today, and do a live broadcast showing what has been done, what still has to be done, and talk to the people involved. They thought it was fine human-interest story."

Marty beamed with pleasure and waited to hear what Beth would say.

Beth was pleasantly surprised and let her enthusiasm show. "Everyone will like that, Marty, and it should encourage more people to volunteer. I'll let the council know, and probably some of them will want to be there. Thanks a lot."

"I want our team to win," Marty said.

"We're doing our best."

Back at her desk Beth called Rhonda to tell her the news and get official permission. "The other council members will be delighted," Rhonda said, "you won't have to worry about that. What did Cy say?"

"I haven't called him yet," Beth said. "I wanted to be sure it was all right with you."

"If the rest of the work goes like this first room did, it's going to be a tremendous success," Rhonda said. "You and Cy make a fine team. I'm so glad you agreed to help, Beth."

"Do you like it now that you're into it?" This was a question Rhonda, who had known Beth for years, had been wanting to ask. She'd been curious about when her girlfriend would discover something in life other than shopping and entertainment. She knew Beth had the potential to do much more.

"I like it more than I ever thought I would. I can begin to understand why people like you and Cy get so involved with other people. I'll see you later at the center."

Cy's secretary said he would be away from his desk all day and would she like to leave a message. Beth declined knowing she could tell him later.

When she walked into the center at seven, she was surprised to see the full crew already there and at work.

"Am I late?" she asked Rhonda.

"No, you aren't. I got here fifteen minutes ago to open up, and most of them were waiting for me then," Rhonda said. "They said they wanted to have time to finish completely without rushing."

"I guess I'd better get to work. Where's David?" Beth looked around for David Walker and wondered if Cy had arrived. She didn't see him in the room.

"David and Cy are in the back," Rhonda said.

Beth was chatting with Emily Walker a few moments later when David and Cy came into the hall each carrying a ladder.

Beth saw Cy look around for her. As their eyes met, she felt the familiar jolt. She turned back to Emily, but all of her awareness was of Cy. She was still upset that he had refused to tell her why he had closed up on Sunday, but that didn't seem to affect the rush of joy she experienced when seeing him. He appeared at her side now after setting down the ladder.

"Hi, Beth."

"Hi." She excused herself to Emily and walked over to a corner with Cy. "Marty told me this morning that he had arranged for Channel Fifteen to come here next Wednesday night. They're going to do a live broadcast about the center."

"That's terrific, Beth. Why didn't you call me?" Cy was well aware of the barrier between them, but he'd hoped it wouldn't affect their Team Four work.

"I did call you right after I cleared it with Rhonda. Your secretary said you'd be away from your desk all day. I decided not to leave a message but to tell you tonight." Beth bristled at what she saw as implied criticism.

Cy laid a hand on her arm placatingly. "Don't be mad, Beth. It's just that I miss talking to you anytime I can. I hate the way we are now. Can we get together soon, please?" His voice was even, but his eyes implored her.

"People are looking at us, Cy. We need to get to work," Beth said. "I'll see you later."

Cy set up his ladder and climbed it to polish the old light fixture. New ones would have been nice, but the old ones still worked, so the decision had been made to use the money for other essentials. The brass polish made them shine as he buffed them and thought of how he had to make up his mind to tell Beth everything. Hold nothing back and pray that it would not separate them.

From his perch on the ladder, he could see her diligently scraping dried paint from the windows. He was so lucky to have met the woman who represented everything he wanted. She was warm, intelligent, and attractive, and she touched him in every way. As he watched her, she turned to get a cloth, saw him looking at her, and smiled at him. Cy felt a wave of desolation at the thought that he might lose her. I must talk to her. Soon.

Beth turned from looking up at Cy on the ladder. I want to see him, but what good will it do us to get together if he won't talk to me? We'll end up like we did Sunday. When we kiss and hold each other, I feel so close, like he's a part of me and I'm a part of him. But that isn't true. Something in him prevents it, and it's too painful to come up against it. The alternative, to see Cy only here at the center, was so depressing that Beth found herself working slower and dropping out of the conversation around her.

After an hour of work, David Walker went around to look at what each person was doing. At the end of his tour, he made an announcement.

"In another twenty minutes all of the work in this hall will be finished. We'll give the floor a final sweeping and, as you complete what you're working on, please take your supplies and equipment to the back room and stack them neatly. Then Emily will lay out the special food she brought, and we'll enjoy ourselves."

A little cheer went up from the twenty people assembled in the hall. A half hour later the large room had been cleared. Chairs were brought in and placed around two long tables in the center of the room. Red and white checked tablecloths and napkins were on the tables. Emily brought out platters of fried chicken and barbecue, bowls of potato salad, and baskets of rolls. There were bottles of soft drinks and a cooler of ice.

"Emily, you shouldn't have gone to all of this trouble," Cy said.

"That's right, but I'm sure glad you did," Dan Burton said as he filled his plate and started right in.

"You make the best fried chicken in town," Rhonda said appreciatively.

"That's what I tell her," David Walker said with pride.

"I can't decide which is better, the chicken or the barbecue, so I'd better have more of each,'' Emily's brother, George, said and held out his plate.

''Family last,'' his wife, Margaret, said playfully, noticing the platters were almost empty.

''There's enough for everyone to have seconds and thirds,'' Emily said as she refilled the platters.

Beth had gone to the restroom while the table was being prepared and, by the time she returned, there were no two empty chairs together. Cy waited to see what she would do. When she sat down beside Matt Logan, Cy politely asked Matt to take another seat. ''Sure, Cy,'' Matt said and moved. Beth watched the maneuver in surprise.

''Sitting beside you is my privilege, not Matt's,'' Cy said firmly.

The color rose in Beth's face, and she was sure they were the center of attention. The potato salad was handed to her by Helen Fort, and she busied herself putting a spoonful carefully on her plate before passing it on to Cy. The bowl was of heavy crockery, and she held it with both hands. Cy took the bowl by putting his hands over hers caressingly. Beth drew in her breath. How could such a slight touch pierce her with its warmth? Reluctantly she raised her eyes, knowing Cy was waiting and would not release her hands until she looked at him.

''Thank you,'' Cy murmured, looking at her with a tenderness he did nothing to hide. He slowly released her hands and, after serving himself, passed the bowl on.

As the meal progressed, the din of conversation increased. Emily produced five homemade apple pies and clean dessert plates.

''Emily's gone way beyond the call of duty with this meal,'' Beth told Cy. ''Will you say something about it on our behalf?''

''I think we both should say something since this is the last time for this crew. Will you tell them about the TV show?''

''I'll be glad to.'' Since talking about the project to a number of groups in an effort to obtain their participation, Beth had developed a certain confidence in her ability to speak. For this group of people who had enthusiastically embraced the center rehabilitation work with loyalty and hard work, she had only admiration. Looking at them now, she was surprised at the bond they had developed. Like Emily Walker. She would always feel closer now to Emily, although they'd known each other all their lives, because they'd shared something different in this work.

David Walker stood and rapped on the table for attention.

"The first thing I want to do is thank my wife for this wonderful meal. It was all her idea. And for all the other food she brought each night."

He turned to Emily with a proud smile and lovingly brought her to stand beside him, his arm around her waist. As everyone applauded, and Emily smiled, Beth couldn't help but wonder how that must feel. Emily had been alone a long time before David Walker had come to Jamison and instantly fell in love with her. It had taken him some time to convince Emily of his love and awaken hers for him, but now they had a happy union and two children. Beth sighed unconsciously and felt Cy link his hand with hers and press it.

"The other thing I want to say on behalf of all of us who have worked on this room is thank you to Cy and Beth. We are all glad to have had this opportunity to have been a part of what we think of as a lasting contribution to the community. It wouldn't have happened without the inspiration and leadership of Cy and Beth."

People began to applaud, but David held up his hand to stop them. He continued. "They not only got it started, they've been here right along with us, putting in their hard work. I know they'll be here until the whole building is done. That takes a real sacrifice of their time and effort. I want them to know they are appreciated." David turned to Cy and Beth. "Now," he said to the others, and the whole group turned to look at Cy and Beth as they gave a long enthusiastic applause.

Beth was overwhelmed. Nothing like this had ever happened to her, and she didn't know how to respond. She didn't feel deserving of it and what it implied. She'd taken on the Team Four concept and was simply following it through. She looked at Cy.

"Want me to respond for us?" he whispered.

"Please."

Cy stood and the applause died down. "Beth and I want to thank you. We all know that an idea is worth nothing unless people are willing to make it a reality. That's what each of you have done in coming here night after night, putting in the physical labor to make this community center beautiful again. What you have done for this hall will be an inspiration for other volunteers as they work on the rest of the building. In connection with that, Beth has an announcement to make."

"This is my first time to be involved in such a project," Beth said. "David, we can't thank you enough for agreeing to be the supervisor for this hall and doing such a superb job. Emily, thank you for the great food that helped keep us going. I personally thank each of you for your work and for showing me what being a volunteer means. Cy and I want to invite you back here next Wednesday night for a television show. Channel Fifteen is doing a live broadcast on our project and will show what has been accomplished. They want to talk to the people who did the work. So as many of you as possible, please be here at seven—and thanks again."

Rhonda stood with Cy and Beth later at the door before closing the center. In place of the scratched-up green walls, the flaky ceiling, and the marked-up floor, there was now a hall with glowing ivory-tone walls, smooth windows, and a gleaming floor. Color was present in the wide floral border around the walls. All of the doors now shone with fresh paint, and the brass light fixtures were polished to look like new. Even the floor of the stage had been redone.

The three looked around the hall then at each other with deep satisfaction. "It looks so good," Rhonda said. Cy and Beth nodded.

"We have Thursday and Friday off, and the next crew is coming what time Saturday?" Rhonda asked.

"Nine o'clock, Deacon German told me," Beth said.

"I'll see you both then," Rhonda said.

"What are you doing Friday, honey? May I come see you,

or will you come over for dinner?'' Cy asked Beth as he walked her to her car.

Beth didn't answer. Cy had made his feelings abundantly clear tonight, but that didn't mean that he was ready to tell her what she needed to know. For the first time she wondered if her imagination had played a trick on her Sunday and invented the emotion in him he later denied. She recalled the moment. Cy had been holding her in his arms, her face on his chest. As if it were her own body, she had felt in him the buildiing of an inner tension and anxiety. His body had become rigid, and when she asked him about it, he made his eyes innocent of feeling and said it was nothing. Her intuition told her otherwise.

No. What Cy had been feeling was real, and there was no point in seeing him unless he was ready to tell her about it.

''Cy,'' Beth said, turning to face him as they arrived at her car, ''there's something bothering you that you aren't telling me.'' She searched his eyes, and this time they were clear and candid.

''I know, Beth, and I'm sorry about Sunday. I didn't mean to turn you off.''

''Does that mean that if I see you Friday that you'll be ready to talk about it?''

Cy made an effort to keep his eyes on Beth and his face unmoved so she wouldn't suspect the premonition that knifed through him. ''Yes, I'll talk about it.'' Even though talking with her about what was between them might very well drive her away, Cy had no choice now. He'd put it off too long, and now he must face the consequences.

Chapter 18

''Beth, your mother and I haven't seen you for so long. Can't you come over and have some dinner with us one day this week?''

Her daddy's voice on the telephone had made Beth feel guilty because it had been more than a week since she'd even talked with her parents and longer still since she'd seen them.

''I'm sorry, Daddy. I've been so busy almost every night with work at the center. I don't have to go on Thursday, and I'll come then. Okay?''

''Okay. We've been hearing about the center, so you can tell us all about it. Maybe we can even come and help sometime.''

''I'll put your names on the list of volunteers. See you on Thursday.''

Beth had to admit it was a relief not to have to go to the center Thursday. She came home from work, leisurely changed into casual clothes, took time to read her mail and water her plants, then drove to her parents' house. She'd deliberately not asked her parents or Aunt Elly's family yet for the first part of the center's work. She knew enough about human nature to understand that volunteers were easier to get for the first part of such a project than later when the initial interest waned.

That's when she intended to draw on her family and her closest friends.

Her mother opened the door as Beth walked up on the porch. "Come in, Beth Ann." Her voice was welcoming and her eyes warm.

"Hi, Mama. How're you feeling?" Beth put a hand on her mother's arm. She was not in the habit of kissing her mother except on rare occasions, since Minnie Jordan had never encouraged demonstrations of affection. They were difficult for her to give and receive.

"I'm doing all right." Minnie looked at her daughter closely. "You look tired."

"I am, a little," Beth admitted. "But I'll get rested. Where's Daddy?"

"Getting the table ready. We're just waiting on you, so come on in the kitchen."

Merdis Jordan put the last plate on the table. "Glad to see you, honey," he said, his eyes lighting up as he gave Beth a vigorous hug.

"Hi, Daddy," Beth said, returning the smile and the hug. "What've you been up to lately?"

"Been building birdhouses for sale. Want one?"

"Sure. How much?"

"For you, nothing. Just promise you'll use it."

"I will—on the tree outside my bedroom."

By this time Minnie had put dinner on the table. As they ate, Beth exclaimed with pleasure at the taste of some of her favorite foods her mother had prepared. "Pot roast, rolls, corn pudding, and steamed cabbage. Mama, you outdid yourself. It all tastes so good!"

Minnie Jordan allowed a small smile around her mouth. "Well, we thought you needed a good home-cooked meal from what we've been hearing of you working every night at the center. I know you haven't had time to do any real cooking."

"Folks at church have been telling us bits and pieces about the center, honey. Fill us in on what you've been doing," Merdis said.

Beth told them in detail about the work and the workers and

how they were recruited. "This Wednesday you might want to come by because Marty Armstrong arranged for Channel Fifteen to do a live broadcast from there, showing what's been done and what still remains to be done," she said.

"Then maybe we'll get to meet this Cy Brewster you're working with," Minnie said. "Dan Burton said he doesn't have eyes for anyone but you." Minnie's voice was mild, but her eyes searched Beth's face.

Beth knew she was blushing, but this time she was not going to be intimidated. She returned her mother's look. "Yes, Cy likes me very much."

"Do you like him, honey?" her daddy asked.

"Yes. I like him more than anyone I've ever known, including Art Woods." Beth hadn't known this was coming up, but since it had, she was determined to make her position clear with her mother from the beginning. She marveled that she was so confident and calm. She said a little thanks in her heart to Cy for helping her to get over the barrier of her mother's accusation. She waited to see her mother's reaction to this new situation.

"We'll be there on Wednesday and look forward to meeting this young man," her mother said pleasantly. "Do you want us to work on Wednesday?"

"No, Mama, I haven't asked any of my family or close friends to volunteer yet because before the center is completed, some people will have lost interest. That's when I hope both of you and all of Aunt Elly's family will be available."

The conversation turned to other matters and, after the peach cobbler had been eaten, Beth offered to help with the dishes before leaving.

"Go home and get some sleep, Beth. We'll clean up like always," her mother said.

Her father walked her to the car. "You know this young man pretty well, honey?"

"I think so, Daddy. We've been seeing each other for a while. His parents retired here from Charleston, George and Iva Brewster. They live on Zinnia Lane. Cy works at Alumax as assistant to the personnel director, Gary Raeford. He's thirty-three and has never been married.''

''Honey, you know my only concern is that you don't get hurt again. I'm glad you found someone you can care for.'' Merdis's face was full of love as he hugged his daughter again and told her to drive safely then watched her leave.

Beth hardly knew how to feel as she thought about the evening. She'd put off mentioning to her parents that she'd met Cy because of what her mother had said about her being flighty. Yet she knew that eventually she'd have to introduce Cy to them. Now not only had it been taken out of her hands due to Dan Burton's gossiping—but wonder of wonders her mother had almost seemed pleased. She'd been able to tell her dad facts, which Beth knew he'd investigate in a discreet manner to satisfy himself because he understood that this relationship was serious to Beth.

Cy called soon after she returned home. ''How was your day, honey?'' His voice was warm and tender.

Beth felt the warmth flowing through her, dispelling the separateness that had existed since Sunday. Whatever Cy had to tell her tomorrow couldn't separate them again, she was certain. Their love was too strong for that. What was important was the honest communication between them. If they had that, nothing else mattered.

''I just came from having dinner with my folks,'' she said.

Cy could hear in her voice that there was more. ''How did it go?'' His stomach muscles tightened at the thought that perhaps Mrs. Jordan had said something wounding to Beth again.

''You won't believe what happened.'' Beth's voice was gay as she told the story. ''They'd been hearing about our work at the center from church friends, and Dan Burton made it his business to tell them that Cy Brewster had eyes for no one but me.'' Beth stopped.

''I don't care for Dan Burton or anyone else spreading my business in the street, but what he said is true. I have eyes, heart, thoughts, and feelings only for you, Beth. You are all the world to me.'' Cy's voice was weighted with emotion. ''Don't you understand that yet?''

Beth hastened to reassure him. ''Oh, Cy, I'm so glad that's true because it's true for me, too. You are everything to me. I love you more than words can say.''

''Why am I here and you there?'' Cy's voice was dark with longing.

''I feel the same way,'' Beth said softly. ''We'll be together tomorrow.'' For a moment there was silence, each one seeing the face and feeling the touch of the beloved.

''What did your mother say, Beth?'' Cy asked gently.

''I'd invited them to come by the center on Wednesday, and Mama said maybe they'd get a chance to meet you. When she repeated what Dan had said, I was surprised, but I looked right at her and said yes, you liked me very much.''

''You're my sweet brave girl,'' Cy said caressingly.

''But that's not all. Daddy said, 'Do you like him?' and I said, 'Yes . . . more than anyone I've ever known,' and then Mama said pleasantly that they'd be looking forward to meeting you on Wednesday!''

''I'm so proud of you, Beth.''

''I was determined to make my feeling clear and not be intimidated. You helped me to be able to do that, Cy, and I truly appreciate it. I also think that maybe Mama has done some thinking, too, and her attitude is changing.''

''I sincerely hope so,'' Cy said. ''My folks are coming Wednesday, too, so you'll meet them. I had dinner with them. Speaking of that, what do you want me to cook for you tomorrow?''

''Surprise me.''

''What time will you be here?''

''Six-thirty okay?''

''Any time you're here is okay, Beth. I want you to promise me something.''

''Of course. What is it?''

''I want you to promise to remember that I love you with all of my heart and soul.'' Cy's voice was compelling in its intensity. ''Do you promise?''

"I promise."

"What do you promise, Beth?"

"I promise to remember that you love me with all of your heart and soul." Beth repeated the words, and the vow sent thrills through her whole being. She heard Cy release his breath.

"Thank you, sweetheart. I'll see you tomorrow," Cy said.

Tomorrow! The word rang in Beth's mind all the rest of the evening. She shivered with the anticipation of being in Cy's arms again, holding him close and listening to their hearts beat as one. That experience was inexpressibly wonderful. It was still new and opened to her emotional insights she'd never known before Cy.

The anxiety about her mother's reaction to Cy could now be dismissed. The security of her parents' approval and Cy's fervent declaration that he loved her with all his heart and soul wrapped around her with comforting bliss. He had exacted from her the promise that she would remember his words with a force that made her wonder a little about his concern. She was overwhelmed at the strength and generosity of his love, so how would she ever doubt it? She'd been happy to make him the promise and would keep it forever.

Beth was hard at work at her computer the next morning and thinking it was time for a break when a deliveryman came into the agency.

"May I help you?" Aretha Symonds said.

"Flowers for Miss Jordan," he said, depositing a tall vase on Aretha's desk and hurrying out.

"Someone is lucky today!" Aretha said as she took the vase over to Beth's desk.

"For me?" Beth asked. She carefully took off the green floral paper to reveal a dozen red roses in a lovely crystal container.

The agents in the office came over to ooh and aah over the flowers. "I don't know which is more striking, the roses or the vase," Jennifer Winters said.

"Whoever picked it out has exquisite taste," Lana James said and looked pointedly at Beth, who looked demure but said nothing.

''Great way to start a weekend,'' Aretha said wistfully.

When the admiration society had disbanded and her desk was hers once more, Beth inhaled the fragrance of the roses with her eyes closed. Then she read the card that had been tucked in the blooms: *Sweet Beth, Promise to remember that I love you with all of my heart and soul. Forever yours, Cy.*

For the rest of the day, the roses were not far from Beth's consciousness. Their fragrance and their beauty enhanced the written message Cy had sent with them.

She found a box in the storage closet to set the vase in so it would be secure on the drive home. After her scented bath she looked in her closet for something special to wear. Her eye fell upon a knit dress that she knew was flattering to her figure and was the color of roses. What could be more appropriate, she thought as she stepped into it and pulled up the back zipper. From her West African jewelry collection, she selected a gold sculptured crescent necklace and earrings, which set off the dress perfectly.

In her full-length mirror, she saw a woman elegantly dressed for an evening out. I'm only going to Cy's apartment for dinner but I don't care. I want to look my best tonight. A final touch to her makeup and hair, a dab of her favorite fragrance, and she was ready.

Cy had been going through hell all day. All of his adult life he had lived honorably, according to his standards. He had worked hard, been a good son, and enjoyed his social life but never at another's expense. He'd given much of his spare time to helping others because that was important to him. He'd been lonely much of the time, yearning for a wife and children, and had learned to channel that yearning into helping young men like Kwesi.

Opportunities to marry had of course presented themselves, but Cy had chosen to wait until he met the woman whom he knew would be the one and only woman for him. Then his car had pulled up beside Beth's at a stoplight. Their eyes had met, and his destiny had found him. He had fallen deeply and irrevocably in love, only to discover that of all the women he could have met, Beth Jordan was the one who would present the greatest obstacle to the fulfillment of his dreams.

But love had seized him, and his hunger for Beth's love had obscured his ability to be totally honest with her from the beginning. All day he could think only of the conversation they would be having after dinner. His moods contrasted between hope that by some miracle she would understand and forgive and despair that she would banish him from her life. In one of the more hopeful moments, he had sent the roses and wondered if the message on the card, a repeat of what he'd said last night on the telephone, would have any meaning for her by the end of the evening.

Now that the moment of reckoning was upon him, he bitterly chastised himself for not taking matters in hand early on in their acquaintance. He wrestled with guilt and shame and could only pray that somehow he could get through the evening without totally destroying whatever feeling Beth had for him.

He finished cleaning up and arranged the roses he'd bought. In the kitchen he prepared the dinner of stuffed pork chops, red rice, and caesar salad, then set his table with his best linen and china. He didn't know if he'd even have Beth at his table again, and so he took particular pains with all of the arrangements. A single red rose in a crystal vase stood between two white candles as a centerpiece. As he gave the table a final look, he remembered the card he'd prepared and put it facedown in front of Beth's plate with her name on it.

He changed into black slacks and a white turtleneck then went to check on the food. The bell rang, and he hurried to the door.

As he opened it, Beth's hand was raised to touch the bell again. Cy took her hand and brought her inside, closing the door with his toe. He put his hands gently on each side of Beth's face and gazed deeply into her eyes, seeking the comfort and assurance he needed. Beth's eyes, wide and bright with loving anticipation, met his.

Her response to his need was instinctive. She put her arms around him and stood on tiptoe to kiss him over and over again while whispering words of endearment. With a muted groan, Cy put his arms under her wrap and pulled her close. She was so sweet, so precious. He tightened his embrace as he kissed her fervently. How could he ever let her go? His hands caressed her slim body, and Beth began to tremble as they clung to each other.

With a deep sigh of frustration, Cy loosened his embrace and lifted his head. He laid his cheek against Beth's hair and breathed in its clean scent. He gently stroked her back until their breathing slowed and calmness returned.

With a shaky little laugh Beth asked, "Do you always greet visitors this way?" She eased herself out of her coat.

"Only you," Cy said, his voice still husky with emotion. With her coat in her his hands, Cy got the full impact of Beth's toilette. His eyes widened in appreciation of her feminine beauty and grace.

"You look marvelous!" His words were vibrant as he took in the allure of the rose knit dress, the jewelry, the silken hose, and the rose pumps. Beth glowed under his adoring gaze.

Cy clutched the wrap he was still holding to help him resist the temptation to take her in his arms and appease his hunger for her.

"All of this for me?" he said softly.

Beth blushed. "Only for you," she wispered.

Cy leaned toward Beth, his burning gaze holding hers. He kept his hands on her wrap, and she put hers behind her back as she moved a tiny step forward.

Their lips met in a kiss of infinite sweetness.

Beth felt she was floating to angelic music Cy knew at that instant what true happiness could be. For an eternity they stood thus, their eyes closed, communing with each other.

Then they moved apart reluctantly, and Cy went to hang Beth's wrap in the closet.

Chapter 19

In the kitchen Beth and Cy were still moving in the atmosphere created by their passionate greeting. Beth felt beautiful and adored and acutely attuned to everything about Cy. She felt like there was an invisible thread holding her to him. She couldn't bear to be far from him as she thanked him for the roses and helped him with dinner. Her appetite had vanished, but the food smelled good, and she was going to try her best to do justice to it for Cy's sake.

Cy was in torture. His senses were overwhelmed with Beth, and all he wanted to do was look at her, be near her, touch her. The dinner he'd prepared had no interest for him, but they had to get through it. Beth was the other half of him. She was his mate. An immense need to tell her so filled him and threatened to make him forget everything else. But first dinner, then he had to keep his promise to her.

When they finally sat at the table, Beth exclaimed at how lovely it looked. Then she saw the card and picked it up curiously. Her name was on the side facing her. On the other side she read: *Promise to remember that I love you with all of my heart and soul. Cy.*

Beth looked across the table. Cy's eyes were intent and

serious. "I promise," Beth said. She held out her hand. When Cy extended his, she held it to her cheek and kissed it. "I do love you so much, Cy," she said.

Beth and Cy made a good show of convincing the other that the chops, rice, and salad were just what they'd been wanting.

"Ready for dessert and coffee?" Cy asked.

"Not now, Cy. I couldn't eat another bite. Maybe later."

Cy was relieved. He doubted if he could force his tied into knots stomach to receive another morsel.

"I'll help you with the dishes," Beth offered.

"They can wait," Cy said and led her to the couch in the living room.

Subdued lighting and soft music added to the atmosphere of the room fragrant with the perfume of roses. Cy sat on the couch and nestled Beth in his arms. She kicked off her shoes and curled up against him in utter contentment.

Beth had not thought beyond the intoxicating discovery of loving Cy. But now it was becoming clearer that perhaps there was a future for them. His masculine strength combined with gentleness and protectiveness was what she'd subconsciously been seeking. He was understanding, caring, and compassionate. Whenever they were together, the electricity that flowed between them was compelling. Like now. She could feel it from her toes up, beginning to make itself felt. Beth knew that Cy was feeling it also.

They looked at each other at the same time and sought the passion of each other's kisses and embraces. Their fervor and ardor grew until Beth felt she could hear and see the sparks that surrounded them. Her lips were bruised with Cy's kisses, and she was finding it hard to breathe. Reluctantly she pulled back and laid her head on Cy's chest and began to draw deep breaths.

Cy let her rest then tipped her face to his. His eyes blazed with love and desire. "I want you forever, Beth." His voice was thick and deep. "You're mine, and I want to love you and care for you all the rest of my life."

"That's what I want, too," Beth said, her face radiant.

''I want more than anything else in the world to ask you to marry me.''

''Why don't you?''

''I can't until I tell you something.''

''Something about what?''

''Something about me.''

''Is it what you were thinking about last Sunday?'' Beth asked.

''Yes.''

Beth thought of the worst thing possible. ''Are you already married or promised?''

''No.''

''You have children you haven't told me about?''

''No.''

Beth gave a great sigh of relief. ''Then I don't know what you could possibly tell me that would change how I feel about you,'' she said confidently. Her eyes held only love and trust as she looked at Cy and waited for him to continue. When he didn't speak, Beth said, ''Tell me what it is.''

''It's so hard for me to tell you because I know it will hurt you,'' Cy said.

Tendrils of fear began to invade Beth. Cy would not say such a thing lightly, and his face was deeply furrowed with anxiety.

''Beth, I was in the car that killed your cousin Bobby.''

Beth's eyes stretched in shock and disbelief. Her face lost its color.

''You killed Bobby?''

Beth instinctively moved back from Cy, and when he reached for her hands she jerked them away.

''No, Beth, I didn't kill Bobby. I was only thirteen. My eighteen-year-old cousin and his friend were visiting us for the weekend, and we went out driving. My cousin was driving the car when Bobby ran in front of it on his bike.''

Cy had always known that when he finally got up the courage to tell this to Beth that it would be difficult, but the look of horror on her face was even worse than he'd imagined.

''My cousin and his friend drove up to Charleston to visit.

That afternoon he wanted to see Jamison because he'd never been here. He had a second-hand car, a heavy old Buick. He was obeying the speed limit when this boy came dashing out of a driveway as fast as he could go, looking back over his shoulder. He ran right in front of the car. My cousin almost stood on his brakes, but it was too late. I'll never forget the sound. I still have nightmares about it."

Beth's face turned ashen. She put both hands over her mouth and rushed to the bathroom. Cy, startled, got up to follow but stopped himself. He heard Beth retching over and over. Then the bathroom door closed quietly.

Cy paced the floor, his hands jammed deep in his pockets. Why had he mentioned the sound? It was bad enough to tell Beth the bare facts. He hadn't meant to add that, it just came out. That sound had produced a trauma he thought he'd never outlive. But he shouldn't have told Beth. He stopped in his pacing to listen but could hear nothing from the bathroom. She'd been in there nearly ten minutes, and he was worried. He'd give her another two minutes.

At the end of the two minutes, Cy knocked softly on the door. "Beth?"

After a moment he heard a faint, "Yes?"

"Are you okay?"

"Yes."

"Can I get you anything?"

"No."

Cy went back to pacing and watching for the door to open. After a short interval he heard the knob turn and Beth appeared. Her eyes were red and puffy. All her makeup had vanished. Her face was drawn and her movements uncertain as she came into the room.

Cy, appalled at her condition, moved toward her. "Let me get you something, Beth. A cup of hot tea while you sit down."

Beth flinched as he approached. "I just want my coat."

As soon as she tried to speak, the tears began again and rolled unceasingly down her face as she refused his holding of her wrap and put it on by herself. Her hand was on the doorknob when Cy stopped her.

"Beth, you're in no condition to drive yourself home. I know you don't want me near you, but I'm not going to let you go home by yourself. Give me your keys. I'll drive you home."

Beth shook her head mutely.

"I'm not going to let you drive, sweetheart," Cy said very gently. "Give me the keys, please."

She fished them out of her purse and Cy took them from her and opened his door. He watched her carefully as she went down his steps slowly and walked to her car. He opened the passengers' door and she got in. When he got into the driver's seat, Beth was hunched in the other corner, her face turned as far away from his as possible. Her obvious misery filled Cy with a degree of fury at himself that he had rarely experienced.

It took only a fast five minutes to get to Beth's apartment. By the time Cy brought the car to a stop, Beth was trembling and he could hear her teeth chattering. He knew that she was suffering from shock.

He opened her door and, despite her protests, put his arm around her and helped her out of the car. "Lean on me, honey," he said as he helped her up the steps to her door, found the right key, and unlocked it.

"IIII'mmmm allll rrright," Beth tried to say through her trembling.

"No, you're not. You need to get warm and to have a hot drink inside you." Cy picked her up and carried her into her bedroom. "You'll soon be warm," he said. He sat her on the bed, took off her coat and shoes. Her feet felt icy, and he massaged them until he felt them begin to warm up. He turned back the covers.

"Lie down, baby," he said, and as she stiffly obeyed he pulled the blankets up over her. "I'm going to make you some hot tea."

In a few minutes he was back with a mug of tea. Beth hadn't moved, and the tears were still coursing down her face.

Cy put one strong arm behind her and raised Beth so she could sip from the mug. He did not allow himself to think or feel but concentrated on getting Beth to take sips of tea, until with a feeble hand she pushed it away and her eyelids began to droop.

Cy laid her down and pulled the blankets up around her neck for the utmost warmth. There was a faint color in her face, and the tears had stopped. He sat by the bed for a while until he was certain that she was asleep.

He knew he couldn't leave Beth like this. He wanted to stay and take care of her himself, but it would make matters worse than they already were if she awakened to find that he had stayed the night.

Cy left a shaded lamp burning in her bedroom and quietly let himself out of the apartment. He walked down the street a few houses and knocked on the door. A motherly looking woman, who reminded him of Beth, opened the door. "Mrs. Richards, I'm Cy Brewster."

"I know who you are," Elly said. "Come in."

Cy followed her into a room where a man who was reading the paper looked up and put the paper down.

"Good evening, Mr. Richards," Cy said.

"This is Cy Brewster, Sim," his wife said.

"It's been twelve years since you came here to see us, but I recognize you," Sim said, looking at Cy searchingly. "Have a seat."

Cy expelled the breath he didn't realize he'd been holding. "Thank you, sir. My parents moved here to Jamison after Dad retired, and I came to be near them. We've been here less than a year."

"I heard that you and Beth are a team for HOP," Elly said.

"Yes, ma'am, we are. That's why I'm here to see you."

"What do you mean?" Elly asked.

"Beth was at my house for dinner tonight. I'm very much in love with her. I told her I wanted to ask her to marry me, but first I had to tell her something. I told her about Bobby. She went into shock. She didn't want me near her, but I couldn't let her drive herself home the way she was. I covered her up in her bed and helped her drink a little hot tea, but that's all I could do. I came to ask if you could see about her, please, Mrs. Richards. She shouldn't be alone."

An expression of surprise on Elly's face was followed by alarm. ''I'll get my coat,'' she said and left the room.

Sim went to the heart of the matter. ''How long have you known Beth was Bobby's cousin, Brewster?''

''Soon after we met, I saw a picture she has and she told me.'' Cy knew he had no defense that Bobby's father would accept for how he'd acted with Beth, but he wasn't going to lie about his feelings.

''Why didn't you tell her when you saw the picture?''

''I was already attracted to her, and I didn't want to cause any problems. The more I grew to love her, the harder it became to say anything. But tonight I knew I couldn't talk about marriage without telling her.''

''Brewster, the first time you came here to ask our forgiveness about Bobby, we were able to give it. You were just a kid who happened to be riding in the car, and you were not to blame in any way.'' Sim's eyes were cold and assessing. ''But now you're a grown man. You should have been honest with Beth from the beginning. She's like another daughter to us, and if your actions are going to make her suffer, you'll have me to answer to. Forgiveness won't come so easy this time. Understand?''

Elly had come into the room with her coat and bag as Sim was speaking. Cy stood. ''I understand,'' he said.

When they were outside Elly said, ''There's just one thing I want to know. Does Beth return your feeling?''

''She told me that she loved me, and I believe her. I think that's part of the reason this has hit her so hard.''

Elly pursed her lips, and Cy saw for the first time a brief resemblance between her and the picture of Beth's mother. Beth's mother! How was she going to react when she found out about this? At the thought of Mrs. Jordan giving Beth more grief on top of what she was already bearing, Cy's jaw clenched and he vowed to do whatever he could to see that didn't happen.

He opened Beth's door for her aunt and went with her into the bedroom to look at Beth. She was in the same position Cy had left her in ten minutes earlier. Elly took one look at the swollen eyes and drawn face then beckoned Cy to follow her out of the bedroom.

Her eyes were accusing as she held out her hand. "You may give me Beth's keys and leave, Mr. Brewster."

Cy put the keys in her hand. "You can't think any worse of me, Mrs. Richards, than I do of myself." He laid a card on the table. "These are my telephone numbers. If there's anything at all I can do, or if Beth gets any worse, please let me know. No matter what you think of me, I love Beth with all of my heart." His eyes held hers steadily, and she could see the lines of worry etched in his face.

"Good night, Mrs. Richards," he said, "and thank you for coming." Cy closed the door behind him and heard the set of the lock.

Outside under the first street lamp, Cy looked at his watch. He couldn't believe it was only a little after eight. It seemed to him that many hours had passed since he'd opened his door to Beth. He was glad it was still early because he had one more thing to do.

The mix of emotion within him fueled his energy, and within fifteen minutes he had walked the distance from Beth's apartment to his. He started his car and in another ten minutes was knocking on the Jordans' door.

A man he recognized as Beth's father opened the door.

"Mr. Jordan," Cy said, "my name is Cy Brewster." Before he could continue, a smile of recognition lit Mr. Jordan's face.

"Come in, Mr. Brewster. I'm glad to meet you," he said as he shook Cy's hand. "Come on in and meet my wife." He led Cy into the family room, where Mrs. Jordan looked up from her magazine in surprise as her husband ushered Cy in.

"Minnie, this is Cy Brewster, Beth's friend."

Cy walked over to where Beth's mother was sitting. "How do you do, Mrs. Jordan," he said pleasantly. Mrs. Jordan's eyes met his, then as if reassured by what she saw she shook hands.

"Please sit down, Mr. Brewster," she said in a friendly voice, indicating a chair across from her. As Cy sat down, she said, "What brings you here, Mr. Brewster?"

All the way over Cy had been wondering how to tell Beth's parents what he had to say. Now that the question had been asked, he had no problem.

''Mr. and Mrs. Jordan, I wanted to tell you both how I feel about Beth,'' he began. ''Beth and I met in January. I was attracted to her the first time I saw her. Then as luck would have it, we were assigned to work on HOP together, and we began to see a lot of each other. The more I was with her, the more I saw to appreciate and admire in her. I fell deeply in love with Beth. I'm thirty-three and have never been married. I felt so lucky to have found her and to know that she loved me too. Your daughter is the woman I've been looking for all of my life.''

Cy took solace from the fact that Mr. Jordan's expression was openly friendly and encouraging. Cy noticed him glance at his wife to see how she was taking this declaration of Cy's love for Beth. Mrs. Jordan was the crucial part of the equation because of her earlier attitude, and Cy now focused on her as he came to the difficult part.

''I made one big mistake,'' he went on evenly, ''for which Beth is in no way to blame. I don't know if Mrs. Richards ever told you, but I'm the kid who was in the car when Bobby got killed.''

The pleasant look on Mr. Jordan's face turned into a frown. Mrs. Jordan's eyes grew chilly, and her mouth tightened.

''My eighteen-year-old cousin was driving, and Bobby ran in front of the car. You may remember that the driver of the car wasn't cited because witnesses said the boy suddenly appeared in the street, and the police determined that the driver was within the speed limit. Of course that doesn't make Bobby's death any less tragic or bearable, I know.''

Cy stopped for a moment. Speaking of the accident was always difficult for him.

''When I turned twenty-one, I went to Mr. and Mrs. Richards and asked their forgiveness because it always weighed on me. They were very understanding and gave it. Now I've fallen in love with the one person who would be most affected by what happened twenty years ago. I should have told Beth as soon as I found out she was Bobby's cousin, but I didn't. I didn't want to drive us apart. The more I loved her, the harder it was to say anything until tonight. She was at my apartment for dinner, and I said I wanted to ask her to marry me, but first I had something to tell her.'' Suddenly Cy saw again how Beth looked when she came out of the bathroom. Pain cut through him like a rapier. He covered his face with his hands and drew a deep breath.

''She took it very hard,'' he continued. ''She didn't want me to, but I drove her home in her car because she was too upset to know what she was doing. I knew she shouldn't be alone tonight, so I got Mrs. Richards to come over. Then I came to let you know what had happened and why.''

''Does Beth know you're here?'' Mr. Jordan asked.

''No, and she'll probably be even angrier with me when she finds out, but I had to let you know. None of this is her fault. It's all mine. I have no excuse except that I love her and don't want to lose her.''

''You think you won't lose her now?'' Mrs. Jordan said.

''Mrs. Jordan, I intend to do everything in my power to hold on to Beth now that I've found her. I will try for as long as it takes to get her to forgive me. I'm not giving her up.''

Mrs. Jordan got up and the men stood also. ''I'm going to call Elly,'' she said and left the room.

The men looked at each other. ''I didn't mean to hurt Beth, Mr. Jordan, and I can't tell you how sorry I am,'' Cy said, hoping that Beth's father knew how deeply he felt.

''That doesn't stop the fact that you should have told her at the first, Brewster.''

''No one understands that better than I do, sir. But right now the only thing that's important is for Beth to have the support of her family. That's why I came over.''

Mrs. Jordan came back in the room. ''I told Elly we'll be over to stay with Beth,'' she told her husband. Then she turned to Cy. ''You were wrong in what you did to Beth, but you were right to come tell us.''

''Thanks for listening to me,'' Cy said. When he got into the Saturn, he turned around and parked up the street from the direction the Jordans would have to go. He waited five minutes, then he saw them come out and drive away. Satisfied that Beth would have the loving care he wasn't permitted to give her, he turned around and went home.

Chapter 20

Beth was roused from troubled sleep at the touch of a soft hand on her cheek. Her eyes felt heavy and sticky, and she couldn't see through them properly. A terrible foreboding filled her being.

"You awake, lovey?" a gentle voice asked.

It sounded like her mother's voice using her pet name for Beth from when Beth was a little girl. Beth was puzzled, but she resisted waking up because she knew something awful was waiting for her. She closed her eyes tight and tried to sink back into sleep.

A warm damp cloth was passed over her eyes several times, and the same voice said, "It's all right, lovey. Mama's here."

I wonder if I was in an accident, Beth thought, and began to cautiously move first one leg then the other. Her body felt like it was in one piece, but her head felt as if it would burst with pain. That must be what happened. My head got hurt. Her subconscious having obligingly repressed reality for her protection, Beth was prepared to drift back into sleep. But the voice wouldn't let her.

"Lovey, you need to wake up enough so I can get you out

of these clothes and put your nightgown on you,'' the voice said persuasively.

Beth cautiously opened her eyes. Her mother's face, worried and sad, slowly came into focus. She was sitting on the bed, and her dad was standing beside the bed.

Beth thought she might be in the hospital, but as her vision took in the room she realized she was in her own bed. But why were her parents here?

''What happened?'' she asked, looking at her mother.

Instead of answering directly, her mother said, ''Merdis, step outside while I get Beth changed.''

Merdis was glad to leave and softly closed the door behind him. Nothing had prepared him for how Beth looked. When they arrived at the apartment, Elly had taken them in and all three had stood looking at Beth in disbelief. Her swollen eyes made her look as if she'd been hit, while the deep lines of pain in her face gave her the appearance of someone who'd been ill for months. ''If I had him here now, I'd make Brewster look the same way,'' Merdis said through clenched teeth. Minnie and Elly wiped the tears from their faces in silence.

Back in the living room, they'd talked about Cy's visits and what had happened between Beth and Cy.

Minnie said, ''Beth must love him very much for it to affect her like this.''

''That's what I've been thinking,'' Elly said, looking at her sister. ''I think it's the first time she's been in love.''

Merdis remembered what Beth had said after Art's letter. ''Yeah, you're right. She said she never loved Woods.''

''Does she need a doctor?'' Merdis asked.

''They don't come anyway, and I'm not going to get her up to take her to sit in an emergency room for two hours,'' Minnie said.

''You're right, Minnie,'' Elly agreed. ''Call her doctor and tell him you need something for shock.''

''I'll go get it, but I want to see her awake first,'' Merdis had said.

''I'll run on home, but you know where I am if there's

anything I can do,'' Elly said. She put her arm around Minnie. ''We'll all get through this.''

''But will Beth?'' Minnie asked, looking at her sister. She knew in her heart of hearts that Elly had more insight in some ways about Beth than she did.

''Beth is strong,'' Elly and Merdis said at the same time. ''We'll help her, and she'll get through it,'' Elly repeated.

Beth looked at her mother's face bent close to hers with an expression of tender solicitude as she used the washcloth on Beth's face again.

Beth still didn't know why she was in bed. ''What happened?'' she asked again.

''You didn't feel good when you came home, lovey. Can you sit up so I can get you undressed?''

Beth pulled herself up slowly. ''Came home from where?''

''You had dinner with Mr. Brewster,'' her mother said cautiously, uncertain of what Beth's reaction would be. She pulled the knit dress over Beth's head.

Comprehension gradually dawned in Beth's face as her memory returned. I was in Cy's arms, and he said he wanted to ask me to marry him. I was ecstatic! He said first he had to tell me something, and he told me about Bobby. Why didn't he tell me before? As soon as he knew Bobby was my cousin. Why didn't he tell me before I loved him?

The tears began again as her mother finished the undressing and helped her into a nightgown. Sharp pangs of grief and pain assaulted Beth. She turned to her mother blindly. ''Why didn't he tell me?'' she cried.

Minnie cradled and comforted her. ''It'll be all right, lovey,'' she said again and again, holding Beth against her and marveling that this was the first time she'd held her daughter close since Beth was a little girl. Minnie's tears flowed silently, not only for Beth's pain but for her own shortcomings.

Gradually the deep wrenching sobbing began to ease, leaving Beth with sore abdominal muscles. ''I have to lie down,

Mama,'' she said. Minnie helped her as tenderly as when she'd been a baby and pulled the blankets up around her.

She brought a freshly warmed damp cloth with which to soothe Beth's eyes and wipe the tearstains away. When she paused to smooth the hair back from Beth's face again, Beth said, ''Mama?''

''What is it, lovey?''

''How come you and Daddy are here?''

''Mr. Brewster came over to the house and told us what had happened.''

Beth couldn't take this in. ''Why?''

''He said you needed someone with you.''

There were more questions Beth wanted to ask, but she couldn't gather the fragments of her thoughts. There was only fogginess and an overwhelming sense of loss. She closed her eyes and put out a hand to her mother. ''Thanks,'' she murmured. Minnie held her daughter's hand and blinked back her tears.

Merdis returned with the prescription from the doctor. ''How is she?'' he asked Minnie.

Beth heard him and opened her eyes. ''Hi, Daddy,'' she said.

''Hi, baby. Dr. Fletcher sent you some medicine so you can get a good night's sleep.'' He opened the bottle and took out two small capsules. Minnie handed him a glass of water.

''These won't be hard to swallow. They're small.'' He helped Beth sit up enough to take the capsules and some water.

''Thanks, Daddy.'' Beth slid down under the covers. Her limbs felt sluggish, and all she wanted was the blessed oblivion of sleep. She shut out everything and drifted off.

Merdis and Minnie turned out the light and went out to the living room. They made up the sofa bed. ''The doctor said he prescribed a strong sedative because what she needed most was sleep. He said she should be okay in the morning.'' Merdis was anxious to reassure his wife.

''That should help her, but I don't think she'll be okay for a long time,'' Minnie said.

* * *

Beth awakened slowly the next morning. Instinctively she looked at the clock radio, whose hands showed seven-thirty. Why hadn't her alarm gone off as usual, she thought as she threw back the covers. Her head felt funny as she stood up, but she stumbled on into the bathroom and to the basin to wash her teeth.

As she reached for the faucet, she casually looked in the mirror above it and was so shocked at what she saw that she had to hold on to the basin. Her eyes were bloodshot with dark smudges under them. There were lines around her mouth and nose that hadn't been visible before, and her hair looked dry and lank.

As she gazed at her face in horror, the memory of the previous evening came rushing back. She began to shake as the tears fell.

There was a knock on the door. "Beth Ann?"

"Yes, Mama."

"You getting up now?"

"Yes, ma'am. I'm getting ready to take a shower."

"Take your time, lovey. I'll be getting breakfast ready."

I'm not going to cry anymore, Beth told herself, blinking fast and swallowing hard. Enough tears. In the shower every time a thought of Cy came, she replaced it with a thought about work or the center. The center. This is Saturday, and Deacon German will be there to begin on the second room at nine o'clock. Oh, God, what shall I do? How can I go looking like this and having to see Cy?

She stood under the shower, waiting for her energy to return as she washed her hair and soaped herself again and again while considering her options. She could get off HOP. The center work would go on because it had a good start, and Cy would just have to carry it by himself. Then she wouldn't have to come into contact with Cy anymore. Or she could carry on with the team as if nothing had happened, but that was impossible. Perhaps she could get someone to take her place. There were still two months to go before the award banquet. Surely Rhonda could find a substitute for Team Four. If she did that, what would she tell Marty? Especially after the glowing report she'd given him a few days ago about the work.

With these thoughts swirling around in her head, she stepped out of the shower, dried herself, dressed, and finished her hair. At least it looks more normal, she thought as she stood again before the mirror after styling it. She applied makeup with great care and more heavily than usual in an effort to hide the lines and smudges. When she was satisfied that she looked almost as usual, she left the mirror and put on jeans and a sweatshirt.

Before she left her bedroom, she stood with her hand on the knob. Help me get through this day, Lord, she prayed.

''We're starting on the second room at the center in about an hour,'' she told her parents as they sat down to breakfast. ''You know Deacon German at Mount Calvary Church. He's bringing a crew to help him.''

''You feel up to that, honey?'' Merdis asked anxiously.

''No,'' Beth said candidly, looking at her mama and daddy, who had been her support last night when she needed them. They already knew the whole story, so she could be totally honest with them.

''I was thinking of the other things I might do about the center so I wouldn't have to come into contact with Cy, but I've decided to stay on Team Four and see the work through because it's more than what happens to two people. I'm not going to let the project down, and I'm not going to let myself down.'' She finished her juice and tried to eat a piece of toast.

''Good,'' Minnie said, looking at Beth with approval. She wanted to ask Beth what she would do about Cy but kept silent on that point. That's where she went wrong before, interfering with Beth and Art. This time she was going to support Beth in whatever Beth decided to do with the firm hope and belief that it would work out right in the end for her daughter.

''Did you remember to take another capsule this morning?'' Merdis asked.

''I didn't take it, Daddy. I don't know if I could keep it down, and they make me feel too groggy,'' Beth protested.

"Dr. Fletcher said it was important to take them for the next few days," Merdis said. He got the bottle and handed it to Beth. "At least carry them with you in case you need one."

As she thanked her parents for coming over and got herself into the car and on the way to the center, Beth went over in her mind how she would handle seeing Cy and organizing the work. They had always worked together almost intuitively, never having to particularly plan who was going to do what.

That would have to change. Beth did not allow herself to feel as she put on her most formal face and manner and went into the building.

"Good morning, Mr. German," she said to the short square man who wore a carpenter's apron with all of its tools around his waist. She smiled pleasantly. "I see you're prepared to start right in." She turned to Rhonda. "Have you met Mr. German, Mrs. Hayes? He's a deacon at Mount Calvary, and he has brought some people from the church to help." Rhonda and the deacon spoke, and he introduced the other crew members, about ten in all including a family called Holloway.

Beth was talking with Jane and Albert Holloway and their two boys when Cy came in the door. She felt his presence immediately. As he came up to the group, the force of his reaching out to her was so strong, she deliberately turned her back and stepped closer to the youngest Holloway boy to listen to his story of a school carpentry project on which he'd worked.

When Beth felt secure again inside her protective shield, she turned to Mr. German.

Cy had not been sure Beth would show up at the center until he saw her car in the parking lot. He knew she was aware of him as he crossed the floor to her by the rigidity in her carriage. He was anxious to see her face, but all he could see was the back of her head as he greeted Rhonda and introduced himself to the man with the apron.

"Mr. German, I'm Cy Brewster. We sure thank you for coming to help us here."

"Glad to do it. I brought some of our congregation with me," Mr. German said and began to introduce them. As Cy acknowledged the introductions to the Holloways, he looked at Beth, who had turned to face him.

"Good morning, Beth," he said pleasantly, his heart contracting with love for her and sadness at the marks of suffering the makeup could not hide from his searching eyes.

"Morning, Cy," she replied, her eyes avoiding his and passing on to Mr. German. "Mr. German, Cy knows what's to be done in the room you and your crew will be working in and can get you started."

She turned to Rhonda. "Rhonda, let's you and I work in the office. We can begin to get it ready for painting."

Rhonda had not missed the tension between Beth and Cy. She thought about it as the groups separated and she followed Beth to where the scrapers and rags were stored. Like Cy, she had seen the marks of distress on Beth's face. Whatever had happened between them must have been serious. Cy Brewster was no Art Woods, and his relationship with Beth was significantly different. Beth knew Rhonda was available, if needed, so she would wait until Beth brought it up. Meanwhile as she worked on the walls in the small office, she introduced a variety of harmless topics to Beth for their conversation.

"Have you spoken with Loraine Dillard lately, Beth?"

"No, I haven't. How's she doing?"

"I see her at least once a week, and the last time I saw her she told me that she has as many children as her license allows. She already has a waiting list."

"I thought she'd be good," Beth said. "I keep intending to go by, but the center has kept me busy. Is her husband pleased too?"

"Loraine said having the extra income has made a big difference, because they so often had trouble meeting the bills that it made a strain on their marriage. Things are better with them now."

Beth was working on a wall, her back to the door, when she heard Rhonda say,"Hi. I was just telling Beth how well Loraine Dillard is doing with her day care. She already has a waiting list."

Beth turned to see Cy standing inside the door. "That's good to hear,'' he said, his eyes on Beth. ''Rhonda, would you excuse us a moment, please?''

''Certainly,'' Rhonda said and left. Cy closed the door after her.

Beth stood against the wall, her eyes cold and distant, daring Cy to come any closer.

Cy came closer and took her hands in his. They were like ice. He removed the scraper she was holding and began to rub them.

''How are you, Beth?'' he asked softly.

Beth continued to stare at a point past him.

''Beth, we have to talk.''

''There's nothing more to say.''

''There's everything to say,'' Cy insisted. ''When may I come over? Tomorrow afternoon or evening?''

''I don't want to see you.''

''Sweetheart, you have to be fair and give me a chance to talk to you.'' Cy hoped that would break through Beth's communication barrier, and it did.

Beth looked at Cy for the first time. ''How dare you speak to me about what's fair?'' she said through her teeth.

''That's just what I want to talk with you about, that and other things,'' Cy said, thankful that the Beth he knew was fully present at last.

''There's nothing you can say to me that I want to hear!''

''You can't know that until you let me talk to you. I'll be over tomorrow night, honey. If you don't let me see you, I'll keep coming over every night until you let me in. Believe that, Beth,'' Cy said with unmistakable authority. He raised her hand to his lips and left the room, opening the door wide again.

It was one o'clock when Beth got home, feeling as if she'd been through a wringer. She took off her shoes, threw on a robe, and lay down on the couch. Five minutes later the bell rang. ''Beth, it's Aunt Elly,'' she heard through the door.

She dragged herself up to let Aunt Elly in.

''You were lying down? Good. I was watching for your car, so I could bring you some of this soup I made.'' She took the pot she was carrying into the kitchen to warm the soup and brought some in a bowl. Pulling a tray table to the couch, she put the soup on it with a plate of crackers.

"Now sit up and eat it while it's hot. I made it fresh this morning, and it's full of good nutrition, but it won't overload your stomach. Where's your capsules?"

Beth was so tired that she hadn't paid much attention to what Aunt Elly was saying. The soup smelled good, and she began to taste it. But the question about the capsules got through to her.

"Mama been talking to you?" Her head had been so full of getting through the morning at the center, she hadn't thought of anything else. But she should have known Mama would tell Aunt Elly about last night. "The capsules are on the dresser, but I don't want any."

Aunt Elly returned with the bottle and some water. "It says take one every four hours. How many have you taken today?"

"None."

Aunt Elly didn't say anything. She waited until the bowl was empty. "That was good, Aunt Elly. Thanks." Aunt Elly held out a capsule and the water. Beth knew from years of experience that resistance was useless. She took the capsule, drank the water, then lay down again.

"Minnie didn't have to tell me what happened last night, Beth. Mr. Brewster came to see us," Aunt Elly said.

Beth's eyes opened wide. "When?"

"After he brought you home." She took Beth's hand in hers. "I never told you about the young man who came to see us about Bobby. He was only thirteen when it happened and was in no way to blame, but it preyed on his mind so much that as soon as he turned twenty-one he looked us up and asked us if we would forgive him. Sim and I both said yes, and we meant it. So he knew us when he came to see us last night."

"What did he tell you?"

"He said you'd been at his house for dinner. He wanted to ask you to marry him, but first he had to tell you about Bobby. You went into shock, so he drove you home and put you to bed. He asked if I could come see about you."

Beth thought back to last night. She could not recall seeing Aunt Elly at all. The bewilderment showed in her face.

"You don't remember everything, Beth?" Aunt Elly's hand was warm and comforting. From long years of dealing with many types of accidents, wounds, aches and pains, she knew the best and quickest way to healing was to drain out anything that could cause festering and poison. What had happened to her dear Beth had made a deep psychological wound. It had to be cleaned at once of any misconceptions, and that part she could help with by making clear for Beth exactly what had taken place. From then on she fervently hoped that between Beth and Cy Brewster they could do the rest—so there would be true healing. Elly Richards had seen too many embittered men and women whose unresolved trauma had affected their whole lives. She didn't want that to happen to her niece.

"Tell me what you do remember, Beth."

"I went to Cy's, and we had dinner," Beth said slowly. "Then we went and sat on the couch in the living room." She stared straight ahead, and tears began to run down her cheeks. "Cy said he loved me, that he wanted more than anything else to ask me to marry him. I said, 'Why don't you?' He said because he had to tell me something first, and he told me about Bobby."

Aunt Elly let a minute pass. Beth said nothing more, so Aunt Elly asked, "Then what happened?"

"I had to run to the bathroom because I was crying and throwing up until there was nothing left to come out, but my stomach was still having spasms. Cy knocked on the door to see if I was all right. When I came out, I wanted to get home as fast as possible because I was so cold and weak and shivering. I thought I might faint any minute. Cy said I couldn't drive, and he drove me here in my car, and that's all I remember."

Beth had not permitted herself to open the door of memory to the misery of last night's events, but now the full flood surged in. She had sat in her car so numbed with pain and shock that when they got here, she must have fainted—because the next thing she knew, Cy was lifting her up to sip hot tea. She must have slept then because the next thing she remembered was her mother sitting on the bedside wiping her face with a washcloth.

"Mr. Brewster covered you up in your bed and gave you hot tea because your teeth were chattering, you were so cold. He wanted to stay with you himself but knew he shouldn't, so he came down to the house and I came back with him. He left and went over to Minnie's and told them what had happened. They came over and I went home."

Elly finished her summary of the night's events. She was satisfied that at least Beth was straight about that.

"Thanks, Aunt Elly," Beth said. She closed her eyes and turned her face away.

Aunt Elly put away the remainder of the soup and quietly let herself out of the door.

As soon as Beth heard the door close, she let out the sobs she'd been holding in. The stomach spasms began, and she hurried to the bathroom in time to lose everything. When she could move again, she wearily crawled into her bed and let sleep deliver her from her grief.

Chapter 21

Cy Brewster wiped the perspiration from his face as he came into the last quarter-mile of his morning's run. The April sun now had warmth in it, and he felt the easing of tension in his muscles. Jamison Park was a popular place for Sunday joggers, and several had passed him with a nod, but he wasn't as much interested in speed at this point as he was in ridding his body of tension.

The trees were full of new spring growth, and the grass was sprouting up green, filling in winter's bald spots. Wish I could bring Beth here, he thought. We could have a picnic, then we could have our race, which I would win, and give her a sweet kiss as a consolation prize. The smile that curved his mouth at that image faded as the image of Beth confronting him in the office yesterday took its place. He had a long way to go before Beth would ever race with him again.

But at least the worst was over. She knew about Bobby. That was one of the hardest things he'd ever had to do. Now he had his work cut out for him in helping her get through it by taking whatever she needed to hurl at him to assuage her hurt. That part would not be easy, but it had to be done. It's going to be harder to convince her that we belong to each other despite the past, he thought, but I'm not letting her go no matter how long it takes.

As he ran lightly into his driveway and entered his apartment, he went immediately to the telephone to call the florist. By the time he hung up, he was satisfied with the first step in a campaign that might be long, but which he was determined to win.

Cy knocked at Beth's door that evening at seven. Beth opened the door as he was getting ready to knock again.

He was over the first hurdle, he thought with relief. At least he was in. "Hi, Beth," he said.

"Come in, Cy."

Beth's pride had dictated that she do the best she could to hide the distress signals on her face with makeup, but she had decided she would not dress up for Cy. Her jeans were old ones and her shirt faded. "Sit down," she said, seating herself in a chair in the living room and facing him with her back straight and her cold eyes direct. She would let him say whatever he had to say and get it over with, but it would do him no good.

"Beth, the first thing I want to say is how sorry I am that I told you this way. I should have told you a long time ago."

"Why didn't you?" Beth asked tonelessly.

"I thought you wouldn't let me see you again."

"You mean you were a coward," Beth said flatly. She saw the flicker in his eye that showed she'd hit a bull's-eye.

"Yes, I was a coward," Cy agreed. "But I was already so attracted to you, and I didn't want to lose the chance of getting to know you better." He saw no response of any sort in Beth's eyes or face. He'd have to do better.

"Beth, I'm almost thirty-four. I've been around a long time. I've been going out since high school, but I've been tired of the singles scene for a while now. Home has become lonely for me because I want a wife and my own family. I never found the woman I wanted for my wife until I met you." He thought he saw a gleam come into her eyes, and he leaned forward to press his case.

"The moment I saw you something clicked, and I couldn't get you out of my mind. If I hadn't had the enormous luck to be put on the HOP team with you, I would have scoured Jamison to find you. You didn't know that I'd already begun asking people if they knew a young woman who drove a green Honda."

No, I didn't know that, thought Beth. Cy's recital of his feelings was beginning to let a hint of warmth seep into the ice that had formed around Beth's emotions. She didn't want that to happen, so she made herself think only of her anger and hurt pride.

"When we met at Rhonda's, I knew you were my destiny. You were the woman I'd been looking for and waiting for. You were the woman I wanted for my wife. Every time we were together after that just strengthened the feeling."

There was a quiet sincerity in Cy's statements, and Beth knew he believed in what he was saying. However, what he was saying was not the core of the issue, so the anger remained.

Cy could no longer sit still. Beth watched him get up and go stand by the window, then he came back to the table where the picture of Beth and her cousins stood.

"The first time I was here and you showed me this picture, Beth, I was stunned. How could I have met the one woman for me and that woman turn out to be Bobby's closest cousin!" He turned to Beth pleadingly. "I know I should have told you right then, but can't you understand how I felt, Beth?"

He pulled the chair up close to Beth and reached out to take her hands, but she pulled them up away from him. She saw the hurt in his eyes and was glad.

"I was wrong, I know I was wrong—but I couldn't bring myself to say, 'Oh, by the way, it was my cousin and I who were in the car when Bobby was killed.' I just couldn't do it, Beth. Can't you see that?" Surely she would give him some kind of answer, Cy thought. He kept his eyes on her and waited.

Finally, Beth said in a cold, dispassionate voice, "You could have told me later. You could have written a letter if you didn't want to say it."

"That's true," Cy said, "but each time I was with you, it got harder and harder to do. The more I loved you, the thought of losing you was something I didn't want to face."

"You're facing it now," Beth hissed, her anger burning hard

and bright. ''You brought it on yourself, Cy. You played me for a fool.''

Cy jumped to his feet. His eyes blazed, and his voice was full of outrage. ''Played you for a fool? How can you say such a ridiculous thing?''

Beth was on her feet also. She stepped behind her chair and held on to it as she looked at Cy with scorn. ''You must have thought I was a fool, that I wasn't worthy of having the knowledge of the facts that you had. Only you could have that knowledge. I wasn't capable of taking the facts and coming to my own decision about it. Only you could do that. You speak of love, but the truth is I mattered so little in your estimation that you couldn't treat me as an equal by telling me the facts and letting me deal with it.'' By the time Beth got through she was spitting out the words to Cy.

Cy was horrified. How could Beth possibly think that he held her in such low esteem as she was saying? ''But that is not how I felt!'' He was furious that she could see his actions in such a light. It put him in the same category as her mother—and hadn't he, the last time he was in this very room, held Beth and comforted her and helped her understand how wrong her mother was?

He marched toward her. She backed away from the chair, but he kept coming until he reached her and grasped her arms. His face was an inch away from hers, and she tried to lean back from its intensity. Beth could see a vein throbbing in his neck.

''Haven't you heard anything I've been saying to you, Beth Jordan?'' His dark eyes bored into her. ''Don't you understand that I love you, that I admire you, that I want you, that I need you, that anything wrong I've done comes from that? You mean more to me than anything else in the world.''

Cy's great fear had been that somehow by telling Beth about Bobby he would lose her and her love. Now he knew he was not going to permit that to happen. He was going to fight for her. He could not lose Beth any more than he could lose his breath. She was his and he was hers. Forever. He knew that with absolute certainty, and the sooner she knew it the better.

Somehow they would get through this, and when they did they would be together. For always.

''Understand me, Beth. We belong together, and I'm not going to let you go.'' Beth felt scorched by the blaze in his eyes. She instinctively closed hers to shut it out. The next second his lips came down on hers firmly, possessively.

No, no, Beth was thinking even as deep down inside a traitorous part of her was trying to respond to Cy's passionate entreaty and kiss. She willed herself to give nothing back to Cy. When he released her, she stepped away and looked at him.

''What I understand, Cy, is that you knew something I should have known. By not telling me you betrayed my trust in you and in our relationship. You were dishonest and you belittled me. That's what I understand.''

She understood more, but she would never tell Cy. Like Cy she had finally found the person she could love, and she had welcomed that love with all of her heart. Life had suddenly become full of promise and happiness. She dreamed of what the years ahead with Cy would be like. Before Cy, she'd thought she'd always just miss out on the man who could make her fall in love and who would love her back. She'd thought perhaps her mother was right. She was too flighty and shallow to attract and hold a ''real'' man. Then Cy had appeared, and they'd been pulled together irresistibly. He'd put all her fears to rest when he said he loved her.

Then with one sentence he'd destroyed it all. That agony was so deep, she could not speak of it to Cy. She could hardly acknowledge it to herself. She had to repress it so she could function.

Dishonest? Betrayed? Belittled? Cy heard these words, but he couldn't understand them as applying to him. What he could accept was that Beth was hurting. He searched for what he could say to alleviate that hurt.

''Beth, I know I misjudged the situation. I should have told you. There are no words to tell you how sorry I am for doing it all wrong and causing you to hurt. What can I do to make it up to you?''

''Nothing,'' Beth said. She needed Cy out of the apartment,

and to make the point clear that his time was up she walked to the door. "Thank you for coming," she said, her voice cold, her face expressionless.

Cy could not pretend to be as unmoved as Beth. "Thank you for letting me come, Beth." His eyes caressed her lovingly. "I'm not going to let this be the end for us, sweetheart." His voice was tender as he raised her hand to his cheek then kissed it. "I'll see you at the center."

Beth closed the door behind him and leaned against it. She covered her mouth with both hands to keep the sobs from escaping. Her stomach ached as the grief she felt at sending away the man she loved swept through her.

It had taken every iota of her will to remain unmoved by Cy's plea, but she could not ignore the fact that he had been involved in Bobby's death and had deliberately withheld that fact, even though he knew they were falling in love with each other. He'd been so protective of her when she'd told him how her mother's comments and attitude had affected her, and he had given her of his strength and tenderness. She had never felt so secure, so loved, so treasured. Why hadn't he used that same strength and protection against this agony instead of causing it?

Beth bent double with the ache in her stomach. She dragged herself to the bedroom and into the bed, where she could give vent to her sorrow without worrying about her neighbors hearing her. Beth wept for her lost love until all her tears were gone. Dry-eyed and hollow she took stock of how to get through the remaining weeks until the project was over. Once the center was finished, she would leave Jamison.

Chapter 22

On his way home from Beth's, Cy remembered promising his parents to see them sometime on Sunday. It wasn't yet eight-thirty, so he knew it wasn't too late.

"We'd given you up," his dad said as he let him in. "We're in the kitchen, having dessert."

Iva Brewster looked up as her husband and son came in. She caught her breath as she noted the unusual signs of stress in Cy's face. "Have you been overdoing it with that work at the center, Cy? You look like you haven't slept for a week," she said in concern as he came over to greet her.

She told him to sit and placed before him a slice of sweet potato pie and a cup of coffee.

George Brewster watched his wife fuss over Cy. He didn't think the center work had anything to do with Cy's worried look. The boy was accustomed to hard work and long hours. No, he'd bet it was that girl Cy had mentioned to them, the one who beat him in the race. When his wife sat down again, George looked at Cy and said, "Something wrong between you and the girl who beat you in the race?"

"Beth Jordan." Iva Brewster supplied the name quietly, her eyes on her son.

Disarmed by the atmosphere of unconditional love he'd always had from his parents and their intuitive sense of the source of his anxiety, Cy felt a sting of moisture in his eyes and blinked several times. Then he told them all that had happened since Friday night when Beth had dinner at his apartment. There was silence when the recital ended as George and Iva took in the significance of what had happened. Iva reached over and patted Cy's hand.

"You still didn't tell Beth everything, did you?"

"What do you mean?" Cy asked.

"You didn't tell her of the trouble you kept getting into at school up until that time and that afterward you changed your ways. You didn't tell her how you've spent the years since then trying to make up for it by helping young people."

"I wasn't looking for any sympathy from Beth, Mom, for what I went through after the accident. I only want her to understand how much she means to me."

"Tough break, son," George said compassionately. He shook his head. "Tough break. Puts you between a rock and a hard place."

There was silence in the warm kitchen. A clock ticked, and the fragrance of the sweet potato pie drifted in the air. George and Iva waited for whatever Cy wanted to say next.

Cy looked unseeingly at the floral table cover. "What scares me most," he said almost to himself, "is that she'll link me with Bobby's death and somehow identify me with killing him."

George was instantly indignant, but he kept his voice low and his tone mild. "How could she do that, son? The police told Elly and Sim in no uncertain terms that your cousin was not to blame. You were only a passenger, not even the driver, so how could she hold you responsible?"

"She's not thinking logically, George," his wife replied. "She's reacting emotionally." She turned to Cy. "Even if she thinks that right now, I don't think it'll last."

"You don't know Beth," Cy said despondently.

"No, I don't, but I do know that if she loves you like she said, that in the end that is what will bring her through this."

"Will we get to meet her Wednesday at the center?" George asked.

"Yes. Her parents will be there also."

On his way home Cy found himself feeling better. Talking important matters over with his parents had been a habit ever since the accident. His high spirits, energy, and strong will had made him rebellious in school, and he'd been in and out of the kinds of trouble that were beginning to become serious when the accident occurred. The trauma he'd suffered had been profound. For a year he'd gone to counseling, and the Cy that had emerged had been the one who was able to gradually use his energy and will in positive directions. Through it all he'd been able to talk with his parents, and it had helped. He hoped his mom had been right about Beth. Only time would tell.

When Beth arrived at work on Monday, she found that three properties had been sold over the weekend. She was glad to have a lot to do and was busy at the computer when a deliveryman brought to her desk a pot of brightly colored primroses. The card said: *With love always, Cy.* Beth was surprised. The flowers with their pink, white, lavender, and yellow blooms were so delicately lovely, she couldn't help but be pleased at their beauty. But she stiffened her resolve against allowing them to influence her where Cy was concerned.

That night at the center, she and Rhonda continued to work away from the main group. She spoke to Cy briefly but did not acknowledge the receipt of the flowers. Tuesday was the same.

Wednesday evening the center was filled with people and excitement. Most of the original crew had come as well as the workers from Mount Calvary Church. Bill Barnes and other council members were there. The Channel Fifteen people were busy arranging their hookups and chatting with Beth and with Cy. Marty Armstrong was talking with the Jordans, and nearby were the Brewsters and the Richards.

Beth had decided to be very professional for the camera

when she had to be in front of it but to avoid Cy as much as possible.

"We're ready to begin, Miss Jordan and Mr. Brewster," the interviewer said. "Could you both stand here, please? I'd like you to tell me informally how this project came about."

Cy glanced at Beth. She gave him a little nod. "We were looking for something to do for the community as Team Four on the Helping Ourselves Project, and we'd both been coming to the center for youth activities and noticed that it needed a lot of work." That was enough to get the ball rolling, Cy thought, and turned to Beth.

Beth picked up the ball smoothly. "We talked about it together and made a plan about what needed to be done then we met with the center's council members." Beth felt herself falling back instinctively into easy rapport with Cy. They finished the whole story, talking back and forth, sometimes finishing each other's sentences. The council members were introduced, and Bill Barnes spoke succinctly about the contribution Team Four was making with the project. Rhonda Hayes described her work as liaison and how volunteers, supplies, and donations were needed. Cy brought up David and Emily Walker and described their work. Beth said they couldn't forget the wonderful food Emily had provided. The camera panned around the room, dwelling on various aspects of the work as the interviewer spoke with the person who'd done that particular task.

"Now Miss Jordan and Mr. Brewster, could you tell us what is next?" The camera followed Cy and Beth as they went into the room where the Mount Calvary crew was working and then to the office and finally ended with all of the other rooms yet to be done. They gave a telephone number for people who wished to help. Back in the hall the interviewer spoke to Marty Armstrong, who explained how the business community was supporting HOP.

To conclude the story, the interviewer began to speak to people at random. One of the men selected identified himself as George Brewster.

"Any relation to Cy Brewster?" the interviewer asked.

"He's my son."

"What do you think of what he's doing here?"

"I'm real proud of what he and Miss Jordan are doing for and with the community."

As the interviewer moved on to another person, George went to where Beth was standing and introduced himself.

"Miss Jordan, I'm Cy's father, and I meant what I said. You and Cy are both doing something good in giving your time to this work." As they shook hands, he said with concern, "I just hope you're not wearing yourself out."

"I'm trying not to," Beth said, looking at him with interest despite herself. Before she could say anything else, a woman appeared at Mr. Brewster's side. This had to be Cy's mother. She could see the resemblance in the eyes and mouth.

"I'm Iva Brewster, Cy's mother," she said and gave Beth a warm and affectionate look. "The hall looks wonderful," Iva said, "but there's still so much to be done, and George and I want to volunteer. We told Cy, but I don't know if he's put us on the list. So now we're telling you."

"Thanks, Mrs. Brewster, I'll be sure to put you down. We're going to need many more workers before we're done."

"Your folks here this evening, Beth?" George Brewster asked.

"They're standing over there with my aunt and uncle," Beth answered, indicating the group with a nod of her head.

"We'll go over and say hello and let you go on to do whatever else you have to do."

"You take care of yourself now," Iva Brewster said, "and we hope to see you soon, Beth."

"What'd you think of the TV crew, Beth? Didn't they do a great job?" Marty Armstrong was anxious to share his enthusiasm about the show. Fortunately Len Nesbit and David Walker joined him, freeing Beth to listen with half an ear and look interested while watching Cy's parents talking with her mom and dad and Aunt Elly and Uncle Sim. The message of friendliness and concern from Mr. and Mrs. Brewster had been pointed and unmistakable. What would their attitude be once they knew what Cy had done and the alienation it had caused? Would they be friendly then?

Beth excused herself from the men and, after thanking the work crews, escaped into the office in which she and Rhonda had been working. She would go back out in a while to talk with her family but not while they were being so cozy with Cy's folks. She couldn't dissemble and be part of that with all of the turmoil inside her.

''Beth?'' She looked up to see Cy in the doorway. He came in and leaned against the wall. ''What did you think of the TV show?''

''It went well.'' Beth continued working.

''I thought so too.'' Cy watched Beth's circular motions as she wiped away years of dust and wear from a small section of the wall. Her movements were graceful and efficient. Some dust landed on her face. With the back of her hand, she flicked it away, leaving a smudge on her nose. She looked so absurd and endearing, so forlorn yet dignified, that Cy wanted to protect her, make love to her, and rage at her all at the same time.

He wasn't aware that he'd moved, but suddenly he was holding her by her arms. ''Sweetheart, can't you forgive me?'' His voice was husky, his eyes pleading.

Beth shut her eyes against his plea. She couldn't trust her voice, so she shook her head no. Cy gritted his teeth to resist the urge he'd felt all evening to kiss her until she listened to reason. When they'd been on camera talking about their work, the old rapport they'd always had reasserted itself, and Cy's heart had leapt with hope. Later from across the room, he'd seen his parents talking with Beth and saw her eyes follow them when they went to talk to the Jordans. The TV crew on their way out had engaged his attention, and when he was free Beth had disappeared. He found her hiding here in the office, and he'd hoped perhaps she was feeling her way to a better frame of mind.

He'd been fooling himself. But he knew she was not indifferent. He could feel the emotional tension in her body as he held her arms. She refused to respond, and he gave a great sigh and moved away. Frustrated and depressed, he left the room.

Beth leaned against the wall to support her trembling legs. Each confrontation with Cy left her depleted. All of her energy was taken in resisting him. Through the open door she could hear footsteps approaching. She straightened and began rubbing down the wall again.

"Here she is," Merdis Jordan said, poking his head through the door. "I found her." He came into the office followed by his wife and Aunt Elly and Uncle Sim.

"Hi," Beth said, putting down her cleaning cloth. "I was coming to find you in a minute. Let me take you around and show you what we're planning."

In the hall Emily was discussing the evening's proceedings with Rhonda. "This publicity should help, Rhonda, but is there anything else David and I can do?"

"I've been thinking that once all the work is done, the council will be wanting to have an Open House, Emily. Could your place provide the refreshments?"

"What did you have in mind?"

After discussing a menu and an estimated cost, Emily said, "Rhonda, what's happened to Beth and Cy? I couldn't help noticing there's something wrong between them."

"I'm not sure, Emily. All I know is that Beth seems to want to stay as far from Cy as she can when we're here in the evenings. He is very unhappy about it."

"What a pity! They seemed so well matched and so happy together."

"Whatever it is, I sure hope they'll be able to work it out," Rhonda said. "It would be terrible for Beth to have to go through another disappointment."

Cy came into the hall and over to them. "How do you think it went tonight? Will the publicity bring in more workers and supplies?"

"I don't know why it wouldn't," Rhonda said. "It covered all the work in a most interesting way."

"You and Beth were very convincing," Emily said.

A shadow crossed Cy's face. "I hope so because there's still so much to do. I don't want this project to fail."

He seemed anxious for the first time to Rhonda. Always

before, Cy had been confident and assured of success. It was Beth that was worrying him, she was certain, not the job itself. However, as liaison person for Team Four, she felt as responsible for the success of the project as Cy did. As she watched him walk away, she wondered what she could do to make sure that at the award banquet her Team Four would walk away with the prize.

Chapter 23

''Where do you want these pound cakes, Emily?'' Beth asked, carefully handling a wide shallow box that held four cakes. She'd collected them earlier that Saturday morning from her mother and Aunt Elly before they'd set out with their husbands for a fishing day down by Beaufort.

''Pies and cakes go over there on this table.'' Emily Walker pointed to a long table against the far wall of her restaurant.

Beth set down the box. ''I haven't been in here since you completed the expansion. What a difference it makes!'' She looked around admiringly.

''You know, when I began Letters and Lunch a few years ago, I leased what used to be Conway's restaurant and had Sandye Parker right in here to do my clerical service while Mabel Joyner and I did the lunch part. But fortunately the food business grew so rapidly that when the building next door became available, David and I decided to take a risk. We bought this property and the one next door and put them together. Do you really think it's better?''

They began cutting slices of cake and pie and putting them on small paper plates, then covering them with plastic.

''Yes, because you've upgraded the restaurant without taking it out of the price league of most of your clientele. Have you taken on more employees?''

''We had to add one person in the kitchen and one out here. We're thankful that business has been steady because it means we can pay the mortgage. David and I worry about that sometimes.''

''Where'd your clerical service go?''

''Sandye's down the street in that office building.''

''Holding the fund-raiser here for the center is not only a generous idea on your part but will also bring in a lot of folks who can take a look at your new place.''

''I've got to admit that has crossed my mind,'' Emily said with a smile.

Beth looked around appreciatively at the pale yellow walls, the periwinkle curtains at the large windows, and the many golden light fixtures. The large room was filled with twenty tables and ten booths. There were flowers on the tables and coverings that matched the curtains. The whole room had a feeling of sunshine and warmth.

''It lifts my spirits when I come in here. Then I eat some of your wonderful food, Emily, and I really feel good.''

Emily looked at Beth with concern. ''You need to come more often, Beth, dear, and let me put some meat on your bones. You are much too thin.''

''A few weeks ago I had a really bad cold, and I haven't gotten my appetite back yet,'' Beth said brightly. Her stock answer to explain to friends about her obvious weight loss slipped out easily. She'd had to give it often since her breakup with Cy.

Anxious to change the subject, Beth looked up at the name of the restaurant over the door. ''I'll bet the new name was David's idea.''

Emily smiled fondly. ''When the office part moved out, David and Mabel said we'd have to change the name. They both insisted it be called Emily's and so did my family.''

''It was all your work, so it's appropriate. Is the rest of the food here yet?''

''Mrs. Willis and Mrs. Porter brought the greens yesterday.

We did the barbecue ribs yesterday, the corn bread is in the oven now, and Miss Mabel is frying the last of the chicken. Some ladies from my church are bringing potato salad and macaroni and cheese. They should be here in the next fifteen minutes, according to my watch."

"Did the supermarket bring you all the ribs they promised?"

"Yes, and they're meaty ones too. What really surprised me, Beth, is how you and Cy got these people to donate all of this. We got thirty pounds of ribs and forty pounds of chicken quarters."

"We told them they'd be getting publicity from it, and after all these are the markets where most of our community shops, so they don't want us telling folks they didn't contribute to such a good cause."

"You've gotten to be quite a strategist, haven't you?" Emily said admiringly.

"Open the door," someone called, and Beth and Emily both went to help bring in the pans of macaroni and cheese and the bowls of potato salad.

When Rhonda had first proposed some kind of fund-raiser to get money for the center work, Beth had been too weary to give it much attention. Rhonda made the arrangements with Emily and the council to have a day-long sale of food with all of the money going to the center. The big part was to get all of the food donated. Beth had found herself involved in that part with Cy.

At the center one evening, Rhonda had sat them down in the office and told them about the plans. Cy and Beth had been glad to know more money would be coming in addition to the funds supplied as a result of the TV show. Rhonda had given them a list of what would be needed and said it would be widely publicized. They expected to sell the food on the last Saturday in April.

"What I need you two to do is go around to the markets to get as much of the meat donated as you possibly can and also to line up the cooked food through the churches or wherever. Okay?"

Cy looked at Beth, who looked at Rhonda. "Okay," they said.

"Good. I've got something in the car I want you to see." Rhonda left the room, and Cy immediately turned to Beth. This was the only time he'd been alone with her since the night of the TV show. She'd seen to that.

"Can we go see these people together, Beth?" he asked.

"No. You go the markets about the meat, and I'll see about the rest." She did not meet his eyes but looked down at the list.

"Beth, you're killing me," Cy said, his voice low and grating.

Beth, startled, looked at him. He did not try to hide from her the anguish he was feeling. In his face and eyes, she saw a reflection of the depth of her own suffering. "How long must this go on?"

"I don't know," Beth said honestly. Long enough for you to understand what you did to me and to our love. Long enough for that love to be resurrected if it can be. The feeling that it might already be too late made a bleakness settle in her. She was looking directly at Cy for the first time, and he felt the hopelessness in her.

When Rhonda returned, they were sitting silently, each in his or her isolated space. She'd hoped that by leaving them alone they might begin some helpful dialogue, but obviously it hadn't happened. If anything the atmosphere between them was worse. She showed them the flyer for the dinner, then Cy left the room.

At the restaurant other helpers began to arrive, and soon the place was filled with the activity of setting out the food and then filling the orders as they came in.

By noon Beth began to feel empty. She'd had only coffee before leaving home. Several other people were eating, and Emily put a plate in front of Beth. "Eat, Beth," Emily said.

Beth took her plate and went through the kitchen to sit in the quiet and the sunlight of the restaurant's small backyard space. She took a bite of the chicken. It was moist and delicately flavored and crisp. A sip of iced tea and a bite of corn bread next. Emily was a truly talented cook. It was no wonder that her restaurant had become a success.

Beth continued to eat, remembering the Emily Brooks she used to know before David Walker came to Jamison. That Emily had been immersed in taking care of her parents, her son, and the family home with no thought of herself. David had fallen in love with her instantly and had courted her gently but persistently, causing Emily to blossom into the woman she now was, assured and confident in the love she and David shared reflected in their two children.

Beth put the plate on the grass and laid her head back against the chair, her eyes closed. All of the time I was watching Emily with her David at the center, I thought that someday I would be like that with Cy. I would possess and return that kind of love: strong, deep, and constant. Passionate and tender. The kind I've never had. I could see its promise in the way Cy looked at me and in his touch. All that I'd heard others say about love was finally going to be mine. I was so happy. Now it's gone.

The bright sun continued to pour its benign warmth on Beth's upturned face, but agitation began deep inside her. Her stomach muscles began to contract, and the contents of her meal roiled, causing her stomach to ache and cramp. She got up hurriedly and went as far from the back door as possible to bend over and lose her dinner. The spasmodic retching continued until nothing was left to come up. She felt exhausted and dizzy from the effort to be quiet so no one would come out to investigate.

She leaned against the fence, wondering if this physical reaction was ever going to stop. When the bleakness of her lonely and loveless future came to the top of her consciousness, it often triggered the retching. That's why she was so thin her clothes no longer fit.

Back in the restaurant she busied herself filling dinner orders. David Walker, Dan Burton, and Mr. German brought their cars to deliver them. Beth was cutting another pie when she heard a familiar voice.

"Hi, Miss Beth." She turned around to see Kwesi Michaels at her table. Kwesi had been helping out at the center as often as he could. Several times he had sought Beth out to exchange a few words with her or to ask her a question. Beth had responded to his overtures of friendship. Once he had asked her seriously about the techniques of computer learning because he thought he might be good at it.

"How you doing, Kwesi?" she said. Usually when Kwesi was around, Cy was not far behind, but she kept her eyes on Kwesi.

"I came to help with deliveries. Mrs. Walker said you had some to go."

"I've got ten ready. If you take the iced tea and pie, I'll bring the dinner boxes."

Kwesi carefully took the two boxes with the Styrofoam cups of tea wedged in so they would stay upright and a cardboard box of stacked pie servings. Beth followed with the dinner boxes. Kwesi reached the car first and set his burden on the trunk.

The dizziness Beth had felt earlier came again but stronger. She swayed and closed her eyes involuntarily just as she reached the car. She missed the step down, wedging her left foot tightly between the tire and the curb. Instinctively she thrust the boxes toward Kwesi, who caught them as she tried to brace herself against the car. She was overwhelmed by the intense pain in her foot and ankle. She gave a little cry and began to slide downward to the pavement as she lost consciousness.

Cy had been sitting in the car, waiting for Kwesi. He watched as Beth and Kwesi came out with the food. He had purposely not gone into the restaurant because seeing Beth avoid him had become an exercise in despair that he didn't need. He watched her walk toward the car with her boxes and remembered the pleasure of having her in the seat beside him. She reached the car and suddenly disappeared from his view. He heard her make a sound. In an instant he was out of the car and around it to catch her just as her head hit the pavement.

"Go get Mrs. Walker," he told Kwesi.

Beth's face was ashen and her breathing shallow. She was

lying in an awkward position because of her wedged foot. David and Emily came running out. Emily rubbed Beth's face and called her name softly, while David and Cy tried to figure out how to release her foot from the tight place it was in without doing more damage to it. David carefully shifted her so she was lying more in line with her leg, but that didn't help. They couldn't take off her shoe.

By this time a crowd of people had gathered, and Cy instructed the men to help him pull the car away from Beth. He couldn't drive it because of the danger of crushing her foot. The men managed to shift the car just enough for Cy to pull Beth's foot out. The ankle had already begun to swell.

"David," Cy said, "can I exchange cars with you? Yours has four doors and mine doesn't. Help me put Beth in your backseat. I'm taking her to emergency. Kwesi, you sit in the back with her."

Beth had opened her eyes, and Cy spoke to her before they lifted her. "You sprained your ankle and fainted, Beth, and I'm taking you to the emergency room."

"Do you need me, Cy?" Emily asked.

"This might take hours, Emily, and you're needed here, but thanks. Kwesi and I'll take care of her."

Emily handed in Beth's bag, which a thoughtful lady had brought from the restaurant.

When they arrived at the hospital, Kwesi went in for a wheelchair, and they lifted Beth into it. She was still pale and dizzy. Kwesi stayed with her while Cy quickly parked the car and came running back in to help Beth through the registration procedure. There were other people waiting and, after they registered, Beth was left in the wheelchair until a nurse could get to her.

"I'll go call your parents, Beth," Cy said.

"They're not home. They went fishing down to Beaufort with Aunt Elly and Uncle Sim."

Cy thought for a moment. "Who's your doctor?"

"Dr. Fletcher on Hill Street." Her voice was weak, and she kept her eyes closed and her head laid back against the chair.

"Does it still hurt a lot?"

"Yes." Beth was trying to be brave, but the pain was intense. She began to feel dizzy again, and her head slumped.

"Kwesi, watch her," Cy said softly and ran to the desk. "My friend is fainting. She needs to be lying down." His authoritative manner and voice made the woman at the desk get up and come to look at Beth. She immediately wheeled her to a bed and pulled the curtain while she summoned an aide and whisked Cy and Kwesi away with her hand.

Cy went to the telephone. This was Saturday, and he didn't know if Dr. Fletcher had hours on the weekend, but he called anyway.

"Dr. Fletcher's office."

"May I speak with him, please?"

"Doctor's with a patient. May I help you?"

"This is an emergency, and I need to talk with him about a patient of his who's in the emergency room at the hospital."

When Dr. Fletcher came on the line, Cy introduced himself as a friend who'd taken Beth Jordan to the hospital. He explained what had happened. "The reason I'm calling you, Doctor, is because Beth keeps fainting. She's lost a lot of weight lately, and I'm very worried about her."

"Did Miss Jordan ask you to call me, Mr. Brewster?"

"I asked her who her doctor was, and she gave me your name. Then she fainted again."

"Thanks for calling, Mr. Brewster. I'll be over to see her."

Cy went back to where they'd taken Beth, but the nurse was busy with her. She told Cy to sit in one of the five chairs in that section, but he didn't know what was going on behind the curtain.

"Did you see a doctor go in there?" he asked Kwesi.

"I couldn't tell if it was a doctor, but some woman went in wearing a stethoscope," Kwesi said. "Is she going to be all right?" He looked at Cy anxiously.

"She'll be all right, but it may take some time. I don't know if she just sprained her ankle or if she might have broken some bones in her foot."

Cy kept watching the activities around the curtained bed. There were several people going and coming for the first fifteen minutes then no one. He waited for several minutes then quickly crossed the room and stepped inside the curtain.

Beth was lying quietly, her eyes closed. She still looked pale, and Cy's heart turned over when she opened her eyes and looked at him. He took her hand in his. "How do you feel, honey?"

"I feel so weak for some reason, Cy. They think I broke my foot."

He brushed her hair back caressingly. "Are they taking you to get it X-rayed?"

"I think that's next. Someone will be coming to get me, the nurse said." Her fingers clung around his, and Cy could feel his heart in his throat.

"I talked to Dr. Fletcher, Beth, and told him what had happened. He said he'll be over. Is he a good doctor?"

"Yes."

"How did you happen to fall?" Cy had been wondering what made the accident happen.

"Just as I got to the car with the boxes, I had a dizzy spell, which made me close my eyes. I missed the step down. That's all I know."

"Have you be getting dizzy a lot lately?"

Beth smiled faintly and said, "You sound like the nurse who just asked me a lot of questions, Cy."

One part of Cy wanted to jump and shout. Beth had smiled at him and teased him and was holding his hand. Another part said you should be ashamed of yourself to feel so good when she is lying here in the hospital. But he couldn't help feeling glad and thankful that they were on friendly terms. He kept a little conversation going while holding her hand. "I'll keep calling your parents until I get them."

"I ought to be out of here in the next couple of hours," Beth said.

"I don't know, Beth. They'll have to put some kind of cast on your foot eventually."

The curtain was pulled back, and a portly man in his sixties came in. His long face carried a bushy mustache, and his brown eyes were clear and friendly. Cy liked him at once, especially as he greeted Beth with a smile and said, ''Now Beth, what'd you go and do this for? Trying to stay home from work are you?'' He looked across Beth and, extending his hand to Cy said, ''I presume you're Mr. Brewster?''

''Yes, sir.''

''Well, Mr. Brewster, if you'll wait outside, we'll see what the problem is here.'' The clear brown eyes gave Cy a friendly dismissal.

At the end of another hour, Beth had been taken to X-ray and returned. Dr. Fletcher came out to Cy. ''Beth tells me none of her family is in town today, and that it's all right if I tell you what I found and what I'm going to do.''

''Thank you,'' Cy said, returning Dr. Fletcher's probing gaze.

''I'm not pleased with Beth's general condition. Her whole system is run down and needs a little building up, so I'm putting her in the hospital for a day or two. Her foot has two broken bones, and her ankle was badly wrenched. She'll be off her feet for a while.''

''May I see her?''

''Yes. She'll be going up to her room shortly.''

As soon as she heard the curtain move, Beth opened her eyes. She put out her hand. ''He's putting me in the hospital.''

Cy enfolded her hand in his. She sounded so vulnerable and sad. ''I know, baby,'' he said tenderly. ''But it's only for a little while, a day or two, he said, for you to build up your strength.''

Strength. Beth's mind fastened on that word. Strength was what she had felt slipping away from her ever since the first dizziness early in the day. She had become weak, almost to the point of disorientation. When Cy had appeared beside her bed here in the emergency room, her need for the strength and protectiveness he'd always given her blotted out everything else. She had not wanted to let him out of her sight. He was her anchor, and she felt secure if he was near.

Cy put both arms around her as best he could and laid his cheek against hers. ''I'm going to stay with you all the way, baby,'' he whispered.

"You will?"

"Wild horses couldn't tear me away, honey. Believe me."

The aides came in to transfer Beth from the emergency room to a room on the third floor with Cy and Kwesi trailing behind. The floor nurse came in to get Beth settled.

"I'll be back as soon as they let me," Cy promised Beth. Her eyes followed him as he left the room.

"I'm staying here, Kwesi, so let's see what we can do about getting you back." Cy called Emily and explained the situation. It was arranged that as soon as David returned, he would bring Cy's car to the hospital and pick up his. "We'll be sure Kwesi gets home," she said. "You just take care of Beth."

"You can count on that, Emily, and thanks again."

He called the Jordans again but still no answer. Cy sent Kwesi to the cafeteria to get himself something to eat while he sat in the corridor to watch for the nurse to finish with Beth.

She let him back in after some twenty minutes. Beth was wearing a white hospital gown tied in the back. She'd been watching the door with an anxious look, which disappeared as soon as she saw him. Her foot and ankle were now in a cast, but Cy could still see traces of pain in her face.

He pulled a chair up and put it as close to her bed as he could. "Have they given you some medication?" he asked as he settled himself and took her hand.

"I've had one pain pill."

"I thought so. Your eyes are sort of heavy. Why don't you try to sleep?"

"I was waiting till you got back," she said sleepily.

Cy was watching her sleep when David and Kwesi came in. He carefully slipped his hand away from Beth's and went out of the room to talk.

"How is she?" David asked.

"She still has some pain, and they gave her a pain pill. She just went to sleep. Dr. Fletcher said he's keeping her because she's run-down, and he wants to build up her strength."

"You and Beth have both been overworking at the center, Cy." David's eyes were filled with concern. "You need a break."

"As long as I can sleep at night, I'm all right," Cy said. He turned to Kwesi. "Thanks for staying with me, Kwesi. You were a great help."

Kwesi flushed with pleasure. In the time since he'd gone to Vesey House, he had lost most of his anger about being sent away to live with his uncle. He still wanted to go home, but having to live and go to school in Jamison had become bearable because of the activities he'd become involved in through Cy Brewster. Cy was the first adult he'd known and admired who gave him a sense of respect. Today Cy had treated him like an equal in helping with and caring for Miss Beth. It made Kwesi feel ten feet tall.

He couldn't express all of this in words, but he thought Cy understood as they looked at each other. Cy squeezed his shoulder as Kwesi said, "Glad I could do it."

Back in the room Cy settled again beside Beth. Her sleep was so quiet that for a moment Cy was alarmed. He bent close to see if he could hear her breathing, and when he did smiled at his own foolishness.

Beth had kept herself away from him for so long that he was hungry for the sight of her. Now he could feast his eyes on her without interruption. She was so precious to him, so dear. How strange it was that the first moment he'd seen her he'd sensed a connection, and he'd known he had to find her. Destiny was a mystery. He had almost come home another way that day when their cars stopped at the light. But if he had missed her then, he was still destined to work with her on the HOP team. There was no doubt in his mind that he and Beth were meant to find each other.

I've been waiting for her, and she's been waiting for me. The Bobby accident is a quirk of fate, and who knows why such things happen, but it's not going to keep us apart.

Cy did not delude himself in thinking that because he was now sitting beside Beth that their problems were over. He understood that Beth's physical condition made her vulnerable to him. Before he told her about Bobby, they had become so close that their loving interdependence was a fact they had begun to take for granted. He knew that Beth had repressed and denied their unity afterward, but today because of her pain and because he was there with her, it had reasserted itself. For this Cy was thankful.

His continual need and hunger for Beth urged him to take advantage of the circumstance and press for a reconciliation. But this would be wrong and he knew it. Beth had accused him of holding her lightly in his estimation, of belittling her by not letting her have the facts and trusting her to come to her own conclusion about where their relationship should go.

I'm not going to make that mistake twice, sweetheart, he vowed silently as he watched Beth move slightly in her sleep. I am just going to be a friend, and when you get well if you want to go back to where you were this morning, I'm prepared to start all over again—although I hope you won't feel that you can put us both in that hell again. Whatever you decide, I am not giving you up.

Chapter 24

The door opened, and a pink-coated aide brought in a supper tray and, smiling at Cy, set it on the bed table. She was followed by a nurse.

''Could you step outside for a minute while I get Miss Jordan ready for supper?'' she said briskly.

As Cy left, he heard the nurse say, ''Wake up. Time for supper,'' In a few minutes the nurse beckoned Cy back in. Beth was awake, and the nurse had raised the bed so she could sit up to eat.

''The doctor wants you to eat everything on your plate. Are you hungry?'' the nurse said as she adjusted the bed tray to a comfortable position for Beth.

''Not really,'' Beth said in answer to her question.

The nurse turned to Cy. ''You'll help her, won't you?''

''Yes,'' Cy said, wishing the nurse would leave.

When she left, Cy closed the door behind her. ''Did the sleep help, honey?'' he asked as he sat beside her again, her hand in his.

''A little,'' she said, looking at the food, ''but I don't want to eat.''

''Why not?''

"It will come up again like it's been doing," she said with the simplicity of a child.

So that's why she's lost so much weight, he thought, the memory of her retching in his bathroom striking him like a blow.

"I don't think it will, Beth," he said confidently. "I'm sure Dr. Fletcher has prepared for that. Like he said, you can't get strong enough to go home unless you eat." He surveyed the meat loaf, mashed potatoes, broccoli, the dish of pears, and the carton of milk. "It doesn't look too bad, so why don't you start while it's still hot?" While he spoke he cut the meat loaf into bite-sized pieces then handed Beth the fork. He looked at her expectantly.

"I really have to do this?" she asked, looking at him.

"Yes, dear, you do."

She began eating, and he told her stories from his college days and stories about his brothers and sisters, anything that had nothing to do with the center work or with the present. Beth listened and laughed and forgot she was eating until the plate was empty.

"Good job," Cy said as he moved the food tray onto a table.

"It helps when you have your own private entertainer," Beth said dryly, cutting her eyes at Cy.

"Whoops!" Cy said, realizing that Beth had seen through him, and they both laughed.

"Did you call Mama and Daddy?"

"Yes, but still no answer. What time do they get home from a fishing trip?"

"They probably won't be home until around nine or ten. When they go away with Aunt Elly and Uncle Sim, they make a day of it and then stop somewhere for dinner on the way home."

Cy looked at the telephone beside her bed. "We can try them again around nine."

The television set attached above Beth's bed had not been turned on since she'd been in the room. "Want to see the news, or are you ready to go back to sleep?" he asked.

"It's too early to go back to sleep. Let's see the news."

They watched the news and then a sitcom and after that the beginning of a movie. At first, they had exchanged comments about the news and the sitcom. At eight-thirty the nurse brought in Beth's medication, and Cy stepped out while she got Beth ready for the night. When he resumed his seat beside her, she put her hand in his.

''Have you had anything to eat, Cy?''

''Yes, and if I get hungry later I'll get something,'' he said. ''Don't worry about it. You just be sure to be ready to eat that big breakfast they'll give you in the morning.''

''Oh,'' she said. Cy watched a look of anxiety cross her face. He thought he might know what was causing it. He tweaked her nose gently and said, ''I'll be right here to see that you clean your plate.'' Her face cleared. ''You will?''

''Of course. Where else would I be? Anytime you wake up in the night, if you need anything I'll be right here.''

She tried to watch the movie, but Cy could see it was a losing battle. The medication began to take effect and, as her eyes grew heavy, she murmured, ''I'm so tired I could sleep a week.''

Cy turned off the sound completely. He bent down to Beth. ''Why don't you do that, honey.'' He tenderly smoothed her hair and pulled the sheet up to her neck. He felt a thrill when Beth said a soft ''Good night'' and put up her arms for a kiss. He brushed her lips lightly. ''Good night and sweet dreams,'' he said. A faint smile curved her lips as she snuggled under the blanket and went to sleep.

God, give me strength, Cy thought, standing by the window with his hands clenched in his pockets. He stared out blindly across the parking lot at the row of pine trees, tall sentinels in the dark. Had he misread the situation? Why had Beth sought a kiss? All evening they had acted like any long-married couple, looking at the news and a sitcom, laughing and talking about it, content in each other's company. She had wanted to have her hand held almost all of the time. She had never turned away when he caressed her face but had seemed to welcome it.

Had she, in fact, put her anger behind her? He considered

the possibility that it had been wearing her down to the point that when this physical crisis had occurred her energy to hold on to it had dissipated.

He was certain that she loved him. He did not believe that his blunder, enormous though it had been, had destroyed her love any more than her anger and rejection had destroyed his. Her love still existed, but all of these weeks she had been able to deny it because of her pride and because of her pain and disappointment.

Her actions this evening proved him right, thank God. She had been sweet, trusting, and responsive just as she used to be. But would it last? Had she forgiven him? He turned from the window and went to stand by the bed. Beth had made it clear that she wanted him with her during the night and to see him the first thing in the morning. The irony of that situation gave him a wry smile. How many times had he wanted exactly that but hardly in these circumstances!

At nine-thirty Cy left the room quietly and in the hall used a pay telephone to call the Jordans. They had just arrived home. Cy explained the situation first to Beth's father then to her mother. He answered all of their questions and tried in his most tactful manner to address their unspoken questions, like why was he staying with Beth all night when they could be there?

"Dr. Fletcher has given her pain medicine and a sleeping pill. It's finally taken effect, and I think she'll sleep through the night, which is what he's anxious for her to do. I told her I'd be around in case she awakened and wanted anything, and she seemed to be comforted by that."

"Is there a telephone in her room?"

"Yes, Mrs. Jordan. The last thing I told her before she fell asleep was that I'd keep calling until I got you, she didn't need to worry about it. She said she'd call you in the morning."

"Well, I guess that's all right then. Mr. Brewster, thanks for taking care of her."

"No need for thanks, Mrs. Jordan," Cy said. "It's what I want to do for the rest of my life."

From the telephone Cy went down to the lobby, where the machines stood, as the shops and cafeteria were closed. He bought several snacks and a packet of toiletries he intended to use in the morning. He rushed back to the room and was relieved to see that Beth hadn't moved. He turned off the light and turned on the one in the bathroom and cracked the door. Then he resumed his seat beside Beth. He didn't want to be more than a touch away in case she needed him during the night. He didn't know at what hour he dozed off, but when he awakened the morning light was beginning to appear. He went to wash his face and use the toiletries in the packet. Feeling freshened he resumed his seat beside Beth.

He found that at some point he had come to the decision that, until Beth let him know otherwise, he had to assume that she had not forgiven him. He would continue to be as much of a friend as she would permit, but he would cross no lines until she invited him to do so. Whatever happened while she was here in the hospital he would take as being generated by her physical condition, unless she made it clear that it was what she knowingly and truly felt.

Cy was relieved that he had some guidelines to follow and was determined to keep to them.

Beth opened her eyes and looked puzzled. "Good morning, sleepyhead," Cy said with a smile.

Beth turned and looked at him in surprise. Then comprehension began to return as Cy said, "How are you feeling this morning?"

Cy was holding his breath, waiting to see what her attitude would be.

"That must have been some strong pill Dr. Fletcher gave me last night," Beth said. "It put me out like a light."

She rubbed her hand across her face then looked at Cy as if she saw him for the first time. "Did you sleep in that chair all night?"

"I was here like I said I'd be, and I'm feeling fine. How about you? Does your foot hurt?"

"A little. I think it'll hurt much worse when I put my weight on it." Beth was still looking at Cy, and now she stretched out her hand.

Cy took it in his and squeezed it gently.

"Thank you, Cy," she said softly.

"Oh, honey, don't thank me." Cy spoke past the lump in his throat. "Don't you know that whatever I can do for you makes me happy."

Beth curled her fingers in the palm of Cy's hand and closed her eyes again. She could feel the warmth of his regard, his total concern for her, and the forcefulness of his physical presence. She could not figure out how she got from what she had been feeling about their relationship for the past weeks to what she was feeling now. All she knew at this point was that she drew from Cy strength and comfort, that he seemed to be a source of protectiveness, and that she had a great need of him. She would deal with anything else later. But now Cy was here, and she was happy about it. She dozed off again.

Sometime later Beth opened her eyes. "Good morning," she murmured and held out her arms.

Cy leaned to her and put his arms around her gently. "Good morning, Beth," he whispered, reminding himself of his guidelines.

"I spoke with your mother and your father last night about nine-thirty," he said. "They wanted to come over, but I explained that you were already asleep. I told them you had a phone by your bed and would call them the first thing this morning. Do you want to call them now or do you want the nurse?"

"The nurse, please."

The nurse came quickly, and Cy left the room. He poured himself a cup of coffee from the pot on a little table opposite the nurses' station and walked up and down the hall as he drank it. Activity hummed around him as nurses and aides went in and out of rooms, readying patients for the day. He stopped at the end of the hall to look out of the window.

When the Jordans came, he would go home. He needed a shower and fresh clothing. Beth would have a lot of company today like the Richards and the Walkers and Rhonda, so she wouldn't need him. He would plan on being back in time for her evening meal and to stay the night again. He thought of their hours together last evening, and their sweetness filled him with joy. They belonged together—that was the beginning and the end of it.

When he came back into the room, the nurse had gone after helping Beth with her bath. Beth was holding her pocket mirror while combing her hair. She smiled at him and tried to pat a curl in place as he came to his chair. She put the comb and mirror away.

"That's the best I can do," she said. "How do I look?"

Cy wanted to love her with the words that filled his heart about how she looked to him, words like beautiful, wonderful, and desirable. That she looked like she belonged in his arms, next to his heart.

But he said, "You look fine, honey. I'd just like a bit more color in your face. Are you ready for your breakfast?"

"Depends on what it is."

"Now, Beth, last night you promised that you'd eat it."

"Can't you eat some of it?" Her fingers moved restlessly in his hand.

"Sweetheart, you need all of it. Tell you what I'll do. Have you called your folks yet?"

"Not yet."

"While you talk to them, I'll go down to the cafeteria and bring my breakfast up here and we can eat together. Okay?"

"Okay."

Cy moved the telephone from the table onto the bed and turned to go. He was halfway to the door when Beth called him.

"Cy?"

"Yes?" He turned to look at her.

"Hurry back."

"I will," he promised.

The line in the cafeteria was long, and it was fifteen minutes before he was back. Beth had been watching the door, and he saw her eyes light up as he crossed from the door to her bedside.

Cy wanted to say "Miss me?" and then kiss her and flirt with her and play all the sweet lovers' games, she looked so adorable and so available to him.

Instead he said, "Sorry it took so long. There were lots of

people in line.'' He looked at her untouched breakfast tray. ''What did they bring you''

''Orange juice, scrambled eggs, sausage, grits, toast, coffee. What did you get?'' She watched with interest as he took the foil from his plate.

''Scrambled eggs, sausage, grits, toast, coffee.''

Her eyes crinkled with laughter. As Cy picked up his fork, Beth said, ''Wait. We haven't blessed the food.'' They bowed their heads. ''Bless this food, O Lord, unto our use. Please make us grateful. Amen.''

Cy could not trust himself to speak. These simple homely rituals they were sharing as if they had been doing them for a thousand mornings touched him to the core of his being. He dared not look at Beth but busied himself cutting her sausage and pouring her a glass of water from the carafe on the table.

''Now,'' he said as he sat down again beside Beth, ''let's eat.'' Cy made himself keep pace with Beth as she ate. She asked him what the cafeteria was like, and he described it. He asked about her call to her parents. She said they were coming after church at her insistence.

''Mama doesn't like to miss church, and I told her there was no need for her to do so since I'll be here the rest of the day. They're going to bring me some things I need from home.''

''I imagine you'll have plenty of visitors later on,'' he said. ''Especially with this being Sunday.''

He watched her consider this as she slowly took a bite of toast and come to a reluctant conclusion. He was prepared for her next comment.

''I guess you need to go home, don't you?''

''But I'll be back this evening when they've all gone,'' he said gently.

She looked at him then, her eyes soft and warm. ''You will?''

Cy simply nodded his head and drank some coffee. *I'll be back, but God help me if Beth continues to be like this. It's going to be a long and difficult night.*

After breakfast Cy went down to the shops and brought back a pot of yellow daisies, which Beth exclaimed over, and the Sunday paper, which they divided and read. A nurse came in and drew blood for several tests Dr. Fletcher had ordered. Someone from X-ray came to look at the cast and ask Beth how it felt. She said it was uncomfortable.

"I wonder when Dr. Fletcher is coming?" Beth said.

"Probably not until afternoon as it's already late."

Some of the energy Beth had displayed earlier in the morning seemed to have disappeared. "Are you tired?" Cy asked.

"I feel like taking a little nap," Beth acknowledged.

"Why don't you do that?" Cy cleared the papers off of the bed and fussed with the blanket, which had become tangled. He tucked her in then sat beside her again.

Beth pulled her hand from under the cover for Cy to hold.

"You like doing that, don't you?" she said, her eyes on him.

"Yes," he said simply. Their glances held, then with a small sigh Beth closed her eyes.

She was awakened an hour later by the delivery of the noon-day meal. With the help of Cy's persuasion, she managed to eat most of the food. He had just transferred the tray from the bed to a table when the Jordans arrived.

After the greetings were over, Cy asked them about their fishing trip, and they described some of the fish they'd caught. The catch was in the freezer, and they'd like him to have some if he liked fish. Cy said thanks and that he'd be running along now that they were here with Beth.

He turned to Beth. "When you talk to the Walkers, be sure to find out how we did yesterday. Okay?"

"Yes, I will," she said, her eyes intent on him.

"Then you can tell me later."

"Later." Beth extended her hand. Cy raised it to his lips then released it, nodded to the Jordans and left.

Beth's parents wanted to know the whole story all over again. Minnie had brought nightclothes and a robe for Beth from home and her own toiletries, so Merdis was dismissed until Beth could thankfully change. She opened her compact and put on some blusher and a little powder. "Cy said I needed more color in my face," she remarked. "I guess I was pale."

This was the opening Minnie had been hoping for. "It looks

like you and Cy are friendly again,'' she said as she folded up some clothing.

''I haven't figured out yet exactly what we are. I just know he's been a tower of strength, for which I'm grateful.'' Beth hoped that would satisfy her mother, and she changed the subject with a question about what her mother should bring her to wear when the doctor discharged her. Minnie followed her lead by suggesting a denim dress Beth had that buttoned down the front. Beth's reply about Cy had been good enough. Minnie was anxious to relate it to her husband as they'd been wondering ever since Cy had called them.

The afternoon went as Cy had predicted. David and Emily came with the news that the fund-raiser had cleared three hundred and fifty dollars. Rhonda Hayes spent an hour distressed over Beth's accident and was concerned about her. When Beth told her how Cy and Kwesi had brought her to the hospital, Rhonda thought that at least some good had come from the situation. Aunt Elly's family had filled the room with vitality and laughter. Her cousins had never seen Beth in the hospital and, after assuring themselves that she would survive, they made their usual jokes and insisted on writing on her cast. But with all of the friends and family around her, Beth missed Cy. His absence created a void no one else could fill.

Cy had gone straight home to a long and refreshing shower. He called his parents and told them what had happened. His mother said to be sure to tell Beth they hoped she'd be better soon. Then he talked with Gary Raeford about the situation.

''I'm sorry to hear that, Cy. How is Beth?''

''Still weak, and she'll be wearing the cast for weeks.''

''Yes, but she won't have to stay home all that time, will she?''

''No. Listen, Gary, I'm not sure when I'll be in tomorrow.''

''You have any pressing appointments?''

''I have a meeting at eleven, and I'll be in by then.''

''Good enough. You have sick leave and annual leave time you could use, you know.''

''I may need that later. Tell Kimberly about Beth for me, and I'll see you later.''

Cy set his alarm for four o'clock and went to sleep. When the alarm went off, Cy didn't get up. He stretched himself and contemplated the ceiling, his hands behind his head. He wondered what Beth wanted from him or even if she knew herself. He knew what he wanted to give her was his unconditional love and receive the same from her. He wanted to marry her, see her grow big with his child. Raise a family with her. He wanted a long life with her with all of its joys and sorrows, and he wanted it to begin yesterday!

He found himself reviewing all that had happened since he had brought Beth to the hospital, how time after time Beth had demonstrated the same closeness they'd had before. Instead of backing away from any physical contact with him as she'd been doing, she wanted his touch at all times. It was strange, he thought, almost as if the preceding three weeks hadn't occurred or had been a bad dream.

He got out of bed and as he dressed in brown wool slacks, a wheat-colored sport shirt, and a tan single-breasted jacket with a tiny weave in it, he told himself those weeks had not been a dream, and that when Beth had fully recovered her health and strength, they would have to find a way to come to terms with what had happened.

On the way to the hospital, he stopped at the jewelry section of a large department store. He selected a delicate gold bracelet fashioned of tiny hearts linked together. He had it gift wrapped and put the box in his jacket pocket. Arriving at the hospital, he stopped at the florist shop and purchased a small dish garden then went to the cafeteria to get his meal.

He opened the door to Beth's room at precisely five-fifteen. The trolleys with the evening meal were coming off the elevators. Beth's face was turned to the window. She turned around at his entrance. She looked forlorn and weary with shadowed eyes. Cy quickly covered the space between them, put down the dinner and the dish garden, and dropped to his knees beside her.

"Sweetheart, what's the matter? Do you hurt somewhere? Do you want the nurse?"

Beth shook her head and looked at Cy, her dark brown eyes fixed on him. "I missed you so," she said faintly.

Cy was stunned, and for an instant he didn't respond. Then with a stifled groan, he put his arms under the cover and brought her as close to him as he could. She leaned against him, her face nuzzled in his neck. He could feel her relax in his arms, and he held her silently until the sound of the food trolley came down the hall.

He gently laid Beth down and with an effort at lightness said, "I'm here now, honey, and I think your supper is too." He seated himself in his usual chair as the door swung open and an aide brought in Beth's meal.

Her tray held vegetable soup, a hamburger patty, bread with butter, and a dish of grapes. Cy went through his usual routine with her food then raised her bed a little higher. When he sat down, Beth said, "Where's yours?"

Cy took his plate from the table behind him. "I brought mine in with me."

"I didn't see it."

This time Cy said grace and they began to eat. "Did you have something else in your hand? I didn't see what you were carrying, I was just looking at your face," Beth said artlessly.

Cy put his plate down and held up the dish garden for Beth to examine.

"I know just the spot to set that in when I get home," she said, her face lighting up with pleasure. "I like these. They're easy to care for and interesting to look at. Thanks, Cy."

"You're more than welcome. Speaking of when you go home," Cy said as they resumed eating, "did the doctor come, and what did he say about you going home?"

"He came while my parents were still here, which made them happy because they could ask him all the questions they wanted to. My white corpuscle count and my blood pressure are both low, he said. He's having a special eating plan made up that I have to follow, and he says I must get a lot of rest. He thinks he can discharge me tomorrow if he likes the way I look when he comes."

"That's good news."

Beth put a bit of the hamburger patty on her fork and looked at it. She raised her eyes to Cy. ''Yes,'' she said.

Their eyes told each other how precious this time had been for them in this isolated little world of her hospital room.

''Tell me about the rest of your visitors,'' Cy said.

When the meal was over, and the tray had been removed, they sat contentedly holding hands and looked at the evening news. After that the nurse came with the evening medication and prepared Beth for the night. Cy walked the hall, his hands jammed in his pockets. He's been so wrapped up in his nearness to Beth and the emotions he was picking up from her that he'd forgotten about the gift.

When he returned to the room, Beth was wearing a white bed jacket with a narrow satin trim and small pearly buttons. Her hair was freshly combed. This time Cy didn't wait to be asked how she looked.

''You look so pretty, Beth,'' he said.

''Really?'' she asked, holding his hand tightly.

''Really,'' he said, fighting the urge to kiss her. ''I just happen to have something in my coat pocket for a pretty girl,'' he said.

''What is it?'' A smile curved her mouth.

''Why don't you put your hand in my pocket and see?''

Cy deliberately turned slightly so that her searching hand went into the wrong pocket. She pulled out his car keys and held them up.

''This?''

''No. Try again.''

She pulled out a neatly folded linen handkerchief.

''This?''

''Well, no, but if you need one this is clean, and you may have it,'' he said seriously but with a twinkle in his eyes.

Next was a Bic pen. ''This?''

''No.''

By this time Beth was thoroughly into the game and enjoying herself.

''There's nothing more in the pocket,'' she declared.

Cy put on a worried look. ''Are you sure?''

Beth searched again in the corners of the deep pocket. "That's all."

Cy looked dejected and serious. "I was sure," he muttered to himself as he patted the empty pocket and looked at the little pile of items on the bed.

Beth looked worried too. Then to cheer him up, she suggested, "Maybe you put it in the other pocket?"

"Oh," he said as if that hadn't occurred to him. "You can try it," he said doubtfully. He watched her carefully as she put her hand in the pocket in which he'd put the gift.

Chapter 25

Beth looked like a child at Christmas. Her eyes got big as her hand touched what was undoubtedly the shape of a box with a bow on it in Cy's pocket. ''Here it is,'' she said and pulled it out.

Cy sat down, totally enchanted as he watched the play of emotion on Beth's face.

The box was wrapped in red satin paper with a gold ribbon and bow. ''How pretty it is,'' she exclaimed, looking at it from every angle.

''What's in the box?'' she asked Cy, her eyes sparkling.

''You'll have to open it to see,'' he said.

Beth untied the ribbon and the bow and smoothed them out. She took the paper off carefully and folded it. She laid the paper and the ribbons on the table. Cy had given the odd gift here and there on occasion to other women, but none of them had given so much attention to the mere opening of a box.

Beth lifted the lid and laid it on the table. She gently separated the layers of tissue paper to reveal the golden bracelet of linked hearts.

''Oh, Cy, it's so lovely!'' She just sat and looked at it in the box, and all Cy could think of was what a joy it was going to be to give her gifts for the rest of her life.

Beth took the bracelet out of the box and held it up so the golden hearts glistened in the light. She laid it in the palm of her hand and looked at Cy.

"Put it on for me, please, Cy," she said softly.

The bracelet was so delicate and finely wrought it was hard for Cy's large hands to operate the fastening and its safety catch. By the time he succeeded, his fingers were almost trembling. He was so close to Beth he could smell her perfume and feel her warm breath on his face. He knew she was not looking at what he was doing. She was looking at him.

"Kiss me, Cy," she said and wrapped her arms around his neck. Cy held on to his guidelines and brushed her lips with a friendly kiss. Beth accepted it then pulled back and looked into his eyes.

"Now give me a real kiss," she commanded and met him more than halfway.

Beth felt life pulsing into her from Cy's kiss. This was the food she'd been starving for. No wonder she'd been malnourished. She'd been deprived so long! She took another and another of Cy's life-giving kisses then leaned back to rest against her pillow, her cheeks rosy and her breath coming fast. How could it be that she felt both exhilarated and yet calm—as if in her floundering she had found an anchor. How could she explain to Cy what she herself did not comprehend?

Cy's emotions were in turmoil again. Yes, he'd crossed the line he had imposed, but it was at Beth's clear invitation. She asked for a real kiss, accepting the friendly one he offered but deciding it wasn't enough for her. So he'd expressed the love he'd been holding back in the "real" kiss, and she'd asked for more and more. He looked at her from under his lashes. Her eyes were closed, but he could feel her mental wheels turning. He did not want her to feel that she had to make some explanation and perhaps say words she would later regret.

He leaned forward and put a finger gently on her lips. She opened her eyes. "No words," he whispered tenderly and saw the relief in her eyes. "You need to rest."

Cy turned on the television, found a concert on the Public Television channel and, turning the volume low, sat with her hand in his. Once Beth raised her arm to turn it this way and that, admiring the elegant bracelet.

"It's the loveliest gift I've ever had."

"You deserve the best."

She smiled contentedly. After a while Cy saw her fighting against sleep. It was already after ten, and Cy thought she should have been asleep some time ago, but excitement over the bracelet had buoyed her up.

"I'll turn out the light, honey, so you can go to sleep. All right? You must be tired after all the visitors this afternoon."

"I am tired," she agreed. She watched him as he lowered the bed and straightened her covers. When he had finished she said, "You'll be here?"

Cy smiled at her. "Did you need to ask that?"

"No, but I was remembering that tomorrow's Monday, and you have to go to work." Anxiety had returned to her eyes, but she tried to keep it out of her voice.

"I'm not leaving you until after we've had our breakfast together. I need to start off my work week right," he said lightly, hoping to bring a smile to her eyes, and he succeeded.

"Good night, dear heart, and sweet dreams," he whispered as he bent over her.

Beth cupped his face in her soft hands. Cy felt her hands tremble as she pulled him down to give him a long sweet kiss.

"Good night, dear Cy," she said softly, "and thank you for my bracelet."

Cy turned out the light and began his vigil. Gradually the hospital itself settled down for the long night, and eventually Cy dozed off in his chair.

He was awakened by a noise he couldn't identify. It was a strangled cry, he thought. He looked toward the door, thinking it had come from outside, then he heard a moan and some garbled words and realized they were coming from Beth. He jumped up to bend over her. She was thrashing around in the bed, struggling to get away from something.

"Beth! Beth! Wake up, Beth," Cy said, taking hold of her

and shaking her gently. She resisted him, and he realized she was still deep in the nightmare. He pulled her strongly against him and said, "Beth, wake up," in her ear.

She gradually became still. "It's me, Cy," he said as he rubbed her back.

"Something awful was chasing me, and I couldn't get away." She began trembling again.

Cy could feel that she was damp from perspiration. He knew from his own experience how terrifying nightmares could be.

"It's all right now," he said in a soothing voice.

When he thought she was quiet and calm again, Cy began to ease Beth down in the bed.

"No, no." Beth clutched at Cy. "Hold me."

Cy pulled her again into his arms.

"I want you to hold me in your chair," Beth said.

Cy took a deep breath. "Put your arms around my neck, Beth, and be careful of your cast." He put a cover around her then lifted her and carefully sat down in his chair with her in his arms. He hooked another chair with his foot and rested her cast on it.

"Are you warm enough?"

"Yes."

Cy shifted a little. The chair wasn't made for two adults to sit in as they were doing. He raised his arm a little to give her back more support.

"Are you comfortable, honey?"

Beth nestled closer to him. Her arms were loosely linked around his neck, and her hair tickled his chin.

"I am now," she said softly. "How about you?"

"I'm all right." Cy wondered what Beth would say if he fully described the condition of his comfort. Here he was in the middle of the night, holding in his arms the woman he loved beyond any idea he'd had of what love was. She was warm and fragrant and soft and wearing only her nightgown and the cover he'd had the good sense to put around her. She had asked to be kissed, and now she'd asked to be held in his arms like this. Beth seemed to give no thought to cause and effect where male and female intimacy was concerned. Cy thought her innocence came from the fact that, although she was twenty-nine, she had never been in a deeply emotional relationship until now.

"I'm scared to close my eyes," Beth said. "I'm afraid I'll go right back into the dream again."

Cy could feel the tension in her body. "Not while I'm holding you, you won't. You're safe here in my arms, baby," Cy said softly and began to rub her back gently through the blanket just as he would have comforted a child.

"Relax and think of something pleasant," he crooned, "and you'll soon be asleep."

As Cy rubbed her back, he could feel Beth begin to relax. Her even breathing proclaimed her sleep after a while.

Cy began to relax also, but he was afraid to let himself drift off. Suppose he did and the nurse came in and found them? He couldn't put Beth in a position like that, so he held her close and wondered if the time would come when he would hold her like this as his wife.

After an hour of sound sleep on Beth's part, he slowly stood and as gently as possible returned Beth to bed. She mumbled something unintelligible but did not awaken.

Cy walked up and down the room, getting the cricks out of his back then stood by the window. Not in his wildest dreams had he imagined that he would spend two nights alone with Beth. He had to smile inside. Be careful what you ask for. You might get it, but it won't turn out to be like you thought it would be!

He wondered if Beth had nightmares often. Would she remember this one, and if she did would she speak of it in the morning or would she be embarrassed?

He saw at once that she did remember it in the morning. There was a self-consciousness on her part that had been absent before. Her morning greeting was restrained, and she didn't put out her hand for Cy to hold. There was tension between them for the first time.

Cy decided that if it continued it would put up an unnecessary wall between them, so when the nurse came and he left the room to go to the cafeteria, he thought of how he might keep that from happening.

"You look like you're feeling better this morning, honey," he said as they were eating their french toast and bacon.

"I am feeling stronger, and I hope when Dr. Fletcher comes he'll let me go home."

Cy drank some coffee. "You had a little nightmare last night," he said and glanced at her quickly. She didn't look up, but a flush came into her face.

"I woke you up, and you said something awful was chasing you. But then you went back to sleep again. I remember having dreams like that, especially when I was little. My brother still likes to tease me about the time I jumped out of bed and ran around the room, trying to get away. He tried to catch me, and I knocked him down, and he got a big hickey on his head."

By this time Beth had resumed eating and was looking at him, smiling.

"Which reminds me," Cy went right on, "when I was talking to my brother, George, last week he said he's coming down for the weekend if he can get away. He hasn't been home for a while, and Mama's been getting on his case. Maybe I can get some work out of him at the center."

"I wonder when I'll be able to get back to the center?"

"That's the last thing for you to be worrying about now."

"Even if I can't stand up for a long period of time, there's work I can do from a chair," Beth said firmly

Cy began to object then bit his tongue. Don't make judgments for her, that's where you went wrong before. "Yes, you can and as soon as you feel strong enough, it will be great to have you back."

Beth's breakfast tray was removed, then the nurse came in and told Beth they'd be taking her down to examine the cast in a little while. Someone would be up with a wheelchair.

Beth and Cy looked at each other gravely.

"You have to go to work," Beth said.

"Yes."

Now that the time had come to end this precious and unexpected time that had brought them close again, neither one was sure of what to say. Beth had a lot of thinking to do about her feelings where Cy was concerned. Cy was unsure of what Beth wanted to acknowledge about what had taken place here. He decided he would follow whatever lead Beth gave him.

"Daddy said to let him know as soon as the doctor tells me when I can go, and they'll be over to get me," Beth said.

"Do you think the doctor's coming this morning?"

"I hope so. I'm ready to go home."

"I have a meeting to get ready for, so I guess I'd better be going. You're sure you'll get home all right?" She nodded yes.

Cy knelt beside Beth. "I'm sorry you hurt your foot, honey, but it's been wonderful being here with you," he said quietly.

Beth looked at him gravely. "Thank you for all you've done, Cy, and for staying with me." It seemed to Cy her eyes were telling him more.

"May I kiss you, Beth?" he whispered.

Beth's eyes gleamed. "Yes."

Cy intended his kiss to be a brief farewell, but Beth's lips were so sweet. Then she parted them slightly and moved them under his. Cy felt electricity galvanize his body. He deepened the kiss and Beth responded.

It took all Cy's willpower not to take her in his arms and press her back against the pillow with the hungry force of his kisses. He broke the kiss, reluctantly brushed her cheek with his hand, and quickly left the room without looking back.

Beth felt bereaved. The light had gone out of the room with Cy. He hadn't said when she'd see him again, he hadn't even said good-bye. He'd just walked out. She pitied herself and cried, knowing she was acting childish and not caring.

Her common sense finally asserted itself. Cy probably left as he did because he felt as confused and frustrated as she felt. The kiss had just made things worse, stirring up all kinds of emotions as well as marking the end of this hiatus.

Beth picked up the telephone and talked to Marty Armstrong, explaining the accident and responding to his agitated questions. She assured him she'd be back at work the following Monday and to feel free to call her at home about anything.

By the middle of the afternoon, Beth was home. Now that she was here in her familiar surroundings, she felt rejuvenated. She refused to get in the bed, protesting to her mother that she'd spent enough time in bed. She moved around the house in the wheelchair they'd rented on the way home. Her dad had brought in the dish garden and the yellow daisies and set them down. She made room for the dish garden on the kitchen counter, where she could see it frequently and the light was good.

Beth and her mother discussed the food list Dr. Fletcher had given her. Her father said he'd go shopping, and she insisted he use her money.

At five-thirty Cy called.

"How was your day, Cy?"

"Busy but lonely. I missed you so much."

"I missed you too." Then she went on quickly. "Are you on your way to the center now?"

"Yes."

"Tell them all hello for me, and I'm sorry for missing work."

"Beth."

"Yes."

"Will you still be awake when I leave the center/"

"I don't know."

"I know I can't stop by, but may I call you?"

"I'll answer the phone if I'm awake."

Aunt Elly came over after supper, Net and Toria tagging along. The girls tried out the wheelchair as Beth sat on the couch watching them indulgently.

"Our Ladies Circle is having our clothing sale this weekend, Beth. Are you up to going through your closets to see what you can find for the sale?" Aunt Elly knew she could count on her niece to have a bag full of items large and small that would bring in good money.

"That'll give me something to do tomorrow," Beth said.

During the evening she talked with Taresa, Cathy, and Kimberly. They all wanted to know about the accident and how she was feeling. At nine she was deciding to get in bed and read when Cy called.

Beth instinctively held the phone close to her ear and closed her eyes, all of her senses attuned to his voice.

"You're early," she said

"I didn't want to take a chance on missing you, so I'm here in the office with the door closed.

"Had you gone to bed yet, Beth?"

His hushed voice had a quality that made Beth shiver as she said, "No, I had just decided to go. I have a new book to read."

"Oh."

In the silence Beth was remembering the wonderful feeling it gave her to have Cy always within touch, to have him watching and caring for her with tender concern. He made her feel so cherished.

Cy was seeing Beth lift her arms for a morning kiss, smelling her fragrance as he fastened her bracelet, and feeling her soft warm body close to him in his chair.

"I wish I could be there with you, baby." His voice was deep and caressing.

Her sudden intake of breath and her whispered "Yes" came clearly down the line to Cy.

After another moment of silence, Beth said, "Cy, I think this nighttime call is not the best idea."

Cy knew Beth was right, but he wanted to protest. At least they could talk about seeing each other, couldn't they? His heart and his libido said, of course, why not? His head and his intelligence said, restrain yourself. Where is your self-control?

He gave a deep sigh. "I bow to your judgment, sweetheart. Sleep well and I'll talk with you tomorrow."

Beth's telephone rang once more. This time it was Clio. She was shocked to hear about the accidnet and wanted to know all about it.

"You have to be home all week? Listen, I'll drive to Jamison Friday night and see you Saturday for breakfast."

Chapter 26

Beth eased herself out of bed. The temporary plaster cast had been removed from her ankle and a wrapping put on instead. Much of the swelling had already subsided. The real discomfort was her foot. A bone was broken, and the foot was now encased in a fiberglass cast. It had to be held immobile for at least six weeks in order to heal properly. While the wheelchair wasn't an absolute necessity, Dr. Fletcher had recommended she use it this first week while she was home to conserve her strength.

"You're still run down, and I want you to rest while you can. When you return to work, use a footed cane or a crutch and elevate your foot as much as you can," he'd said when he consented to discharge her.

Maneuvering with the cast was awkward, and it took her two to three times as long to do a task. She could see that her time schedule needed drastic altering to accommodate this disability.

But the sun was shining on this Tuesday in the last week of April. The trees were full of green leaves, the morning air blowing through the window was fresh and warm. Beth felt better than she had felt in weeks despite the foot. After breakfast she tackled her bedroom closet with zest for Aunt Elly's sale.

She'd made a tidy pile of tops, pants, belts, and bags. Some she was tired of, some no longer fit the way she wanted them to. There was a good navy jacket that never had hung just right, so it was in the pile. Here was a white dress that was no longer in style and a pink one she used to like, but it no longer suited her taste. After several others, the last dress she took from the closet was the rose knit affair.

Beth took it from its hanger and laid it on her lap. This was the dress she wore when she went to dinner at Cy's, full of love, excitement, and expectation. At the end of the evening, her whole life and future had been changed but not in the positive way she had anticipated.

Cy wanted marriage, but he said he couldn't ask me until he told me it was his cousin's car with him in it that caused Bobby's death. He asked me how could he tell me when he found out Bobby was my cousin and very close to me. Would I have been able to do so had the situation been reversed? If I had just met Cy and was instantly attracted to him, would I have right away told him something that would damage my chances with him?

Maybe not. But there was no excuse for Cy to not tell me later. He could say it in a letter. Say it any kind of way—but he should have told me.

Beth discovered that despite the weekend with Cy, there was still a hurdle caused by what she perceived as Cy's lack of confidence in her ability to make her own decisions. He had been so furious with her mother ignoring Beth as a capable adult who could make her own judgments about her relationships. Couldn't he see he had done the same thing?

Beth found she could examine the situation on this April morning without the terrible feelings that had always seized her heretofore. The destructive anger and the physical sickness were gone, thank God. So where did that leave her with Cy?

Beth wheeled herself into the living room. Lined up along the window were plants and flowers Cy had sent her every week. Some of the blossoms were fading now. She pruned them and carefully used plant food and mist on the rest. The flowers and the view from the window were restful to her spirit as she dealt with her conflict about Cy.

There was no doubt that she loved him still. The past few days had proven that. The icy fortress in which her emotions had been hidden and protected had been quietly vanquished by the sheer warmth and tenderness of Cy's constant care throughout the entire weekend. The hospital room had become a sanctuary for the two of them, and they had regained not only their former rapport but an intimacy whose subtle quality Beth had never before experienced.

This was the core of her conflict. Beth knew that when she and Cy were together from now on that intimacy and closeness could not be denied. Inevitably they would be drawn together if they were honest in their feelings. But she could not forget Cy's lack of trust in her. What kind of future was possible for them if he could not see her as an equal?

Beth's reflections were interrupted by a call from Glennette Ellington.

"Rhonda told me about your accident, Beth. How are you?"

Beth explained what had happened, what the doctor had said, and her present condition. "I'll be back at work next week."

"I'm glad to hear that."

"How are you, Glennette? Baby's due soon, isn't it?"

"Yes, and that's one reason I'm calling, but maybe my idea needs to wait."

"What are you talking about?"

"My doctor wants me to do as little as possible until the baby arrives. Says I'm working too hard, and James is on his side. He and I were talking about my Girls Club, and we were wondering if you could take it over for me."

Beth was so surprised that she said, "Who, me?"

Glennette laughed. "Yes, Beth Jordan. You!"

"But, Glennette, there must be other people you could ask who have experience at that sort of thing."

"Remember who you're talking to, Beth. This is me. I've known you all your life. I know you can do this and anything else you want to do. You just haven't bothered doing it until now. You are the kind of young woman who will be able to keep the girls stimulated and interested. They loved hearing you when you talked with them about computers. They told me how down and cool you were. You and I can get together about the kinds of things I've been doing, and you can take it from there. Will you do it, Beth?''

''You're sure I can do it?''

''Believe me, Beth, I wouldn't have asked you otherwise. I've spent too many years building this Girls Club to entrust it to just anyone. I have confidence in you.''

''Since you put it like that, I guess I'll have to give it a try—and, Glennette, thanks for the compliment. I'll call you about getting together.''

Rhonda came over with a chicken and pasta dish for Beth's meal. When Beth told her about the Girls Club, Rhonda wasn't at all surprised.

''Anyone who can do what you've done for the center has the capacity to do other things as well, Beth. That shouldn't come as a shock to you.''

''You worked with the club when they did the fashion tea several years ago, didn't you?''

''Yes, but most of those girls have gone on, and there are new ones now. What I liked about them is that they're responsive to what you do. Glennette has wisely let the girls' needs and interests largely set the agenda.''

''To tell you the truth, Rhonda, the more I think about it, the more excited I become. I'm sure I'm going to like it.''

Cy called at six. ''How are you, honey?''

''I've had a good day, Cy. You sound tired.''

The concern in Beth's voice lifted his spirits. ''We had a couple of difficult personnel problems come up today, and I've been in and out of meetings with individuals and departments all day. Just got home a half hour ago, and I'll be leaving for the center in a few minutes.''

''Cy, you need a break. Why don't we plan to look at the rest of the work schedule and the volunteer list and see what we can work out? We can do it this weekend. You haven't got people coming Saturday, have you?''

"We were supposed to, but remember the people from the Department of Social Services had to back out because of a conflict with their outreach program?"

"I recall now. Don't put anyone in their place. Okay?"

"Sounds good to me. I admit to feeling a little tired at this point. What's your day been like?"

"Glennette Ellington has asked me to take over the Girls Club. The doctor wants her to curtail her activities."

"Do you want to do it, Beth?"

"I do now. I wasn't sure at first, but she talked me into it, and I've had several ideas about it already. This'll be a new kind of venture for me."

Cy could hear the enthusiasm in her voice.

"You're spreading your wings, aren't you, baby?" he said with pride.

"I guess I am," she said, the pride she heard in his voice filling her with pleasure.

"I have to go, Beth. Sleep well, and I'll talk to you tomorrow."

By Thursday Cy's need to see Beth, instead of just hearing her voice on the telephone, was so great that on impulse he left home early and stopped by her apartment on the way to the center. As he pulled into her driveway, he was reminded of the last time he'd been here. What a terrible night that had been! As he rang the bell, he was hoping that seeing him here wouldn't bring back a memory of that night to Beth.

A young woman with caramel skin, a sleek haircut, arched eyebrows, and full lips opened the door and looked at him inquiringly.

"Hi. Is Beth home? I'm Cy Brewster."

"Come in. I'm Jannie Richards, Beth's cousin."

This is Bobby's sister, Cy realized as he followed her into the living room where Beth was sitting in a wheelchair. As his eyes met hers he saw both a welcome and a little wariness in them.

"How are you, Beth? I thought I'd drop by on my way to

the center to see you. Everyone always wants to know how you're getting along.'' He hoped that would make her relax.

''I'm doing well, Cy. Did you meet my cousin Jannie?''

''I did.'' Cy gave Jannie a pleasant smile, which she returned, then he looked again at Beth. ''How's your appetite?''

''It's returning.''

''Who's cooking for you?''

''I do most of it, and Mama and Aunt Elly bring food over too.''

''Do you need anything, any fruit you've a taste for that I can get at the market? Maybe some seafood?''

''I have plenty, Cy, but thanks.''

Cy was sitting on the edge of the couch near Beth's wheelchair. ''How are you sleeping?'' He couldn't look away from her, and he had to make himself sit still so he wouldn't touch her.

''Straight through the night,'' she said.

They were both caught up in the memory of the night she hadn't slept straight through. *I loved holding you* was the clear message Cy sent. Cy knew the message was received and understood when Beth dropped her lashes and slowly rubbed the bracelet he'd given her. A small smile of masculine satisfaction creased Cy's lips.

''Have you tried walking yet?''

''That's what Jannie and I were doing before you came.''

Cy's focus on Beth had been so complete, he had forgotten Jannie, who was sitting out of his field of vision. ''How's she coming along, Jannie?'' he asked.

''I don't think she can go for a ten-k run anytime soon, but she can get around the house pretty good.'' Jannie had been intrigued by the quiet but emotional interplay between Beth and Cy Brewster. She couldn't wait for him to leave so she could ask Beth about him.

''You have a cane or a crutch?'' Cy asked.

Jannie showed him the three-footed metal cane. ''This is comfortable for you?''

''So far.''

Cy took his leave soon, saying he'd call tomorrow. Jannie let him out then came back into the room.

''So that's Cy Brewster! No one mentioned how attractive he is,'' she said accusingly to Beth.

''You think so?'' Beth teased.

''Any woman would think so, and you know it. He's crazy about you, Beth.''

''What makes you think so?''

''He didn't know I was here after he saw you. And all those questions almost like he was your doctor. I hope if I ever get sick or something that my Timmy will be that concerned about me.''

''Cy is a very caring person. You know he does a lot of work with young people, especially young men.''

''I'm sure he does, but I'm not talking about that. I'm talking about how he cares for you. He was real intense about it.''

Jannie was quiet for a minute, and Beth prepared herself for whatever her curious cousin would say next.

''I want to ask you something, Beth. Are you going to let the accident come between you and Cy? He was so young when it happened, and Mama said he had nothing to do with it.'' She looked at her cousin, who had always been like a big sister to her, and hoped her answer would be no. Beth was one of her favorite people, and she wanted her to be happy with someone who loved her like Cy Brewster did.

''I know he wasn't to blame in any way, Jannie. I don't hold it against him,'' Beth said, realizing the truth of that fact for the first time.

''I'm glad, Beth, because the vibes between you two are really strong and positive.''

''What do you think Nel and Net and Toria would feel about him, Jannie?'' This was a matter Beth had wondered about more than once.

Jannie shrugged. ''It doesn't matter to them any more than it does to me. So many of their friends have much worse things happen, and sometimes they're to blame. Cy wasn't, so he shouldn't have to suffer for it."

Beth listened to this wisdom of her younger cousins and mused about what they might say to her about the one obstacle that was yet to be overcome.

Chapter 27

''Girl, these muffins are wonderful,'' Clio said, tearing one gently apart and lavishing it with butter. ''You know how hard it is to find plain muffins in Atlanta? You can get blueberry, banana-nut, chocolate and strawberry, cinnamon, or almost any other flavor except plain muffins. No one makes them, and that's the kind I like best.'' Her brown eyes sparkling with pleasure, she delicately put a quarter of a muffin in her mouth.

''I made plenty knowing you were coming, and there's some for you to take home,'' Beth said, enjoying the gusto Clio displayed.

The breakfast table also held corned beef hash, scrambled eggs, slices of kosher pickles, and fresh strawberries. This was a favorite Clio combination, and Beth had planned to celebrate Clio's visit with as many of her favorite foods as possible.

It was nine o'clock on Saturday morning, and although Friday had been a flawlessly beautiful spring day, some clouds had moved in overnight. Warm spring showers came down intermittently. ''I'm glad the rain didn't come down while you were on the road,'' Beth said.

''Me, too. I was at Mama's by midnight, and I set my alarm for eight, so we can have a good long day. I know you have lots to tell me. Right?'' She shot a piercing glance at Beth, who this morning was looking rested and fresh in a rose skirt and top.

''Right.'' Beth looked affectionately at her longtime friend and confidante. Clio had a large frame and was generously fleshed without being fat. Her cinnamon skin was smooth and lightly made up to highlight her cheekbones and her large brown eyes. She had a well-shaped mouth that fit her face, and her shoulder-length brown hair waved on the right side of her face. Today she wore a pair of tangerine pants, a white big shirt accented with gold buttons, tangerine strappy sandals with two-inch block heels, and long earrings.

''You're looking great, Clio,'' Beth said admiringly.

''I finally decided to dress the way I wanted to, heels and all. No more subdued colors and flat heels unless that's what I feel like putting on. Maybe I'll never find the big man of my dreams, but life goes on. I'm getting tired of looking for Mr. Right anyway,'' she said defiantly.

''You know the old saying that when you stop looking, what you're looking for comes along.''

''I'll believe that when I see it,'' Clio said.

''Coffee?'' Beth lifted the pot.

''Yes, please, and one more muffin and that's it.''

After breakfast was over and the kitchen put to rights, they adjourned to the living room. Clio had a passion for embroidery and was working on a crazy quilt of silks and satins she had designed. She pulled it out of her tote bag now as she settled herself in a comfortable chair by a lamp.

Beth wheeled over to see what progress had been made since the last time she'd seen it. ''When you get this finished—'' she began.

''If I get it finished,'' Clio interrupted. ''It looks like it's going to be a work in progress for years to come.''

''You'll get it done sooner than you think. As I was saying, when you complete it, you should enter it into one of those quilt shows. The embroidery is exquisite.''

''Maybe I will. Now, Beth, tell me all that has happened with you and Cy.''

"Starting when?"

"Start at the beginning."

"You already know that."

"Yes, but I want to get the whole story in perspective since we have plenty of time. We're not talking long distance."

"I hear you. Well, I'm driving home and this red Saturn like the one I'd just been looking at on the car lot pulls up beside me at a stop light," Beth began.

Clio had heard the story in bits and pieces over the telephone, but she knew there were parts she'd missed. She wanted Beth to put it all together so she, Clio, would have a clearer picture of Cy Brewster's part in all that had happened to Beth. Clio felt the process would also be helpful for Beth.

The telling took nearly an hour, with Clio asking questions and making comments along the way.

Clio's face took on a grim aspect when Beth recounted the crucial evening when Cy told Beth about Bobby. "You remember when you introduced Cy to me over the phone? I warned him then not to be messing with you! I didn't want you to be hurt again, and that's exactly what happened."

Beth found herself defending Cy. "He wasn't playing with me or my feelings. He's been serious from the moment we met and his feelings have always been clear. It was like he said—of all the people he met, the only one he fell in love with turned out to be Bobby's cousin."

"But he did hurt you, didn't he? Much worse than Art did."

"Yes. The weeks after he told me were pure hell." Beth's eyes darkened as she remembered that tortuous period. "I was was sleeping poorly and couldn't keep food down. All that time I was working at the center in the evenings, which meant that I had to see Cy. After a while I was living on my nerves alone. I think that's why it was easy for me to have the accident." She explained in detail how the accident had occurred and that Cy had been waiting in the car for Kwesi to bring out the dinners for delivery.

"It was Cy who took charge and brought me to the hospital. He stayed with me all of the time, except for a few hours on

Sunday afternoon. He left me Monday morning after breakfast to go to work.''

This part Clio hadn't known. She laid her quilt aside to give her whole attention to Beth.

''I don't understand,'' Clio said.

''Don't understand what?''

''All those weeks you'd been so angry and had shut him out of your life. So why did you let him stay with you at the hospital?''

''I know it sounds crazy, Clio.'' Beth sighed. ''That's the question I asked myself, but I was so physically and emotionally exhausted I had no resistance to what he was giving me.''

''What was he giving you?''

For a moment there was a mischievous gleam in Beth's eyes.

''TLC, girl, what we're always looking for.''

''Be serious.''

''Believe me, Clio, I'm serious. I'd never had the tender loving care that I received from Cy. He was there every minute except when the nurse came. He did so many small things like helping me eat when I didn't want to. Fixing my bed to make me comfortable. Putting flowers in my room to cheer me up. Holding my hand. But the main thing was the sense he gave me of strength and peacefulness. He made me feel protected, safe, secure.'' Her voice had softened as she relived the days with Cy in the hospital. ''He made me feel that I was the most precious person in the world to him.''

''Who could resist that?'' Clio said almost enviously.

''When he came back Sunday after all the visitors had gone, he brought me the dish garden you saw in the kitchen. He also brought me this.'' Beth showed Clio the bracelet.

Clio admired it, noting its quality and beauty. ''The brother has good taste,'' she said. ''I guess there's no doubt that he loves you, Beth.''

''I believe he does,'' Beth said.

''The big question is, what do you feel about him?''

''I love him, Clio. I figured out that's why it was so easy for me to have him with me in the hospital. The love hadn't gone away because of what he told me. I had just repressed it."

"If you know you love him, then what's the problem?"

"I can't tell him I love him because he might think everything is back to the way it was before, and it isn't. I want his love, but I also want his respect. He has to be able to see me as an equal."

"I understand how you're looking at it, hon," Clio said soberly. "Stay with me now while we look at it from where he is. He meets you, is instantly attracted and in a few days finds out you're Bobby's close cousin. He hasn't had time to get to know you well or to know how you'd react, so he doesn't tell you. Later when he knows you better, and at the same time is on his way to being deeply in love with you, he knows if he tells you it will make serious trouble and he can't risk it. You with me so far?"

"I'm with you."

"When he gets ready to propose marriage, he tells you—and just what he predicted happens. He's cut off from you. He's out in the cold right by himself. Lost the woman he loves. Lost the prospect of marriage. He realizes how wrong he was. He should've told you and taken the consequences whatever they were."

Clio put up her hand. Beth was listening in fascination to Clio's argument, but as always she noticed Clio's hands: large, shapely, satin smooth, and with beautifully kept nails. Clio ticked off her fingers as she pursued her thought.

"Now let's look at the whole matter from another angle. Number one. Cy didn't leave you on your own that night. He brought you home, cared for you as best he could. Number two. He was responsible and straightforward in telling your aunt and uncle and then getting your parents over here. Lots of people would not have done that. Number three. He came over and tried to explain himself and to give you the opportunity to say what you had to say. Number four. He never gave up. Tried to talk to you, sent you flowers, tried to show you his love. Number five. He took super care of you this past weekend, and as far as you've told me, without asking anything in return. Yes?''

Clio raised an inquiring eyebrow.

''That's right,'' Beth said.

''I don't know about you,'' Clio went on, ''but to me all of that tells me that Cy is a responsible man who loves you deeply but who made one big mistake early on. It seems unlikely to me that he will make such a mistake again. He's an intelligent man and knows what's at stake.''

Having delivered herself of argument and summation, Clio picked up her quilt and resumed work on it while Beth watched, turning over in her mind all that Clio had said. She had never looked at the facts in the way that Clio had lined them up. As she pondered them, she began to feel the first stirring of hope that there might be a way out of her dilemma.

Clio and Beth were in the kitchen preparing a salad lunch when the doorbell rang. Beth grabbed her cane and moved as quickly as she could, arriving at the door after the second ring.

''You're walking!'' Cy said, his face lighting up in a great smile.

''I've been practicing yesterday and today. Come in,'' Beth said, looking past Cy to the large brown-skinned man standing behind Cy and thinking this must be George.

''Beth, this is my brother, George,'' Cy said.

''Am I glad to finally get to meet you,'' George said warmly, his voice a melodious baritone. Refusing to stand on ceremony, he bent down to kiss Beth on the cheek.

Beth blushed and glanced at Cy, who gave an indulgent shrug.

''Well, well, who do we have here?'' George said in a hushed tone, looking past Beth at Clio, who had come into the room to investigate what was happening.

Before Beth could make introductions, George moved around her smoothly. Never taking his eyes from Clio, he went to her and took her hand. ''I'm George Brewster,'' he said.

''Clio Stewart,'' she replied, her large hand feeling dainty and fragile in his.

''Do you live in Jamison too?'' George asked.

"I'm working in Atlanta and just came home this weekend to see Beth."

George kept Clio's hand securely in his and, turning back to where Cy and Beth stood watching this unexpected drama, said, "Have you met my little brother, Clio?"

"We met over the telephone," Clio said, finally managing to look somewhere other than into George's eyes. "I'm glad to see you in person, Cy."

"I'm glad to see you, too, Clio." Cy knew in his bones that Beth had been confiding in Clio about the events of the recent past and wondered what Clio thought about him. Right now he could feel only friendliness emanating from her.

Cy had brought in a bouquet of yellow tulips. "For you, baby," he said softly as he handed them to Beth.

"They're lovely, Cy. Thanks," Beth said as she looked into his eyes, aware of him in every fiber of her being.

"Clio and I were just having a little lunch," she said to George and Cy. "Please come into the kitchen and join us."

"We just had brunch, but we'll come and sit with you," Cy said, happy to be near his dear Beth again.

George made sure he sat beside Clio. Then he turned his attention to Beth. He needed to get a sense of what she was like, this woman who had done what no other woman had been able to do: capture his brother's love. He knew his brother to be a good and decent man. True, Cy had made a stupid mistake by not laying his cards on the table as soon as he'd discovered the relationship between Beth and Bobby, but he didn't see why Cy should have to pay for that misstep the rest of his life.

Beth was attractive, he thought, but there were hundreds of attractive women out there. What he liked was that her face showed character and maturity. Cy had confided in him the entire story, and George could see around Beth's eyes and mouth the evidences of recent suffering. That must mean that she cared deeply about Cy.

"I was sorry to hear about your accident, Beth," he said. "Do you still have any pain?"

"Some but it's bearable," Beth said, thinking that George was a king-sized version of Cy except for the shaved head.

George had a close haircut and no goatee. But you would certainly know they were brothers.

"Cy showed me the center this morning. Very impressive job you two organized."

Beth felt herself flushing with pleasure. "Thanks, George. I'm not sure we appreciated just how much it would demand of us until we got into it. I know I didn't, but once we got it started we had to keep going. It worries me that I'm not going to be able to do my part now because of my foot."

George looked at her with so much interest and understanding that Beth found herself confiding in him.

"It's going to put more of a burden on Cy, you see, and he doesn't need that. I'm worried about him. I think he needs a break and that all work should be suspended for a week. Maybe you can help me persuade him."

She cares for him, George thought as he noted the look of pleased surprise on Cy's face when Beth expressed her concern for him. "I'll certainly help if you need me, Beth, but I think you can probably get my brother to do anything you want him to do." He kept his eyes on Beth but said to Clio, "What do you think, Clio?"

"I wouldn't be surprised," Clio said, figuring she could follow this man's lead in healing the breach between Beth and Cy.

George watched Beth blush and look down at her plate. A satisfied smile touched his mouth as he looked at Cy. You're on your own now, little brother, he signaled and shifted slightly in his chair so he was facing Clio instead of Beth. From the moment he saw her, Clio had become priority number one with George. He intended to give all of his considerable energy and will to that priority.

Chapter 28

''Don't let big brother upset you, honey.'' Cy's soft words were for Beth alone. He took her hand under the table and pressed it tenderly. Beth's composure began to return. When she dared to look at him, he gave her his usual affectionate look.

''I brought the tentative work schedule and the groups we have listed. They're in the car, and we can take a look at them later.''

George had captured Clio's hand again and, looking across the table at Beth and Cy, said, ''How about us taking you ladies out to dinner later?''

Clio looked at Beth, who said, ''Thanks, George, but why don't we stay in. There's lots of food here. Clio and I were going to cook this afternoon.''

George's face lit up. ''What've you got, Beth?''

''Chicken, ribs, chuck roast, potatoes, carrots, broccoli, yams, and several other things.''

''I'm not quite the cook Cy is,'' George said. ''But I know a thing or two about it. You two go and work on your schedules while Clio and I amuse ourselves getting dinner. Okay, Clio?''

Clio raised an eyebrow at Cy. ''Your big brother is a take-charge guy, isn't he?''

''All of his life, I'm afraid,'' Cy said smilingly.

''Not really,'' George said. He voice turned softer as he looked at Clio. ''I know what I want, and when I find it I don't waste any time.''

Clio drew in her breath as she met George's eyes. They were intense and confident. She felt the heat rise in her face, and to break the spell she looked across the table again.

''How many want pot roast and how many want ribs or chicken?''

It was decided the cooking team would prepare both ribs and pot roast and anything else they wanted to.

''Good,'' George said. ''This'll take us all afternoon. Can you bake, Clio?''

''Of course I can bake,'' Clio said indignantly. ''Rolls, biscuits, corn bread, muffins, pie, cake—or what?''

George threw back his head and laughed from sheer pleasure. Then his face sobered. ''To think I almost didn't come this weekend. What a tragedy that would have been!''

''Let's go look at the schedules,'' Beth said to Cy, who helped her up and into a chair in the living room facing the window. He pulled another chair up beside hers then went out to the car for the material.

Beth was thankful to be out of the kitchen and the emotional atmosphere George had set in motion. Everyone had been caught up in it, and she wasn't sure she and Cy were ready for it. Clio was certainly going to have to deal with the tornado that was George Brewster. She wondered how her friend would manage it.

In the kitchen George and Clio were clearing the table.

''I'll wash these, then we can start the cooking,'' Clio said.

George brought the last of the dishes to the sink where she had turned on the water. He shut it off and turned Clio around to face him.

''When it comes to something important, I always lay my cards on the table, Clio—and finding you is the most important thing that's happened to me. I want you to know now that I intend to marry you." His face was serious and his eyes piercingly bright as he looked at Clio.

Clio's eyes opened wide in astonishment. "You do?"

"I knew as soon as I saw you, Clio. I don't expect you to be as certain as I am right this minute, but if the idea doesn't turn you right off could I kiss you, please?"

Clio was a sea of emotion: wonder, doubt, laughter, excitement, and hope. Hope won out. Maybe this is the big man of my dreams, she thought. She had to stand on tiptoe to put her arms around his neck and receive his kiss.

Kissing Clio was exactly what George knew it would be. Her lips were soft and full and sweet, her body filled his arms to perfection.

"Are you by any chance engaged to someone, Clio?"

"No, George."

"Involved with someone?"

"And if I were?"

"Then you'd have to get uninvolved. Fast," he said against her mouth as he kissed her again.

"Are you?" Clio asked when she came up for air.

"Only with you, Clio, now and forever."

Cy opened the trunk and got the folder of schedules. He wondered what the next few hours would bring. He was walking on a tightrope here with Beth. One false step and he would fall off. He knew with certainty that this day would bring a resolution to his future with her. He didn't know why he felt that way, he just knew that it was so. Please let me get it right this time, he thought as he went inside.

Beth smiled as he sat down beside her. "How's the weather?"

"Lots of clouds in the north. I think more rain is coming. I'm glad we're staying here for dinner, honey. Thanks for inviting us."

"I couldn't let all that food go to waste," Beth said, smiling.

"With George around, you never have to worry about that,"

Cy declared as he laid out the schedule of work yet to be done at the center.

"We still have two small meeting rooms, the kitchen, the two bathrooms, the storage space and closets to do, plus the porch."

Beth looked at the volunteer list. "There are only three groups of volunteers we haven't used." She looked at the calendar. "Four weeks before June first."

Cy agreed. "The committee needs time to evaluate the work before the June fifth award banquet."

As far as Beth was concerned, they actually had only three full weeks to get the work completed. Cy and Rhonda and the volunteers had all been at the center five or six times a week in addition to their other jobs and duties. It was too much to ask. She knew how weary she'd been before the accident had given her time off. But Rhonda and Cy had still been working. They had to have a week off!

"If we count the volunteers we have left, there are about twelve in the groups. Then there's your family and mine and Aunt Elly's. People from my job haven't been called on yet nor have my friends you met at the Valentine Dance. I'm sure you have some people you haven't called on, haven't you?"

"Sure. I can always think of a few who wouldn't turn me down."

"That should give us enough people. If it doesn't, I'll get on the phone and get some more," Beth said, making notations on her pad.

"Want to do the meeting rooms first?"

"Up till now, Cy, we've been doing one room at a time. But now that we're down to smaller rooms, we don't need to do that. Why not plan to do all the rest in one week?"

"How would it work?" Cy looked puzzled.

Beth, full of enthusiasm, laid it out with a quick diagram, showing the rooms and describing what needed painting and how many workers it would take. "We'd have all these people and the supplies there on a Monday and assign people to where they'll be working. You, Rhonda, and I will keep circulating, helping and keeping it going. By the end of the week, it should all be done." Her eyes were glowing, her voice vibrant.

"Where would we get enough brushes for all those people?"

"We'd have to buy some more."

"We don't have that much money."

"Then I'll get some more from somewhere. And while we're speaking of money, what are we going to use the money from the fund-raiser for?"

"Paint and whatever else might come up that we don't expect right now, but I sort of want to save it for electrical and plumbing repairs," Cy said.

"I disagree, Cy."

"I thought that's what we said when we first talked about the center," Cy said in surprise.

"There's something more important, I think," Beth said.

"What is it?"

"Have you looked at the outside of the building, looked at it critically? The last time I did, I thought what's the use of doing all this backbreaking work on the inside and then have the outside look so shabby?"

"What are you suggesting, that we get volunteers to paint the whole outside of that building? That's a huge job, Beth. I thought we were only going to do something about the porch not the whole building," Cy protested.

"Well, if we couldn't find enough volunteers, why not use the fund-raiser money and pay someone to do it?"

"I think it would cost a lot more than we have—and besides we need some of that for paint. What about the other things I mentioned, the repairs that might be needed for plumbing and electrical work?"

"My feeling is that comes under maintenance, and we would do better to leave that to the council. We should stick with the painting."

"There're loose boards on the porch that need replacing, and the steps aren't as safe as they can be," Cy said. "Have you noticed that?"

"Yes, I have."

"Why can't we take care of that and paint the porch all around like we said at first?"

"I'm not saying that doesn't need to be done, Cy. What I am saying is that the whole exterior needs to be done. Newly painted porches would make the rest of the building look even worse than it does now."

This was the first time since Beth and Cy had been a team that a serious difference of opinion had occurred over a matter of any importance. Beth saw the whole center, inside and out, gleaming in fresh paint. What an uplifting feeling it would be for the many people who used the center. Doing only the inside was no longer sufficient from her point of view; it was all or nothing. She had no doubt at all that the volunteers could be found as well as the necessary funds. She would stay on the telephone as long as it took to get the commitments she knew were out there. There were still folks she knew in Jamison she had not yet contacted, and she had no hesitancy about doing so. All she needed was to convince Cy!

Cy felt the original plan was large enough, and if they could pull that off they would have done well. Where would they find the people or the money to do the exterior? Did Beth really understand how large a job that was?

A red flag went up in Cy's consciousness: He was about to fall off of the tightrope! Why shouldn't Beth understand the size of such a job? Had he forgotten that she had been working in a real estate agency where these jobs came up as a matter of course? Maybe the idea of indoor repair work could be done by the council unless Team Four could get it donated. What was her other idea about having all the workers come in at the same time and finish the interior in a week. Could we make that work? We could at least give it a try. Right now the essential thing was to give Beth credit for good judgment and together to look at the possibilities in her ideas.

Cy pulled out a fresh pad. "Okay, Beth, let's begin with your idea of painting the exterior and how much that might cost with and without volunteer labor. Then we can work backward from that point to see about the other things. Would that be all right with you?"

Beth's heart was beating fast. Until she was in the midst of their discussion, she hadn't realized that subconsciously she was not only describing what she wanted for the center but was also challenging Cy to see if he could treat her ideas with the same respect she gave his. All her ideas might not work, but they all deserved serious consideration—and Cy had realized that!

It took the rest of the afternoon to work out all of the details. They both realized that the more thought they gave it now, the better chance they had of success. Since this was the last push, they needed to consider every aspect.

Cy agreed to no work for the next week. He and Rhonda would get some rest, and Beth would use her time in finding as much money and as many volunteers as she could. She was certain she could organize a Saturday paint day for the exterior with volunteers and a contractor or two to supervise. They agreed that she would also try to find men to do the repairs and if that didn't work, the council would be left to do it.

One week might not be enough to complete the indoor work, so allowance was made for a few extra days. They made lists of professional people who might help, and Beth even made a few calls to get information about contractors and painters. They planned box lunches for the paint day and snacks for the interior work days. When they were discussing the budget, Beth reminded Cy that Marty was her ace in the hole. She'd get all she could elsewhere then let him know the remaining amount needed. Cy said there could be more also from Alumax.

They were congratulating themselves on how much they'd achieved as they reviewed the many neatly covered pages of their plan when Clio announced dinner.

"About time too," Cy told George. "That brunch we had is long gone."

"I've worked up an appetite too," Beth said. "The food smells so good."

Dinner was a huge success. George claimed the ribs as his masterpiece, and Clio accepted praise for her pot roast with vegetables. The crusty rolls went with both. Clio had insisted on cooking rice in case any good South Carolinian wanted some, and George had made potato salad because that's what you had to have with his ribs.

For dessert Clio had made a pineapple upside-down cake because George said he hadn't had one in years and had bet she couldn't produce one. Clio served him a big slice with whipped cream on it topped with a maraschino cherry. They all watched as George took a sizable bit. He closed his eyes as he savored it. When he opened his eyes, he touched his mouth with his napkin then turned to Clio and kissed her.

"The cake is almost as good as you are," he said.

Clio blushed and looked across the table at Beth. "Don't mind him," she said, "he's incorrigible."

No, Beth thought as they all ate their dessert and talked, George Brewster is a person who knows what he wants and ignores any risk in getting it. He has faith in his own ability. To him, hurdles and obstacles are to be avoided or overcome. They do not stop him.

"As thanks for a wonderful meal, Cy and I will do the dishes," Beth said. "You two are excused from the kitchen."

"I won't argue with that," George said, putting an arm around Clio and leading her from the room.

"How about me washing and you sit in the chair and dry?" Cy suggested after he'd helped Beth put the food away.

There was a quiet and restful companionship between them as they washed and dried and put away the dishes. Beth found that the way they were now was a given in her mind. They found a way to fit like this afternoon. They'd worked matters out until the sharp edges of disagreement were gone.

Cy watched her solicitously as he helped her up from the chair. "How are you, honey? Leg hurt?"

"I'm fine, really," she smiled and leaned against him as he took her into the living room and seated her on the couch.

George was sitting across from Clio, watching her work on her quilt. "Cy, did you know Clio could quilt and do this beautiful embroidery?" His voice was filled with appreciation and pride.

Cy went over to inspect Clio's work. "That's beautiful, Clio. It looks like the work our grandmother used to do when we were small. She would work on it for hours and tell us marvelous stories if we would sit quietly."

"It was my grandmother who taught me," Clio said.

George told them about quilt exhibits he'd gone to in New York and how he'd been fascinated by them because of his grandmother. He'd even recognized some of the stitches she'd done. Clio came to the end of the segment she'd been working on and began to fold the quilt carefully to put in her tote bag.

"I'm going to take Clio out," George said. "We'll use her car so yours will be here for you, Cy."

"Have fun," Cy said.

"You, too," George said with a straight face as he bent to kiss Beth on the cheek. "I'll talk to you, Beth, before I leave—and thanks for this day." His brilliant look told her how much he meant what he said.

"Call me," Beth told Clio.

"Don't worry, girl," Clio said with a mischievous smile.

The room seemed very quiet after George and Clio left. Cy sat beside Beth on the couch and took her hand in his.

"You may find this hard to believe, but I have never seen George act like he has today with Clio."

"I thought maybe that was his usual way."

"He's an outgoing kind of guy, as you can tell, but he's fairly restrained and almost formal with the ladies I've seen him with."

Beth recalled the first time Cy had told her about George.

"I remember you saying that he hadn't married because for him the first choice has to be the only choice."

Cy turned to Beth. "I said that was the reason neither George nor I had married because we both felt the same way. I told you we believe in marriage so strongly that we both decided to take our time in finding the right person—because the first choice has to be the only choice for us."

Cy's eyes held hers. "I remember what you said too."

"What did I say?"

The emotional tension Beth had felt earlier in the kitchen

was here again, only much more urgent. She could feel her heart thudding and her breath quickening.

"You don't remember?"

"Tell me." Beth's voice was soft, and her eyes were deep with emotion.

Cy took both her hands in a warm clasp.

"You said there would have to be a feeling of absolutely belonging to each other to make that possible." Cy leaned toward Beth, propelled by his great need. "Sweetheart, I could never belong to anyone but you. Please say you'll marry me, Beth."

A little shiver of pure feminine satisfaction ran through Beth.

Cy leaned closer until he was only a breath away. "Say yes, dearest."

"Yes," Beth said.

Cy's mouth came down on hers, and he crushed her to him.

Cy cupped Beth's face in his hands, and she felt his eyes were searching her very soul. "Tell me again, Beth."

"Yes, I'll marry you."

"Why will you marry me?"

Beth understood that Cy needed to hear from her the vow he'd made. "Because I could never belong to anyone but you, Cy," she said with all of the sincerity she possessed.

"I promise to love you and honor you with all of my heart, Beth. I misjudged you once, and I will always regret it. But I swear that our marriage will be one of equal partners and mutual respect. Will that suit you?"

"Thank you, Cy," Beth said, happiness flowing through her. Cy's promise—and his actions this afternoon when he gave her ideas equal weight with his—erased the last bit of residue from what had happened earlier. Cy understood the issue now. Beth had faith that if it should arise again, they'd be able to work it out.

She could now say what her heart had been wanting to express. "Oh, dear Cy, I love you so much!"

Cy scooped her up and sat her in his lap. They clung to each other fiercely. "I missed you so, I thought I'd go crazy," Cy said in a hoarse voice. ''Kiss me, my sweet baby.'' Beth's lips parted under his as she kissed him with a blazing hunger.

Cy's hands caressed her lovingly as he rained kisses on her face and neck and throat. Their need to make up for the loneliness and pain of the past weeks drove them until breathless and trembling they drew away from each other.

''Sweetheart?''

''Ummm?''

Cy stroked Beth's hair as she leaned against his chest.

''When you were in the hospital, you put up your arms for me to hug you and you asked me for a 'real' kiss, and when I came back Sunday you said you missed me.''

Beth sighed softly. ''What about it, Cy?''

''Were you loving me then or just being friendly because I was there near you?''

''I never stopped loving you—I realized it then. That's why . . .'' she began and then stopped.

''Why what?'' When Beth didn't immediately respond, Cy tipped her face to his so he could see her eyes. ''Why what, baby?'' he asked softly.

''That's why I wanted you to take me in your arms and hold me that night,'' she said shyly. ''The nightmare was a good excuse.''

Cy's eyes narrowed until they seemed to Beth to be points of fire.

''I'm glad. I tried to tell myself to think of you as my sister. But you were so soft, so warm, so unbearably sweet—and I could feel your heart beating against mine in that quiet, dark room.''

Each whispered word lit a spark in Beth. She had never in her life had such a sensation. She burned and trembled and, no matter how hard she tried, she couldn't get close enough to Cy or kiss him deeply enough.

Cy could bear it no more. He gently set Beth out of his arms and stood up.

He went to the folder and drew out the calendar they'd used in their scheduling. He sat beside Beth again.

''How soon can we be married, sweetheart?''

Beth counted the weeks and pointed to the sixth one down.

''Do we have to wait so long? I want us to get married soon,'' Cy said urgently.

''So do I, honey, but we've got the center to finish and even more important I want to be able to walk down the aisle to you when I become your wife. This cast has to be off.''

''It doesn't matter to me if you have the cast on.''

''It does to me, Cy,'' she said tenderly as she touched his face. ''It's important and the weeks will go quickly. You'll see.''

''Not quickly enough,'' Cy said, ''but I bow to your judgment.'' He took her in his arms again. Beth surrendered to his fervent kiss, secure in the knowledge that the promise of love was now hers forever.

EPILOGUE

"Stand still and let me fix your tie," George growled to Cy. "I think you're more nervous than the bride."

"Just wait till you're in my shoes next month when it's you and Clio. You'll see," Cy said.

In the vestry Beth's maid of honor, Clio, and Rhonda, her matron of honor, were fussing with Beth's veil and train. Beth, oblivious to their flutterings, thought of the past weeks. The plans she and Cy had made that wonderful day of their reconciliation had seemed to be touched with the same magic as their coming together. Money and volunteers had been found for the interior and exterior work.

At the award banquet she and Cy had won top honors. When pictures of the beautiful white center had been flashed on a screen, the people in the audience had risen to their feet and cheered.

What they had overcome together to arrive at that moment of success gave a deeper satisfaction to them both than the award itself. They had looked at each other and clasped hands tightly as they accepted the ovation.

That moment had been exciting. But now it seemed to Beth

that everything in her life had brought her to this supreme moment of becoming united with Cy.

The organ sounded. In the minister's room George said, "That's our cue. Let's go."

There was an expectant hush in the packed church as the robed minister and the groom and best man, elegant in their black and white, took their places. Down the aisle came Jannie, escorted by a stiffly erect and proud Kwesi, then Rhonda on the arm of Gary Raeford, and Clio, escorted by Cy's brother, Winston, from Atlanta.

George looked across the aisle to Clio and winked. She smiled back. Then the organist began the bridal march, and all eyes turned to the back of the church.

Beth, radiant in white, and serene in her beauty, floated down the aisle on her father's arm, her eyes seeking only Cy's. When she reached the minister and stood beside Cy, she was filled with inexpressible happiness and peace.

The minister began, "Dearly beloved, we are gathered here," and Beth was suddenly reminded of the "community" sculpture in Cy's apartment. She could sense the goodwill of the congregation reaching out to them.

Cy turned to face her, his hands holding her in a tight grip as if he was afraid to lose her, and began, "I, Cyrus, take thee, Beth." Each word of his vows reverberated with passion and pride.

Everything around her disappeared, leaving only Cy and her, holding to each other, safe home at last, as she answered, "I, Beth, take thee, Cyrus, to be my wedded husband."

It was the following Easter in New York, and George and Clio had just returned from seeing the Easter Parade when the call came.

"It's a boy!" Cy said, his voice full of excitement. George whooped for joy and yelled the news to Clio, who picked up the other telephone. "How's Beth?"

"Tired but happy. She said to tell you two to come down

week after next to meet your godson and for the christening.''

''What's his name—as if I didn't know?'' asked George.

''First name Cyrus, of course. Second name, Robert. We'll call him Bobby.''

ABOUT THE AUTHOR

Adrienne Ellis Reeves is a natural traveler. Born in Altamont, Illinois, she graduated from Du Sable High School in nearby Chicago. She went to college in Phoenix, Arizona, and met her husband, William, in Greensboro, North Carolina. They lived in New York City then moved to California, where they raised their family. Her travels in connection with the Baha'i Faith have taken her to Bermuda, Canada, Iceland, and throughout the United States. Now she and her husband have retired to South Carolina. Adrienne has published articles and children's books. Her other interests include music, cooking, and quilting.

Dear Reader,

Your many letters are a constant pleasure to me, and I thank you for them.

In PROMISE OF LOVE some of your questions about what happened to Emily and David Walker in CHANGE OF HEART, the first Jamison book, are answered. Glennette Percy and her James Ellington from HEAVEN KNOWS also appear as do Kimberly and Gary Raeford from KEEPSAKE.

They all have a part to play in this story of Beth Jordan, who first appeared in HEAVEN KNOWS, as Beth tries to find her true love.

I'll be anxiously waiting to hear your opinion. Write to me, and I will answer you. Thank you for reading our Arabesque books and pass the word to others.

Adrienne Ellis Reeves
975 Bacons Bridge Road
Suite 164 Box 122
Summerville, SC 29485

COMING IN DECEMBER . . .

FOOLISH HEART (0-7860-0593-9, $4.99/$6.50)
by Felicia Mason
CEO Coleman Heart III inherited his family's chain of department stores and focused only on saving it from bankruptcy. Business consultant Sonja Pride became the only person he felt he could trust. But Sonja had a debt to pay the Heart family, and being close to Coleman seemed the perfect way to make them pay. Until she found out he was a caring, honorable man to whom she could give away her heart.

DARK INTERLUDE (0-7860-0594-7, $4.99/$6.50)
by Dianne Mayhew
Sissi Adams and Percy Duvall had a relationship based on trust. But when Sissi admitted that she didn't want children, Percy was devastated. And when they discovered that Sissi was pregnant and that she miscarried, Percy broke off the relationship believing she aborted their child. Years later, Sissi is unhappily engaged to another, unable to forget her true love. She places Percy on the guest list of a celebration for her upcoming wedding for one last chance to see if they were made for each other.

SECRETS (0-7860-0595-5, $4.99/$6.50)
by Marilyn Tyner
Samantha Desmond raised her young stepsister, Jessica. To keep Jessica from calculating relatives, Samantha pretends Jessica is her daughter and relocates. When she meets pediatrician Alex Mackenzie, she fights the attraction between them to keep him from getting too close. But Alex finds out the truth about Jessica and his trust in Samantha is broken. They soon learn that neither can do without each other and their love.

OUT OF THE BLUE (0-7860-0596-3, $4.99/$6.50)
by Janice Sims
On a research trip to frigid Russian waters in pursuit of the blue whale, marine biologist Gaea Maxwell doesn't expect to meet corporate attorney Micah Cavanaugh—a man capable of thawing her frozen heart. Micah was asked to recruit Gaea for a teaching position at a private college. He didn't expect her to be a beautiful, charming woman. She refuses the position and returns home to Key West, Florida. Micah is more than disappointed. He follows her to Florida, determined to show that his love runs as deep as the ocean.

Available wherever paperbacks are sold, or order direct from the Publisher. Send cover price plus 50¢ per copy for mailing and handling to Kensington Publishing Corp., Consumer Orders, or call (toll free) 888-345-BOOK, to place your order using Mastercard or Visa. Residents of New York and Tennessee must include sales tax. DO NOT SEND CASH.

AND FOR THE HOLIDAYS . . .

SEASON'S GREETINGS (0-7860-0601-3, $4.99/$6.50)
by Margie Walker, Roberta Gayle and Courtni Wright
Margie Walker provides hope to a scrooge in form of a woman in her moving Christmas tale. When Hope Ellison and her young son melt Stone Henderson's frozen heart, he will do anything to keep them . . . including go up against her ex-love. In Roberta Gayle's perky Kwanzaa celebration, Geri Tambray-Smith looks for a date before matchmaking uncles interfere. Luckily, Professor Wilton Greer is a willing accomplice in it for research purposes, who finally learns what love is all about. Courtni Wright rings in the New Year with a new love for Pat Bowles, who is looking to get away on a New Year's Caribbean cruise and finds love with a seductive stranger.

CHANCES ARE (0-7860-0602-1, $4.99/$6.50)
by Donna Hill
Dione Williams, founder of a home for teenage mothers and their babies, and television producer, Garrett Lawrence, were drawn to each other from the start. Only she was a young mother herself and Garrett's cynical view of ''irresponsible'' teen mothers puts them at extreme odds. But 'tis the season of hope and a chance at new beginnings.

LOVE'S CELEBRATION (0-7860-0603-X, $4.99/$6.50)
by Monica Jackson
Two years have passed since Teddi Henderson's husband picked up and left her and her daughter behind with no explanation. She had returned to her hometown in Kansas to start anew, but the Kwanzaa celebration always brought memories of J.T. This time it has brought him back in person . . . with dangerous secrets—he is a government agent. Can Teddi put her faith in him again and start anew with the man she has always loved?

A RESOLUTION OF LOVE (0-7860-0604-8, $4.99/$6.50)
by Jacquelin Thomas
Daryl Larsen's biological clock was telling her it was time to settle down and have children. This New Year's she's determined to find Mr. Right, and she is sure she sees him in pro basketball player Sheldon Turner. Even though he has a reputation as a ladies man, and he sees nothing amiss with a life of beautiful women and momentary passion. Sheldon soon begins to feel something special for Daryl, whose persistent caring and honesty has him seeing life differently.

Available wherever paperbacks are sold, or order direct from the Publisher. Send cover price plus 50¢ per copy for mailing and handling to Kensington Publishing Corp., Consumer Orders, or call (toll free) 888-345-BOOK, to place your order using Mastercard or Visa. Residents of New York and Tennessee must include sales tax. DO NOT SEND CASH.